Incite
Scars of Lumierna
Kelsea Koope
I0712395

Pronunciations:

Stirling Bakere	Stur-ling Bake-eer
Amiria Rey	Aa-meer-ee-aa Ray
Ignis	Ig-nus
Taika	T-eye-kuh
Calix Gautier	Kay-lix Goe-tee-air
Ealdian Dietrich	Aal-Dee-un Dee-trik
Kinsey Gautier	Kin-zee Goe-tee-air
Giles Bakere	Jeye-ls Bake-eer
Quilan	Kwil-uhn
Aether	Ay-th-er
Dicun	Deye-kun
Quetzecoatl	Ket-suhl-koh-at-uhl
Per'yanny svir	Per-yawn-nee-s-veer
Amphipteres	Am-fih-teer
Wyverna	Weye-ver-nuh
Lumierna	Loo-meer-nuh
Tillfalya	Till-faal-yuh
Uviktiland	Oo-vik-ti-land
Leucasia	Loo-caw-zee-uh
Patu	Paw-too

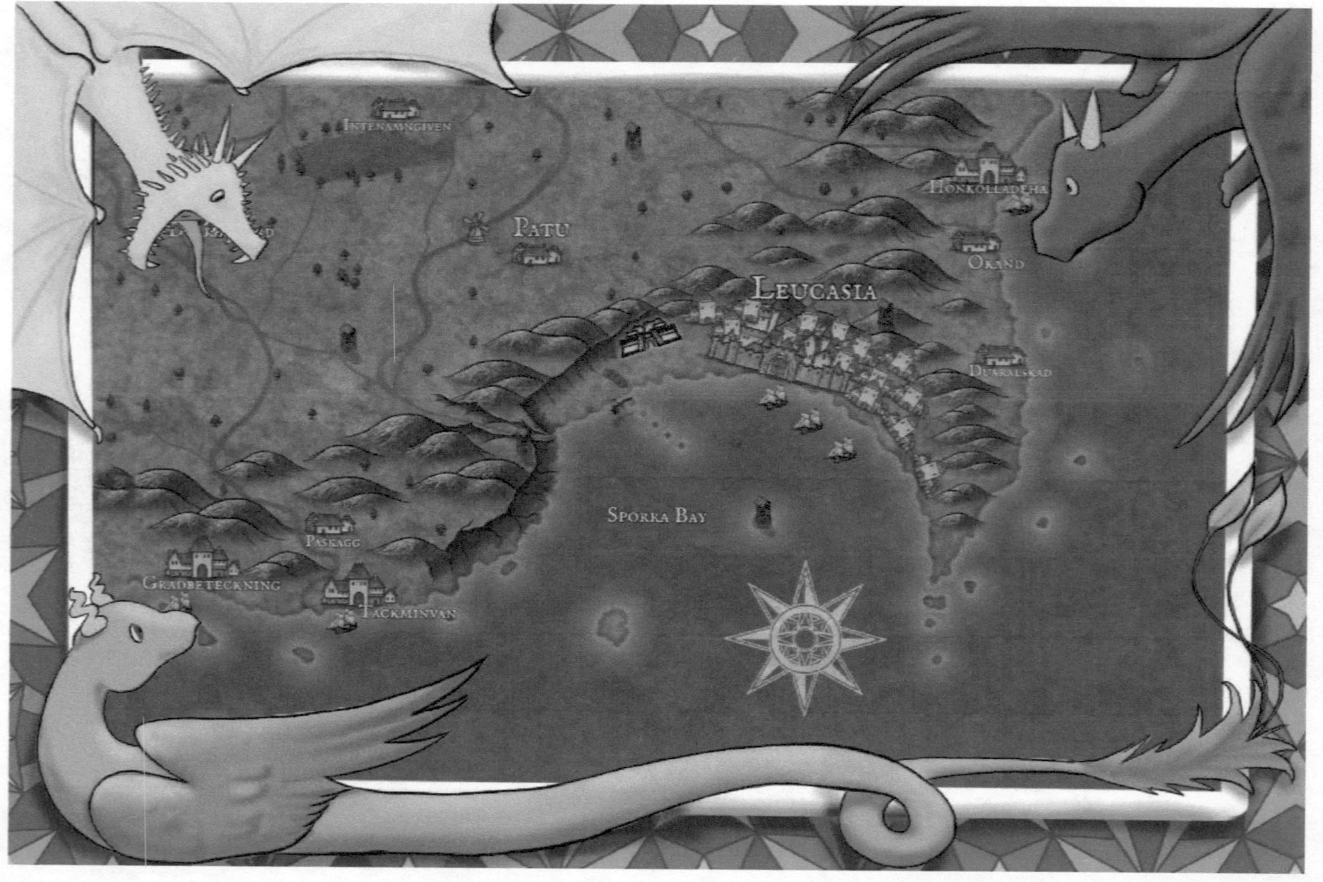

INTENAMNGIVEN
DUARALSKAD
PATU
HONKOLLADEHA
OKAND
LEUCASIA
DUARALSKAD
PASKAGG
SPORKA BAY
GRADBETECKNING
TACKMINVAN

UVITILAND
KINGDOM OF TILLFALLYA
Isles of Wyvern
Anica's Path
Sterling's Path

One

*H*ow *many villages are we going to pass until we finally get to stop?"* Ignis whines as they fly over hills, rivers, and one of the many small villages nestled between them. *"We've been traveling for over two weeks. Just pick one,"* he gripes.

Nearly dying from the flames of the Winged Cavalry, Stirling and Ignis had managed to escape the Isles of Wyverna with minor injuries in comparison to what could have been. The skin on the back of Stirling's hands was seared off. Stirling's clever idea to reveal he has been alive for the past three years to his father before he left took a drastic turn for the worse. How his father thought of him as a demon and threatened his life. He was chased into the street for everyone to bear witness to the unfolding of a new chapter, a new outlook on life in Wyverna. Ignis, exposing his existence, flew over Lumierna to rescue Stirling setting off the alarms, and deployed Amiria's team into a manhunt in the clouds. A manhunt that Stirling

barely survived and escaped onto the shores of
Uviktiland.

Without looking back, they kept to their decision, the
only information he provided Amiria, and they flew
southeast. Unsure of their environment and whom to
trust they haven't conversed with any of the local citizens
in this new foreign land. They can only presume
Uviktiland does not stretch on forever, and they will
eventually reach a new kingdom. Their question now is,
have they passed the border, and if so, where are they?

They've passed countless small villages, but when a
city appears on the horizon, they've gone out of their way
to avoid being spotted, afraid a replay of Lumierna will
happen.

Squinting through his lenses, Stirling searches the land
stretching on before them. In the distance, small misty
peaks pop over the horizon. "I guess we've traveled far
enough. I haven't seen another dragon since we left. How
about at the bottom of those mountains? No matter the
village, we'll stop. It's just comforting to be near
mountains again."

*"Hold on. Wait a moment. I've realized something peculiar. If
we were the only dragon flying over these villages, why haven't we
heard any of the people make any kind of commotion,"* Ignis
brings up.

Stirling blinks slowly as the thought finally occurs to
him. "Wait, you're right. I know people have seen us.
They've looked up as we passed overhead now that I
think about it. But they always returned to whatever task
they were doing. It didn't occur to me that we were not
on the island anymore. Dragon sightings are not a regular
occurrence. But even the people back home didn't react
so nonchalantly about it."

"What do you think it means?"

"I have absolutely no clue," Stirling admits.

They approach the mountains that are dwarfed in comparison to the towering peaks around Wyverna but are still mountains on their own. Like the forests and grasslands, they have been flying over, there seems to be an absence of pine trees that appear to touch the clouds, but the landscape is rich with oaks, maple, chestnut, shorter pines like juniper, and trees he has never seen before.

Smokestacks rise from a quaint-sized village settled at the base with a single dirt road cutting through the center and up the incline of the mountain.

The village's homes are spaced out from each other in what at first appears to be scattered at random, but this is due to the fact the shack-sized houses are lining up with wells, avoiding spots tending to flood, and locations known to have frost pockets chilling the land sooner and longer than the rest.

Stirling remembers the market he grew up in. The buildings mashed together, each home supporting their neighbors' rotting structure. Below the jetties of the second floors are permanently flooded alleys too narrow for a grown man to fit his shoulders through. How the people who never leave and an ever-expanding population with each generation, packed themselves into the street, squeezed tight like a bundle of hay.

The homes here are mostly single stories, several possessing a higher roof to make room for a loft. They are small one or two-room homes made of piled stones. The tops of the walls are uneven leaving openings and gaps beneath the planked wood roofs laid across. There are simple fences made from various stones and branches enclosing individual gardens, chicken coops, and a few pens where goats nibble at the grass on the other side of the fence after already devouring what grew inside the pen. Dogs lay beside the front steps of multiple homes keeping guard while the humans leave or mill about their days.

"Let's land in this pasture by the river and walk in. It's less of a startling entrance if they haven't seen a dragon before," Stirling suggests.

"*Whatever you say,*" Ignis says, gradually beginning his descent.

Wooden gears complain as water pushes them to keep turning year after year are audible as they pass over the mill to the overgrown meadow.

A small herd of cows groans as they shuffle out of the way of the orange dragon. His wings send powerful gales as they steadily lower into the long, lush grass flowing like the rippling surface of a calm pond. His hind legs contact the marshy earth first. Tucking in his wings he catches the rest of his body by landing on his front legs, his claws sinking into the mud.

"*Yuck.*" Ignis shivers at the wet soil seeping between his toes.

"My legs are so sore," Stirling gripes as he slides off Ignis' back, his legs below his knees disappearing into the emerald sea.

"*You're sore? I've been doing all the work while you just sit there,*" Ignis retaliates.

"I am not *just* sitting there. I've been holding on for dear life! After constricting your muscles for a long period of time they start to cramp and hurt. It takes a lot of energy trying to not fall to your death," Stirling argues, throwing his hands up in the air. He runs his hands down his face, "Keep your head down, maybe we can pass you as an ugly horse."

"*I'm beautiful, remember?*" Ignis gloats, lifting his head higher.

"Don't you start with that again? Come on, let's go. I'm not even sure how we will communicate. I don't know what language these people speak." Stirling pulls his goggles down letting them hang around his neck. With a nod of his head in the direction of the quaint village, they begin trucking through the thick grass.

After struggling their way through the field Stirling steps out onto the pressed dirt road. Deep hoof prints made when the earth was saturated by rain retained their shape as the sun stole the water. Stirling follows the groves leading the way to the village.

There are only two buildings residing on the side of the road directly across from one another, not more than a stone's throw away. Connected to what appears to be a tavern or alehouse is a small stable to tie up your horse while you stop for the night.

"Look! A racer! A racer!" a young boy approximately five or six years of age squeals as he pulls his hand free from his sister's—who is only a few years older—grasp.

"Wait, Gregory! You can't run up to people like that," she shouts after him. With his arms raised to the air, he doesn't listen to his sister's instructions as he bolts towards Stirling and Ignis.

Stirling halts in place as Gregory sprints up to him. The small child skids to a stop before colliding into Stirling's legs, his slower sister in tow. With his chin to his chest, Stirling leans back to see the boy practically standing on his toes staring up at him starry-eyed.

"Can I pet your dragon? Can I? Can I?" Gregory asks, impatiently bouncing on his heels with his hands clasped together near his chest in a pleading manner.

Stirling is taken back. Confused about how he can understand the child despite having a thick accent that is heavier on the vowels but soft on the consonants.

Stirling stammers out, "I uh…you know what dragons are?"

"Sorry about these rascals." A bear of a man with a thick beard dressed in a simple garb of a worn-out brown tunic and a red merchant's hat slouching on his balding head comes jogging over from one of the buildings lining the road.

Stirling is tall, but he is slender. The man standing before him is taller in height by a hair and is double in girth. Stirling gawks bewildered. He was expecting some sort of reaction from the villagers to Ignis, but it wasn't whatever this is.

"I'm Bernard. These are my children Delilah and Gregory. Competitors don't normally pass through here. He got a little excited." His voice is deep and heavy with a foreign accent. He reaches down, tussling Gregory's hair.

Bernard's children huddle around Stirling's knees fascinated by the goggles hanging from his neck, the belt with a "T" shaped hook, and Ignis' entirety. The girl stands on her tippy toes trying to touch the engraved brass of his goggles shining like a necklace in the sunlight.

With his eyes still on Bernard Stirling clasps his hand protectively around the goggles pulling them slightly away. He raises an eyebrow, "Racer? Competitor?"

"You know, for the games next week," Bernard states.

"Stirling, Stirling. They're touching me with their little grimy hands," Ignis says, lifting his leg in disgust at Gregory who had stepped around Stirling and is currently stroking the scales on Ignis' front leg.

Stirling's face is blank, his mouth hanging open slightly, he turns his whole body to face Ignis behind him. Glancing back over his shoulder, he questions, "Games?"

"Boy, do you understand a word I'm saying?" Bernard asks.

"Shockingly, yes," Stirling utters.

"So, you own a dragon, but you don't know about the games? It's like owning a mill but not knowing about flour. Where have you been living? In a cave?"

He shrugs, "Yes, for three years." Bernard stares absently. Feeling awkward, Stirling begins to tap his fingers to his thumb in a nervous habit. "So, what are these games?"

Bernard cocks his head, "You must not be from around here if you are serious about not knowing about the games. Even the neighboring kingdoms to the north and east know about it and sometimes participate. Unless you're from—" He scratches his beard knitting his bristly eyebrows together. "The west? You do have an unusual accent."

"I guess you can say that," Stirling tells his shoes. "What–What do I sound like?"

"Like you are forgetting to pronounce parts of your words, you're a bit, how can I put it, choppy?"

"Choppy?"

"As long as you don't talk too fast, I can understand you. Now, tell me." Bernard leans in intrigued. "What do I sound like?"

"There are a lot of ups and downs, but also like you're talking in the back of your throat sometimes."

"Huh, I don't hear what you mean but it's still interesting. It's been a long time since I've heard a new accent. Well then–" he claps and throws his hands out, "Welcome to Patu the best village in the Kingdom of Tillfallya."

"Tillfallya?"

"Yep, but tell me, if you're not a professional rider then how did you come upon buying such an expensive imported dragon? Unless you have the riches of a lord, you would have to sell everything you own and then some," he laughs.

Stirling blinks long and slow, so deeply lost in the progress of the conversation that he doesn't know how to catch up. Every time this burly man speaks, he is only filled with more questions.

Bernard's laughing comes to a stop as he becomes fully aware of Stirling's confusion. "Do you not even know the species of your dragon?"

Stirling shakes his head. "I've always thought of him as a freak of nature."

"*Excuse me,*" Ignis scoffs.

Stirling acts as if he didn't hear him. "I've only known one species, the Wyverns."

"Well, boy, that is definitely not a wyvern. I've seen a few of those at the games, but they are rare. They're too aggressive for most to handle. The majority of people ride our common dragons, dracos for short. They've got wings like wyverns, but four legs like yours here," Bernard informs.

"We have riders back home and all they fly is Wyvern," Stirling adds.

"They must be very extraordinary riders to control such an intense creature. Takes a strong soul," Bernard says.

"You don't even know," Stirling states. "But, if you know so much about dragons then what is he?" he adds, referring to Ignis who is pulling his wings up and out of the reach of the children.

"He appears to be a per'yanny svir," Bernard answers, inspecting Ignis.

"A what?" Stirling says, turning back to Ignis who only tilts his head in response.

"Per'yanny svir is what they call them. They aren't native here. They are more common in the northeast where it's colder. That's why they have feathered wings. I haven't seen one since I was a lad," Bernard expands.

"Do people not fly them down here?" Stirling asks, still confused.

"No, not commonly. They are extremely intelligent creatures but compared to other dragons, they are very high-maintenance. They tend to be owned by only those who can afford the pricey bill," Bernard rambles. "So, they are more for wealth status and not for labor or sport."

Stirling stares at Ignis who returns the same expression of puzzlement. *"So all along you've just been a noble person's pet?"*

"An extremely intelligent, elegant pet, thank you," Ignis says in a snide tone.

"Oi, boy, you listening?" Bernard says, snapping his fingers in front of Stirling's face. Stirling jerks his head back startled. "I was saying why don't you come into the alehouse with me? I'll tell you about the games and you tell me about where you've really come from. I know it ain't anywhere in this region." He suggests throwing his arm around Stirling's shoulders. Without giving Stirling time to protest, he begins leading him to the only two-story building in town with a few wooden tables set up outside, warped and abused by years of weather exposure and use.

Several more children and their mothers begin to close the gap around Ignis.

"Wait, don't leave me alone," he calls out to Stirling who is being guided away by Bernard.

"The Games, my child, are held once every year. The official name is Leucasia's Skylit Endeavor, but that's too much of a mouthful, so the Games it is. Here, riding a dragon is a sport, a profession done by the wealthier folk who can afford to purchase a beast. I'm serious if you thought horses were expensive—here, let me put it in perspective, you can buy an entire herd before you pay off a dragon." He waves his hand in a broad arch through the air.

Bernard continues to explain, reaching the door to the alehouse, "Well, throughout the year all over the region are small tournaments for professionals or teams to compete in, but none of that compares to the Games.

You see, anyone can enter the games. Professional, newbie, rich, poor."

Using his free hand Bernard swings the door open and shoves Stirling through with his other. Stepping inside awkwardly Stirling glances around taking in the atmosphere.

Standing behind Stirling, Bernard inhales through his nose breathing in the beloved scent. His chest expanding as far as it goes, he lets out his breath satisfied through his mouth and carries forth his explanation, "It doesn't matter where you came from or if your first time flying was yesterday. If you own a dragon you can enter. There are levels of course. Beginners won't be flying against the elite."

The alehouse is bustling. It seems as if every man in the village is here sitting around on wooden benches lined at tables across the dirt floor with scattered rush and straw to absorb the spilling ale. Large wooden tankards fill the tables in front of them as they laugh at each other's stories. In the corner of the room, a few men play a gambling game with dice. The hoppy aroma fills the air with the lingering smell of perpetual stew simmering about the coals in a pot hung above the fire stuffing the air like humidity on a summer day.

"Anyone can enter?" Stirling repeats, his attention turning back to Bernard.

"Do you ever listen? As I said, if you got a beast and you got the entrance coin you can enter," Bernard answers.

Raising his hand in the direction of the alehouse maid calling out, "Oi two!"

A young woman with warm brown skin and black ringlet hair pulled back in a wrap and arms full of tankards scowls. Her honey brown eyes narrow in at Stirling who meanders across the room to the far wall distracted by a tapestry map of the known continent pinned to the wood.

He is lost in the map. Lost in a world he never knew existed. An entire coastline south of the mainland reaches east to west. There are markings of significant hills, prairies, and rivers he must have flown over and dots representing towns with scribbles he assumes are their names beside them. He's mesmerized by the unrecognizable land displayed before him. How big is the world?

"Is your town on here? If not, we can add it." Stirling jumps at Bernard's voice speaking directly over his shoulder, "We're a trading village right outside the capital. So, we get all kinds of people traveling through. They help us fill out the map."

"Um no, no it's not," Stirling admits. "Where are we exactly?"

Bernard cocks an eyebrow. "You flew here, and you don't even know where you are? I might be saying things that confuse you, but you sure are confusing me."

Staring blankly, Stirling doesn't reply.

Bernard sighs. "We're right here," he says, reaching past him and placing the tip of his finger on a small dot labeled "Patu" near the bottom of a stubby peninsula right above a small mountain range. "And here is the capital." Bernard continues as he drags his finger to the other side of the mountain to a star on the coast. Sliding his finger up and to the right, he lands on a crown. "Except the royal family lives on a massive enclosed estate here."

Stirling leans in closer. They are on some kind of land mass jutting out into the ocean from the rest of the continent. The land itself seemed to curl out into the ocean towards the southeast. The ocean is to the west, south, and east of them. It's like an island, but not quite. The land is still attached to one side.

"I can't read. What is it called?" Stirling asks.

Bernard sounds it out for him. "Le-u-ca-sia. And this lovely place is Patu."

Stirling turns his focus back to the map, on the Kingdom of Tillfallya. There is nothing past the capital Leucasia except the never-ending ocean besides several small islands.

We did it. Southeast until we can't go anymore. He thinks to himself, reaching out to the map.

His fingers run along the coast feeling the rough canvas with layers of paint a mixture of bumpy and smooth from years of constant interaction with the human hand adding, changing, and working together to complete the world they know.

"You're an odd one," Bernard blurts as he examines the previously unnoticed fresh webbing of scars still pink on the back of Stirling's hands.

Bernard's gaze falls from his hands to the three large burn marks covering some sort of symbol on the inside of his right arm.

"Can you even point to where your town might be?" he asks, suddenly wary of the newcomer who is scarred, marked, and knows nothing of the land he is in.

Keeping his finger placed on the map Stirling scans the tapestry up to the northwest where the Kingdom of Uviktiland is labeled bordering the entire west coast. He drags his finger across the prairies, forests, hills, and towns he had flown over passing the Uvkitland's port town they traded with. His nail caked with dirt stops in the middle of the ocean.

Bernard scratches his beard. "Have you hit your head or something? There's nothing out there."

Stirling doesn't budge, his eyes stuck staring at the empty water. "No. You're wrong. There's a channel of islands. One particularly the size of a whole kingdom surrounded by a mountain region. It's just over a week's long ride on horseback to cross it. We have towns, cities, a capital, a king…a military."

"You don't say?" Bernard rubs his fingers across his eyes and pinches the brim of his nose. "But you are speaking the same language as us, despite your thick accent." Bernard adds intrigued, "I wonder how that is possible?"

Stirling drops his hand.

The realization of how cut off they are from the rest of the world dawns on him. "I don't know. Our maps don't even show past Uviktiland. None of this world exists to us."

"We don't have any trade routes or connections with them. Before even my great grandparents' time, Uviktiland invaded from the north conquering the entire coastline. We were able to fend them off with aid from our neighboring brothers, that Kingdom is known for its savagery—Well, in the end, they signed a treaty creating the new borders you see here as long as we never step foot over them. That cut all ties we had with the West. Our trade routes only go east and north now," Bernard explains.

Stirling's fingers catch in the tangled knots of his hair as he runs them through it, "We used to be the western coastal Kingdom. A large sum of our people escaped and relocated to the island. I guess they kept us a secret. They are still controlling us even after they stole our land. They've made themselves our only trade route. Here I was thinking we had power over them, that we were the stronger country. No, we're nothing more than animals corralled into a cage we learned to call home."

Bernard nods his head confused. "Uh-huh."

"Ahem," the young maid cuts in. They turn around to her holding up the two tankards wearing a disinterested face.

"Just add it to my tab," Bernard tells her, taking both ales from her with a gracious grin. Rolling her eyes, the young woman does not return the smile as she steps back disappearing into the crowd.

"You didn't need to," Stirling insists.

Bernard hands him one of the tankards, the foam running down the side as it sloshes with the movement, and motions for Stirling to have a seat on the bench closest to the map. Stirling licks the foam crawling down his fingers and follows him.

Nodding to a few of the other men sitting at the table Bernard sits beside Stirling. "Don't worry, I run the trading business in this town. So, I'm used to greeting all of the travelers coming through and I enjoy talking about where they came from over a drink. That's why I started that map."

"I imagined a trading town outside of a major city to be a little **difficult?**" Stirling admits.

Bernard leans into Stirling as if he is about to tell him a secret. "It is. most people will continue to try to make a better deal inside Leucasia. But the people who stop here like to sell items that are old or damaged. Basically junk people don't want to carry around and wont pass in the city."

"Is that your family's trade?" Stirling asks.

"Yeah." Bernard shrugs and sips his ale. "That shops has been here as long as the village has. Leucasia wasn't always so massive. It once was a small harbor town and Patu wasn't forgotten about. But we love it here and are never leaving."

"Wow," Stirling pauses, his mind returning to Wyverna and its set-in-stone laws. "We didn't have anything like that happening back in Wyverna," he almost retracts his statement as he remembers the leather workshop being the only victim of major theft in Lumierna.

Bernard pushes air out through his teeth, making a "chh" sound. "You're still young, you probably just didn't know about it."

"No really, we didn't. There weren't any major crimes, no unemployment, no homelessness, well, except for me. I ended up becoming the only one listed under all three of those in the end. I guess I am their worst criminal in history."

The other men around the table start becoming interested in Stirling's tale and lean in.

"None? Across the whole board? I doubt that. Sounds too good to be true," one of them states.

"He needs to talk slower, I'm only getting part of what he is saying," another adds.

"No there's a total of one on the board, didn't you hear him? We've got ourselves a little outlaw here," Bernard mocks.

Stirling pushes his ale to the side, laying his right arm on the table revealing his insignia. "I'm being serious, everyone is assigned an occupation and it's marked on their arm forever. This is the symbol of the bakery trade. Well, it was the symbol before I got injured."

"This system of yours doesn't seem so bad. Appears to be successful in my eyes." Bernard states, confirming with his comrades around the table who nod in agreement as they examine Stirling's arm.

Pulling his arm back Stirling touches his fingertips to the bumpy scars. "It looks good on the outside, but it has some major cons. It's illegal to practice any other trade besides your own. Just speaking about the idea of it can land you in stocks, but to actually go through with it will put you at the gallows." He doesn't peel his eyes up from his scar as more men gather around the table to listen. "That's why, when I found Ignis."

"Is that your dragon?" Bernard interrupts.

"Yes," Stirling confirms, "I had to keep him a secret for most of my life, so I didn't end up hung, drawn, and quartered. To illegally ride a dragon is treated as the most heinous crime you can commit in the Wyverna. I distanced myself from everyone, it was safer for me, and for them. Eventually, I ran away and hid in the mountains. The Winged Cavalry searched for me, but never found me. Our king didn't want to admit I was able to successfully run away and live homeless, so he lied and told everyone I died. My very existence became a secret. There was this girl though."

"Ohhh?"

"She was in the Winged Cavalry, but—" he hides his hand below the table tapping his fingers to his thumb. "She saw things, how I saw them. How it's not right to control people's lives. No freewill. So, I ended up becoming her secret."

"The Winged Cavalry?" a man standing behind Stirling asks.

Stirling checks around to see who had spoken. "It's the highest rank in our military, they ride dragon back, our knights of the sky. Lords are honored to sit with, but they are trained from childhood to only know bloodshed."

"A dragon army! Well, now I've heard it all. That's terrifying," one shouts from the crowd.

"I'm still stuck on how you became her little secret. Who's this girl?" one sitting at the table across from Stirling asks with his head resting on his hands. "She must have really liked you to commit mutiny like that."

Stirling blushes, his body sinking into the bench. "Yeah, I really like her, too. She was my best friend besides Ignis. But I did something unforgivable to her."

"And what was that?" Bernard asks.

"I abandoned her there for my own sake. I convinced myself I was doing it for her so she can go live a normal life. Though in reality, I was saving myself." Stirling drops his head to the table, his forehead hitting with a soft thump of remorse.

Bernard senses the distress emanating from Stirling and changes the topic. "Well, our Tillfallya hasn't really tried putting the dragons into the military. But we also haven't had any battles since we protected our borders from Uviktiland. We also definitely don't have any rule about only having one trade. Your home must lack small villages because there's not enough people to only have one job. Here we do everything for ourselves. Then if you're unable to grow it, fix it, or make it yourself, then you go ask a neighbor and trade with them. If not still, we make the trip into the city. We help our neighbors because we want to, not because we were told to."

A drunken man calls out, "This village is just one large family!"

"I can drink to that!" another cheers, holding up his drink.

"To Patu! The best damn village there is!" the man across from Stirling toasts.

"AAYYYY!" all the men in the room cheer, throwing their tankards into the air, liquid sloshing, and jumping out of the wooden borders.

"I say another round!"

"Oi! Round for the house!" Bernard calls out.

The men throw their arms around their neighbors, singing, "Drink! Drink! Gather at the tavern and drink! Place a bet and roll the dice and drink!"

Stirling can't contain himself as the laugh bubbles out of him. They act closer than any family he has ever known. All the times he snuck past the tavern back home, not once did he hear anyone singing that wasn't the hired musicians. If anyone began to become rowdy or even shout, they were asking for the guards to show up and remove them.

Several men at a table in the corner of the room pick up instruments worn down with love and begin to play. Dozens of sets of hands begin to clap along with the beat and matching sets of feet dance around the tables still singing, "Work all day, for no coin and Drink! Don't tell my Mrs, she'll holler as I drink! Drink!

Bernard jumps up pulling Stirling up with him laughing as they join the drunken batch of men parading around the room. "Gather at the tavern and drink!"

Two

Time begins to slow around Stirling. A smile stretches from ear to ear with glee as he bounces on the balls of his feet. He doesn't even care about the cramp forming in his abdomen from the constant constriction of movement and laughter.

The engagement is exhilarating; everyone acting merry and foolish, their drinks spilling as they jump and turn. Putting his head back he lets the brewed liquid race into his mouth overflowing and pouring out of the corners. Setting the tankard back on the table beside him he wipes his mouth dry with the back of his arm.

A large hand slaps Stirling on the back causing him to lurch forward. "That's the spirit!" Bernard encourages.

Stirling coughs choking on his ale still hunching over at the waist. He puts one hand up signaling to Bernard he's fine.

At this moment, Stirling is better than fine, he never wants to leave this alehouse. He only recently met these

villagers yet even after admitting he is a criminal back
home, they threw their arms around him and invited him
into their group.

"It's going to be a moment Ignis."

Ignis lies outside in the setting sun, the women and the
children sitting around him stroking his velvet feathers.

"Take your time," he lazily replies.

The sun now long gone and replaced by the lingering
moon, round after round had been served in the
alehouse. With each tankard, the volume of the men grew
increasingly louder.

The owner of the alehouse, a homely man with dark
rich skin going by the name of Gilgamesh steps up onto a
stool with a pot and ladle held over his head. The
boisterous room disregards the obnoxious clanging
passing through their eardrums and over their neighbor's
head.

"Aye! Listen up! Everyone shut up!" he shouts. The
clamoring of the crowd breaks apart as the blundering
men finish up their sentences. Wobbling and swaying eyes
turn to acknowledge Gilgamesh. "Next week is Leucasia's
Skylit Endeavor, many of our regular athletes have already
signed up so you know what that means?"

"Time for my wife to kick me out again?" a man jokes.

"Exactly!" Gilgamesh agrees. "It's time to open the
alehouse bets not to confuse it with the official games
bets in Leucasia. You all know the rules. Pick the athlete
and placement they'll be taking in each game. Don't
forget their levels, beginner, intermediate, advanced, and
elite. I'm looking at you, Edward."

Edward the miller shrugs, "Common mistake."

"The Games," Stirling mumbles to himself, his face
flushed with alcohol.

It is a sport dominated by the wealthy class, but there is no rule against him entering. If you have a dragon and the entry coin, you can participate. This is his shot. This is the opportunity he sacrificed everything for, days with his mother, his father…Amiria. All for an opportunity to show the people he can touch the sky.

"I'm going to join the games," he utters, barely audible to himself.

"What was that?" Bernard asks.

"I'm going to join the games!" Stirling announces with all heads snapping to him.

"The new kid is going to join the games! Hazah!" a drunken man shouts.

"HAZAH!" they all cheer in unison clapping their hands.

Stirling throws his hands balled into fists into the air. "I'M GOING TO ENTER THE GAMES!"

Swaying as he shouts, he leans too far to one side and loses his balance. Tipping over he clumsily attempts to catch himself by slapping the table and knocking over a few tankards. He lands on the side of his hip and leans back beneath the edge of the table. The liquid flows in a path across the wood and pours from the corner, spilling onto Stirling's curls.

The room bursts into a roar of laughter. "I'm placing my money on the boy who can't hold his ale!" One of the men who is sitting at Stirling's original table when he told his story calls out.

Stirling joins in howling with laughter. He can't contain himself. The humor spreading to him is like a contagious virus. The world around him is hilarious and he doesn't understand why.

"Young man, you and your fancy northeastern dragon better make a good name for this village," another adds.

"What, the town nickname *lost and found* doesn't suit you?" Gilgamesh mocks.

"Well, the boy was lost, and we found him, so it's still suitable," Bernard inserts. Bernard hunches over Stirling. "Here, boy, take my hand," he offers, extending out his hand. Clasping it Stirling is pulled to his feet, his legs wobbling unsteadily beneath him as if he is an infant learning to walk.

Jumping off the stool, Gilgamesh pushes through the villagers to Bernard who loops Stirling's arm around his neck to help stabilize him.

"He can stay the night here, we can't let him wander around like this," Gilgamesh tells Bernard, referring to Stirling whose neck can no longer support his bobbing head.

"Did you hear that?" Bernard shakes him. "You won yourself a night stay at the glorious alehouse inn."

Stirling hiccups and leans into Bernard. "Where's Ignis going to sleep?"

"Who?"

"Ignis, Ignis, my dragon Ignis," Stirling reminds.

"Oh, right. There's the stable right outside he can sleep in. Right now, we're focused on getting you to bed," Bernard informs.

"But we'd always sleep in the same place," Stirling expands, finding it difficult to string together a proper sentence.

"What? He'll be right outside. I'm taking you upstairs," Bernard adjusts his grip and chauffeurs the drunken boy to the front door. With one linked around Stirling's waist, guiding him forward, and the other holding Stirling up, Bernard uses his shoulder to push open the weak boards of the door.

Ignis' head immediately pops up. His serene body spread out across the road no longer surrounded by company, where he fell asleep from the relaxing touch of the mothers and children petting his feathers.

"*Stirling?*" he says.

Stirling's head bobs as his glossy eyes find his friend, his wild curls latching onto Bernard's beard in their close proximity. Stirling's eyes strain to focus on the blurry orange figure.

"*Are you drunk?*" Ignis asks.

'No, you're drunk," Stirling rebuts wittily.

Bernard cranks his neck pulling his head back keeping Stirling's hair from his mouth as he speaks. "Did you just tell a dragon it's drunk? Clearly, you are the intoxicated one here."

Stirling shakes his head repeatedly, "Noooo, he calls me drunk first." His words slur.

"You're more of a lightweight than I thought." Bernard laughs.

"No, no, talk, he unerstan, wetalk, Ignisan I talk—But wid our minds!" Stirling tries to explain, pointing to his head.

"Grab the railing," Bernard instructs as they reach the stairs. Stirling slaps his hand out at the railing, missing he slumps forward still held up by Bernard.

"Hahaha, I missssssed.," he laughs.

Ignis holds back his laughter, "*You're making a fool of yourself.*"

"You shudyour face!" Stirling snaps back, scrunching his nose in Ignis' direction, and grabs the railing firmly.

Blinking long and slow Bernard sighs, "You're messing with me, right? People can't understand dragons. That's impossible."

Stirling leans into Bernard, his forehead bopping into Bernard's with his lack of spatial judgment. "It is paudible. All about bond. You don't buy—you bond— become eachobers eberyting."

The burly man shifts his grip on Stirling so his bobblehead lobs to the other side and no longer leans against his own. "I don't know what you are trying to convey to me, boy, but it all sounds like a tall tale. Even quetzalcoatl are known to be the wisest of the species, but no one has ever been able to speak with one."

Lifting his foot with the expectancy of another step, Stirling's foot slips through the empty space. Bernard tightens his grip on the falling boy as the sole of Stirling's patch-worked leather shoe slaps hard down on the weathered wood.

"Be careful now," Bernard tells Stirling as he guides him across the balcony to the first of two doors. The second door at the end of the balcony leads to a private room for those who can afford to pay for it.

"Weeeeelllll, maybe dey never try," Stirling suggests, his mind still on being told people can't speak to dragons.

"I think you need to try to get some sleep," Bernard nudges open the communal room door.

Several wooden box frames filled with straw line the room, each accompanied by a small trunk for the traveler to store and lock their belongings. The heat radiating up from the alehouse and kitchen below warms the room as if there was a fireplace built in.

Bernard leads Stirling over to the closest bed, "Your bags will be fine with you dragon, no one will try to take them. Let's at least get that costrel off of you and your belt, we don't want that hook jabbing you in the middle of the night."

Swaying without the support of Bernard, Stirling pulls the costrel strap over his head and drops it to the floor. He fumbles blindly, undoing the belt worn over his tunic, adding it beside the costrel. Pausing, Stirling stands waiting for the next directive.

"Want to hand over those goggles? We can lock them in the trunk," he asks, reaching out for them expecting Stirling to drop them onto the ground as he had done with the other items.

"Noooooo!" Stirling complains, stepping backward with a shake of his head. His foot catches on the costrel's strap, his body beginning to tip.

Bernard reflexively grabs Stirling's outstretched arm stopping him from falling. "All right. Wear them. I don't care. Just lie down."

Stirling's hands protectively encase the goggles. Feeling the comfort of the metal digging into his skin, he shuffles over to the bed. He loses what control he has of his muscles and flops down onto it, his long legs hanging hallway off. Bernard tilts his head as he watches the odd boy pass out with his hand still clutching the bronze goggles with a heartbroken smile.

"Good night, kid," he says softly.

Three

The castle's courtyard is a well-tended botanical garden with more colors than the average person can name. Red and gold railings surround the courtyard with a covered walkway with walls painted with an array of scenery; people farming in a small village, a ship unloading its merchandise, dragons flying in formation, and an ocean view of the island.

Amiria sits on a marble bench in the center of the garden. She used to come here whenever she could as a child, anytime she was able to escape from training she would end up here to play alone, to pretend she was exploring new lands.

She hasn't left the Castle grounds since that night several weeks ago. She misses the forest and the mountains. She misses the freedom nature offers to anyone who is willing to take the moment to listen.

She hates these surrounding walls. No matter the number of murals painted and strung up tapestries to cover the naturally depressing color of the castle hallways, they will never compare to the real beauty the world has to offer.

This place is no more than a birdcage. A creature given the gift of flight only to be confined to a metal cage. No matter how you decorate it, a cage is a cage.

"Amiria, there you are. I had to ask you handmaiden where you were. I don't have time to search all over the castle grounds for you," her father calls out from behind her, stepping out onto the cobbled stoned path leading from the terrace to the center of the garden.

"It shouldn't be that hard to find me. Anyone who knows me would know this is my favorite place in the castle," she peers over her shoulder from the bench surrounded by a bed of primroses.

"Well, I guess no one knows you," he says in a candid tone. Amiria's posture droops. "The only person who has any clue on where you might be is paid to know you. Maybe you should stop spending all your free time alone. It's bad for your image." He lectures strolling out to her, "This is precisely the reason I came to speak to you. You're not a child anymore. You're nineteen. You should have married three years ago and yet here you are still without any form of marriage lined up. You need to wed soon before you become too old to bear children."

"Who says I want children?" Amiria's face twists at the idea.

"It doesn't matter what you want. You have a duty to continue my bloodline. You need to get over it and grow up, and since you have no intention of finding your own spouse I'm taking it upon myself to help you. You will be attending the ball next week and you will be matched with a suitor." He lays out for her.

She spins around to him wildly, "You can't do that!"

"I can and I will. It is my right as your father to give away your hand," he says, raising his voice. "You might be a Winged Rider, but you are still a woman."

Amiria is speechless, baffled at the information being slapped across her face.

"If you don't show up to the ball and speak to the gentlemen yourself, I will pick whomever I deem fit."

Amiria is on fire. Her body reaching its melting point, the olive skin liquefies and pools into a sullen puddle on the carved bench. Slowly it drips into the soft soil below her feet watering the primroses.

Overwhelmed with anger and frustration Amiria follows her melting body and slides off the bench to the flower bed burying her face into her hands.

Her father pulls his lips into a straight line, the creases on his forehead deepen as he furrows his eyebrows, irritated. Sighing through his nostrils embarrassed by her behavior he turns silently leaving her to her self pity.

She listens to her father's footsteps dissipate through her pounding eardrums. She pulls her face vibrant with fury away from her hands. In a fit of emotion, she rips a handful of primroses from the garden and chucks them. The flowers scatter out into the air like confetti.

Three noble women eye her from the opposing terrace wearing bliauts, dresses form fitting around the waist with long loose sleeves, and jeweled ceintures hanging as knotted belts around their hips.

One of the women in a purple bliaut leans over to her friend, cupping her hand over her friend's ear she whispers, then both glance over in sync. The friend holds up her hand stifling back a laugh.

"If you have something to say, come over here and say it!" Amiria shouts, leaping up to her feet.

The women's eyes bug out as the third friend in a blue bliaut pulls them both away and out of sight. Amiria drops back to the soil with a slump. Angry she kicks out at the ground in front of her scuffing up the once nicely planted garden.

Leaning her head back, she rests it on the marble bench and watches the passing clouds.

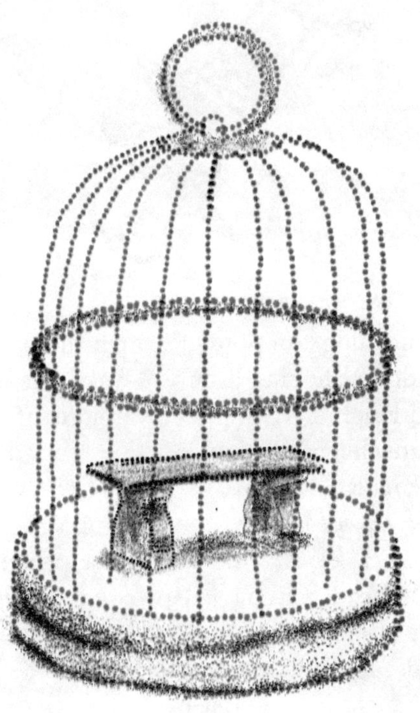

Four

The morning sun pours through the open window. Blinking his eyes awake, the bright light heightens Stirling's awareness of his splintering headache. He squints peering around the room to recall where he is.

The inn above the alehouse.

"Are you going to sleep all day?" Ignis asks, popping into Stirling's aching head. Stirling groans covering his eyes with the crook of his arm. *"Come on, sleepy head. Don't be rude to your hosts."* Ignis taunts.

Stirling mutters a reply under his breath and rolls out of bed, pieces of straw stuck in his mangled curls. Swaying with each step, he wobbles across the room and out onto the balcony.

He grimaces, shielding his eyes from the blinding white light of the sun with his hand. The temperature is significantly warmer than on the island. It isn't muggy, but as he flew south, he reached a point he no longer required a jacket even at night. He was content lying beside the fire under the open sky.

"Hey, you're finally awake!" Bernard calls, waving his hand from the dirt road below, a large bucket full of water from the nearby river held firmly in his other hand.

Smiling politely, Stirling waves back. From his viewpoint, he can see the village folk in the neighboring homes scattered about already amid their morning chores.

What he can't see is any distinguishable shop signs above any of the buildings close to the alehouse he is standing above. The only sign beside the one with a painted mug and bed is hanging from the shop across the road with a painted scale. The image fading and chipping off the cracking wood. Attached to the shop is a small garden, a chicken coop, and a single goat like the rest of the homes.

"Ignis, you woke me up, now where are you?" Stirling asks, checking around.

"Went to find myself some breakfast. I might not have to eat every day. But I need to eat at some point and you took so long to wake up," Ignis explains.

"Oi! Boy! You spacing out again?" Bernard calls up.

Motioning with his hands, Stirling answers, "No, I was talking to Ignis."

"You still going with that? I thought you were saying drunken nonsense." Bernard shouts.

"It's not nonsense!" Stirling yells back as he hops down the staircase two steps at a time.

"What's nonsense other than the way he speaks?" Eve, the alehouse maid from the prior night, asks pausing from her chore of sweeping the old rush, trampled and soaked in ale, from the alehouse's floor to replace it with a new dry layer.

"This boy claims he can speak to dragons," Bernard informs, jabbing his thumb in the direction of Stirling who has reached the bottom of the stairs.

"Not drag*ons*, drag*on*. Only him," Stirling defends.

"Yeah, and I can turn rocks into gold. No one can speak to dragons. They're just beasts," Eve mocks.

"Has anyone tried? Because where I come from they aren't *just* beasts. They are our warriors, our protectors, and our friends," Stirling enlightens.

"Whatever makes you happy, kid. You talk to your dragon. Hey, maybe if you win the games you might start some kind of trend," Bernard teases.

"I need to sign up before I start thinking about winning or losing," Stirling adds.

"Don't let the competitors know about your, uh, gift," Eve states, circling her hand in the air as she searches for the last word.

"Why?" Stirling asks, confused. "Back home, someone with this ability was seen as a master in the art of flying."

Eve pops her hip, "To be honest, with the poor characteristics you've already displayed you're going to be the kindling to their fire of ridicule, you don't want to give them any more fuel." With a shrug stating it is how it is, she turns back into the alehouse to finish cleaning.

Stirling dismisses her comment, focusing on Bernard. "I've spent my whole life hiding who I am for the fear of the death penalty. Some name-calling isn't going to bother me."

"So you really are serious about going to the games?" Bernard's eyes widen beneath his bristly eyebrows.

"More than you know," Stirling grins.

Nodding, Bernard leans back, sizing Stirling up. After a long pause, he asks, "You hungry? My missus made some oats earlier. There's still some warm on the fire. It's way better than your typical porridge. I'll let you in on a secret."

Bernard motions for Stirling to lean in. "She likes to go heavy on the honey. I didn't get this belly from eating carrots." He chuckles, slapping his stomach.

Stirling's stomach growls in response, "That sounds amazing, thank you."

"This is actually my place right here across the way," Bernard points out, nodding his chin at the shop Stirling was reading the sign for.

"*So, that must be their trader's guilds sign,*" he ponders the obvious in hindsight as he follows behind Bernard.

"You can wash your hands and face off in the trough here," Bernard instructs.

Stirling does as he's told and leans over the trough set up beside the side of the house in a perfect position to collect rainwater from the wood-shingled roof. He disregards his unkempt reflection as he cleans himself off.

Still holding the water pail, Bernard pushes open the crudely built door constructed from multiple strips of wood held together by two metal brackets.

Stirling steps inside the shanty shop. The interior doesn't surprise him. It is no different from the alehouse, the floor or lack of flooring is compacted dirt layered with rush and hay to absorb any liquids and help insulate. If he is being honest, it is a step above the cold rock flooring of the cave he spent three years in. He remembers how all the homes and shops back home sat on a raised foundation with wooden floors. Is that a factor of the city or the whole kingdom? Stirling struggles to recall his grandparents' bakery out in the center of the island. They too had wooden floors. His family is more well off than he took for granted at the time.

Wall to wall of the shop is overflowing with trinkets. He imagines himself stepping inside a treasure chest for scavengers, filled to the brim with items that would have assisted him the last several years. Miscellaneous textiles lay in uneven stacks on shelves. Hung from stands near the front of the shop like fruits from a tree are hats and glinting metal of cheap jewelry. Gloves like mounds of dirt lay piled beneath the accessory stands.

The sleeve of Stirling's shirt catches on one of the chipped swords poking out of a barrel. He can see a second barrel with staffs and spears shoved in the corner. He stops at a table cluttered with tools of all sorts.

Stirling touches the hand-worn leather-wrapped handle of a dagger. He thinks of Amiria, how she held the dagger delicately in her nimble hand. An artist with her paintbrush. She had attempted to teach him how to fight with one or at least protect himself, but it had the same result with swordsmanship, he was terrible at it. He managed to hold himself if she held back and only in defense. When it came to striking back he was useless. His movements are hesitant and clunky. He isn't aggressive. He doesn't have it in him to attack someone. In the eyes of the Cavalry, he is weak.

Bernard stops in front of a door in the back of the room, "You like any of this junk?"

"Oh, I was just browsing. It reminded me of someone," Stirling admits.

"That girl you spoke of last night?" Bernard guesses.

"How did you know?" Stirling questions.

"I can see it on your face," Bernard points out, making Stirling subconsciously touch his cheeks. Bernard changes the topic back to the shop items. "Well, most of this stuff isn't worth much. I have a few valuables, but I keep those hidden until a customer comes along offering something else of value—Well—" He nods his head at the door behind him, "Let's get you fed."

He opens the door to a single-room home. Each corner is designated as different sections of a house. A bed barely large enough to fit two adults fills an entire corner of the space with two storage chests. On the opposite side is a small table pushed against the wall with a bench seat, near a fireplace with a pot hanging inside. The corner closest to the door is stacked with small crates of collected vegetables, grains, and herbs.

The room is the opposite of the store when it comes to material items. It only contains the bare necessity of household supplies.

Bernard's wife Roesia, a tawny skinned woman with round cheeks and her dark hair tied up into a knot on her head, jumps up from the table. "Oh, good, so they didn't drink you to death. They can get themselves pretty carried away at times."

Stirling is alarmed as she takes his hands in hers, they are warm like her smile. "Yeah. I was a bit outmatched in there," he tells her.

"Let me get you a bowl of oats," she says, patting his hands in a way meaning she won't take no for an answer, "If I knew we were having a guest I would have used the almond milk. This is just made with goat milk."

"Oh, no worries. I'm not finicky," Stirling says awkwardly.

"Roesia, it's confirmed this boy really does want to join the games," Bernard announces.

Taking the ladle, she scoops a large helping into a wooden bowl. "Oh? We have a games participant here in our little abode? We are honored. Are you any good?" Her brown eyes blink up at Stirling as if he had left and returned as a newly established man. Her shimmering gaze is now full of admiration and astonishment.

Riddled with embarrassment, Stirling ashamedly admits, "Well, I don't really know. I only have one friend back home to compare myself to. Also, I haven't signed up yet, but don't get me wrong I do want to, but Bernard said there is a registration fee?"

Bernard eyes Stirling who is rubbing the back of his neck awkwardly.

"I don't have much, but maybe there is something I can sell to you? I have those leather bags and cloak, but they are a bit water damaged. I fell into the ocean a few weeks ago. The bow I have is really nice, but it broke in half," Stirling touches his goggles. "What about these? How much are these worth?"

Bernard crosses his arms, his forearms resting on his gut. Closing his eyes, he travels deep into thought. Roesia shoves the bowl of oats into Stirling's hands, implying there's enough for seconds.

Bernard opens his eyes, "The goggles are of high quality, I can see from here someone took the time and effort into their craft. They would get you enough coin to pay the fee twice and then some, but I'm sorry kid. I will not purchase them from you. You will be needing them for the games."

Stirling shakes his head frustrated, "But I have nothing else to offer though." He reaches up, gripping the goggles in one hand, "And I don't even know where to start with the burned harness. I've just been riding bareback, but I can't compete like that."

Bernard and his wife share a mutual glance before speaking up. "I propose a deal?"

"A deal?"

"Yes, a deal. I will loan you the registration fee. I also have an idea of how to fix your harness. But you have to promise me to register under this village's name. You will be Stirling of Patu. Let's show those noble folk that we exist, too," Bernard offers.

Confused, Stirling asks, "What about my family name?"

"Family name?"

"Bakere, my family name, the one that gets passed down through the men in the family. I'm Stirling Bakere," he explains.

Bernard frowns and lays out, "We don't have second names here. That's only for nobles. People know who you are by where you are from. Bernard of Patu and she is Roesia of Patu, you can always add the wife of Bernard so no one tries to marry this wonderful woman." A smile emerges on his face as he ganders lovingly down at his cheeky spouse. Peeling his adoring gaze away from Roesia he returns to Stirling. "So, do you accept the deal?"

"I-I can't accept so much, while all I'm giving you is altering my name," Stirling declines.

"Well, I'm not asking you, I'm telling you. Registration ends in a few days. We can build your harness today and you can be there to sign up tomorrow morning." Bernard tells him.

Stirling is unsure of how to respond, overtaken by Bernard's generosity. They had only met yesterday, yet here he is already putting this much trust and faith into him. Does he not think there's a possibility he might take the money and run? They would never be able to catch up to him. He can use the money to join the games, but not use the village's name, he can use the capitols instead. What would they even do if he did?

Stirling's shoulders slack, he can never betray these people. They have shown more hospitality to him than he has ever even been shown by his own family. What is it they have to gain from him? Better status to their town's name?

"Why are you doing this for me?" Stirling confronts.

Bernard shrugs. "From what I have gathered from your story, all you've needed in life was a chance to prove yourself. But I'll be honest with you. This isn't just for you. This is also for this village. It would be good for our name if you ride under it, whether or not you win. We can at least show them this village has more to offer than a place to drop off broken goods. So, in reality, my offer to you is selfish." The truth falls from his lips.

"Oh," Stirling's eyes drop.

Bernard squeezes Stirling's shoulder, "I'm a tradesman, I'm about benefiting both of us. Now go on and eat before the food gets cold from you standing there holding it."

After Stirling finishes breakfast and a second helping forced upon him by Roesia and with his stretched stomach aching for the first time in several years he follows Bernard back into the shop.

"I have a few ideas to tie you over until you win enough coin to purchase a real saddle," Bernard suggests, picking up a cattle harness.

Stirling stands in the center of the room holding a few more heavy-duty leather straps that Bernard strewed across his arms. "Do they make some for what did you say he is again, a per'yanny svir? But he's not a commonly ridden species?"

"Yes and no. They will make you a saddle, but it will have to be a custom purchase. They don't carry those in stock since no one rides a per'yanny svir. It'll cost you extra," Bernard explains.

"Great," Stirling mumbles.

"Okay, I think these should be enough straps to fit around his body. Can you grab those hides draped over the bench with the slippers on top?"

Stirling scans the room landing on the bench Bernard is referring to.

Squatting down, Stirling moves the several pairs of slippers off to the side exposing the large cow hides below. Rolling three hides together he tests the weight. Seeming manageable he heaves the hides up onto his shoulder with an "Oof."

"Can you whistle for your dragon or do we need to go looking for him?" Bernard asks.

With an exaggerated sigh, Stirling says, "Yeah, I can get him to come to us."

"Oh, right, you can talk to him, with your mind," Bernard repeats in a mocking tone tapping his temple.

Annoyance vibrates through Stirling. Brushing it off he calls out, *"Ignis. Meet me back in the village."*

"Right now?" Ignis responds immediately. He stands knee-deep in the river, a fish flopping in his clamped jaw.

"Yes, right now!" Stirling says more frustrated than he should, the words accidentally coming out audibly.

"I don't know, maybe. What's in it for me?"

Bernard chuckles. Stirling self-consciously turns away. *"Ignis,"* he hisses.

Bernard pushes open the front door to the shop. "Is your beast coming?"

"Yeah, he's stubborn and his name is Ignis."

"I told you per'yanny svirs can be high maintenance."

A large shadow casts over them. Tilting their heads up to the sun, they squint up at Ignis as they walk to the center of the road. Ignis circles down to them descending slowly. With a flutter of his wings above the compacted earth, he nullifies his landing to a gentle drop. His feet firmly on the ground he tosses the fish still in his jaws up into the air and catches it in the back of his throat letting it slide down whole like a pelican.

"You summoned me, Your Majesty?" Ignis says with a mocking bow of his head.

"Shut up, Ignis" Stirling bounces the hides on his shoulder. "We're going to make you a new harness."

"That's what you ruined my fishing for? A harness? I don't need a harness, you need a harness. I can fly fine without one," Ignis argues.

"Oh, get over it. Bernard is right. Your species is high maintenance," Stirling replies, sticking out his tongue.

Bernard's eyes furrow, skeptical of the possibility a human can talk to a dragon. "Yeah, this talking to your dragon like it's a person. This is exactly what we were saying you shouldn't do in front of people. It's weird."

Stirling frowns.

Shaking his head, Bernard moves on. "Here's my idea. Toss the hide over the back of Ignis so we can measure this out. Last night after you fell asleep, I examined your old harness and the one still strapped to Ignis. We're going to construct a similar framework but have these thicker straps for more reliability and hides to sit on for comfort. We can add some support for your legs too. Seems like you've been flying without a horn or cantle which is good because we don't have the time to construct those."

"As long as I'm buckled down, and I have handles to hold onto I will be perfectly fine," Stirling adds.

"No reins?" Bernard questions, "Don't make me regret investing in you."

Stirling throws the leather over Ignis' back, "I guess we'll just have to prove to you we're worth it."

Bernard smiles. He appreciates the kid's outlook. He doesn't care about money or the craft of his gear. The boy's scraggly appearance shows as if he has crawled out of a hole in the ground. His tunic faded to a degree he is unsure if it used to be blue or it's a shade of grey and a pair of leather patchwork shoes that didn't grow as he did.

He has heard thousands of stories during his time owning the trades shop, but he has never heard a story as intense as this kid's. Beaten and broken he keeps getting up. His stubborn soul drives him forward solely on ambition. Refusing to let anyone dictate his life.

Maybe in reality he wants to live vicariously through Stirling. He was raised watching the games. There is nothing he loves more than learning about the professional racers and their dragons. He understood he would never be a racer, but his dream was to work with the racers. To be a hostler or stableman. To help them prepare for their competitions and help maintain their dragons. He took over his family's business and started a family of his own giving up on his dreams.

Brought back to being fourteen constructing his first harness for Ignis, Stirling walks with a new pep in his step. He stops beside Ignis and throws the hides over the dragon's back. Grinning widely, he turns to Bernard for the next direction.

The older man scratches his beard. "Okay, this is what we're going to do."

By the time supper rolls around the new harness is finished. "*What do you think?*" Stirling asks Ignis, admiring their handiwork.

Ignis shimmies his body testing the feel of the new gear, "*Hmm, I'll get used to the stuff across my back, but I guess it'll soften your knees digging into my shoulders.*"

Stirling rolls his eyes, "*You literally have armored skin. So, I call bull on that.*"

Eve leans against the alehouse wall beside Bernard, "Should we have someone check that boy's head?"

"You know what? His little quirk is starting to grow on me. Gives him character." Bernard tells her while they watch Stirling converse silently with Ignis.

Eve curls her upper lip. "Yeah, the characteristics of a madman."

Five

The next morning, Stirling stands well-fed at the edge of town after breakfast of fried eggs and bread warmed on the fire made by Roesia. The small family of four huddles perfectly together with Bernard's arm around Roesia's shoulders and his hand on his son's, ready to watch Stirling off.

Stirling's arm nearly bumps Ignis' shoulder as he points south with Bernard, Roesia, and their two children. "Just over the hill, big arena to the right. I can't miss it," Stirling repeats aloud. Over breakfast, Bernard had provided Stirling with a rundown of Leucasia's layout and his itinerary for when he arrives.

"Right. There will be a stand with the game's emblem, the five dragon species, not including per'yannny svir, there's the knucker, lung, amphiptere, and quetzalcoatl. The stand will have an employee sitting there with papers and a box of capes," Bernard informs.

Roesia motions to Stirling to lean down to her height. "You missed a spot on your face." Licking her thumb she wipes a spot on his cheek he had neglected after he had rinsed his face and hands the best he could in the trough. Stirling doesn't flinch, letting her take the motherly role of preparing her son for the world. "You know under this mess of hair and old clothes is a very handsome man. Here's some small village advice for the city." She leans close as if to tell him a secret. "Ignore them."

"Ignore them?" He pulls back, raising his eyebrow.

"It doesn't matter what they say or how they look at you, It doesn't mean anything when it comes to actually competing. Remember this Stirling. Do. Not. Let them get to you. And never, *never* stoop to their level. Keep being you until the very end. If it gets rough, just remember why you joined the games," she advises.

"Because I love flying?" Stirling states.

Giving him an encouraging squeeze on the shoulder, Roesia smiles softly. "Exactly."

"Also, Stirling," Bernard speaks up. "There is an accommodation the racers are required to stay at near the stadium, but it isn't free. You can try to book a room now, but they might want the money upfront."

"Wait, you're telling me this now?" Stirling stands up to full height.

"Well then, you'll have to at least place third in your first match, then you will easily have enough to stay there the whole month and still have profit," Bernard adds.

Stirling's eyes dart back and forth, unsure. "Wait, what happens if I don't stay there?"

Bernard shakes his head. "Not sure. No one in the games hasn't been able to afford the inn. You might have to pay an inconvenience fee—yes those exist. They prefer everyone to be in one location for easy access if they need you. The rooms are at an extreme discount since everyone is forced to stay there.

"Awesome," he grumbles. "Well, I appreciate it again. I can't convey how much your help means to me. I'll be back soon," Stirling says, pulling himself onto Ignis.

Roesia pulls her children close to her as they wave goodbye giddily.

Separating them from the family, Ignis picks up his pace turning from a trot into a sprint across the fields. With a jumping start, he climbs into the clear blue sky. The mountain is small, someone in an hour can leisurely walk to the summit from the center of the village. From the view, in the sky, the nearly treeless mountains are velvety soft like the fabric clumped and bubbled on the tailor's table.

The small village disappears behind the green mounds as they roll over the top. Ignis sputters in the air falling momentarily as his wings skip a beat. He stops short, and the beauty of the city landscape on a horseshoe-shaped harbor comes into view. The gradual climb on one side of the mountain ends at the summit and drops off to sheer cliffs, except for several swooping locations with roads carved out for easy access and departure from the city.

Stirling has never imagined anything like it. Following all the way to the tip of the cape, Leucasia is a stunning sprawl of white lime-washed walls with red clay shingles. The buildings on the oceanside cliff stack one on top of the other. Narrow paths layered with crushed stone line the building walkways, each connected by staircases carved of cut stone.

The ocean.

Stirling inhales sharply, the realization of how much he missed the ocean is evident, hitting him like a wall. She glimmers before him like an endless diamond meadow. Her dazzling teal waters stretch as far as he can see.

He watches with eager curiosity as Leucasia's citizens file in and out of the city's arching gates at the bottom where the land levels out. Following the trampled pathways is a rainbow of booths and tents twisting and twirling. They pool around a massive stadium the size of a village carved halfway into the mountainside. His eyes follow the path continuing past the stadium to bleachers running perpendicular to the mountains. Out in the ocean, massive numbered pillars placed in a straight line erect from the deep water.

Dragons of all shapes and colors cling to the walls, fly through the sky, and crawl across the ground.

Ba-dump.

Stirling feels his whole chest constrict in a single breath.

Ba-dump.

His breathing picks up becoming ragged gasps.

Ba-dump.

His hands are trembling.

Ba-dump. He can't breathe. *Ba-dump.* HE CAN'T BREATHE.

"Ignis stop," he panics, gripping the fabric over his heart, his nails digging holes into the worn-out tunic.

"Stop what?" Ignis hovers in the air confused.

"STOP! JUST LAND! PLEASE JUST LAND!" he screams in his head, his lungs unable to push out enough air to give him a voice. His spine arches, doubling his body over. His heart is going to give out, death is imminent.

"Okay, okay. Calm down.," Ignis lowers them gently to a spot on the top of the mountain.

The hooked-shaped claws barely skim the surface before Stirling unbuckles and throws himself to the ground. He lands half-crumpled on his hands and knees. The muscles under his skin violently tense and spasm controlling the bones they encase on their own accord.

"Hey! What's wrong with you?" Ignis worries.

Soil squeezes out in clumps between Stirling's fingers as they claw into the earth. With rigid movements he lowers his forehead, feeling the cool turf against his skin. *SIRENS.* Releasing the dirt he cups his hands over his ears. *ALARMS.* His body curls into itself, his chest

pressing against his knees. *FIRE*. His stomach twists to
an extent that it's one degree from spewing all its
contents.

*The sound of the creaking rope as the tailor's body swung in the
breeze.*

"*Stirling?*" Ignis lowers his face down close to him,
"*Are you okay?*"

*Once flowing silk hair caught up in the twisted necklace,
hovering toes still covered in soil, point down to the earth no longer
living off her nutrients.*

Their golden eyes meet, but Stirling only sees the end
of the rainbow. It blows in the wind at the top of a
trampled daisy hill in the form of a colorful skirt.

"*This isn't Lumierna. We can fly here,*" Ignis reminds him.
Stirling's fears ooze out and seep into his thoughts.

Stirling's eyes gloss over. Images of his father
clenching the paddle, the Cavalry pursuing him, and the
dark depths of the ocean surrounding him. The water
crashing in. Everything is crashing in. Fingernails draw
red lines down his throat to his chest. He can't breathe,
he's suffocating.

Gasping and wheezing, Stirling struggles to pull air
into his lungs, his face a vibrant red.

"*SNAP OUT OF IT!*" Ignis nudges Stirling's side with
his snout tipping him over. Stirling sprawls out on his
side, his eyes watery with leaking memories. "*We're not in
Wyverna anymore. We've made it to where they will never find us.
We did what you wanted. We're as far southeast as we can get.
This is a brand new kingdom with a brand new way of life that
accepts what we have to offer. Now get up so we can show them.*"

Dead-eyed, Stirling blinks Ignis back into view. His
ragged breaths begin to even out. *What happened?* His
awareness gradually returns like the sun breaking through
a thick fog.

Biting the back of Stirling's shirt Ignis pulls him up to
an unsteady standing position. Held up solely by Ignis, his

knees bow under his weight. The seams of his worn-out tunic inform him they are ready to let go with sounds of tearing.

Breathe in. Breathe out. Breathe. Breathe.

Gathering himself, Stirling shakes his head embarrassed. What had come over him? The sight of the city had seized him, it held him down and forced him to rewatch the horrors of his life.

"You all right to keep going?" Ignis asks, concerned.

"Yes and no," Stirling confides. With his body still jittery, he hesitantly climbs back onto Ignis.

"You sure?" Ignis presses. Stirling hazily nods his head. *"All right, because we're not turning back now."* Ignis leaps into the sky no longer allowing Stirling a chance to change his mind.

Ignis lands in the fenced-off patch of land designated for arrival and departure. Fighting the urge to fold in on himself, Stirling squeezes his eyes shut. He imagines forcing the desire to run down into a box and closes the lid. He won't run, he doesn't need to run. So why does every scar holding him together scream to take flight and disappear? Why do his eyes play tricks on his mind by putting *threat* above everyone's head?

He sits timidly on Ignis' back, unable to dismount as he scans his surroundings. He was surrounded by festivities. Dragons of several different species and every shade of color sit hitched to heavy stone or cling to the sea cliff above. Children sit on the wooden fence watching the arrival of men on dragon back. With toothy grins, they point at Stirling and Ignis and clap before their eyes are caught by another racer. A mother pats her child's head without regarding Stirling and Ignis.

A man in a brightly colored tunic and matching flags in each hand waves them at Stirling. Stirling's nerves ignite, his body tensing at the man waving the flags.

"Disembark over here," he instructs, one hand motioning Stirling forward and the other pointing to a spot out of the landing zone where another man is currently dismounting his draco species of dragon.

Stirling's uneasiness begins to quell. They only see another owner of a dragon. Dragons can be bought by *anyone* here. He is *allowed* to be here. He can be here, it's okay. He can be here, it's okay. It's okay. It will be okay.

While Stirling argues with his instincts, Ignis follows the flagger's directions and leads them out of the pen making room for the next dragon landing.

Fascination lays over his uncertainty like a wool blanket snuffing out a fire. He cautiously dismounts. Finding his footing, he loops his fingers through Ignis' harness for support and they set off through the maze of colorful canvas booths and tents. Item after item catching his eye, his head whips back and forth unable to stay put on a single object.

There are merchants selling blankets, capes, and cloaks stitched with silhouettes of dragons. Metal cloak clasps shaped as wings and claws glint against the fabric displays. The smell of bread baked into the shape of dragon heads and a side view of the whole body wafts through the air. Every booth offers trinkets to take home as a reminder of the annual event, there are soaps, candles, bowls, and mugs. Every item and each booth is in some way dragon-themed.

Bernard taught him the names and descriptions of the different species but seeing them now in person leaves Stirling speechless.

Emerging from the main density of the tents they step out to a wider space where the majority of the competitors are walking about with their dragons. Racers and non-racers stand at enlarged booths compared to those selling memorabilia to the citizens. They lean over scrutinizing the gear questioning, the comfort of new saddles, the quality of reins, the structure of helmets, and the padding of shin guards.

Stirling's gaze lingers on a stand selling goggles made from various metals, copper, iron, bronze, and even silver and gold. Each with leather straps dyed to compliment the tones in the metal. He absent-mindedly touches the cool metal hanging around his neck before turning his focus to the species of dragons around him.

Close to all of the dragons walk on four legs like Ignis with membrane wings similar to the Wyverns though unlike Ignis their legs are stalky. Their chests swaying close to the ground. Dracos. Stirling runs the names through his head as he spots each species.

Amphipteres. Legless creatures curled up like snakes beside their owners. Their membrane wings tucked close against their scaly bodies.

A long thin dragon called a knucker with short front legs and long hind legs trots past a breed called Lung. A species that resembles the amphipteres where Stirling can't tell where their bodies stop, and their tails begin. Their major difference is they have four legs that are too short to lift their bodies. Their elongated bellies drag and slither along the ground like a skink.

"Incredible," he utters.

"I'm not the brightest color anymore either. They're every shade of the rainbow," Ignis adds, staring at a yellow knucker.

"I believe that's it," Stirling says, pointing to a stand-alone tent with a flag sectioned into fifths fluttering in the breeze, each portion a different color with a silhouette of each species. "Wait here." Stirling motions for Ignis to stay and approaches it.

A man in his mid-twenties stands centered at the table conversing with the young woman running the registration.

"Here's your cape with your number. Remember it is to be worn at all times during the games," the woman informs him.

"This isn't my first year. I'm very aware of that," the man grumbles impolitely, snatching the green and blue shoulder-length cape. Turning to leave, the man pauses on Stirling, glaring.

Stirling shrinks under the man's presence. Wishing to hide from the judgment, Stirling submits diverting his gaze down to the table. His scarred hands are hidden from view behind his back.

"They do just let anyone sign up," the man sneers. Shaking his head, he shambles away from the tent. Every several steps he glances back over his shoulder to see if he had seen Stirling correctly.

Struggling to ignore the sting of the man's comment, Stirling turns his attention to the woman. She scrunches her nose at him, "If you're here for handouts, I don't have anything. This is the registration. So, I need you to step aside for the professionals."

"What?" Stirling shakes his head. "No. I'm not here for handouts."

"Excuse me what?" The woman's eyebrows touch as she struggles to understand Stirling, "What are you saying, talk slower."

Stirling sighs and slows his words, "I'm here to reg—"

The woman cuts him short. "You can't register for other people."

"Huh?"

"Racers can't have their lackeys come and sign up for them. I need the actual competitor here to sign the paperwork," she explains bluntly, tapping her finger on the desk.

Stirling shakes his head confused, "Lackey? No, I'm here to sign myself up."

The girl raises her eyebrows, "It's required you own a dragon to participate in the games."

"I do have one," Stirling motions towards Ignis who is staring intently at a butterfly fluttering around the grass nearby.

"A per'yanny svir?" she says with disbelief. "You can't borrow other people's dragons either. It has to be your own."

Stirling's initial hurt is slowly melting into frustration, "He is mine. He's been my partner for nine years now. Can I just sign up already?"

The girl lifts her chin as if she has discovered a way to checkmate Stirling, "There's a registration fee. If you can't pay right now, upfront, you can't sign up."

Stirling pulls the coins from his bag laying them across the table, "Here. Happy? Now can I sign up?"

Lips curling, she bares her teeth. "Fine. Here's the paperwork." She hisses, tossing the papers across the table. Picking up the sheets Stirling frowns. "What can't you read?" She smirks. Ashamed Stirling shakes his head. "Of course, you can't." She scoffs. "Now I'm going to have to help fill it out for you." She twirls the quill in her fingers annoyed, "Your name for a start?"

"Stirling of Patu."

She lets out a short laugh after hearing the village's name, "Explains the speech." Continuing with the form she asks, "Age?"

"Nineteen."

"Species of dragon?"

"Per' ss—yanny something."

"You can't even pronounce the species correctly," she mutters to herself.

"Dragon's age?"

"Uh, I guess the same as me. We grew up together, but I'm not exactly sure."

Exhaling, she turns her head, cracking her neck, and finishes jotting down Stirling's answers, now and then muttering under her breath as she looks at Ignis for his color and guesses his approximate size and weight.

Completing, she looks back up at Stirling. "Since this is your first time and you have no prior experience. I will be placing you in the beginner's category. If, emphasize the IF you win and deem yourself suitable to the judges you can advance to the more experienced categories. Here is a paper with all the rules, schedules, and any general information about the overall games and lodging," she informs, sliding a paper scribbled from top to bottom with writing. "Of course, you'll need to find someone to read it for you though. Because I will not."

Rummaging through a crate beside her she pulls out an orange cape with the number zero stitched onto the front and back in white.

"Solid Orange?" he questions.

"Yes, it matches your dragon–" her smile is wide and fake, "The number is random. Most of the numbers have been claimed permanently by the veteran riders, and I'm out of other colors."

Over the table, Stirling can easily see into the crates beside her, still plentiful of capes in different colors and number combinations. He spots several oranges with secondary colors.

"Oh, okay," he grumbles, accepting the orange cape with his right hand exposing the inside of his arm.

The woman's eyes lock on his scars. Repulsed, she releases her grip on the cape, yanking her hand back to the safety of her side of the table. Demeaned, Stirling tugs the undershirt sleeve down over his insignia for the first time for any other reason besides warmth. He drapes the cape over his arm as an extra barrier pulling it protectively into his chest. Without saying a word, he hangs his head and lumbers back to Ignis.

"*We signed up?*" Ignis asks Stirling as he approaches.

"Yeah," his replies are short. "Beginners."

"*Only beginners?*" Ignis inquires.

"*Yep,*" Stirling says, switching to his thoughts suddenly self-aware of the people already starting to notice him. Keeping his chin down, Stirling refrains from meeting the prying eyes. He watches his feet progress him forward one at a time. Bernard and Roesia are right. It might be legal for him to ride, but he is still a pariah. He isn't part of their world.

"*Ignore them,*" Ignis advises, ushering Stirling along in the direction they believe the inn is in.

"*It's easier said than done,*" Stirling kicks a small rock with the inside of his foot.

"*I think you're reading into what people think too much. Lighten up and focus on the races,*" Ignis repeats the knowledge the villagers have been guiding him on. "*WHOA! WAIT HOLD ON!*" Ignis hollers abruptly.

Stirling jumps, startled. "*What! What is it!?*

"*There, look there. It is the most beautiful dragon I have ever been granted to lay my eyes upon,*" Ignis says pointing his snout in the direction of a crowd of people. Stirling peers around Ignis.

An all-feathered dragon as blue as the summer sky rises above them, white specks in its feather coat glisten like melting ice. It has no legs like the amphipteres from earlier. Its elegant wings with sapphire undertones spread out in display with feathers the length of an adult woman. The crowd cheers at the sight. Its large royal eyes scan the audience before it, its racer obscured behind the masses.

"That must be the quetzalcoatl," Stirling blurts out loud. "I wonder who it's racer is? He must be popular, bringing in a crowd like that."

"*I don't care who the racer is. I want to know who the dragon is,*" Ignis says, practically drooling.

"*Do you even know if it's a guy or girl?*" Stirling asks, tugging on Ignis' harness to get moving.

Ignis doesn't budge. "*Don't know, don't care.*"

Stirling yanks on the harness with futile attempts. Groaning, Stirling rolls his eyes, "*All right we get it. You like the dragon. Now stop staring. Let's get going.*" He yanks again impatiently. "*I want to check out the inn and get away from all these people for a bit.*" His eyes shift across the huddled groups of spectators witnessing Stirling's struggle to command his dragon.

Ignis protests, "*Oh, come on, you had nine years to stare at a pretty girl, let me have this.*"

"*They'll be in the races. You'll see them then,*" Stirling argues. "*Also, I didn't stare at Amiria. She is my friend.*"

"*Not for the first six years, stalker,*" Ignis heckles.

Stirling glances at the groups. "*Please, let's go. People are watching. It looks like I don't have any control of you.*"

"*You don't have any control of me,*" Ignis stubbornly plants his feet.

Stirling can feel the heat in his cheeks, each set of eyes a hot dagger raising his body temperature. "*Ignis! Let's go!*" he demands, jerking the harness.

Ignis lays off, cluing in on the dynamics of their surroundings. Giving in, he follows Stirling's lead. Unable to resist the urge to steal one last view of the quetzalcoatl, Ignis twists his neck keeping his eyes locked on them for as long as possible. Closing his eyes he paints the dragon on his heart, memorizing the details of their stunning appearance.

Six

Past the competition grounds and the festival tents is a large plain of open land stretching from the base of the mountain wall to where the grass appears to drop off into the ocean.

The inn rests in the center of the two, the building four times the size of the alehouse back in Patu. Stables designed for dragons extending from the smaller horse stalls run the length between the inn and the mountains. It cuts around back with plenty of roaming in between the two separate structures. A farm can be seen behind the buildings and a stone structure Stirling can't identify sits off to the ocean side of the inn.

A teenage girl with auburn hair and a face speckled with freckles sits on a bench outside the front door of the inn hemming a torn pillow.

She hears the shuffling of feet and sets the pillow off to the side of her. Her eyes darting back and forth between Stirling and Ignis, "Is the racer here himself? He can't send his serfs ahead to check in for him."

"I am—!" Stirling begins before biting his tongue. "I am the racer," he says, starting over calmer. "See here's my cape and my paper," he adds, holding up the two items as evidence.

The girl is stricken. "My apologies, sir. I mistook you because of your appearance. We can get you washed up and changed right away. Was the trip here rough? Where are you from?"

"Yes, well no, this isn't because of travel–I'm from Patu" Stirling starts, but decides against explaining further.

Leaving the pillow on the bench, the girl smiles and jumps up eager to serve a customer. "I'm Farah, my family owns the inn here. I can check you in if you are ready. Will you be staying here this week also, or will you only be here once the games begin?"

Stirling bites his lower lip. "Well, here's the thing. I don't have any coin yet. I won't be able to pay until I win one of the rounds."

Farah puts up her hand signaling him to stop talking. Her welcoming smile is suddenly absent. "This isn't a charity house. We do not accept any I owe yous. This is the one time a year we make our real profit. This is how we make a living to support ourselves for the rest of the year. We've experienced too many people not paying after the games and leaving us high and dry. We're a family with six children. Do you understand?"

"Okay, okay I get it," Stirling says, backing down. "You could have said No and left it at that."

Pinching the brim of her nose, she sighs. "Look. Try to win one of the first rounds and I'll gladly set you up with a bed. Hopefully, the games coordinator won't even know you weren't here on those starting days and fine you." She holds, waiting to see if Stirling has anything to say. Forgetting the basics of conversations he stands there idle.

She raises an eyebrow at his silence and returns to talking. "We will be completely booked for the single-man rooms by then, but we can always squeeze another cot into the communal room. Most racers try to book in advance to get their own rooms, which is why I made that comment earlier."

Afraid she will flip personalities again, switching from defensive, to helping then and back to defensive. Stirling dips his head, keeping his answer short. "Thanks for your advice."

He had expected her to remain hostile towards him as the registration woman had, leaving him unsure of how to respond to her when she changed the dynamics of her speech so fluently.

Her shoulders soften. "I do wish you luck though. It's nice to see someone so—someone so relatable to the majority of us finally steps up to the racing line."

"Oh." Stirling shifts, uncomfortable with his own body. "I should be going then." He crosses his arms unsure of what to do with his hands. "Thanks again." Backing away, Stirling turns and follows a path leading away from the inn

"See not everyone over here is bad," Ignis reassures.

"Yeah, but I'm not sure if she is nice or mean. She confuses me," Stirling brings up.

"Oh well, who cares. As long as she checks us in after, we win," Ignis insists, optimistic. *"Do you want to look at the stadium? Or at any of the booths?"*

"No, I'm going to pass on the crowds for now," Stirling answers, turning Ignis' suggestions down. Why does the congestion bother him? He grew up in a crowded city, but he had never felt as helpless as he did on the summit above Leucasia. How the memories strangled him. Was it because he spent too much time alone? Or is it because the last crowd he was in he had to run for his life?

"Let's go check out the water. I did miss the ocean," Stirling suggests.

They walk in silence, the only sound coming from the crunching of the pebbles beneath their feet. There isn't any form of a beach. No sand to walk along while the rolling waves wipe away your footprints. The grassy landscape breaks off, eroded by the constant slap of tides leaving behind large rocks disappearing into the deep harbor.

Hopping down the knee-high dirt ledge, Stirling stands balanced on the slippery rocks emerging from the crystal clear water. Sitting on his haunches Stirling cocks his head, fascinated by how quickly the water drops down into a lapras abyss. Studying eyes switch from the mysterious depths to the minnow swimming around his feet, darting in and out of the plant life flowing with the subtle tide. A calloused hand reaches down to the surface. The lukewarm liquid latches itself to his fingertips as he pets the calm waters. The memories of the frigid waters come flooding in, filling the capacity of his lungs and choking him. He yanks his hand back from the sticky water.

With a dull ache of the mental strain, he shoves the nightmare out of his mind, replacing it with the memory of the subterranean lake with Amiria. How the magic blue lights danced off her skin making her shine brighter than any of King Dietrich's wyvernites.

"What's that?" He asks himself as a pink object in the water catches his eye. Reaching down into the water below his feet, he pokes the pink object with five points coming off of it. "It's not a rock."

Gripping the object and with a little force, he tugs it free from the rock. The side he is holding is covered in rough bumps with smooth sections in between. He turns it over and yelps. Dropping the unknown object back into the water.

"What is it!?" Ignis asks, stretching his head over the edge of the bank to take a peek.

"I think that pink thing is alive. It had thousands of little moving finger feet on the bottom side." Stirling shivers.

"You dropped it, now we'll never know what it is," Ignis complains.

The water settles, his distorted reflection returning to its original form. When he lived in the cave, he commonly rinsed off in a stream nearby, but he never cared to control his hair. There wasn't any more effort given than running his fingers through to pull apart the thick tangles.

Amiria always did a better job when she would help trim it for him. How she would call him a baby when he complained about her pulling his hair out. He had been so focused on running away that his appearance was the last thought on his mind. That's just an excuse, he reminds himself. He has never really cared about what he looked like even before this, it's not as if the bakery or the forest had mirrors. The only two beings who had to see his face were Ignis and Amiria.

Stirling prods his face, poking at his nose that maybe is a little too big, pulling at the corners of his drooping eyes. He pulls out a smile for himself and drops it, watching his reflection frown back at him. Why did he ever think Amiria would want him as more than a friend?

Frustrated with himself, Stirling combs his fingers through his hair. Each finger catching, hooking, and snagging unable to find a clear path out.

"Don't look so surprised. You've always been that ugly." Ignis says nonchalantly. Stirling pulls his hand free and glares up at him. *"What!? Don't look at me like that. I'm the only one who isn't afraid to tell you the truth."* Ignis says, turning his head away, breaking their eye contact. His eyes jump back to Stirling's disgruntled face.

"Aren't you comforting? You really know how to boost someone's self-esteem," Stirling jabs.

"Maybe you are crazy, and I am just in your head. So you're actually the one saying this too—"

The end is cut off as Stirling puts up his hand. *"Let's not go to some dark deep meaning of self-loathing…"* He straightens his legs and with his head down begins to climb back up to the grass, *"Let's head back to the village. I'm done here."*

"Back so soon?" Bernard calls out to Stirling and Ignis as they stroll back into town after politely landing on the outskirts, "You don't want to join in on any of the pregame festivities? Did you at least sign up? What did the inn say?"

"No, yes, and I need to pay upfront," Stirling answers. "I'm registered, but Roesia was right about the people looking at me differently than the other contestants."

"Oh, they're a bunch of prudes," Bernard says, swatting his hand in front of his face, "They'll lighten up eventually after they see that talent of yours."

Stirling pulls out his informational sheet. "It's not only my appearance. I would never have guessed literacy was such a common practice. I've never had any reason to learn how to read, let alone that your script is different from ours. I am pretty proficient in math to help run the bakery, but that's it."

The paper is plucked from Stirling's hand. He blinks up at Bernard who holds it up to his face. "Yeah, I'm not much of a reader myself. I know enough to read the names on the maps. Gilgamesh knows a little too. We might be able to decipher this for you. Luckily the games never change so this shouldn't be too hard to understand."

"Thanks. I apparently can't do anything without your help." Stirling stabs at himself.

"I believe you would be able to figure something out to get this done on your own. You don't appear to be the type that gives up easily. But it's not a shameful thing to ask for help. No reason to make things unnecessarily hard when you have friends around." Bernard inclines his head.

Stirling suppresses a smile. *Friends.* "So now what? There's still a week until the games."

"We'll it's past the halfway point of the day and most of the chores are done already. So how about you and I relax outside the alehouse till the wife calls," Bernard suggests. Stirling nods in approval.

Approaching the alehouse, Stirling peers through the opened window. It is mostly empty with two men sitting together playing a strategy game with painted pebbles.

The old bench on the opposite side of the entryway from the staircase complains as Bernard takes a seat. He leans back against the wall and motions for Stirling to sit beside him. "So tell me," he starts. "Have any useful talents besides riding a dragon?"

"Like what?" Stirling asks quizzically.

"Well, Gilgamesh has agreed to let you spend the remainder of the week here, but you'll need to help around the place as payment. Any household chores you specialize in?" Bernard expands.

Stirling tilts his head up as he thinks, "I survived in the woods alone for three years. So basically, I can do any menial tasks." He pauses and smiles, "I also grew up in a bakery."

"Perfect!" Bernard slaps his knee and points at Stirling, "The inn has a large oven out back. Maybe you can do a better job than any of us can."

Stirling laughs at Bernard's enthusiasm. "Great. I fly across the world to escape life as a baker and here I am offering that very service."

Eve pokes her head out of the alehouse's door. "Bernard, is there anything I can get for you?" She stops, peering past Bernard at Stirling. "You're already working off your pay to stay here so I'm not serving you."

Stirling slowly blinks. Disregarding Eve, he rests his head back against the wall without responding.

"He's still a guest so cut your attitude for once and play nice," Bernard lectures.

Eve sticks out her tongue and disappears back into the alehouse.

"Don't mind her. She's like that to everyone," Bernard states.

"It's fine. She actually reminds me of someone back home," Stirling says, closing his eyes. The sounds of the village flow around him; several children shouting and playing in the distance, the bell on a goat chiming and birds singing their midday songs. Other than that it is relatively quiet compared to the city, but not anywhere as close to the solitude of the forest. The perfect median. He could get used to life here.

He sits there beside Bernard listening to him rant about each of the villagers. He asks questions sparingly, but he mostly listens. There's something enjoyable about learning the traits that make up each of them. The afternoon disappears as Bernard talks it away until the moment Roesia calls for him to help prepare supper.

After Bernard departs, Eve steps out of the alehouse, "If you're going to bake here I recommend cleaning out the oven now. It's been a while since the last time we used it and it will save you time in the morning."

Stirling tilts his head. "Were you eavesdropping earlier?"

"No! I just overheard you." She quickly excuses herself with a puff of her cheeks. "It's around back. Are you able to find it yourself or do you need someone to show you how to walk around a building?"

Stirling's face remains flat. "I can manage on my own. Thanks though."

Eve crosses her arms. "Good, because I can't do my job and babysit you all week."

With nothing more than a scowl Stirling brushes her off and slopes around the side of the alehouse. But before he can vanish behind the corner, Eve's eyes drop, scanning the length of Stirling's body.

She hasn't been here in weeks. Amiria knows she had promised Giles she would see him next week, but after what happened that following night, she couldn't bring herself to look him in the face. Not when the hatred she felt towards Stirling is so fresh it is still seeping and oozing from the opened wound in her back, soaking through any bandage she tried to cover it up with.

She needs familiarity. She needs a fallback. She needs someone to talk to again. Her father is going to marry her off, she is going to be forced to start a family. She is losing every ounce of freedom she has left.

She still has this. She still has Giles and this little bakery. This might have been Stirling's cage, but it is her only safe haven, like a child pulling the covers over their face to hide from the monsters in the night. When the bakery door is closed and she is tucked away inside. It is the only time she is hidden from the world.

The hood of her maroon cloak hangs low over her eyes concealing everything but her long dark hair flowing out the front. Because of that night, she can no longer walk casually through the market to this bakery without raising suspicion. The market locals no longer see her as the frequent face here to only pick up picnic supplies, but Giles deserves to know the truth. What truly happened behind the closed door is a mystery. The only story coming from witness accounts. She can only hope the news coming from her won't have the same outcome as seeing Stirling. A man's life can only be upturned so many times before he loses himself.

She opens the bakery door popping her head inside, "Mr. Bakere?" Her voice is soft and quiet as if she is intruding.

"I know that voice!" Giles exclaims dropping the dough he is holding onto the table. "Amiria!"

Amiria scoots around the door, closing it quickly behind her, "Yeah. I'm sorry I've missed my weekly visits."

"It's okay." His lip quivers beneath his scruff, "It's just good to see you again."

Using both her hands Amiria gently removes the hood of her cloak. She pauses fiddling with the gold dragon fang clasp, "How—how are you doing?"

Giles' shoulders drop as he stares down at the dusty floor, "I don't know—I—" He covers his eyes with his hand. Shaking his head he wipes his hand down his face pulling on the ends of his beard. Drained Giles falls into the chair.

"Mr. Bakere?" Amiria takes a concerned step forward. "Mr. Bakere?"

"I don't know what's real anymore." Rewatching the past, his brown eyes stare distantly at the stairs.

She lays her hand supportively on his shoulder, "Real or not, tell me what happened."

Hunching over with his elbows on his knees Giles hides his face, "I don't know. It's only the makings of a dream or more like a nightmare." His body shudders, keeping the lid of his emotions shut. He squeezes his eyelids closed. "I don't want to talk about it."

Amiria's eyes travel across the room, evidence of hardship apparent on every surface, misshapen pretzels, charred rolls, and unswept dust. She finally lands on the gingerbread sitting pristine beside the dilapidated loaves, "Do you remember the boy I went on picnics with?"

Eyes puffy and red turn up to her, "Yes, but what does he have to do with this?"

"Everything," she admits, pulling away from the gingerbread to meet his eye "Giles, I have a confession."

Giles leans away from her, "Amiria, what is this about?"

"He—It was—" His name lodges in her throat as if it is covered in barbs. Speaking his name was forbidden for so many years, conjuring up the sounds feels impossible.

Brushing her hand from his shoulder, Giles stands up creating distance between them filling it with his alarming suspicions, "*Who* is this guy? What has he done?"

"It was—S-Stirling," she finally coughs out.

The color drains from Giles, his skin prickling in the sudden cold. Maybe he was right about not knowing what was real or not. Maybe he has been the one dead all along and it's Stirling and Jannell who live on. He turns, obscuring his face. "Get out."

"Mr. Bakere?"

"GET OUT!" Bursts from his mouth, his face now heated with his distress.

Amiria flinches at the uproar, she holds her voice calm and steady, "Mr. Bakere, listen to me."

"You're the same as the rest," he spits.

Her voice breaks with the anguish on her face, "What I'm telling you is the truth."

Shaking his head vigorously, Giles tilts unsteady on his feet, "No, no, no. You're just messing more with my head. I trusted you." He grabs the table for stability and cries out, "I trusted you!"

"And you still should," Amiria pleads. "Stirling is my best friend. The food was for him. It's been for Stirling this whole time."

"Stirling is dead." His voice is an echo of itself, a repeated sentence now lost in meaning.

Amiria cautiously steps forward, "No, no he's not." Testing the waters she reaches out to place her hand on his but Giles pulls it into himself before she can. Hurt on her face, Amiria continues. "Mr. Bakere, You've been lied to, not once, but twice."

Lowering himself to the ground, Giles mutters under his breath about the impossibilities. His eyes wide and dilated searching the room or his memories, Amiria doesn't know. She follows him down resting her knees on the ground and sits back on her heels. The grieving father crumbles broken on the bakery floor.

"You're a liar," Giles says in denial with tears running down his face and into his beard. "Why are you doing this to me?"

"I'm being honest with you—now." Amiria bites her lip.

"Please go." His voice is soft and broken.

Amiria sits cross-legged on the ground before him, "No. Mr. Bakere, I won't go. You are my friend, the only one I have now." Bringing his knees to his chest like a small child, Giles turns away from her. Amiria continues, "For the past three years, I've been helping him. We met the day before he ran away from home. King Dietrich, he lied to you." She drops her eyes. "I lied to you." She returns her gaze to Giles' shoulders shuddering with heartache. "I couldn't tell you, to keep both of you safe." She wipes at tears that never seem to fall from her eyes, always trapped and blurring her vision, "He became my first true friend, so I protected him. I came here to watch over you because he loves and misses you."

"This can't be," Giles utters.

"I know this belonged to him," Amiria says, pulling the wooden dragon out from her bag hidden beneath her cloak.

Peering over his shoulder at the toy, Giles' eyebrows furrow. "Plenty of children played with those."

Amiria pulls up her sleeve just enough to expose the leather bracelet. "This was his mother's."

"Jannell," he whispers, reaching out to touch the bracelet. He thumbs the autumn-colored leather. The bracelet had caught her eye during one of their supply runs. The bracelet he secretly saved for. The bracelet that she never took off until the day she lost it.

His dilated pupils constrict finding Amiria. "She lost it the same day…"

"Lost it the same day Stirling received those *claw-like* wounds on his arm?" Amiria expands. Giles stares up at her in disbelief. Amiria continues, "Tell me, how do you really think he got that wound?"

He fumbles, in reality, shifting in a new tide, "An accident on a farm, a pitchfork perhaps."

Her voice is blunt, "A dragon."

Straining himself as if he was climbing a mountain, Giles uses the table to pull himself back to his feet. Shaking his head he refuses to let the truth sink in, refusing to get his hopes up once again. He begins to pace around the room fiddling with objects to occupy his hands, to occupy his mind.

"It's the truth, Mr. Bakere," Amiria straightens up, her eyes trailing him. "If you think about it, really think about it. It was obvious. He had a strange animal-like wound, he was defiant and never home. Always smelled of the forest. That's because he was out in the mountains teaching himself to fly."

Giles picks up the dough from before and begins kneading it, "Just coincidences. All—coincidences," he says, barely believing his own justifications.

Her fingers spread out on the table as she leans over the wood, "I'm not making this up. I had caught him, but . . .there was something oddly inspiring about him. I heard him out and let him tell his story. I—"

She stops, her voice beginning to falter as the fury rises back into her. Giles pauses checking her. She is staring at the ceiling with her mouth hanging open, "I broke the law for him for three years and he deserted me."

"Amiria."

Amiria doesn't hear Giles. "That was him several weeks ago," she breaks off, her jaw tense. "I was so angry. So betrayed, so tempted…" She clenches her fists at the memory, her body seething. "So ready to blow my horn and give him away when I spotted him during our search." She releases her muscles, nearly collapsing. "But I couldn't. I betrayed my team, my kingdom," her voice is a struggling gasp, "My father."

Before Amiria can react, Giles is across the room pulling her into an embrace. She blinks wide-eyed with shock. "Mr. Bakere?"

His arms tighten, securing themselves around her, "You didn't betray your friend despite all those facts. At that moment you made a life-altering choice on who mattered more to you. If this is all true, my son is alive because of you. Thank you."

It's warm. She thinks to herself. Her body is rigid in his hold, unsure of how to respond. This is a hug. *This* is a hug.

With her head pressed to his chest, Amiria feels something land in her hair. She peers up at the man, *He's crying again.* Tears slowly make their way through Giles' unshaven face and drip from his beard. Amiria raises her arms as fast as sap flows from a tree, she loops them around his back returning the embrace.

"I miss him so much," he sobs, confiding in her.

Amiria thinks it over before responding. How does she feel? How can she ever forgive Stirling for deserting her here? How can she put this empty pit she feels at the bottom of her stomach into words?

"I miss him too," she mumbles into the fraying tunic.

Amiria pulls the hood low over her face as she slips out of the bakery. No one is paying attention to her as she blends into the crowd. She stops short, her eyes catching a glimpse of a man walking past her. Spinning around she tries to find him again in the mass of people. He's already vanished, but she can swear she'd just seen her father.

# Eight

He is filthy and shaggy, and the scars on his hands and arms are borderline grotesque. He isn't handsome, not like some of the famous racers with flawless features. His face, or what she can tell of his face beneath his curls and dirt, is more humble. The features of a friendly face you wouldn't give a second glance to.

Eve takes her time spreading the chicken feed behind the alehouse as she steals glimpses of Stirling who is helping her brother grind down the grain they had harvested. What she doesn't understand is why can't she stop watching him. Her gaze is drawn to him like a moth to a flame.

Scolding herself she had decided to try ignoring him after that first night he was here. To not even bother warming up to him because he is going to join the games and most likely going to be a laughing stock. There's no way they will ever take someone like him seriously. He's nothing more than another traveler who will disappear after they try their shot to make it big in the capital.

Ignore him. She lectures herself again. Even if he isn't terrible at racing and he isn't a jester for the crowd to mock. If he somehow makes it to fame he will still leave this village behind, move into a manor like the other winners and find himself a wife whose father is a lord.

She glances over again. Stirling is grinning at some joke her brother made. So why does the idea of another girl holding his hand make her blood boil? Why does she wish it was her that is making him smile when all she can do is make him frown?

His entire reality had shifted beneath his feet. Stirling is *alive.* Giles' head throbs overloaded with the information Amiria had dumped on him. Stirling is *ALIVE.* He had been alive this entire time. He didn't just chase off his son for a second time, he almost *killed* him. His arms hug around his torso, his feet carrying him far from the bakery. After Amiria had left, the air inside the small room was suffocating. The patch over the door sealed the tomb as a permanent reminder of what he had almost done that night.

He shakes his head trying to rid the thoughts plaguing his mind. He forces himself to think of the topic Amiria had confided in him before departing. Her father was readying to marry her off against her will. He is only providing her a short amount of time for her to choose a suitor or he will pick one for her. She confessed to him there was no one on the island she wanted to marry, but it was the way she specified *on the island* that brought a smile to a broken man's face.

Three years. For three years he had listened to her talk about the boy she brought the bread to. Knowing now who the boy is, Giles wonders if there is someone *not* on the island she was interested in courting.

Numb to his surroundings. Giles makes his way through the emptying streets to the closest tavern.

Pushing through the door, he scans the busy room for an empty spot. Passing all the tables with men chatting amongst their neighbors he takes a seat at the half-empty table closest to the musicians playing on a small stage lifting them to the height of the benches.

Raising his hand, he politely grabs the maiden's attention. She bounces over happily and takes his order of mead and the special of the day. He turns around repositioning himself on the bench to lean back on the table. Exhausted, his body sags with the weight of stress no one besides Amiria can help him carry. His overworked mind dwindles letting the musicians take over; the sounds of the tabor drumming away, the trimble setting the tempo to tap your hand to, and the singing of the recorder serenading the room.

A woman's nimble fingers pluck away at the citole's strings. The chords are a dancing melody full of vibrant life. Strands of her red hair fall loose from her coif sweeping over her porcelain skin. She can't be much younger than himself.

He is entranced. The last time he had been struck like this by a woman was the last time he had seen Jannell, the woman who always had his undivided attention. He breaks his focus as the maiden drops off his supper and mead. He thanks her and drops the coin into her opened palm.

He turns his back to the musicians and faces the table and begins to dig into his roasted chicken as the citole's notes played by the enticing woman vibrate through him. He feels as if the chords are running through his body and lifting his soul.

Nine

S tirling. Stirling dear," Roesia calls as she walks around the alehouse looking for him.

He steps out of the stables setting down a pitchfork, "Yeah?"

"It's your last day before the games," she states.

Stirling brushes off straw and dust from his clothing and meets her partway, "Yeah, I guess it already is."

"But we can't have you going looking like that," she says, inspecting him. Stirling's shoulders droop as he tugs at his ruined attire. Roesia holds up a small basket, "Take this and head down to the river." Stirling instinctively accepts the basket she holds out to him. She begins pointing to the items as she talks, "There's soap I made myself, it's got lots of goodies in it; ash, nettles, mint. Then there's a bottle with rosemary water for your hair, make sure you let it soak for a bit before you wash it out. Then there's a change of clothes and shoes, too."

"Clothes! No, I can't accept anymore," Stirling pushes the basket back to her.

"Oh, don't worry," she dismisses. "They're secondhand from some of the men around town, we made sure it was similar to what you are wearing now. We want you to look nice for tomorrow but also feel comfortable. First impressions are important, you know?" With a pleasant smile, she practically shoves the basket back into Stirling's arms informing him she will not take no for an answer.

"I appreciate it," Stirling smiles graciously, feeling like a helpless child.

"Go on. Get washed up then come back here to me. I'm gonna see what I can do with that hair of yours," she demands.

Defeated, Stirling takes off on a stroll toward the river and begins trudging across the flowing grass of the fields.

Ignis peeks up at Stirling from his nearby resting spot and trots over, *"What are you doing?"*

"I'm going to bathe," Stirling informs. He kicks a pebble watching it plop into the lulling water as they walk along the riverbank in search of a decent spot. The water is a steady flow, perfect for swimming and bathing, absent of harsh currents. It is nothing stronger than a gentle push to casually travel past the small village on its way to the ocean.

He comes to a concealed location hidden by a wall of shrubbery, "This is going to have to do." He turns to Ignis, "This was way less awkward in the mountains. I wasn't worried about someone walking up on me out there."

"Well, it's time to get over it because you stink," Ignis pokes fun at him.

Stirling's brows furrow, "Why are you here anyway? You creep. Go chase some rabbits or whatever it is you do for fun while I'm working."

As Ignis saunters off Stirling strips off his clothing. Folding them neatly he sets them next to the basket and takes out a clay bottle. Uncorking it the rosemary water with apple cider vinegar aroma wafts out tingling his nose. Pouring it slowly over his head he massages the cleansing liquid into his tangled hair.

Testing the water with his toes he shivers, sending goosebumps across his arms. It might be cold, but it is warmer than the water in the mountains. He is also grateful for the hot temperature of the day making the cool water refreshing over torturous. He grew up cleaning himself in troughs, it was common practice to keep your hands and face clean, especially before meals. But his family never had the coin to go to a bathhouse where maidens would fill wooden tubs with warm water while you soak. He wonders what kind of bathhouses Leucasia has and if he will ever be able to afford them.

He wades out into the freshwater, scooping handfuls of water and wiping them on his arms and chest to adjust his skin to the chill temperature.

Examining the dirt caked under his nails, Stirling remembers how Amiria's skin and hair was always clean. She had constant access to the royal bath houses though she never commented on Stirling's appearance. She would trim his hair and separate a few of the tangled curls but said nothing else.

Waist deep in the water, Stirling lowers himself to his chest. The cool water surrounds him forcing an involuntary deep gasp as he sucks in air. Taking the soap he scrubs at the dirt staining his body. He watches the ash scrub the grime from his arms and be carried away with the current. His insignia no longer hidden beneath dirt comes alive on his light and freckled skin

He lathers up more of the mint-smelling soap onto his hands and scrubs his face and neck. With a deep breath, he submerges himself under the river, rinsing out his hair. Popping back up he whips his shaggy hair like a dog drying off before double-checking the entirety of his body. Afraid Roesia will send him back for round two, he rewashes his face and neck.

All clean and clear, he wades back up to the riverbank and dries off with a towel from the prepped basket.

A new white under-tunic and a waist-long yellow short-sleeve tunic are pulled from the basket. The tunic is of a higher quality than his faded blue one had ever been. He pinches the soft fabric in his fingers, unable to make out what it is. All he knows for certain is neither the wool nor linen he was used to. There are brown accents along the edges of the sleeves and collar that tie closed with a matching brown string. Already in favor of the new lighter fabric, he pulls on a clean pair of braies and brown trousers with drawstring ties around the ankles.

He tugs on his new leather turnshoes and out of habit pushes up the long undershirt's sleeves to his elbows. Staring down at his right arm he turns it outwards exposing his scars then turns it back by pressing it to his side. With a sigh, he pulls the sleeve back down covering up the label of his old life.

"I knew there was a handsome boy under all that dirt. Look at you. Do a spin for me," seated at a table outside the alehouse, Roesia compliments Stirling as he returns, walking down the road through the center of the village.

"I'm not going to spin," Stirling turns down.

"Oh, come on, spin spin," she claps.

"Fine," Stirling throws his head back, giving in. Awkwardly, he holds his hands out walking in a small circle.

"Close enough," she giggles.

"I don't think I've ever smelled this good," Stirling smiles pulling down a lock of hair close to his nose, the smell of rosemary and apple cider vinegar still clinging to him.

"Good, good, come here. Come sit here," she waves, gesturing to the bench seat at the table. She stands up as Stirling steps up to her.

"What are we doing?" he questions as she hoists herself to sit up on top of the table.

"I'm going to comb those knots out of your hair while it's still wet, but you are too tall for me, so I need to sit above you."

Stirling sits directly in front of her like a child, his back resting against her knees. She lifts a thick-toothed comb carved from wood, "Ok son, I'm going to go gently and work these knots out. So, you're going to have to bear with me."

"Yes ma'am," Stirling obliges.

She picks a random matted lock to start with and begins working at the end slowly moving into the root as she detangles it. "They might be loose curls, but they are still curls. I'll give you this comb but don't comb your hair dry. It will only frizz. If it is dry just get your hair wet again and it'll correct itself."

"Ow!" Stirling cries as the hair snags in the comb pulling his scalp.

"Oh, don't be a baby. You wouldn't be in this mess if you took better care of yourself," She lectures continuing with her combing.

"Tale of my life," Stirling mutters.

Stirling shakes his head, his hair dampened from the trough's water spraying droplets in every direction. His curls spring back to life after their grueling fight. Waiting for the water to settle, he leans over to check out his reflection.

For the first time in his life, his sandy curls are tangle free. They fall soft and move freely around his head, a few wild ones still defy gravity and stick up towards the sky feather light in the wind.

"Stirling! I need help fetching water from the river!" he hears Eve call out. He turns around, his hazel eyes popping with the lush green backdrop. Eve's jaw drops along with the two pails she is holding. This is not the same boy she has been working with all week.

"Sure!" Stirling calls back, jogging the short distance across the road.

"Um yeah, yeah okay," she says, fumbling over her words as her heart begins to pick up. She leans over to pick up the pails.

"No, I'll get them, I'll get them," he offers.

She straightens herself as Stirling gathers the pails for her with a wide goofy grin. "Shall we?" He smiles motioning towards the river.

Tucking her lips inwards, she bites down on them holding back her blushing smile as they stroll side by side to the river, "So how do you feel about the games opening ceremony tomorrow?"

Stirling swallows the lump rising in his throat, "Nervous."

"Are you any good?" she asks in what she believes is a polite tone.

"I like to think so," Stirling shrugs humbly.

"Not to put any more pressure on you, but people are placing bets on you to win."

"Oh no," Stirling whines, hanging his head. "That doesn't make me feel any better."

"Sorry, sometimes I have a problem with saying whatever pops into my head." She pauses sorting through her thoughts to find one to lighten the conversation, "We get a *lot* of travelers, a bunch of people passing through. Yet, you're the most exciting one this village has ever seen."

"Exciting? I'm not exciting," his voice is genuine. Viewing himself from a third person, he sees himself as nothing but a burden, a hindrance to those around him.

"You're not a normal person. You're going to be a participant in the games! Half of us don't have time to see a single match let alone become friends with one of the racers," she says, practically bouncing with each word. "That's if you see us as friends because the village folk sees you that way."

"I do, really, I do. I've come to love this village." Reaching the river, he closes his eyes momentarily, thinking back on his life. Every moment, every win, and every loss that has brought him to this place in time. It's true. It has not been an ordinary life. "I guess my life has been pretty exciting…It came at a hefty price though."

He loves this village. Eve replays in her mind. She takes a pail from him and dips it into the water. "Nothing is free. The more you want the more it will cost."

Stirling squats beside her, filling his own pail. "Have you ever given anything up?"

They fill the pails to the rim and stand back up. Eve holds the heavy pale's handle in both hands. She shakes her head slowly. "No." Her eyes drag across the landscape looking away from Stirling, "But that's probably the reason I'm still in this village working at my family's inn. Not much of a risk taker."

"If you want something, go for it," Stirling advises, his eyes distant over the prairie.

She smiles at the back of his head. "I think I will." Shaking the thoughts away, she suggests, "Let's get these back. The whole town will be at the alehouse tonight."

Smiling, Stirling offers, "Here, I'll carry it for you."

Eve hands the pail over, accepting, "Such a gentleman."

"It's no problem," he brushes off with a shrug.

***

Each table in the alehouse is centered with a loaf of bread muddied in orange. The smell of ginger sweetened with honey wafts in the air filling the noses of the villagers with its delectable scent.

People crowd the tables. Their shoulders between neighbors molded together, shifting in unison as the other moves. Antsy children struggle on their parent's lap eager to play with their friends. The family-like village sits comfortably, unconcerned with overlapping one another. Laughter and chatter are a static noise as each voice speaks over the other.

"What is this you made?" Bernard asks, cutting the first slice to serve to those at their table.

"Gingerbread," Stirling informs, still standing after he finished serving each table, "I found all the ingredients and my mother used to make it for me on special occasions. So, I found it fitting."

"Well, you are right! It's time for a celebration! Let's get a huzzah for Stirling!"

"HUZZAH!" the room cheers in unison.

The tips of his ears burning with embarrassment, Stirling squeezes himself onto the bench seat across from Bernard and beside Eve. Her honey-colored eyes the size of saucers bat flirtatiously as she makes room for him.

"I hope it tastes all right. It's been a few years since I've made it. I had a hard time recalling the measurements," Stirling apologizes.

Eve leans into him. "I'm sure it tastes fine. You've already proved yourself quite the cook and all-around handyman."

Whoa! Look who's handing out flattery. Can I get one of those, it's been quite a while," Bernard taunts.

Eve snaps abrasively, "Because you don't do anything that warrants one."

"Aw, there's the Eve I know and love."

Stirling laughs along with his peers. They talk about past games and what is their favorite race. They mention several of the racers that Stirling had already forgotten the names of. Every last crumb of the gingerbread was devoured as the sun leaves to rest for the night. The warmth of the villager's presence coddles him like a mother telling him everything is going to be fine.

Tomorrow is his new beginning.

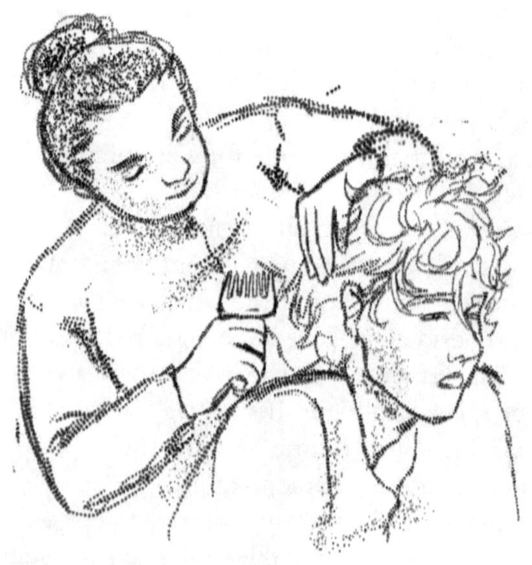

Ten

With her skin crawling, Amiria silences her alarms. She pretends she doesn't hear the warning bells as she clenches her jaw and doesn't pull away. The clink of metal is audible as his rings make contact with her spaulder. There isn't enough iron in the world to form an adequate barrier to keep her from wishing to escape. To run to the cleansing baths after King Dietrich rests his hand on her shoulder.

He stands directly behind her, and with a stoic expression, Amiria holds her act as the perfect soldier. The spaulder on her other shoulder shifts as he lays his hand upon it. Playing his piece in a war that had started long before she was born. King Dietrich's eyes lock with Field Marshal Rey's.

With a calculated smile placed on his face, King Dietrich speaks over Amiria's head to her father, "Heard you were finally looking for a suitor." Amiria watches her father's fingers twitch at his sides. "Such a prize she is, the next field marshal, ready to carry on the Rey lineage."

Rey lifts his chin. "Why did you summon me here."

They stand in King Dietrich's personal cabinet. Missing three of her unit's members, Amiria has been tied to King Dietrich's side with no one but Calix and Dicun to split the responsibility with. He does not need them beside him every hour of every day. He does not need *her* standing as decoration in his cabinet when she should be training for their upcoming mission. He doesn't keep her attentive at his side for protection.

Amiria can see King Dietrich's features written back to her on her father's face. They are ordered to stand here in bright polished armor to mock her father. Their unit, their crest, is a slap in his face. *She* is an incapacitating strike to his chest.

"You're dismissed Amiria." King Dietrich pats her shoulder before releasing his hold. Amiria takes a tentative step forward and then turns about face to King Dietrich. Without looking higher than his collar she bows.

Her father steps aside from the doorway letting her pass. She keeps her head up and her shoulders back, she gives him no indication of what is behind her armor. How her unease around the king has grown into an ugly fear that tears at her insides whenever she is around him. Fear he will discover her truths, fear he already knows, fear of what he has planned behind his artful grin.

Amiria stops short on the threshold of the door. General Gautier's pinched face scowls at her. "Amiria Rey."

"My apologies." Amiria bows her head and stands aside letting the general through. Slipping out into the hall she catches the king's greeting before the door closes.

"Aww, yes, General, you're here. We will be discussing the direction this kingdom is taking."

Eleven

Lying on his back in the inn, Stirling watches a finch fly in through the open window and land on a nest built into the high point of the ceiling. It was a sleepless night. His mind ran rampant with the possibilities for the upcoming morning. Each time he blinked the room grew brighter with the departing night and the arrival of the day.

As if the light took hold of his collar, it pulls him up into a sitting position in bed.

It's time.

With a deep breath, he shrugs his new tunic on and picks up his new harness. It is no longer a single belt around his hips. He slides his legs through the updated leg hoops to help disperse his weight. His fingers begin tapping rapidly at his side and his eyes squeeze shut. He is brought back to the chase. He can feel the leather belt digging into the small of his back as Ignis rears back vertically in the night clouds. The pink scars stretch across his knuckles as he clenches his hands into a fist.

With his eyes still closed his fingertips touch the cool metal of the goggles filling his heart with ease. Looping his tie to her around his neck he picks up his orange cape. With a deep breath in through his nose and out through his mouth, he ties it around his shoulders as he walks out the door.

"*Ready!?*" Ignis shouts at him from the road.

Arms crossed, Stirling slowly descends the stairs, a pit already forming in his stomach, "*Ready as I can be.*"

Full of impatience for the opening ceremony Ignis' massive frame bobs unable to stand still, his saddle already fastened around him.

Ready to watch Stirling off, Bernard, Roesia and their two children stand near Ignis with enough distance to keep them from being knocked over.

"Oi! Looks like your beast is ready to head out," Bernard jabs his thumb at Ignis, "He definitely appears more eager than you."

Stirling's fingers play with the fabric of his pants. "Will you guys be there for the opening?"

"Of course! Half the village will be there. They're getting themselves ready at this moment," Bernard assures.

"The games! The games!" Gregory chants with enthusiasm.

"Yes, the games. Our friend is going to be in the games," Bernard tells Gregory. He turns his attention back to Stirling. "Most of the town can't afford to leave their chores unattended and can't make it to the races. But I will be at every race cheering for you and let the rest of these guys know how you're doing. Don't worry. We won't leave you alone."

"Thanks. That's actually pretty comforting." Stirling's body slacks and his voice fades to a whisper. "To be honest. I'm more than nervous. I'm scared."

Bernard clasps both of Stirling's shoulders, "It's okay. It's only human to be scared, especially something as big as this. Push through those jitters and focus on flying. Ignore the audience. Ignore the other racers and fly."

"I'll be there, too!" Eve waves from the alehouse's door.

"Well, look at you!" Bernard calls back over Stirling.

Turning around Stirling doesn't see a frowning young maiden who works long days at her family's alehouse. Standing at the threshold is a girl who is glowing in the early morning light. Her pale-yellow kirtle, a form-fitting sleeveless dress with ties synching the sides over a tight white undershirt, is lit by soft light. Her umber hair free from the coil is now intricately braided in a crown around her head with ringlets springing free around her face.

Her father, Gilgamesh, hovers behind her, "Fine, go and leave all the work to your brother."

"Father," she draws out the word. shifting her eyes from Stirling back to him.

He chuckles, pulling her in to kiss her on the forehead, "Have fun darling."

Bernard sighs. "Well, boy, you should get going. We'll be there shortly. We've got two wagons to pull ourselves in, which will get us there faster than walking."

"*Calm down for a second.*" Stirling grips Ignis' saddle. Ignis contains himself just long enough for Stirling to climb up and buckle himself before proceeding to gyrate. Stirling smiles, "Thanks for everything, I really mean it." He turns to the mountains envisioning the city beyond, and his smile fades. Swallowing hard, he tells Bernard and Roesia, "I'll see you there."

"GOOD LUCK!" Eve hollers waving both her hands in the air.

The smile the city stole is brought back to his face as Stirling replies with a nod. Ignis takes his cue and begins to trot, leaving behind the group. With the small family shrinking as they separate themselves from the village, Ignis gains speed turning his trot into a gallop. Throwing his body into the air he pumps his wings, sending them into the sky and over the small mountain.

Stirling's legs refuse to remain still. His heels bounce rapidly as he sits in the waiting area built beneath the stadium's stands. The area is a maze of stone halls and rooms carved into the mountainside. Fingernails disappear as his teeth nervously gnaw them into extinction. Any minute his name will be called.

He is thankful he was placed in the beginner's group. His suffering of anticipation will end that much sooner. The beginners go first starting off the ceremony after the opening display, then the intermediate, advance then finally ending with the elites. The opening presentation was a spectacular display of choreographed actors and dancers dressed in elaborate dragon-themed costumes, but Stirling couldn't get his legs to respond to his command to get up and watch. Instead, he sits there listening to the crowd react, their echoing cheers running rampant through the stone halls. Unsettled, he hunches forward, rubbing his hands around one another, his heart in his throat and his stomach in knots.

Names have begun to be called by the announcer introducing the participant with their species of dragon. The racers step out from the archway beneath the stands into the center of the arena and using their whistle, command their dragon to appear from the opposing entrance or to fly in from the sky.

Stirling closes his eyes muttering to himself, "There's no one there, there's not thousands of people watching. There's not thousands of people watching." He doubles over, burying his face into his hands. "Oh God. There's thousands of people watching."

Index. Middle. Ring. Pinky. Middle. Ring. Index. He replaces the image of the people watching with repeating of his fingers.

"You're next," a coordinator instructs.

Stirling feels his lungs implode. He looks up from his halved position, his face a sickly grey.

The coordinator checks their paper again. "You're Stirling of Patu, right?"

His throat squeezes shut from the vacuum in his chest, so he responds with a nod.

"Then get up and wait just inside the entrance to the arena out of view. They'll be calling you."

Wobbling legs bow beneath him as he palms the coarse wall to keep himself from collapsing. His vision tunnels, narrowing down to nothing but the spot between the coordinator's back as he follows him down the hall.

His toes stopping at the edge of the shadow, Stirling can see out through the large arching entrance into the stadium's arena. With the crowd vaulted, only the wall surrounding the ground perimeter is visible from his line of sight.

He watches as the racer before him bows alongside their draco before mounting the creature and taking off out of view.

The announcer stands on a high rise built above the stands. An oval piece attached to a long metal tube cups his mouth. The tube is a long brass horn extending from the announcer to the ground held in place by brackets and a stand. With a loud enunciating voice coming deep from his diaphragm the horn amplifies his words for the entire stadium to hear, "Next we have a first timer at the age of nineteen, Stirling of Patu, and his per'yanny svir!"

Silence.

The claps and hollers from the villagers are drowned out by the deafening silence.

Step by agonizing step, he travels across the deathly landscape until his feet come to a stop in the middle of the sandy arena. Open and vulnerable, surrounded by disapproving eyes. Stirling begins to tremble, both of his hands tapping their fingers to their thumbs at his sides. His breathing is an unsteady quick and halting pattern.

They watch his every movement. Face after face, staring, watching, murmuring, all blending into one single tidal wave with the height and strength to level an entire town.

He's going to pass out. They are all going to witness him collapse. Witness his failure before he even starts. He can't move. He's frozen beneath this wave like a rock sticking out from the ocean he can do nothing but let it crash into him.

He can't hear them, but their voices echo in his head.

"What is a peasant doing out there?" Shut up. *"Who let someone like him sign up?"* Shut up. *"Doesn't he know his place?"* Shut up. *"He's tainting the games."* Shut up, shut up.

The judging townsfolk back home watched him as he ran away from home when he was sixteen. *Shut up.* How they stared petrified hugging their children as if he was a monster. *Shut up.* How they witnessed the heroic Calvary descend upon him as he escaped for his life. *Shut up.* Their gaze still lingers behind like a spiderweb he can't get rid of. *Shut Up!*

His father.

SHUT UP!

CATCH HIM! CONDEMN HIM! HANG HIM!

People shouting. Dogs barking. Alarms howling.

Stirling grips his ears, the scars on his hands burning. "Please stop." He cries out in a whisper.

"Oh no." Bernard realizes from his seat high in the stands.

"This is why this is a dignified sport that should be left to the upperclassmen." A man within earshot of Bernard grumbles.

"A small villager can never handle the pressure. Look, he's already cracking."

"Where did a poor farmer even get a per'yanny svir from?"

"If he even has one, because I don't see it."

On cue, an orange dragon dives from the cotton clouds like a meteor, landing in front of a Stirling in a plume of dust and sand.

Casting his wings out to the sides he tilts the feathers up to the sky fanning them out. His body crouched, and his jaws unhinged. A dragon's roar rips through the crowd. Everyone's mouths clamp shut. Stunned and unsure.

Ignis inches closer to Stirling, his tail curling around him. He turns his head striking out like a snake at the people behind him completing the protective barrier around Stirling.

"Get me out of here," Stirling begs. His stomach lurches, ready to display its contents.

"Of course," Ignis promises. In the cover of Ignis' mass, Stirling slides his arms through the saddle's straps. With a few hopping steps, Ignis catapults up and out of the stadium leaving the audience confused and speechless.

Roesia nudges Bernard's shoulder. "Go find the poor boy. I'll stay here with the kids."

"Yeah, okay. I'll meet you by the wagons when it's over." Bernard kisses Roesia and pats Gregory and Delilah on the head as he stands up.

"Bernard, wait!" Eve throws herself from her seat grabbing the hem of his tunic.

He rolls his eyes already aware of what she is going to ask. "All right, come on." Beaming Eve releases the fabric and trails behind him as they pick their way through the stands.

The gritty texture of the stadium wall digs divots into Stirling's palm, his other hand clenched around his stomach. Ignis had carried him to the back corner where the building collides and melds with the mountainside.

His abdominal muscles squeeze and constrict to the point they hurt with exhaustion. He has finished vomiting, but his body refuses to stop dry heaving. He struggles with choking gasps between each convulsion. His body betrays him by denying him the oxygen it needs.

Ignis shakes his head. *"That's disgusting."*

Drained of energy, Stirling wipes his mouth with the back of his hand. His face shines with perspiration and dampening his curls. Straightening up, he stumbles to the side several steps before sliding his back down the wall. His knees tuck into his chest, they work as a curtain to hide his face in shame.

"There you are." Bernard appears before him with Eve peeking around his hefty waistline. Pulling his lips into a sympathetic grimace, he kneels in front of Stirling, "You all right, kid?"

Stirling peeks up from his knees. "I don't understand what happened. I just—I just freaked out."

"There are some things that time doesn't truly heal. Some events are so deeply seeded into you, you forget they're even there until they finally sprout again." Stirling stares up at him dumbfounded. "You're braver than you think, boy." Bernard extends his hand out. "Now let's get up and keep going."

"I'm sorry," Stirling utters, accepting the hand graciously.

The burly man pulls him to his feet. "For what? Being human. You should never apologize for that. Boy, you know you could lose every match and we will continue to support you. We enjoy you as a person and not because of this—" He swipes a hand out at the festivities. "So I don't want to hear any more apologies."

"But if you want to try to win that's also an option, you know," Eve interrupts.

Bernard shoots her a glare with the unwritten instructions to stop talking. He steps to the side, his frame eclipsing in front of her cutting her out of the conversation. "You know what I saw down there?"

"What?"

"Companionship."

"Companionship?" Stirling asks, not understanding.

Bernard enlightens, "Here, dragons are no more than tools. This is a game, and a dragon is merely a factor. Your beast—" They both look over at Ignis who is watching curiously. "I mean Ignis. He knew you were in distress even though he was nowhere in sight. He came to rescue you. Your dragon is willing to defend you. You made that very apparent to everyone there. I honestly cannot name another racer in these games that can relate."

"Oh." Stirling ponders over the information, his mood lightening he suggests, "The opening ceremonies are still going on if you want to go finish watching?"

"Nah, let's go get you something to eat. Looks like you have nothing left in your stomach," Bernard says.

"Yeah, sounds good," Stirling agrees, laying his hand over his stomach.

Bernard places his hand on Stirling's shoulder guiding him toward the food stands. Eve skips up to Stirling's side grinning up at him.

The three of them maneuver their way through the festival crowd. His stomach growling, Stirling instantly becomes engaged with the savory aromas carried in the breeze from the nearby booths. Closing his eyes, he inhales a deep breath of fried dough.

Young girls squeal, crying out a male name.

Opening his eyes, Stirling doesn't have time to react as a man only a couple of years older than himself with pale blonde hair and deep ocean eyes plows through the narrow space between him and Eve. His stride radiates impatience and importance.

Stirling's shoulder is flung backward like an opening door knocking him back a step. Eve's foot catches on her dress. Reacting, Stirling reaches out, catching her by the crook of her arm.

He looks up furious at the man. "Hey! You just pushed over a girl! You need to come back and apologize!"

The young man is good five or more fingers shorter than Stirling, wearing a thin loose navy-blue top with a swooping collar and buttoned cuffs turns around slowly. The curves of his face run soft and elegantly making him strikingly beautiful, but his eyes, his dark blue expressionless eyes, are vortexes pulling whatever is in their sight into them and freezing them at their icy core.

"Then don't be in my way," he replies in a monotonous voice. Stirling's jaw drops as he watches the man march away through the parting crowd.

"Are you okay?" he asks, steading Eve.

"Yes, thank you. What a jerk that guy was. Who does he even think he is?"

"Quilan," Bernard informs.

"Quilan! Like Quilan of Leucasia!" Eve shouts.

"Who?" Stirling asks.

Bernard sighs, "The top racer. Mr. Number One, Mr. Every Girl Wants To Marry, and Every Guy Wants To Be. He has held the title of undefeated since he beat his father the prior undefeated champion in his second year at age sixteen. His father retired right after that to focus on coaching his son. But I don't see why he needs to coach someone who beat him. But that's not my place to argue."

"If he is an elite competitor, doesn't he need to be at the stadium?" Stirling questions.

"You're in for a rude awakening. Quilan doesn't follow the game's schedule. The games follow him," Bernard says.

"Isn't he just humble?" Stirling grunts.

"Forget about him," Bernard tells Stirling, "You're not going to have to worry about him for a while. Let's focus on food. I'm in the mood for roasted chickpeas and maybe some honeyed almonds for Roesia. Have you ever had olives?"

"Olives?"

"They're good, kind of salty, but good. You'll like it, let's go," he ushers.

Still holding her shoulder, Eve doesn't hear Bernard tell them to start walking. She is preoccupied with listening to something else. Hanging her head, she looks away from a group of girls within earshot. Stirling overhears them laughing about how he and Eve were almost taken down by Quilan. They snicker the words insignificant, invisible, nobodies. They claim it was criminal they didn't step out of Quilan's way. He should never have to apologize to anyone.

Stirling's arms wrap around her shoulders, his scarred hand visible to them. The girl's lips curl up in disgust as they lean into each other whispering about his disfigurement.

An embarrassed tear slips from the corner of her eye and silently runs down her cheek. She tilts her head up to the curly-haired boy holding her. It has not even been an hour since he humiliated himself in front of tens of thousands of people. Never in her life will she experience that level of embarrassment. Yet, even after she had been disrespectful to him this past week and he knows nothing

about her past the shallow shell, he is willing to take her
shame and fully direct it at himself.

Feeling safe in his arms she leans into him.

Twelve

The woman's muffled sobs leak through the slits of her fingers, her nails already turned white with the pressure of her hands clasped over her mouth. The orange light of the candlelit room sneaks through the crack of the wardrobe lining a flickering streak across one side of her face. She can hear the heavy footfalls of the armored guards wearing blue gambesons.

"Can you explain to us why you are awake at this hour?" Thomas, one of the two guards asks.

"P-painting, I'm a painter. It isn't too late. The tavern isn't even closed yet." A man sitting on a stool in the middle of the room beside an easel tells the circling guards.

"Don't get smart with me!" Thomas yells. The painter flinches as if anticipating a strike.

The second guard, Wyot, inspects the surrounding room, "Wouldn't painting be better during the day than in candlelight?"

"I get my best inspirations at night. I'll make a quick draft at night then, then I'll redo it or I'll touch up the colors in the morning." The painter fibs.

"Then what is this second one for?" Thomas asks, referring to a poor-quality painting beside the original.

"What do you mean?" The painter asks, playing ignorant.

Thomas stands behind the canvas tapping the top of the frame, "I can tell by the other paintings in this room that this one is not done by you."

"I have children. My eldest son. It's his work," The painter tells him.

The wandering guard turns to his partner. "Aye. I saw two children with whom I'm assuming is his wife in the bedroom. The story checks out."

Thomas snarls, "Keep your painting to the daylight hours so you don't waste our time."

The painter doesn't exhale. Ignoring the pain in his lungs, he holds his breath until the door to his home is securely shut. Shaking, he looks over to the wardrobe with a ghost of a smile.

Thirteen

The morning marine layer has dispersed, broken through by the never-failing sun. They are stationed on top of the cliffs awaiting their first meet. Nervous palms saturate the worn straps. Stirling grips onto Ignis' saddle and presses his forehead into the leather, *"The first meet. It's a race."*

"You ready?" Ignis asks.

"My stomach is in knots, but not as bad as I felt yesterday," Stirling admits.

"Good thing you're not the one flying. I am. So you just hang on," Ignis reassures.

"Thanks," Stirling means it. If it wasn't for Ignis, the opening ceremony would have been even more of a catastrophe.

A voice interrupts their conversation. "Hey, hey! Look, who am I?" A racer in a green and yellow checkered cape says laughing with a few other participants. He proceeds to make mock vomiting actions. The group laughs and peers over at Stirling.

"Why would you cover your ears when no one is even cheering?"

"I think the city guards should take him in."

Stirling's heart drops.

"For what?"

"For being a danger to society. I've never seen someone silence an entire crowd before," the small group cackles with laughter.

Stirling curls his fingers to his hands to keep them from twitching as he hangs his head.

"RACERS! MOUNT YOUR DRAGONS!" the referee shouts, walking down the line, "READY YOURSELVES AT THE STARTING LINE!"

Stirling pulls himself onto Ignis. Glancing over he inspects the racer beside him in an all-black cape. He sits on a brick red knucker dragon, its long slender frame with front legs significantly shorter than the rear. The racer checks his black gloves and red wrist guards that match his knee and shin padding. His legs in their locked position similar to the ones the Winged Cavalry uses, only modified to fit the species with an extended horn to keep the rider from slipping forward on the dragon's sloping frame. The racer pulls his goggles over his black leather helm and returns Stirling's gaze.

He analyzes Stirling's lack of gear and simple garb. No real harness and saddle, but ones thrown together with scraps. He stifles a laugh, "Good luck, orange. Hope your gear doesn't fall apart on that pet of yours."

"*Pet?*" Ignis repeats

Stirling pulls his goggles down over his eyes and faces front. The realization of the orange cape is now strongly apparent. Almost every color when displayed on a flag or coat of arms has a meaning. Blue for loyalty and truth. Red for military and power. Green for hope and joy. Then purple for royalty and justice. Stirling isn't sure if the colors are the same here, but he knows back in Wyverna orange was excluded from the list.

She did not give it to him because she was low on capes or because it matches Ignis. She gave it to him because orange is a color with no meaning. It symbolized nothing. They are calling him "a nothing racer".

The nervous cells in his body become agitated, mutating into a rage. He has not spent more than a day in this city, and he has already become furious with the citizens.

They are acting irrationally by choice. They truly believe he should not be in this race. Not because the laws forbids it, but because they on a personal level don't approve. They are gaining amusement from belittling someone they see as lesser than them. Maybe this is how people are. Maybe this is human nature. To always try to be above one another.

Then there are people like Amiria, Bernard, Roesia, and the rest of the villagers…Faerydae…his mother. People who are kind-hearted, people who want to help, and people who care. Everyone is different, so choose those whom you want near and keep them close. No one else's opinion matters but theirs.

Stirling glances back and forth checking the rest of the line. He notices one more thing. There are no female racers. He stares not understanding. Surely there would have to at least be one female competing in the beginners. Are there any in the higher ranks? Past the line of racers, a robin egg cape ripples around slender navy-blue shoulders.

Quilan. Stirling registers. *Is he scoping out the crowd?*

Qiulan stands away from the racers with his toes dangerously on the edge of the cliff. He's disengaged from the activity around him as he stares unblinking down to where the citizens wait eagerly for the races to begin.

"RACERS!" Stirling jumps at the referee shouting. "I will repeat the rules for you one final time. Do not leap from this post until you hear the horn. You will fly out to the furthest pillar in the water and return to the pillar placed at the bottom of this cliff!" The referee instructs.

Stirling leans as far as he can to peek over the ledge.

The referee continues, "There will be five laps. The hitting of another racer will lead to disqualification, the failure to at least reach the pillar will be disqualification! RACERS! ARE YOU READY!"

"ON YOUR MARKS!"

Stirling presses himself against Ignis.

"GO!"

A horn blares.

Frozen.

A landslide of scales unfurl from the cliff's edge diving into the race. Stirling and Ignis remain petrified at the blaring sound of the horn. They are a stone gargoyle mounted on a cathedral, a ghastly creature frozen in time.

The racers catch themselves before crashing head-first into the ground, sending a tempest of wind across the wooden bleachers lined up on each side of the runway of land stretching between the mountain and the ocean. The crowd shrieks with delight as they hold onto their caps and coifs.

"Come on kid," Bernard mumbles to himself in the crowd.

The distorted world being stretched into a muted blur reaches its limit and snaps back into place. Shaking his head, Ignis sees the rest of the racers flying out over the water. With a growl in the back of his throat he throws himself from the cliff with such velocity, fissures crack in the light-colored stone. The rush of familiar wind stinging his cheeks brings Stirling back to the first time Ignis had leaped from the cave mouth and they plunged towards the ocean's waves together.

"Where we belong," Stirling says, still lost in his memory.

"Shall we?" Ignis asks with a smirk.

"Let's do it."

With a thrust of his wings, Ignis twists his body, spinning them past the crowd and out over the water. He straightens himself out, pumping his wings with determination.

"There you go, kid. You don't need first. Just catch up," Bernard commentates.

Bouncing in her seat, Eve tucks a strand of hair that had fallen loose from her braid behind her ear and claps with overly animated excitement, "Go, Stirling, GO!"

The beginner's level. The largest group of competitors in the annual games. Stirling counts the racers in front of him. Twenty. The leader is already banking their dragon sharply to the side to force themselves around the pillar as tight as possible.

Stirling is gaining on the back of the pack. *"You thinking what I'm thinking?"* Stirling asks Ignis.

"Usually. Sometimes not by choice."

Ignis aims straight at the pillar. Tucking his head, his body contorts to follow the path. Ignis' feet strike the massive pillar and he vaults off whipping past the last five racers. Fifteen more to go.

"That's illegal!" A man sitting towards the top of the stands shouts.

"Yeah! He can't do that!" A woman adds

"Cheater!"

"Disqualify!" The onlookers shriek.

A crier stands in front of his segment of the crowd, he looks up at the judges sitting above everyone. The row of judges lean toward each other in discussion. The judge holds his hand out straight like a blade close to the judge's table and raises it up and towards the water.

"IT WILL BE PERMITTED!" The crier announces. The next criers hear him and pass the news down to the audience.

An encore of booing ensues across the upper level of the stands. People shout their disgruntlement with their agreeing neighbors to only have their angered words drown out by the wind of the lapping dragons.

Stirling and Ignis pass three more racers during the straight stretch. Twelve more to go. Ignis pushes off the pillar shooting past two. Ten to go with three more laps.

The audience watches apprehensively as the gigantic structure shudders under Ignis' weight.

Bernard crosses his arms. "I don't know about you, but that move appears more advanced to me." The man sitting beside him raises an eyebrow. "Just saying." Bernard shrugs.

Eve cups her mouth and hollers, "LET'S GO STIRLING!"

Two more laps, five to go.

One more lap and two racers.

He's in third place. Third place will provide enough winnings to pay for his entire stay at the inn for the next year. But this is no longer about the money. This is about proving to them he is not someone to trifle with. He will not be underestimated. He is not someone they can continue to mock as if he is the game's jester.

"*I'm meant to be here,*" he reassures himself as he passes into second place. Recognizing the green and yellow cape, striking eye contact and with a friendly wave, he passes him.

The man turns beet red with rage flicking his reins, demanding his dragon to pick up the pace. Stirling can see the black cape flowing in front of him. Him and the green and yellow caped racer pivot to either side passing the last-place racer. They swing back together, Stirling slightly behind the other racer.

Scoffing, Ignis rocks to the left swerving around a yellow dragon. Flying sideways he continues to gain on the brick red knuckler. With a pump and twist of his wings, Ignis turns upside down traveling up and over the first-place racer. Stirling looks up—which has become down—at the racer with the black cape. His face is contorted as he leers up at them.

Finishing their spiral they lunge for the finish line. Employees scamper across the raceway stretching out a banner indicating the end. A gale of wind rips at the thin fabric threatening to pull free from the worker's hands as they cling to the banner. Ascending upward to the top of the cliff Ignis lands with a soft thud.

They did it. They won.

Overly animated, Eve leaps up from her seat squealing with delight. She digs into Bernard's shoulder as she bounces up and down shaking him. "HE DID IT! HE DID IT! HE DID IT!"

The Lower half of the stands cheer ecstatically. They have never seen anyone in dead last pick their way up to first place. Stirling started last in the take-off he should have finished last or best hoped for nineteenth or eighteenth place.

The games are predictable. The same racers, the same matches, the same outcomes.

Stirling was shrugged off because he is new and lacks professional training. They expected nothing from him. They anticipated for him to fail. They predicted the regular standards. Today was a change in the tides, a rip tide pulling them out into the unknown waters

They clap, cheer and holler with the unforeseen. The overdue change to the routine they unknowingly longed for. A line in the crowd's reaction divides them in half. The two halves are polar opposites. The men and woman on the top half boo and hiss, calling Stirling a cheat and to remove him from the games.

Stirling is instructed by the referee to ride his dragon down to the middle of the race track. Ignis hangs back between the brick red dragon and the draco belonging to the rider in the green and yellow cape.

Taking his place, Stirling stands between the second and third-place riders directly in front of their corresponding dragons.

"And in first place, we have Stirling of Patu!"

Stirling is glowing. He can't control the ever-expanding grin across his face. He tilts his head up to the wispy cloud sky. *First of many.*

"Here are your winnings," the announcer says, holding out a canvas drawstring bag.

Stirling cups his hands underneath the bag. The announcer releases it letting it drop into his palms. His hands bob from the weight of the coins. He is still learning their currency, but he is positive this is more than the bakery earns annually. He wriggles his fingers feeling the metal shift inside the fabric.

Still playing with the coins, Stirling sprints his eyes across the audience before hiding them away in the safety of Ignis. Dipping his chin he's unsure on what to make of the opposite dynamic in moods.

The winners are escorted off the raceway in preparation for the intermediate competitor's race to begin.

Stirling's feet barely cross the threshold through a walkway under the bleachers into the civilian side when Eve ambushes him. Leaping into him she wraps her arms around his neck pulling him tightly into her. "You did it! You did it!"

Momentarily stunned Stirling puts one arm around her half returning her embrace. She is significantly taller than Amiria, her face nuzzling perfectly into the crook of his neck. The top of her head is at nose height where Amiria's head barely reaches his chin.

Eve releases Stirling, backing away in time for Bernard to throw his arm around Stirling's shoulders. Tousling his hair, Bernard tells him, "Boy, you were incredible. Way to bend the rules out there. Though you gave us quite a scare there in the beginning. You all right? What happened?"

"Yeah," Stirling says, half truthful. He squirms out from Bernard's arm. "The horn. It startled me. I should be…fine now, now that I know what to expect…But the race." His face brightens. "The race, it was exhilarating! This is what I unknowingly wanted my whole life and I never want it to stop."

Fighting was never something he saw himself doing. He was never inspired to join the Cavalry so he could serve and protect. He doesn't enjoy the idea of raising a sword against another person. All he wanted in life was to fly, to be able to be weightless and touch the sky. Now he can do that freely. With this new alternative brought to his awareness, he has no reason to ever return home. He never belonged in that world. The only thread still connecting him to that place is Amiria. Amiria who made her own choice. She chose Wyverna and King Dietrich.

"Oh, by the way." Stirling reaches into the drawstring bag he attached to his belt, taking out a small handful of coins.

He extends his hand out to Bernard who asks, "What's this?"

"Payment for the registration fee and all the food you gave me," Stirling explains. Bernard holds out his cupped hand allowing Stirling to drop the sum into it.

Bernard shakes his head, not needing to count. "This is way more than what I loaned you."

"Consider it interest." Stirling smiles.

Bernard chuckles, "You're a good kid. Let's go celebrate our first win." Bernard holds up his fist clenched around the coins, "On me."

"I think you just approve of any excuse to enjoy festivities. Do you not want to watch the rest of the races?" Stirling brings up.

"I guess. We've probably lost our spot by now. It can get kinda cramped at the bottom," Bernard advises.

Stirling stares at him blankly.

Bernard expands, "Unlike the regular competitions throughout the year, the Games are free to watch, but the wealthy still get the better seats. Whether they sit lower and closer to the racer like during the opening ceremonies, or they sit higher to have a more level view of the flying." Bernard pauses. "There's actually a row assigned to participants."

"But I'm guessing you're not allowed to sit with me?" Stirling already knows the answer.

"No," Bernard confirms.

"I'd rather sit with you guys."

Bernard grins. "Don't say I didn't warn ya. Let's go finish watching."

Returning to the bleachers, Stirling follows Bernard and Eve up the stairs popping out on a walkway across the front row. Scanning the audience Bernard searches for an open space for three, "Seems like there's some room down that way."

The three of them shuffle and slide their way past the onlookers who turn to acknowledge the people scooting past them. Their annoyed faces turn awestruck as they recognize Stirling.

"Didn't he just win?"

"What is he doing down here?"

"He's from that little village over the hill."

Stirling takes his seat between Bernard and Eve. Straining his neck to look up he can see the intermediate racers prepared to leap from the edge when the alarm sounds.

The horn blares from the cliffside. Stirling winces, his resting hands squeeze his knees. Eve follows his gripping hands up to his eyes closed in pain. She doesn't watch as the racers plunge from the starting line, diving nose-first toward the sandy land. The wall of wind runs over them seconds after the dragons pass. He opens his eyes and catches Eve's before she bounces back to the racers. Releasing the grip on his knees he focuses his breathing and distracts himself with the race that instantly ensnares him.

Stirling sat captivated through the intermediate and the advanced races. But they are nowhere close to beholding the elite race happening now. Stirling can't remove his eyes from the blue dragon, the way its feathers shimmer like a melting icicle as it travels through the air.

This is a quetzalcoatl. *This is* Quilan's dragon. The rarest breed. They are elegant, intelligent, and incredibly swift. You can purchase a herd of Dracos for the same price as a single quetzalcoatl. Purchasing a quetzalcoatl is purchasing your win. They are unbeatable. Stirling sees this firsthand as he watches the way it's able to wrap around the pillar as it turns like rope sliding around a beam.

Each of the contenders in the elite division would be able to lap every single rider in the beginner's round.

"Maybe we'll get a chance to race him one day," Stirling tells Ignis who is watching from a designated area to store your dragon back on the top of the cliffs.

"I'd be okay with that. I'd like to place second so we can just fly behind that dragon the whole time," Ignis replies with a mental wink.

Stirling's whole body sighs. *"Why do I bother with you at times."*

"Because you love me as much as life itself," Ignis gloats.

"Shut up, Ignis."

Fourteen

Ignis lopes behind the group as Bernard and Eve accompany Stirling partway to the Inn he is required to stay at before they return home themselves. Luckily for Bernard and Eve, Stirling's scheduled events were not daily. The matches spanning over the next month give the dragons and racers ample time to rest and enjoy the festivities.

"Bernard, why are there no female racers?" Stirling inquires.

Bernard doesn't hesitate with his answer. "Because women are too fragile to fly a dragon."

"Fragile? I don't want to be the person who tells that to Amiria." Stirling laughs to Ignis, then says aloud to Bernard, "Are they allowed?"

"No, definitely not," he states. "It's like jousting or any knight's game. Women can't be knights, it's too dangerous for them. But they can help do their part by working at the games or caring for the professionals."

"I think they'd be better than you'd think. If you give them the same training and the same standards, I bet you'll have some of the top flyers who are female." Stirling says, disagreeing with Bernard's point.

"Look at you." Eve nudges Stirling. "Standing up for women."

Stirling blushes. "It's, well, my friend back home, she can outfly everyone here. We have plenty of women as knights and guards. They didn't care what you were, you are assigned the job so you better figure out how to do it."

Eve hangs back. "Oh? Was she a girlfriend?"

"NO–No, we're close friends—What's that?" Stirling diverts the conversation to a crowd surrounding a large wooden display board.

Bernard smirks at Stirling's quick change of topic. "That is one of the reasons we're walking with you. You, my young man, made the village extremely happy."

Ignis slows to a stop, knowing he can't proceed any further. Stirling leaves Ignis behind and approaches the crowd. Standing on his toes he can see clearly over everyone's head, "What do you mean?"

The board is indecipherable as he jumps around the markings, colors, and numbers. Small blocks numbered and color-coded are slid into slots lining one side of the board. Seeing an orange tab with a white zero painted on it answers one of Stirling's questions. Though he still can't decode what all the numbers beside the racer's tabs mean.

"Boy, this is a betting board. All those numbers are your odds based on prior experience and prior training, which is none for you. Then how many people placed a bet on you and for what position," Bernard explains.

"I'm not following." Stirling cocks his head to the side, "Why is my number so high?"

"It means out of. For example, one out of three means, one out of three races you have a chance at getting first place. You had one out of a thousand and only one person bet on you."

"Did you guys bet on me?" Stirling raises an eyebrow at Bernard's purpling face as he struggles to contain his explosive excitement.

"Yes!" He bursts. "Yes, we did! The town played it smart and we all pitched in and placed a single bet. The only bet placed on you winning first place." Bernard slaps Stirling on the back, "You, boy, just won the village a large sum of coin. We can live comfortably this year. We knew we saw something in you." Bernard rubs his hands together. "Now it's time to collect. Excuse me, I'll be right back." Bernard shakes Stirling again with proud enthusiasm and disappears pushing his way through the crowd.

"Hey! It's the cheater!" a man in riding gear and a halved black and white cape yells.

Confused, Stirling searches the faces around him. The betting board no longer exists, unblinking eyes poke and prod from every angle. Dread washes over him as he returns to the man in black and white. His accusatory eyes inject ice into Stirling's veins, sending pinpricks down his body. Stirling shrinks as the confronting racer squares his shoulders. Behind him, Stirling counts three more racers who came in close to last poised with their arms crossed.

Stirling takes half a step back raising his hands to chest level, "Hey, it was ruled in. I didn't cheat. I was just playing by the rules I was told."

"Don't play dumb with us. Maybe you're not playing, you can't even pronounce your words correctly." The man sneers, shoving Stirling in the chest. Stirling stumbles back a few steps. Then spectators immediately around them gasp, sending out an invite for more to watch.

Eve grabs Stirling's arm steadying him, her face puffed with fury, "Hey! It's not his fault you were too stupid to think of it!"

"You better watch your mouth girly, remember your place." The man snaps at her.

"Leave her out of this," Stirling defends stepping in between them, "This is between us. Plus, didn't you come in around tenth place? You weren't going to win anyway."

The man's movements are a flash. Within a blink, the crowd shows a display of every emotion. Women cover their mouths while others snicker. Men cross their arms with disapproval at those making heckling remarks in the racer's favor. No one besides Eve defends Stirling as he doubles over. Grimacing in pain he wraps his arms around his stomach and drops to his knees.

"Stirling!" Eve panics, stooping down beside him with her arm cradled around him, "GUARDS!"

"*I'll roast him,*" Ignis calls out.

"*Stay back, Ignis,*" Stirling instructs, still clenching his stomach.

"Go back to your fields, peasant." He spits, the wad landing in Stirling's hair and splattering in Eve's face. "Look at you—pathetic."

"If I'm pathetic, but I beat you in a race, what does that make you?"

Eve barely leaps up in time to keep her balance as the man snatches Stirling's cape, yanking him up to him, "Yeah? You cheat your way to first and you think you're some big shot now? Mr. Zero, Mr. Nothing, I've been competing for five years, so you talk to your veterans with respect."

Stirling coughs a wounded smile. "Five years? And you're still in the beginners?"

With a surge of rage, the man pulls back his fist. Stirling grabs the wrist holding firm to his cape and grimaces in anticipation.

"BREAK IT UP!" a guard orders.

"RELEASE HIM!" another demands as the crowd parts ways letting them through.

Complying with the guards' orders he releases Stirling's cape by throwing him to the ground. Stirling winces as his shoulder scrapes across the gravel.

"All right, Grimni, you've had your fill now move along. Leave the kid alone," the first guard instructs.

Grimni waves the guards off. "He asked for it."

"Go on, get on with your day. He's not worth getting kicked out of the games."

"Fine." Grimni shoots Stirling a warning glare. "You've got off easy for what you've done." He signals to his compatriots and vanishes into the numerous faces of the surrounding people.

The crowd already losing interest and dissipating, Bernard shoves himself to the front of the remaining audience, "Oi! You all right?" He slides to Stirling's side as Eve helps him sit up. Leaning over he cups Stirling under the armpits like an infant and lifts him to his feet.

The Guard turns to Stirling, "You're lucky you didn't hit back or we would report you to the board."

Eve puts her hands on her hips, "Oh? But the man who came out of nowhere and assaulted him doesn't even get a reprimand?"

The Guard blinks slowly, glancing at Eve then returns to Stirling, "I'd control your girl if I were you, or we're going to have problems. And you should be glad it's only disqualification. If you were a regular citizen I would have to apprehend you."

"Yes, sir," Stirling mumbles, dropping his gaze to the guard's shoes.

Bernard waits for the Guards to leave, "So it was one of the racers."

"Yeah, I guess people are the same no matter where you go." Stirling sucks in a sharp breath through his teeth as he touches his stomach, "You guys should head back to the village before it gets too late. You've got good news to spread." Stirling nods at the sack of coins hanging from a cord across Bernard's chest.

"You sure? It looks like you can use the company?" Bernard invites.

"Yeah, but once I get back to Ignis' side, I should be fine." Stirling shakes his head, turning the offer down.

"Maybe we can see if you're allowed to stay back in the village." Eve's soft hand curls around Stirling's with concern.

He takes a moment to observe his rough and scarred hand in hers. "They want all the racers to stay there for easier access if they do need to speak to us."

"Eve, let the boy go. People can only handle you in small doses anyway," Bernard says, tugging on her shoulder.

Eve slaps his hand away. "Fine, but I want some honey-soaked peaches and a wild berry pastry for the ride home."

"Yes, Your Highness," Bernard teases.

With a soft sigh, Stirling waves as they part their separate ways. Slouching his shoulders, Stirling distances himself from the mass of people returning to his place beside Ignis.

"How's your stomach?" Ignis questions.

"It hurts, but not as much as being hit with a stick by Amiria," Stirling claims.

Walking down the desolate road compacted by the heavy footprints of dragons, they stroll in silence. Stirling can still hear the laughter and joyous conversations of the people exploring the festival grounds as they near the inn.

A middle-aged woman throws a sheet over a line and acknowledges Stirling's quiet arrival. "Oh! You must be the new one."

Stirling nods. "I am. How did you know?"

"My husband owns this inn. I know all the racers sweetie. Go on in and my daughter will be able to help you out. If you need anything, I'm Ceola."

"Thank you, ma'am," Stirling responds with a dip of his chin. Leaving Ignis to wait outside, Stirling heads into the front room of the inn.

Farah with a face splattered with freckles sits behind a table that is more loose paperwork than the tabletop. "Well, look who returns."

"Yeah. I got the coin like you asked," Stirling says, awkwardly holding up the small bag.

"Well then, let me properly introduce myself. I'm Farah, may I get you a room?" She offers.

"Stirling of—of Patu," he introduces. "Yeah, uh, what do you have left?"

She picks up some of the papers in front of her and flips through them. Her eyes skim the words in front of her. Stirling sees nothing but scribbles and numbers. "We only have two beds in one of the communal rooms left. It's a large room with five beds. You each get a lockable trunk to keep your belongings in. I keep suggesting to my father we need to start expanding. But he always answers with, "Next year.""

"This communal room. What level are the people staying in there," Stirling asks cautiously.

She looks back down at the paper. "Beginners. So they are the guys you raced with today." She smiles cheerily.

Stirling frowns. "That's what I'm afraid of."

Her smile fades. "Oh—" She catches on to what Stirling is insinuating.

"Word travels fast, but I have not yet heard about your race. I do know from the opening ceremonies people are having mixed feelings about you. No one from the working class has even ridden a dragon before, and I'm not counting when you're a kid and the professionals let you sit on their dragons."

She watches as Stirling sinks into himself. Trying to fix the road the conversation is taking, she continues, "There's not just negatives in mixed feelings, well there's a lot of negatives, but there's also positives. The working class is ecstatic to see one of their own out there even if you froze and threw up at the ceremonies." She waves her hands, panicking. "It's not a bad thing, it shows us racers are human, too."

"Thanks," Stirling mutters, not feeling any better about himself.

Farah mentally hits herself. Biting her tongue from saying anything else she will regret she forces a smile through gritted teeth.

Leaning to check out the window, Stirling asks, "The stables, is there an open one farther from the rest?"

"Are you asking to stay in the stables?" She raises an eyebrow.

"Well, you see…" Stirling starts fumbling for the appropriate words, afraid she will find him stranger than she already does. "I'm used to sleeping beside my dragon. I didn't always have a home. I feel a lot more comfortable when he's around."

"I see. Well, we have our old stables behind the new ones. Parts of them are dilapidated from years of neglect. But there's some stalls still in fair condition. I'll only charge you half price for it. Meals and the use of the bathhouse are included," she informs him.

"That sounds perfect," Stirling answers with a sigh of relief.

Farah stares at him unsure, she puts on her best smile, "You can either follow the gravel path and cut through the new stables which is faster, or walk out and around them. You'll see the old ones right away. My brothers will bring out a new batch of straw for bedding, and we'll provide you with several blankets. It gets a little cold at night from the coastal breeze, but please do not start any fires inside there. It's very flammable from its age. If you want to make a fire pit away from the building that will be fine."

The old stables sit in half ruins. Portions have collapsed in on themselves as termites ate through the supporting walls. Stirling and Ignis step up to the small segment still mostly intact. A large barn entrance designed to fit dragons stands open where a door once stood. One of the door remnants lies decomposing in the grass nearby. The other leans against the outer wall as if there were intentions to be repaired. Inside, Stirling will be able to claim one of the stalls as his own, but as the only resident, it hardly mattered which one.

Two of the Inn Keeper's sons have brought a large wagon of straw to begin cleaning out the old remnants and replace it with fresh bedding. The younger of the brothers swings a pitchfork over his shoulders and heads inside to start.

Picking at the decaying entrance frame, Stirling's thumbnail catches at the splinter of wood. Placing his hand on the rough grains while the brothers work he falls deep into thought wishing he can tell his mother about his recent success. This isn't only for the village, this is also for his own sake, but most of all this is for her. She understood him before anyone else. Even when she thought his dreams would remain just as that, she still encouraged him to keep going. She believed in him until her last breath.

"Hey ma, we won our first race. I can't believe it either. I wish you were here to see us...I wish Father was here to see us— Amiria—We've got plenty more wins coming our way—"

"Only if this place doesn't cave in on us." Ignis interrupts.

"Shut up, Ignis. Those were private thoughts." Stirling taps his forehead on the graying wood annoyed.

Fifteen

Amiria's toes curl in the brown fur of the imported bear rug placed in the middle of her room. Wearing a long sleeve white tunic and a pair of long braies pinching off at her knees she watches the dark fur stick out between her toes.

"Ms. Rey?" her personal Handmaiden, a girl only two years younger than Amiria, says.

The fur moving around her toes remains in Amiria's focus, she knows what her handmaiden wants. She is only prolonging the inevitable truth of her duties tonight.

The well-furnished room is coated in a variety of shades of purple. A pastel wardrobe containing her cotehardies and dark armor sits near a bookshelf filled with scripture about the history of the nation, the Winged Cavalry, and military strategies. A storage trunk stuffed with dresses, shoes, and accessories she refuses to wear, sits neglected gathering dust in the corner.

Against the wall above her heavy framed bed with a goose feather mattress and the thick quilt is a headboard displaying wood carvings of a wyvern dragon. Adding the illusion of a wall of windows, tapestries hang in line telling the story of the sun's life cycle. All in an attempt to keep the natural, cave-like structure warm with her personal fireplace.

Besides the brown bear currently padding the ground beneath her feet near the hearth, animal hides carpet her floor. Most are a mixture of red, fallow, and sika deer she hunted herself.

"Mairead, I'm going to end up stabbing someone if I have to wear that all night," she states, referring to the gown hanging from a hook on a privacy wall. The tone of her voice is indistinguishable between sarcasm and seriousness.

"Ms. Rey, your father instructed you to wear this," Mairead pleads. "I can't disobey his orders. I need to dress you for the ball."

Amiria chews on her lip wishing she can stay in the comfort of her usual attire. "Fine," she grunts, snatching the dress down. The wall wobbles from the overly dramatic yank of the fabric. "Let's get this over with."

"Ms. Rey, you need to put this on first," Mairead informs, holding up a long silk undertunic.

Amiria's eyes narrow; she's never been fond of feminine clothing. "No one is going to see what I'm wearing under my dress, I'm keeping the braies."

"Yes, you are right." Mairead drapes the slip on the back of a chair.

"What's that supposed to mean?" Bashfulness plays on the surface of Amiria's skin as she tugs off her linen tunic and drops it into a clump at her feet.

"Nothing." Mairead bites back a teasing smile. "Now put out your arms."

Amiria scrunches her nose in response and extends her arms out straight letting Mairead slip the orchid silk dress onto her arms. With a raise of her hands above her head, the contraption of fabric is pulled past Amiria's face and fitted into place. Her arms drop with an audible *swish* as her sleeves brush her skirt.

"Back up." Mairead taps Amiria's hand.

"There's more?" Amiria raises an eyebrow.

"Yes, there's more," Mairead says mockingly and retrieves the top layer of the kirtle, a front-laced golden gown of stiff taffeta fabric.

"It's hideous." Amiria's shoulders slump, defeated.

"Says the girl who wears oiled armor." Mairead side glances at Amiria while slipping the kirtle over her.

"Armor protects me," Amiria mutters under her breath.

"But you're strong without it." Mairead ties the gold twine of the kirtle's front closed, receiving a disgruntled expression from Amiria. Amiria's tight long orchid sleeves remain exposed beneath the shorter-sleeved top layer matching the purple flowering vines crawling from the neckline to the hem and accompanied by a belt of pearls.

She tugs at the kirtles neckline pressing into the bottom of her throat. "It's too tight. I can't breathe." Amiria whines in a breathy voice, her fingers fumbling down to the cords across her stomach keeping her lungs from fully expanding.

"Oh, you'll be fine," Mairead says, patting Amiria on the shoulder.

"No, I think I'll die." Amiria holds firm to her pout, refusing to smile until her young handmaiden turns away to pick up several hairpins from a case on the desk.

As Mairead lays out the pins and hair ornaments, Amiria tests out her articulation in the dress by lunging and stretching out her arms. Just as she thought. It's terrible. The kirtle's fabric has no give to the movements, her sleeves digging into her arms stopping her from raising them to their full extent. The hems hang heavily around her feet asking to be tripped on as soon as she reaches the first flight of stairs.

"I hate it."

"I love it. It's stunning. The light colors with your dark hair and tan complexion. I wish I could wear a gown like this," Mairead compliments.

"Trust me." Amiria grimaces as she sits herself stiffly down into the chair, "I'd rather you be wearing this instead, too."

"If only," she says dreamily as she swoops the top layer of Amiria's hair back letting the bottom half fall free in thick waves. Pinning gold ribbon to each side of Amiria's head. she rolls the strands of hair twisting the ribbon in with it. Banding it together at the back of her head, Mairead twists it into an eight-strand braid. Topping off the hairstyle she adds small amethysts glued to hairpins throughout.

"All right, just slip on your shoes and you're ready to go," Mairead says, pinning the last amethyst in Amiria's hair.

Amiria scrunches her nose at a pair of golden slippers. "Yeah, about that."

Sixteen

The golden slippers hide beneath the brown tunic gown worn by Mairead as she follows behind Amiria. Her face glowing from the new gift. The most valuable item she has ever owned. Even though no one can see them she will always cherish them.

Amiria's boots, comfortable and molded to her feet support her to her undesired destination. With the dress hindering her stride she kicks the heavy fabric with each step forward to keep from tripping on it. She hasn't made it to the great hall and she is already miserable.

Mairead hurries her pace to reach the double doors before Amiria does. With both hands, she pulls open one of the heavy doors leading inside the great hall.

"Thank you," Amiria says, stepping inside with Mairead slipping in behind her. She peers over at her handmaiden one last time pleadingly as the young girl slips into an open space against the wall to wait until the ball is over. Amiria wishes she can join the wallflowers.

An exaggerated hearth of textured stones and dragon carvings stands at a height of full grown man lights the hall in a golden hue. Floating over a table stretching across the center of the room, chandeliers flicker like dying stars.

A banquet with enough food to feed the entire population of Lumierna is spread across the table. Plates, bowls, and platters are piled on top of one another not leaving a single spot to set down your chalice.

There are pies filled with pork and eggs topped with honey and pepper, fish and fruit, sausage and meatballs, and egg topped with whole chicken pieces. Entire bodies of roasted heron, roasted swans, and peacocks sit lined like a mountain range. Each of the birds was cooked in wine sauces and glazed in batter. People help themselves to lamb stewed with sage and parsley, venison ribs in wine, stuffed porpoise stomach, and shellfish in a thick almond sauce.

Stuffed between the savory dishes are baskets of white bread served with onion-ale soup, honey and pine nuts, and wine sauce. Side dishes of stuffed eggs and quiches, fried beans, spinach and carrots, and pea porridge with onion are scattered about.

In the center of it all: a roasted pig.

Barrels of wine, ale, mead, and cider clutter an entire corner of the room, and warm mugs of posset are handed out to toast to good health. Wearing their finest fabrics guests stand socializing in segregated clicks, gossiping amongst their peers.

"Amiria!" A stern voice erupts from the crowd. "You are late!"

Her father emerges from thin air in a red and gold doublet jacket with a damask print. His golden sword glints in the scabbard at his hip. "You know better than to keep a gentleman waiting. I have a list of fine suitors here solely to meet you."

"Aren't I just a lucky girl?" The sarcasm rolls off her tongue with fluency.

"Amiria Rey, I'm going to tell you this only one time," he says, his voice only loud enough for her to hear. Amiria's eyes shift away scanning the crowd. "Amiria, look at me while I'm speaking to you," he growls. Her eyes shoot back up to his. "I'm only going to tell you this once. Not only are you a Winged Rider tonight, you're also a lady so conduct yourself accordingly. Do not embarrass me. It's a shame, you're a beautiful girl, it's your personality that is the problem here and it needs to be fixed," he lectures.

"Yes, sir," she recoils. Her eyes scan the room, she doesn't feel his presence, "Is King Dietrich here? Isn't this his ball?"

Rey scoffs, "You work beside him. Have you ever seen him attend a dance?"

"No?" She is now questioning her memory.

"Neither have I. The queen puts these gatherings on. She was here earlier with the princesses and prince, but with your tardiness you missed her." He scowls at the last words. Exhaling sharply through his nose signaling he is done with small talk, his attention turns elsewhere. "Barric!" her father calls out, ushering a man in royal garb to step forward. Amiria recognizes him as Earl Barric, a second cousin of King Dietrich.

Marrying him she would not only take over as the field marshal in the Cavalry, but she would also be a countess merging the Rey's into the royal family. *I see your game father.* She thinks to herself.

Earl Barric bows to Amiria, one hand scooped across his stomach and the other flaring out behind him. Amiria remains stationary, her father steps up beside her facing the opposite way so Earl Barric cannot see his face. She can hear the rustling of her sleeve as it conects with his.

He glares down at her from the corner of his eye. "Show respect."

Amiria doesn't blink, her eyes fixated forward.

Forcing a smile, she bares her teeth. Her nails dig into her dress as she curtseys. Her father's stare lingers on her failed attempt at a formal greeting before he departs giving the two young adults privacy.

Earl Barric immediately begins the conversation, jumping straight to describing himself and his daily routine. Not once switching the topic or leaving room for Amiria to speak.

Her eyes gloss over as he tells her about his position as an Earl. He is far down the line of heirs and has no interest in becoming king and is glad he isn't the king's direct son and only a cousin. He enjoys watching over his countship though. Then he tells her about the time he was in such a hurry to make it in time to a dinner party he wore two different pointed slippers, one was navy blue while the other was black. He was mortified.

From these stories alone, Amiria can take it that other than his carriage ride from his manor in his countryside to the king's castle he hasn't stepped a foot off royal ground. Not even to participate in a royal hunt.

She watches the feather attached to his hat. The way the frilly object bounces and flows with the movement of his head as he talks.

"It was pretty scary when all those alarms went off. Remember that? It woke me up. I've never had such a fright. You're in the Winged Cavalry, right? As King Dietrich's little guard? Did it wake you? Or were you on watch? How do you feel about it all? Scary huh? Someone not under King Dietrich's watch is in control of a dragon. It's a terrifying thought. Can you imagine what they could have done? I'm so relieved he was shot down. Truly for the better." He says touching his chin in thought.

Amiria blinks. The action is so deliberately slow, she almost doesn't open her eyes because she knows he will still be standing there. She opens her mouth to speak but pauses. Her face falls knowing there is no point to her words. Clamping her mouth shut, she turns and leaves.

"Ms. Rey? Ms. Rey! Where are you going?" he calls out.

Ignoring him, Amiria pushes her way through the crowd with nowhere specific in mind. Her only goal is to be out of earshot of this Earl Barric.

Wearing a pale blue doublet that glows against his tan skin, Calix leans against the wall beside the hearth, the light accentuating his tracking eyes. The fire's light casts a heavy contrast of shadows over half his face. He sips his sweet red wine from his silver chalice, his eyes never leaving Amiria.

Amiria hooks the fingers of both hands in the collar of her kirtle alleviating the pressure. Steel plates are easier to move in than this. She drops her arms as she stops at the table set to the side of the room full of desserts.

Her mouth waters as she stares down at the honey crisps, custard tarts, and bread pudding. She scans over fritters of every kind; almond, apple, honey glazed. An elderflower and rosewater cheesecake topped with wild berries sits beautifully between piles of shortbread knots, donets, and wafers beside a marzipan cake.

Her stomach growls. "How do you people stand this?" Amiria complains, referring to the ties down the front of her gown.

The women standing around the dessert table turn in unison, their faces covered in silent judgment.

One speaks up, "It's not about comfort. It's about fashion and how you appear to those around you and a little advice." Her voice snide, "You look lousy picking at your gown like that."

Amiria holds her tongue, *This is why I avoid these events.*

Acting as if the comment didn't scratch her armor, she picks up a pancake, the dough pan-fried in oil with uneven and crispy edges. Her fingers twitch, hesitating as her eyes linger on the loaf of gingerbread sitting beside the platter.

I hate gingerbread.

Shoving half of the pancake into her mouth, she ignores the crumbs falling onto her chest and dress. She chews slowly, savoring the sweet fried dough.

The girls laugh, "Who eats likes that."

"Let the men stuff their faces. We're only here to look pretty."

"You don't look familiar, have you ever been to one of these events before?"

Amiria takes another bite of the treat, "No. I've been busy working."

"Gross, working class," the girls hiss as they migrate their group away from Amiria.

Now standing alone, Amira wipes her face with her sleeve, discreetly eyeing the social life surrounding her. She didn't want to make small talk with them anyway, her stomach is her primary focus. She is starving, she purposely skipped lunch so she can indulge herself with the banquette.

"You must be Ms. Rey." A man says behind her. She turns around to see one of the second lieutenants of the Winged Cavalry. "You're almost unrecognizable without your gear on. You should wear dresses more often. Who knew you would be so beautiful," he compliments.

He bows to her like Earl Barric, but instead of flaring his hand backward, he holds it out forwards palm facing up with his intentions being for her to place her hand in his so he may kiss it. Amiria does not respond this way. The Second Lt looks up from his bow to behold a half-eaten pancake sitting in his palm.

"Thanks. I wasn't sure where to put that," Amiria says. "I've got this itch." The unforgiving fabric of her sleeves digs into her skin as she struggles to reach the middle of her back.

The Second Lt straightens up, blinking blankly at the pancake in his hand. "Umm." He lets out as he observes Amiria as she presses her hand to her opposing elbow, stretching it to reach the spot on her back. He sets the pancake on the table, whipping his hand on the cloth. "Ms. Rey? Are you all right?"

"No. I can't reach it," Amiria says, spinning. With a huff of defeat, she snags a knife from the table. "These stupid sleeves," she gripes to herself, exasperated, holding the dull side of the blade using the hilt to reach between her shoulder blades.

"You know, you're acting a fool right?" he says with a raise of his lip.

Amiria points the knife as she speaks. "What am I supposed to do? Use the wall?" Her eyes widen at the idea and scans the wall for something useful.

"Uh." The Second Lt pretends to notice some friends and waves. "It was, um, nice talking to you. I'll see you around, Ms. Rey."

Amiria barely nods a goodbye as she spots a smaller door frame leading to the kitchens. "Perfect." Stabbing the knife into the gingerbread she sets off in the direction making it only two steps before she stops short.

"Ms. Rey, care to dance?" a gentleman appearing in front of her asks, holding out his hand to her with a chalice of wine in the other.

She can't get a break. "Well, yeah, I kind of do." She leans to peer around the man to the door that will save her.

Instead of the door, she spots her father leering at her from across the room. "Actually, maybe dancing doesn't sound bad right now." She reaches out, stealing the chalice from his hand. "Let me borrow this."

Stealing the silver chalice from his hand, she dumps the contents at their feet. She shivers with delight as she relieves the itch with the brim of the chalice. Tossing the chalice on the table, she takes his hand. "All right. Let's go."

Pulling him out to the dance circle near the musicians in front of the mosaic windows, Amiria already regrets her choice. Everyone is holding hands. Their laughing faces spin across the floor. Their arms swing to the beat of the band.

Amiria hates dancing. The same dances every time, nothing new, nothing original. The choreography is simple and basic. Not a single drop of individuality as everyone moves in synchronization.

The dance circle opens a gap wide enough for her and the man whom she dragged over without bothering to learn his name to fit in. She takes the hand of the person next to her and side steps to the left nearly stepping on their toes.

The circle stops and they start spinning to the right. They stop again. Still holding hands the group steps in closing the circle. They raise their hands to head height. Pulling out away from the center they step back in with one foot then back out. She thinks, after all the years of training to master the grace and fluidity of swordsmanship she would be able to dance.

Amiria knocks into the person beside her as the group changes direction, earning her a sideways glare.

Great. She thinks as the group slows to a stop again. Every other person including Amiria lets go of the hands and bounces to the beat as they dance into the middle of the circle.

Amiria fakes her smile as she bobs awkwardly to the middle with the other half of the dancers. Putting their right hands into the air their fingertips touch as they circle. The larger outer ring remains still waiting for their partners to return. Amiria's group finishes their dance and she takes the cue to follow everyone back into line.

Girls in the room snicker as Amiria's boots are exposed while jumping side to side. "Yuck, look at those ratty things."

"How disrespectful to wear something so hideous to the king's ball."

"Is she expecting to win over a nobleman like that? A man marries a woman because she is a lady, not because she acts like another man."

Amiria's face is flushed. Her body heat caught inside the unbreathable fabric. She knows the heat and sweat radiating from her face can cook a small meal. Releases her hands, she fans her face as she steps away from the dancing circle.

Peeling the collar of her dress away from her skin she attempts to circulate air flow for any sort of relief. Amiria groans in frustration as she can barely pull the fabric around her arms and torso away from her skin.

"I need something to drink. Can we get something to drink?"

The man steps out of the dance circle to check on her. "Now? We can get something to drink after we're done dancing," he instructs, grabbing her hand to drag her back to the ongoing circle.

Amiria yanks her hand free. "I'm done dancing. *I'm* getting something to drink." Turning on her heels, she stalks across the room directly for the wine barrels.

Picking up an empty chalice she fills it to the brim. Downing the drink like it's water she fills it up a second time. Mid-chug a man clears his throat attempting to grab her attention. Amiria doesn't take the drink away from her lips.

"Excuse me, miss. Don't you think you should slow down? Did your mother not teach you how to sip?"

Amiria's eyes narrow. She glares sideways at him around the metal rim.

"Or you can carry on. Sorry to bother you," he says, retracting his initial statement and slowly retreating into the crowd.

After her fourth drink, the room begins to blur. She feels better.

Anyone not within arms reach of her is lost from her vision. Her surroundings are no more than a smudged oil painting. She leans against the wall alone. Tilting her chalice, she watches the scarlet liquid twirl around its prison.

A hand slips around her waist. The touch is so slow and subtle that she can barely register the pressure of it until it's too late. She is pulled tight against his chest.

"A beauty such as you shouldn't be standing alone." He flirts, a slur in his voice signaling he has had too much to drink.

She looks up trying to focus her vision on his face. She doesn't recognize him. "Let me go!" She demands, firmly pushing against him with her free hand. Her drink sloshes in the other leaving blood-like droplets at his feet.

"Ah come on. Let's have some fun," he seduces, pulling her in tighter.

He leans down into her, his face invading her personal space. She can feel the warm air of his breath on her neck and ear. The stench of cider is strong in her nose.

"I said let go!" she shouts, throwing the rest of her drink in his face.

He jumps back surprised. His grip loosens around her waist. Taking advantage of the opportunity she steps back freeing herself from his enclosing arm. Before she can gain another step away he grabs her forearm. His hand is large enough to fully enclose her thin wrist. He tugs her forward out muscling her.

"HEY YOU! STOP!" a voice calls out.

"You're going to pay for that." He holds her arm up as if he is holding a torch.

She's pulled forward off balance. The pain in her arm screams and begs for her to make the crushing grip stop before the bone breaks.

"UNHAND HER!" the same voice shouts. A young guard only a year older than Amiria, pushes through the developing audience, but he doesn't reach them before Amiria reacts.

"I SAID LET GO!" she howls. Using the heel of her hand she strikes, hitting the man in the nose.

The world succumbs to tears. He drops Amiria, his hands shooting to his face. Blood gushes from his nose adding to the red wine stains on his top and the floor around them.

"You wench!" he curses, spitting blood that has run into his mouth from his nose.

The man's friends rush to his side as they hand him handkerchiefs to stanch the bleeding, but the shorter guard with straight auburn hair is at his side.

"Hands behind your back!" the guard, William, demands reaching for him.

The drunken man blinks back the tears clouding his vision and swats his hand at William, who takes hold of his wrist and presses his other arm to the man's bicep and takes a step to the side and back, throwing the man to the floor.

With William apprehending the man, a taller guard with short dark hair named Robert, seizes Amiria by the arm.

She rips her arm from his grasp, "Don't touch me!" she screams. Robert recoils at the recognition of who she is. "None of you have the authority to touch me!" She stumbles back with her swaying vision.

The room pauses, frozen in time. No one is sure on how to react to the scene that is playing out before them.

"Ms. Rey, I'm going to need you to vacate the hall," exclaims the guard alarmed by her outburst toward him.

He is lost on how else to handle the situation. She is correct and he does not have the authority to lay a hand on someone with her title. His eyes find the Winged Cavalry brass standing idly by in the crowd. They are the only ones who have the ability to seize her, but none of them move a finger.

"Best thing I've heard all night." She sighs with a sag of her shoulders.

Every eye following, their faces showing signs of ease that this pariah is done spoiling their night. Mairead peels herself from the wall and glues herself back to Amiria's side as she flees the hall.

Field Marshal Rey stands in a group with the Lt General and Colonel of the Winged Cavalry. They remain silent holding their tongues until the large double doors are shut once again.

"Was that your daughter?" the Lt General asks.

"I'm afraid so," he answers by holding back any emotion.

"Women in the Calvary are a breed of their own aren't they," The Colonel jokes. They all laugh except Field Marshal Rey who frowns at their humor.

Across the room, Captain Guatier stands close to the General. She raises her lip in distaste at the space Amiria last occupied. Captain Gautier rests his hand on her shoulder. "I know, but she is the only one in line for field marshal."

"The Reys are a dying family who feel as if they are untouchable. They need the Gautiers to take control and run this Calvary efficiently," General Gautier says smugly.

Seventeen

"AHHHHHHHHH!!!" Amiria belts, releasing her frustration. Her voice echoes off the corridor as she stumbles down the hall.

"Ms. Rey! Ms. Rey! Let me help you walk!" Mairead calls over the hollers and reaches out to steady Amiria.

"I don't need your help." Amiria's voice lowers. She dodges Mairead's helping hands, "I don't need anyone." Anger returns, "What I need is this damn dress off." She hikes up her skirt and searches the interior of her boot revealing a dagger.

"Of course, you have that." Mairead throws her hands. "What are you going to do? Cut the sleeves off?"

Amiria presses the tip of the blade into the seam at her shoulder.

"Amiria, don't."

Amiria gives a sly grin.

"Amiria," Mairead warns. "Amiria drop the knife." Her orders fall useless to the floor between them as she watches helplessly while the threads of the gown are severed. Then with a significant *rip,* Amiria tears both of her sleeves free, the shorter falling to her feet as the longer under-sleeve bunches at her wrist.

Mairead comments sarcastically as Amiria continues to the next. "Well, you need them to match."

Letting the sleeve hang like the first Amiria's hands go up to the front lace of the kirtle. "Amiria! No! Bad!" Mairead leaps forward to stop Amiria's fingers struggling to untie the knot.

With her grace returning, Amiria spins away bumping Mairead's arms away with her shoulder. Her voice grows soft as she speaks to the empty air in front of her. "People don't truly want to be with you. They only want something. Once they get what they want, they leave. I like you Mairead, but you're only here because you're paid." Unsuccessful with the knot Amiria takes her knife and cuts the ribbon, letting the kirtle fall open like a vest. "So, you should just leave too."

Mairead nervously looks up and down the corridor, "Ms. Rey. Please stop this. Let's get you covered and take you back to your room."

Dropping down onto the ground, Amiria pulls the purple fabric taught with her legs and punctures a hole. Wiggling the dagger, she saws at the fabric starting the tear. Returning the blade to her boot, she finishes the tear ripping it the entire way around exposing the bottom half of her legs.

"What am I to do?" Mairead slaps her hand to her face.

Amiria leaps up now free of her shackles. She sways slightly from the quick movement, the jagged remnants of the dress hanging loose around her knees.

Facing away from Mairead, Amiria rests her cheek on her shoulder and speaks with a distant voice. "Don't follow me."

"Amiria?"

"Please."

Mairead stands beside the discarded scraps of gown as she watches the fragmented girl hold herself together and walk alone.

With crossed arms, Amiria lopes through the courtyard of sleeping flowers lit by crystal moonlight from the cloudless sky. She can still hear the faint music following her down the corridor she had escaped from.

Her body collapses to the marble bench surrounded by primroses. Slumping forward she hides her head in her hands. The muscles beneath her prickled skin shudder in the cool night air.

"What do *you* want?" She mumbles angrily into her hands.

Calix stops beside the bench, his eyes as pale as the moonlight. "How did you know it was me?"

She looks up at him from her hands. The bundle of fabric still around her wrists, "I know the footfalls of all our teammates. You need to recognize if it's friend or foe behind you."

Calix nods as if he agrees, but his face shows he hasn't thought of that before. "May I?" he asks, gesturing to the space beside her.

"Whatever," she grunts, scooting over to make room. She waits for Calix to take the open seat beside her before continuing. "Why did you come out here? You want to make fun of me too? Sorry, I wasn't raised to be a *lady*. You can't drop me into a place like that and expect me to blend in," she vents.

Calix shakes his head. "No. I didn't come out here to mock you. I thought your punch was pretty impressive. It was a great shot. I'm positive you broke his nose."

Amiria smiles. "You think so?"

"Yeah." He pauses, twisting his hands in his lap.

"Truth is, I came out here to apologize to you." He takes a deep breath. It fogs in front of his face as he lets it out slowly, "I saw the way you were treated in there. It made me reflect on myself a bit. The way I have acted towards you." He meets her eye, "I'm sorry Amiria. I truly am, you deserve better than—" He motions to himself. "*This.*"

Amiria blinks dumbstruck. Calix…is apologizing? He gave her a compliment that wasn't about her appearance? The same Calix who thinks he is above everyone else. The same Calix who acts as if she is nothing more than an object he needs to obtain is the same Calix who is apologizing to her about *his* behavior. This is the first time she knows of since meeting him that he has admitted to doing *anything* wrong.

Amiria shivers again as the breeze comes down from the rooftop and fills the garden.

"Here," Calix says, removing his pourpoint, and drapes it over her bare shoulders.

"One apology can't change all the times you've harassed me with your persistence," she tells him.

Calix now only in his long sleeve black tunic drops his shoulders with a sigh, "I know. I don't expect you to forgive me after only one apology. To be honest I'm not the best with people. I was brought up and taught that if I want something, the only option is to take it. My father can be…well, you know how he is."

Amiria remembers spying on them around the corner. How his father belittled him there in the middle of the castle corridor. If that is how he treats him out in the open for anyone to witness, she can't imagine what has happened behind closed doors.

She scrunches the ruined sleeve away from her forearm examining the red mark where the drunken man had gripped her, but instead sees her scars of battle. Small white lines and marks cover her arms from years of training and now fighting. They aren't the most noticeable at first glance, but she knows they don't stop at her arms. Her skin will never be beautiful.

Dropping the sleeve, she pulls the pourpoint in close around her. The smell of chamomile and mint wafts up to her. She knows what can leave scars upon one's skin, but what scars the soul?

"I do like you Amiria. I've never liked anyone how I like you."

Amiria is no longer cold as he drives the confession through her. He *likes* her? Why? Is this another one of his ploys? Is this a grand scheme to win her over and then leave?

She never believed him when he sought her out, always assuming his intention was for the power in her name. Other than her name, what reason does she have? Girls fawn over him daily while he soaks in the attention. Then there are the occasional girls that exit his room in the morning. For the past three years, Amiria has never known him to be in a serious relationship with anyone.

Lacing his fingers and untwining them over and over, Calix speaks down to his hands, "I like how you make sword fighting look like an art. I like how you don't care how people perceive you, including your father. Something I can never achieve. I love how brave and fearless you are, you're always ready to defend others no matter the opponent."

"Noooo." Amiria groans, hiding her face in her hands.

The oversized pourpoint conceals the entire top half of her body. No one has ever confessed feelings for her before. No one besides Stirling has ever wanted to be called her friend. Calix has always shown his hand in the past, his intentions to win her, but has never expressed true feelings.

He has just said the words she has always longed to hear. She's spent years watching the other girls get courted from the sidelines. She would convince herself she didn't want a man to give her flowers and tell her how he feels, but she was doing nothing but lying to herself. Now it has finally happened and of all people, it has come from Calix. The one person she despises over the rest. Though she loathed him because he only expressed interest in her status. He behaved as if he didn't take who she is as a person into consideration.

Maybe that was all a front.

"Do you truly hate me that much?" He asks, still not having enough courage to look at her.

Still doubled over, she peers up at him. His face is soft and a little heartbroken. Is it because of the "no" comment? She always says no to his advancements. That's nothing new. Is it because this time he is being sincere and opening up the truth about his emotions?

"Yes." She blurts out of habit. She bites her tongue deeply regretting her inability to think before she speaks. His face falls as if she had told him he lost everything he's ever cared about. "Sorry." She apologizes, "I'm not good at talking to people. To be frank, the way you treated me and spoke down to me is everything I hate."

"That isn't the real me. It's really not. I'm just trying to portray the person my father wants me to be. But I am not him, and I can't keep pretending I'm something I'm not. Especially when it's driving someone I care about away. You mean more to me than my father's opinion." Calix reveals to her.

How does one respond to that? Amiria sits silently blinking. What do you say when someone exposes themselves to you? What do you do when they open their chest to show you their beating heart? She only knows how to attack, how to exploit weakness.

After a moment of listening to the music, he finally faces her and smiles, "By the way. I like what you did with the dress. It didn't suit you anyway. I think damaged armor decorated with blood is more your style."

Amiria snorts a laugh, a new grin spread across her face. Twisting her wrists back and forth she spins the bunched fabric around. Leaning back she kicks out her dirty boot, the shredded fabric falling around her extended leg, "You think so?"

The fast tempo of the distant music slows. Calix stands offering his hand to Amiria, "May I have at least one dance?"

"I don't know the steps to this one," Amiria replies, trying to place the song.

"It doesn't matter, we can make up our own steps."

Curling her lips in, Amiria tries to hide her smile as she accepts his hand and is whisked off her feet. The pourpoint slipping off her shoulders lands in the bed of primroses.

With a twirl, Amiria is pulled close to Calix, her hand reflexively shoots up landing on his chest. He gently slips his hand around the small of her back. She can feel the warmth of his light hand through the back of her dress sending a shiver up her spine. His touch is merely a guide as they step side to side in the courtyard.

Her sleeve slips down her arm hiding the five-finger bruise. Her hand runs up his chest to the nape of his neck. His body is solid and strong from years of training.

His steps carry them gracefully backward as the intertwined bodies begin to circle. They spin in the diamond light, their footsteps on the gravel walkway and the drumming of their hearts joining in with the soft beat of the music.

They slow to a sway as the song ends and a faster one begins. Amiria rests her head against his chest. The thumping of his heart setting the new tempo to their dance.

Maybe this won't be so bad.

Eighteen

Winning several more of the beginner-level matches over the week by a landslide the judges bumped Stirling up to the intermediate level. He sits in the competitor's tent as he waits for his turn in the trick competition. They congregate inside the closed canvas room with their field of view blocked to prevent any unfair advantages from going last.

The intermediate like the beginner group has a large number of contestants. With only a few racers left, the total amounts to sixteen participants.

The men who are packed into the tent don't act as if they are waiting for their names to be called. Practically sitting on top of one another as they throw out jokes and friendly banter filling the tight space with laughter. Men who have been close friends for years.

Sitting with his fidgeting fingers in his lap in the front corner is Stirling. In the small crowded tent, he has plenty of space. He lifts the collar of his shirt and discreetly smells it. Nope, he still smells clean, regularly taking advantage of the bathhouse and laundry service.

He leans his head back resting it on the canvas wall, *"How's it going out there?"*

"Lame. It's as if they are all doing the same routine. How boring." Ignis replies from his station with the other dragons.

"That might suck for the audience, but it's good for us." Stirling ensures.

"Stirling of Patu!" The coordinator shouts into the room holding back the entrance flap, scanning back and forth at the group of racers. Stirling perks up, sitting just off to the side of the flap. "You're up next." He instructs jabbing a finger at him.

"Hey!" One of the other competitors calls out from the group, "Break a leg!"

"Or both!" Another adds. The group of peers laugh.

"What?" Stirling wonders confused. Shaking his head, he steps out of the waiting area.

Stirling appears from below the stands, walking out into the middle of the racetrack from his first race. The bottom half of the crowd cheers at the sight of him. The common folk are magnetized to him, the underdog to root for.

Someone to believe in. Someone relatable.

Girls scream his name as he walks and stops in the center. Staring down at the ground, he nervously waves. Unless he is on the back of Ignis he is unable to face the audience with confidence. Seeing the dizzying number of eyes watching him still churns his stomach.

The spectators in the top half of the stands roll their eyes. "I can't believe they let him advance. Completely ridiculous."

"There are people with years more seniority and they still refuse to let them step up."

"He's a cheat. There's no way someone from a poor village can afford a per'yanny svir."

"Don't worry everyone knows amphiptere always win this one, they can move their bodies in such a mesmerizing way."

Stirling braves a glance up at the crowd searching for Bernard and Eve. He finds them sitting in the front row where Bernard told them they would be before they separated in the morning. With trembling hands he gives them a thumbs up, a symbol meaning he is ready for battle.

Eve's heart flutters as they make eye contact. The girls sitting around her go wild unaware his attention is directed at a specific individual. With a low growl in the back of her throat, Eve eyes the competition around her.

Bernard cups his hands over his mouth and shouts, "YOU CAN DO THIS!"

"You heard Bernard, let's do this," Stirling tells Ignis who arrives over the top of the bleachers, his claws nearly clipping the flags mounted to the judge's podium.

People instinctively duck their heads. Dodging the beast as it sails low over the crowd. As he reaches the churned-up dirt from dozens of dragon's claws, he twists his body into a barrel roll. Timing his turn precisely so his back is facing downward as he passes over Stirling.

Grabbing the handle of the harness, Stirling is wrenched off his feet with the momentum of Ignis's mass. Ignis right sides himself and banks sharp to the water feeling Stirling settle into place on his back. Goggles already on and his cape flapping in the wind, Stirling secures himself signaling to Ignis the ready mark. With heavy thrusts of feathered wings, Ignis begins his climb.

The crowd roars. Brought to their feet from the lively entrance. They have never seen a racer be picked up by their dragon. Every racer is set into old routines. They walk out to the center waving to their fans then climb atop their beast. No one has diverted from the idea that

they are required to mount regularly onto the dragon's
back before beginning their choreography.

*"We need to do something they have never seen before. We didn't
have all year to plan like they did,"* Stirling advises as they fill
in their time with flips and turns.

"I've got an idea," Stirling says.

"I like what you're thinking," Ignis agrees.

Ignis pulls up, ascending vertically through the air.
Bending backward, he begins arching in an exaggerated
loop.

"Please, catch me," Stirling says, his body already rising
off Ignis as they start to fly upside down, reaching the top
peak of the loop. His harness digs into his skin as it
prevents him from being overtaken by gravity.

With his legs floating freely in the wind he loops his
arms through the saddle's handle and pulls up to unhook
his harness. His hips drop automatically pulled by earth
herself. She is telling him he shouldn't be up there,
shouldn't be amongst the clouds. She is calling for him to
return to her.

Breathe. Breathe. Breathe. Ignis will catch me.

"I will always catch you," Ignis promises.

Stirling releases his arms and slips away. The roaring
sound of sea air fills his ears as it rips and tears at his
clothing. Flipping himself over he faces the approaching
blue wall.

*Ignis will catch me. Remember diving into the canyon. Ignis will
catch me.*

"HE FELL!" someone in the crowd screams in
horror.

Eve's nails dig into Bernard's arm as she watches in
terror. Ignoring the pain, Bernard's jaw hangs open in
shock.

Ignis beats his wings on his descent downward,
desperately trying to pick up speed, racing Stirling to the
bottom. Blue is all Stirling can now see in his peripheral

vision. No sky, no land. Nothing but the rapidly approaching blue and the metal rim around his eyes. From the corner of his eye, Stirling sees Ignis in the distance appear around the brim of his goggles as he passes Stirling by.

Rounding out the rest of the loop, Ignis aims for Stirling who reaches out bracing for impact. Swooping beneath him Stirling, who misses grabbing the front of Ignis' harness. He panics and grapples the saddle sliding down Ignis' back until his fingers loop around the hind leg straps.

Swaying from the impact, Ignis' claws barely clip the white caps of the tide. Mist sprays into the air from the turbulence beneath his powerful wings.

With his heart pounding in his ears, Stirling crawls up the saddle with shaking hands. He's alive. He's still somehow alive. Before he has to retract that statement, Stirling quickly secures himself to Ignis'.

The audience stares idly. Their minds slowly process what they have witnessed.

"He's not dead? He's not dead! It is all part of his trick!" Eve registers as she watches Ignis rocket back up into the sky. With a sharp turn, he corkscrews in a tight spiral directly back down at the water

"Wait for it…Wait for it," Stirling tells Ignis calculating the vanishing distance between them and the deep blue waters.

"NOW!" he commands.

Ignis opens his jaws letting out a stream of blazing fire. A swirling vortex of orange and yellow. Steam erupts into the air concealing them behind a thick cloud reaching all the way to the ocean banks.

It is not unknown Per'yanny svir's have the ability to create fire. They are a breed of dragon from a colder climate. It is common knowledge that they and quetzalcoatls can do what is impossible to any other creature. What shocks the crowd is that never in the history of Leucasia's Skylit Endeavor has anyone made it into a spectacular display.

The audience squints through the shifting mountain of mist. Searching and waiting for the daring rookie they lean forward with anticipation. Their bodies retract, their bending spines straightening with surprise as Ignis and Stirling burst from the cloud. With a crash landing, Ignis skids to a stop. His claws ripping through the churned-up dirt send plumes of dust rising into the air around his legs.

Unclipping himself once again, Stirling leaps up into a standing position on Ignis's back and throws his head back looking straight up at the overpassing clouds.

Stirling hangs onto one of Ignis' horns for balance and in unison, he throws a fist into the air as Ignis lets out a jet of flames. The citizens shield their faces from the blinding light as their skin turns warm like on a hot summer day.

Ignis clamps his jaws shut, cutting off the flames.

The nails holding the wooden structure together test their grip as the bleachers shudder beneath the audience's weight. They leap to their feet in a roar of excited cheers, including half of the upper class.

"Did you see him! Did you see him!" Eve shouts, shaking Bernard, "He was incredible!"

"I know, I saw, I saw. I'm right here." Bernard huffs, "That boy sure can give an old man a fright."

Above the audience in a private box seating for the elite racers only, eyelids narrow over dark blue eyes. Quilan crosses his arms with an undisclosed expression.

Lucan, in a purple and white striped cape with a number four and his feet propped up, spits his words, "There's no way someone from *Patu* can pull off tricks like that."

The second youngest elite racer scratches his chin. "What are you suggesting? He lied about where he's from?"

"Who in their right mind would claim they're from *Patu*." Firmin, one of the more veteran racers with a number five cape of white and black diamonds, grumbles.

Aylmar, the most senior, nods in agreement, "They would have to admit they live in huts with dirt floors."

Quilan keeps his eyes focused forward and ignores when they try to grab his attention asking what he thinks.

"Ay! Quilan! Too good to join the conversation?"

Quilan's eyes roll over to them, "Indeed."

People, so many people.

What do I do with my hands? How am I supposed to stand? Am I too stiff? I should be smiling. I need to smile. I can't smile. They are surrounding me. Please stop touching me, please stop touching me. Stop touching me!

Standing petrified as a group of fans surround him, Stirling squeezes his eyes shut. He can hear their congratulations and feel as they take his rigid hands in theirs shaking them proudly, but he lets his mind take him somewhere else. Somewhere safe. Somewhere alone.

The first-place coins rattle in the bag attached to his hip as he silently quivers. His eyes are wide and dilated as he is forced to shake another stranger's hand.

"Excuse me. Excuse me." Bernard's deep voice rumbles over the adoring fans, "His friend is coming through." Stirling stares at him with dazed eyes. "All right kid, away, we—" Bernard hunches over wrapping his arms around Stirling's midsection. Straightening back up he lifts Stirling from his trapped location. "Go."

The fans look to each other for clarity as Bernard hobbles away with his arms around Stirling like a toddler carrying their favorite doll.

"There we go, now take a deep breath." Bernard sets Stirling back onto his own unsteady feet beside Eve who is vibrating with excitement.

"Contain yourself," Bernard instructs her. Taking several calming breaths, Stirling curls in on himself and sits down on his haunches. Eve squats down beside him, brushing a curl back from his eyes as she asks, "Are you okay."

He nods unconvincingly, his fingers beginning to twitch, "I-I don't know why, but—the crowds."

Bernard lowers himself to kneel on the ground joining Stirling and Eve. He rests his hand on Stirling's shoulder, "You don't have to face them alone. Remember that, we're here for you."

Eve takes his scarred hand in hers. "Was it scary? To fall like that?"

"Terrifying." He closes his eyes seeing the flashes of orange artificial lightning glow in the night clouds. "I still have nightmares of when I fell for real," Stirling admits, his voice low as if he is afraid of someone overhearing him.

Eve squeezes his hand. "You're here, you made it."

"Yeah, the entire town is proud of you, you know that right? You've surpassed our expectations by a landslide. We never guessed you were actually good. You're quite the racer." Bernard hooks his hand under Stirling's arm and hoists him to his feet. Keeping her hand linked to Stirling's, Eve follows.

Stirling dips his chin hiding his face behind his curls. "Thank you."

"How are the other racers?" Eve asks, still holding onto him, her golden-brown eyes big and hopeful. "You make any friends yet?"

He slips his hand away from hers and clears his throat. "No—no not yet." He watches her face fall. He clammers for an excuse. "You know—I'm new—and they've all

156

known each other for a while now—But I think they're starting to warm up to me."

Eve frowns, seeing through his lie, "Do you have a roommate?"

"No, I requested a single room," Stirling says with shifty eyes.

Bernard takes Stirling in close, wrapping his arm around his shoulders. He leans in to whisper, "Hey if any of them are giving you any trouble." He holds a confident fist. "Family has each other's back."

Bernard pauses checking over at Eve.

He turns them both away from her to give themselves privacy, "Even Eve. She might appear abrasive, but that's what happens as the only daughter of an innkeeper. Her brother does all the labor and she is stuck with us drunkards. But she cares about us and she cares about you. So, remember, we're here okay?"

"Okay," Stirling mumbles.

"What are you guys whispering about?" Eve asks, poking her nose into their business, "It's rude to leave someone out."

She attempts to step in front of them, but Bernard laughs, turning himself and Stirling away from her again. They pivot as if they are on a turntable, moving each time she tries to step in front of them.

"Oh, come on! You're such a jerk, Bernard!" Eve whines with a smile.

Stirling can't hold back his laughter as he is pulled around by Bernard.

Nineteen

The accommodation's tavern is a mess hall designed to feed the entire registry of competitors in the Skylit Endeavor. It's a vast seating area below vaulted ceilings lit by small metal chandeliers hanging from thick crossbeams.

Eight tables line the room, each comfortably able to accommodate six men. A long counter stretches across one end of the room separating the guests from the family working the kitchen. Several cooking appliances line the wall; cooking pots of stew, charcoaling meats, and baking bread. A latched wooden door sits to the side of the kitchen leading down to the larder where perishables are kept cool.

The room is bustling with laughter from the forty-four men sitting shoulder to shoulder, eating a hearty meal complimentary to them with the cost of their room.

Stirling sits without his cape in the farthest corner alone, having almost an entire table to himself except for two other men facing each other at the very end. Absentmindedly, Stirling pushes around a grain he had learned was called rice beside a fish seared in olive oil and topped with tomato sauce cooked with parsley, chives, and garlic.

He listens to the chatter among friends with no hard feelings after a long day of competing. Leaning his shoulder against the wall he takes another bite of fish.

When he received his meal and sat down at the table the several men currently occupying it decided the other filled tables would be a better option to finish their dinner leaving Stirling alone.

His eyes have not left his food since he sat down. Arriving in Patu with worn-out clothing and matted hair didn't make him feel this repulsive. The two men still residing at the table are the two unlucky ones who arrived last for supper.

"*This sucks,*" Stirling mopes to Ignis.

"*Why?*"

"*I've spent years isolated in a cave, but I never once felt as lonely as I do here in this crowded room,*" Stirling admits. The hoards of people crowding him at the stands sends a panic through his bones, but he wouldn't mind the company of at least one person to talk to.

"*Why is that?*" Ignis ponders genuinely curious about the matter.

"*I had you and I had Amiria. I never once felt alone. I didn't know any different. But here, seeing all of them together while I'm excluded really puts it in perspective,*" Stirling explains.

"*You have Bernard, Eve, and the whole village now,*" Ignis points out.

"*Yeah, as soon as these games are over I'm building a house and we'll settle down in Patu,*" He pauses. "*I wish Amiria came with us. She would kick their butts on and off the course.*" Stirling chuckles to himself as he imagines the men cowering beneath the dining tables after they tell Amiria, *women are too fragile to fly a dragon.*

"What are you laughing about loner?" A threatening tone cuts across the aisle from the next table. A rider from the advanced division named Mere, wearing a red and white cape, had discarded his spoon as if Stirling had disturbed his appetite.

"Nothing, just thinking of something funny," Stirling says, quickly shutting his mouth.

"What's funny? You think the games are a joke, peasant!" Merek's voice grows louder with each word, while the room falls silent.

"No."

"Are we a joke to you then? You feel so high and mighty sitting here with us!"

The whole room is watching.

"N—No."

"Learn your place villager. I bet if you were in the advanced level racing against us big boys, you wouldn't find all this so funny," Merek lectures demeaningly.

Stirling's face feels as if it is being struck by Ignis' flames. With his skin turning red with embarrassment he shoots up abruptly with his unfinished meal.

The room is muted. No one moves. Only their eyes follow Stirling. Each one of his footfalls is a cataclysmic earth-shattering boom. Everyone sees him. Everyone is judging him.

Rice rolls around on his trembling pewter plate. A single hand snakes out from the blending bodies and attacks the bottom of the plate, flipping it upward out of Stirling's hands. The sound of the metal clashing against the ground echoes across the room, its contents sliding down Stirling's tunic.

"Oh no! That's probably his only one," an anonymous voice mocks.

The room burst into laughter. Stirling brushes off the rice stuck to his shirt smearing the tomato sauce in the process.

Momentarily feeling brave, Stirling rebuttals, "Actually, I do have the coin because unlike all of you, I've been winning my matches."

Merek stands in the center aisle of the tables. "Ave bin winnen" he mocks Stirling's accent. His laughing face quickly turns cold. "Watch how you speak to us. You shouldn't even be here, you're a nothing, a nobody who needs to stay in his place."

Stirling opens his mouth to speak back but stops. The cold feeling of liquid dampening his hair and soaking through to his head jams the words in his throat. The smell of fermented berries and honey fills his nose as the dark red mead runs down his face staining the collar and shoulders of his tunic.

A guy behind him laughs. "Maybe this will help with that mess you call hair."

He can't face them. The room erupts in laughter, each cackle is a stone pelted in his direction. He hangs his head in frustrated shame. Through his dripping hair, he looks over at Farah amongst the rest of the innkeeper's children who are helping cook and clean. She holds a serving tray over her mouth stifling her laugh.

"You…okay?" she asks between chuckling breaths.

Stirling's shoulders slump with betrayal. "Leave me alone. Everyone, just leave me alone." Leaving the plate on the ground he avoids eye contact with everyone in the room as he shows himself out.

Stirling stomps across the gravel pathway leading to each separate building of the accommodation.

"*Hey! What happened?*" Ignis' voice asks with urgency.

"*Nothing! Nothing happened. I'm going to the bathhouse,*" Stirling replies defensively.

Stirling shoves open the first door of the bathhouse leading into the changing room, a room no larger than a box lit with skylights containing stone benches and metal hooks on the wall to hang up your clothes while you bathe.

Stirling grabs the back of his tunic with one hand and tugs it up over his head. He holds it out examining the damage. This tunic was a gift from the villagers and now it is dyed purple and red. No amount of washing will get rid of these stains. It's forever ruined.

Sighing, he finishes undressing and wraps a towel around his waist. With his hair still dripping with mead, he pushes open the second door stepping into the bathing room. The door seals firmly behind him keeping the steam from escaping.

A large waist-deep pool takes up the entire center of the room leaving a walking ledge around the perimeter. A circle skylight sits in the direct center allowing the sun to heat the space along with the well-planned structure. The mosaic pool floor is a platform held up by small stone-layered pillars. Warm air from an underground wood furnace heats up beneath the bath and rises through slots in the walls.

Pale hair reflects in the white stream of the sunlight shining down on him like heaven's call.

Dark opaque eyes look up at him, his voice flat and monotone, "Tired of the feeding frenzy?"

Stirling doesn't take any offense to the comment after seeing how they behave in the dining hall. "In a way."

He catches Quilan's locked eyes on him then down to his towel. He steps down onto the bath's seat knee-deep in the water. Concealing himself, he removes his towel and swiftly sits down in the mineral-rich water.

"You're Quilan aren't you? I didn't know the Elite also stayed here."

"Obviously," Quilan says, finally breaking his eye contact on Stirling to inspect his fingernails.

Charming, Stirling thinks to himself sarcastically. His eyes wander through the otherwise empty room. He hasn't seen any of the other elite racers around the complex. How was that supposed to be obvious? Or was he stating obvious at the comment of who he is? Stirling feels heat rising in his cheeks and not from the warm water of the bath. He must appear like a naive child who had stumbled onto the racing grounds in comparison to him, someone who had grown up on the track.

"Tell me," Stirling jumps at Quilan's lackadaisical voice. Getting comfortable, Quilan rests his arms on the bath's edge, his soft features languid, unshifting as he talks up to the skylight. "Your dragon. How?"

Shaking his head confused, Stirling struggles to comprehend the question. Why doesn't he form entire sentences? "How? How what?"

The unreadable eyes return to Stirling half-lidded. Listless, jaded, or irritated, Stirling is unable to decipher. His nervous tick returns under the water of the pool. His trembling fingers tap to his thumb under the pressure of the number one racer. Fear of what hateful thoughts are filling his head.

Stirling's mind fails him in Quilan's intimidating presence, his words coming out in a croak. "I—" Stirling clears his throat and begins again, "I found him as fletchling. Then I taught myself." Gulping, he hunches his shoulders trying to hide himself.

"Hmm," Quilan says, his eyes narrowing further into slits.

Stirling shifts uneasily in the water. Quilan surveys him, his eyes pressing into him like metal stamps.

Does this guy ever blink? Stirling wonders.

Scooping a cup of water in his hand, Quilan watches it run back into the bath. He turns back to Stirling and points at his own hair. This language Stirling can understand. He reaches up tugging on the matted bang sticky with mead.

Still holding onto the clump, he drops his gaze, "The other racers."

Stirling's body flinches at the abrupt movement, anticipating a behavior he's growing accustomed to. Quilan stands facing him in the bath, his hand raised, signaling to Stirling no need to explain further. His face growing hotter than the bath water, Stirling blushes and drops his line of sight fixating on the steaming water.

Quilan's words are guttural sounds deep in his throat as he speaks under his breath. "They're all losers." He wades across the bath to the bench where Stirling sits by the exit.

Reaching the underwater bench, Quilan moves to step up and out as Stirling rises to meet him.

With his left hand concealing himself and his right hand extended out to shake, Stirling stands awkwardly while desperately trying to maintain eye contact, "I'm Stirling by the way."

Without moving his head, Quilan's eyes fall to Stirling's arm. His lip raises in the only expression he has shown this entire encounter, disgust. Pulling his arm against his chest disheartened, Stirling lowers quietly back down in the water letting the warm water hug his insecurity.

Quilan utters, "I know," and exits the bathing room.

Stirling steals a glance over his shoulder at the exit while subconsciously rubbing his thumb over his insignia. With a broken sigh, he dunks his head under the water.

Twenty

Amiria walks alone in her silver armor, her only company is the sound of her boots following her through the place-of-arms, a covered assembly point for guards and at times the Winged Cavalry. She can't wait to be rid of her armor. To shed the reflective shell she hides inside, to leave it in her team's personal armory. A room tucked away in a discreet passage leading to their wing built in the northwest tower.

Her dark armor, which has seen more blood spilled than runs through her veins, is stored away in her bed chamber. The metal is wrapped in an oilcloth to keep from rusting waiting for the next time she is called out into the night.

Team Requaero consisting of Eda, Armundus, and Everard, was dispatched approximately a week ago and is already surveying Uviktiland. They've been gaining intel on the whereabouts of the fugitive known as Stirling Bakere from the lower-class market. In a month their extensive deployment will come to a conclusion and Calix, Dicun and Amiria will meet at an undisclosed rendezvous point.

Sweat dampens her brow, small beads dripping from beneath her helm. She's exhausted after a day of her team's build-up and training for their upcoming mission. They've been specializing in high-flying advanced reconnaissance; using an eagle eye technique to read trail markings from the sky, how to properly track in an unknown land, and how to successfully trap and apprehend.

"Oh, good, you're exactly where I thought you'd be," her father states, walking in her direction wearing his regular gold brigandine with wyvernite crystal buttons.

"Well, I did just get out of training that you scheduled so it's not that hard to figure out," Amiria says, already done with their conversation before it started.

"Watch your tone. I am not only your father. I am your Field Marshal," he snaps.

"My apologies." Amiria backs down.

"Despite the mockery you presented as yourself at the ball, there was a single man who wasn't repulsed by your display of ill manners and violent tendencies. I have already conversed with him and he has agreed to accept your hand."

Amiria's eyes widened. "You asked someone! Who was it!" Her brain and heart are a muddied mess of wavering excitement and animosity. There is someone who agreed to marry her? Someone likes her? Someone wants to be with her!

"Your teammate Calix. I saw the two of you in the courtyard. You should feel grateful that a gentleman such as him would be willing to take your hand." Her father's disapproving eyes read into her mixed expressions.

Someone wants to marry her!

She is going to be forced into marriage.

This someone is Calix.

Amiria feels as if the heavy stone ceiling arched above her head is crashing around her. She desperately wishes one of the stone slabs would land and crush them both. Her gaze drops to the ground.

"He's a good suit for you. Soon you will be Field Marshal and he will either take his father's place as captain or if he can prove himself over his siblings he will replace his mother as general by your side. It can not be more of a perfect match. I'll enlighten you on the fact, he is such a gentleman he initially denied my request because he believed it was not the way you would want a proposal."

Still refusing to look up at her father, Amiria's ears perk up at his last sentence.

Her father continues, proud of himself, "But I was able to persuade him." She is lightheaded, her body beginning to sway as the words go in one ear and out the other. "I would like you to wed before your deployment, but I don't think I can get the wedding planned and the dress tailored in time. But don't fret. It will be prepared by the time you arrive home."

Her father fades from view, everything a blur of running watercolors. She believes the out-of-focus object of her father is still speaking to her, but she doesn't care anymore. Without excusing herself, she steps around her father and leaves.

He can be calling her name right now for all she knows, but she can't hear him. The only sound is the blood rushing through her veins. Staggering, she swings open the locked door to their armory slamming it closed behind her. The sound of metal rattles from the vibration throughout the room.

Breathing heavily through her nostrils, she steadies her muscles enough to gently remove her helm from her head. Her hair tumbles in waves down her back.

With a white knuckle grip, she examines her reflection in the silver metal. She had one moment. One small moment where she didn't see Calix as scum to step around and now she is being forced to marry the man. He had not said anything during their training exercises.

At least someone wants to stay by her side.

Seething, rage bubbles up from her center and is starting to leak from her pores. Who does she hate more, Stirling? Calix? Her Father?

She screams letting out her frustration. Chucking her helm across the room it slams into a line of longswords hung perfectly against the wall. Several are knocked off falling with a shattering clang of metal hitting stone. Her dampened hair covers half of her face as she heaves catching her breath. Flipping her hair back over her shoulder she composes herself.

Opening her storage cabinet that is taller than her, Amiria removes her armor hanging it up properly on the wooden hooks that stands inside. Picking up her helm she places it in the cabinet and shuts the door gingerly. Without taking a second glance at the scattered swords she departs the armory.

Her dark hair flows out the front of her maroon hood as she pushes her way through the bustling market streets. Keeping her head down, Amiria has lost the direction she is walking in. Seeing nothing but the shoes of townsfolk and wheels of carts, she turns down streets and alleys as if guided by the masses.

She only has one goal. Get away from the castle grounds. Get far away before she runs into Calix.

How can she face him? *Her* betrothed. Her *betrothed*. *Betrothed. Hers.* She runs the word through her head until it loses all meaning, nothing more than a foreign sound repeating in her thoughts. Her mind is knitted wool beginning to fray. The strings hooking and snagging on her life, slowly unraveling with each teetering step.

Her ears perk at the sound of a commotion farther up the road. Holding her hood down she shimmies her thin frame through the tightly packed crowd.

"EVERYONE STAY BACK OR YOU WILL BE JOINING THEM!" an aggravated voice commands the crowd.

The nobody girl in a maroon cloak squeezes herself through the shoulders of the horrified onlookers. She pops free of the dense mass. Stumbling a step forward her eyes dilate as they take in the scene before her. Her body reacts on instinct and leaps back against the wall of people.

With his knee digging into a man's spine the guard in his early twenties, Jerrad, wears a cross expression as he binds the man's hands behind his back with rope.

The man cries out in pain as Jerrad's knee bores into his vertebrae, "Stop, please! It hurts!"

"What does it matter, you're going to hang soon anyway." Jerrad spits, only pressing harder.

A whaling cry escapes the building with the butcher's trade crest above the door. Clyde, from Amiria's class, emerges from the building holding a young woman by her hair.

Tears stream down her blotchy red face, her legs frantically kicking in a desperate attempt to find footing. Breaking fingernails dig into the gloved hand controlling her head as he drags her across the threshold. With the rise of a lip, Clyde throws the woman down the steps without a care.

Landing on her shoulder and face, she skids to a stop. A man launches from the crowd, "KATHERINE!"

"STAY BACK!" Jerrad, still kneeling on the man, rises to his feet drawing his sword. He steps between the citizen and the woman named Katherine who looks up at him with a muddy face.

"This is all of them," Clyde announces as two more people are pushed out of the doorway by a third guard.

They tumble to the ground beside Katherine. Instinctively they crawl together, cowering in a huddled pile like cornered animals.

Clyde looks down the bridge of his nose at them. "Run and you'll die here in the streets."

One of the men begins to stand up. Katherine grabs his hand with begging eyes for him to stop. Amiria tries to step back, her body already pressing against the wall of people. Unsuccessful in her escape, she tugs her hood down, further obstructing her face.

The man stares up at the cumulus clouds far past the crowd and the rooftops, a current of wind far above them pushes the clouds along. They will travel over the castle, over the mountains, and out across the ocean. Far away into places unknown.

He looks back down at Katherine's pleading expression. With an accepting smile, he lunges. The force of his hand ripping from Katherine's drags her back to the ground. She reaches out again. Her hand stops as time slows, a frozen claw holding nothing but air.

In a rolling sweep across the crowd like a shock wave starting at the center, the crowd's curiosity turns to terror.

The air escapes from Amiria's lungs. She stands there mortified.

She can't move. Petrified as the point of the broadsword protruding out from just below the man's sternum is barely even half an arm's length away. She watches as the man coughs blood spraying specks of scarlet across her face. Gargling, he chokes on the warm blood overflowing from his mouth.

Tipping backward without the wall behind her anymore, she lands in the mud of the road. Her fingertips dig into the saturated dirt as she pulls and kicks herself back, unable to take her eyes off the dying man.

The frenzied crowd scatters in every direction.

Everyone is screaming.

Ear-splitting sounds rupture her ability to hear as her vision tunnels in on the man. Someone's husband, someone's father. It took decades to grow into the man who woke up today and seconds to ensure he wouldn't ever again.

A middle-aged woman wails in heartbreaking agony as she calls out the dying man's name.

Jerrad rips the sword free of the man's torso. His limp body folds as he slowly slumps to the ground with agonizing groans. Bent in an abnormal way he stares up at her with earnest eyes as the life in them dims. The blood on his tunic blooms like a spring rose.

Kneeling, Jerrad wipes his sword clean on the dead man's tunic.

Clyde stands over the third man who is protectively cradling Katherine. The woman overtaken with emotion has inverted into a comatose state of panic. Grabbing the back of the man's tunic as the other guard grabs the woman, they tear the two apart.

The man screams profanities at Clyde while his arms are wrenched behind his back.

"Shut up!" Clyde yells, punching the man in the side of the face as he struggles to turn and look up at him.

Blood bubbles and drips from his mouth as he spits out a tooth knocked loose into the dirt.

The woman stares blankly, her mind already given up as her wrists are bound together.

Amiria finds her footing and climbs up off the ground to join the crowd fleeing down the market road. Her hood flies back as it's caught by the wind revealing her. She doesn't care, no one is watching her. She is another citizen running away for safety.

They need her, they are defenseless, but she is useless. She can't help them. She can't save them.

Skidding around a corner, she dives into a narrow alley barely able to fit her slender frame. Her forearms and palms drag against the walls catching herself between them. The sleeves of her cotehardie protect her forearms from grinding against the daubed mud walls as her momentum drags her down.

Coughing, she leans against the wall choking on her own breaths. Her trembling knees begin to buckle and barely lucid, she presses her scraped palms against the adjacent wall to hold herself stead. With her mind already numbing, her unblinking eyes stare at the calloused hands pressed against the white wall now stained with mildew from the everlasting shadows.

A drop of drying blood leaves behind a flaking trail across the back of her hand.

How much blood is on her hands? How many men has she stolen from families who love them back in Uviktiland?

The woman's wail as she cries for her loved one drums against her skull consuming her thoughts. Her fingernails claw the wall as she slides down into a squat, her legs no longer able to support her. She rests her forehead against the wall suddenly sick.

She is not like them, is she? She does not fight to impose power over the weak. She fights to protect, right? She lives to protect them, but she did nothing to stop their murder. She has sworn to herself she would not bear arms against the innocent. In the end, she ran away. Failing to stand up and protect those in need means she is as guilty as those who raised their swords against them.

If there is a criminal on these streets, it is her. She wears the mask of loyalty to King Dietrich, but she has defiled her contract. She raised her head meeting Wyverna's eye as she burned their laws. She has not been sentenced, instead, she has only been rewarded.

Still palming the wall with her stinging hands she pulls herself up. With weak knees and boots sinking into the muck she drags herself through the rest of the alley.

Leaning out of the shadows on the parallel street she scans her surroundings. Everyone's doors and windows shut. Crows have replaced the people spreading out across the deserted road picking at the evidence of recent human activity of dropped crumbs and grains.

She is on the bakery's street. It's only a couple of blocks away.

Twenty-One

Lifting off his seat, Giles jumps spooked as a familiar girl plows her way through the bakery door and slams it behind her, "Amiria! What is the emergency!"

Her back slides down the door as she slumps into a seated position. Her legs sprawled out in front of her. Her voice is distant, "They killed a man. Killed him. Right there in the middle of the street. No judgment, no trial. Just a man and a sword."

"They found more, haven't they?" Giles starts.

Amiria tilts her chin up confused. Removing himself from his seat, Giles kneels beside her. His voice is soft as if he is talking to a child, "People have a new sense of courage. They are starting to secretly practice other trades and arts."

"Why?"

Giles frowns. He shifts himself against the door and sits beside Amiria. He leans his head back talking up to the ceiling, "I think Stirling started something that can't be undone."

"That stupid idiot." She thumps the back of her head against the door, joining Giles in staring up at the cross beams, "He set a fire and left us to burn."

They sit there momentarily listening to the emptiness of the street. Still, without taking his eyes off the ceiling, he informs, "You know you have some red on your face."

Her fingertips run over dried liquid, pieces flake and fall from her cheek. In a moment of fret, she desperately whipes her face with the fabric of her cloak. With her face still buried in the thick fabric, her body shudders with tears that will never come.

Giles can barely hear her as she mumbles, "I was unsure of where else to go. Mr. Bakere, I let that man die. I stood there and did nothing. It's my fault, too. Not just Stirling's, I'm responsible for their deaths."

"It's neither of your faults," Giles places his hand on her arm cradled around her head, "You're not making anyone do anything. These people are making their own choices well aware of the consequences."

She doesn't lift her head as she replies with a grunt.

Giles sighs, "Let's change the subject. Why were you down in the market today?"

Amiria groans.

"Not good, huh?"

Her voice is muffled by her woolen cloak, "My father, he has chosen to give my hand away. He didn't even consult me with his choice. He went ahead and offered me up." Giles nods, not wanting to interrupt. She peeks up from her cloak. "I'm conflicted now."

"About what? The marriage?"

"The guy."

"Why is that?"

"I've despised him for so many years because I've thought he was a certain way, but now I've seen a new side of him and I have—" she pauses as if the next words pain her to speak, "Trouble with opening up to people on an emotional level."

"You open up to me perfectly fine."

"Only you and one other, but this guy. He isn't who I've been picturing myself marrying, but...at least *someone* wants to."

"Who did you picture yourself marrying?" Giles asks, watching her from the corner of his eye.

Amiria blushes, refusing to make eye contact, "No one in particular."

Giles smiles knowingly, "Since there is no one in particular, can you ever see yourself developing feelings for this boy?"

"I don't know, I hate him, but he's been sweet lately. But I don't want to marry him, but he does show me affection," Amiria says, arguing with herself.

Giles reaches over, putting his arm around her, "Let me give you some fatherly advice. Never try to force anything, especially when it comes to feelings. They will either develop on their own time or not at all. It's not fair to either of you to lie to yourself. It'll only end in resentment. I tried to force Stirling to be someone he's not and now I've lost him."

"I don't know what to do anymore," Amiria says, throwing her arms down to the ground in a small tantrum.

"Does anyone really know what they are doing? Don't give up because you've hit some bumps in the road. The road is full of them and it's the only way to get to your destination. So, adjust your wheel and keep going."

Amiria pouts, "I don't like it."

"None of us like it. Welcome to growing up," he shakes her gently. "You seem like you can use some rest before heading home."

Slipping his arm free he stands up and offers out his hand, "You can use Stirling's old bed. It's right upstairs in the corner of the room."

Amiria accepts his hand allowing him to help her to her feet. She has never been to the second floor of the bakery before. She stands at the bottom of the staircase staring up the steps, each with its worn groove in the center where Giles steps every day.

She rests her hands on the railing and looks back at Giles.

"It's all right, you can go up by yourself. Just let me know when you're leaving before you do. Now rest up," Giles assures.

With a deep breath, she ascends the stairs.

Reaching the top she scans the small room. A small fire able to fit a single pot, a wooden table with bench seats, storage crates, and almost bare shelving units. She takes a step forward.

The wood creaks beneath her foot.

She strolls across the groaning wood to a stool sitting beneath the windowsill. A thick layer of dust coats the top as if it hasn't been touched in years. She runs her fingers along the windowsill leaving behind her mark in the dust. She imagines Stirling daydreaming out of the window after being stuck in the bakery all day.

A pang forms deep in her chest.

She turns to a mattress which is no more than a linen sheet sewn closed and stuffed with straw. She can see from the open end, strands of straw still littering the floor from recently being changed. Shaking her head, she shoves away images of Stirling curling up after a day of training with Ignis.

Exhausted, her body collapses into the blankets and curls into a ball inside her cloak.

Twenty-Two

Feet barely moving, Stirling turns in a circle. He is in the dining hall. Through the windows, it's darker outside than a new moon. He stands in the center lit by a faint glow emanating from the smooth surface beneath his feet. Colored capes worn by the racers surround him.

"What do you want from me?" his voice quivers.

He has nowhere to back up, nowhere to run.

The men's mouths stretch back to a gruesome smile touching their ears, their pupiless eyes close into bowing slits.

The masses begin to snicker, their uncanny laughs slowly escalate into sinister cackles around him. Faces distort and stretch into unnatural and obscene angles. The distinct features fade and morph into ghostly silhouettes in the colors of their capes.

The roof of the hall lifts, expanding up as they grow to towering heights above him. Their laughing faces are carved into their flat shadow-like bodies.

"LEAVE ME ALONE!" Stirling screams covering his face.

Something loops around his neck. Startled, he pulls his hands away to see a scratchy braided rope strung around his collarbone. He spins to see Merek standing behind him. The other end of the rope is held mercilessly in his hand. Stirling's eyes follow the rope up to the rafters stories above.

Before Stirling can yell for him to stop, Merek yanks down on the rope.

Stirling gasps awake clawing at his neck. He is lying beside Ignis in the stables. His muscles relax, his arms falling limp onto his chest. His heart, filled with adrenaline, continues to run circles.

Checking around the room from his current position he makes sure they are still alone. Grabbing the feathers of Ignis' wing he pulls it, tenting himself in.

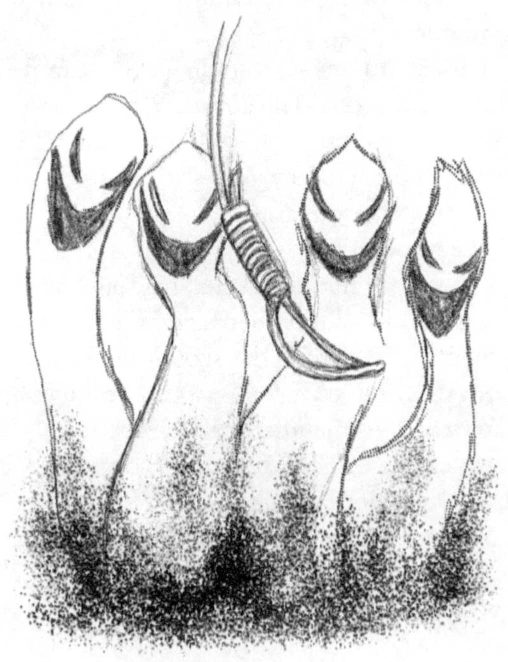

Twenty-Three

The light of the setting sun turns the window a fiery orange.

"Where am I?" Amiria utters, drowsily waking up in an unfamiliar room.

Her eyes focus on her surroundings. She can feel the icy presence in the room. The air inside the four walls grows colder each passing year without a family's warmth. A stool sitting in the window's sill shadow once let a small boy escape to his dreams.

"Oh," she remembers.

Sitting halfway up her disheveled hair falls out from her hood, partially obscuring her face. With only one eye she spots them. Small circles the size of the ball of a person's foot can be seen worn into the wood grains. Insignificant tracks to the untrained eye.

She removes herself from the unforgotten bed. The old wood creaks under her light weight. Tilting her head she shifts her foot to the worn print and presses down.

Silence.

She covers her face with a single hand as she laughs to herself.

Following the path of Stirling's ghost, she crosses the room and heads back down the stairs.

Giles looks up from his plate of roasted potatoes and carrots. "How do you feel?"

"Better. Thanks for letting me rest here," Amiria says, stepping off the last step.

"You will always have a place to lay your head here," Giles reassures.

"Thank you, Mr. Bakere." Her smile rises from the bottom of her heart.

Getting up to show her out, he stalls before opening the door, "Here, take this for the road."

"What is it?" Amiria asks, eyeing the wrapped item in his hand.

"It's bread, but I baked it with cheese inside. I think I'm onto something," Giles gloats.

"Sounds delicious!" Amiria says gratefully accepting the package.

Giles opens the front door. "Take care Amiria, also try not to stress yourself out too much. I know Stirling isn't here but try finding someone you can laugh with. That's what is important in life."

"Thank you," she nods before ducking out into the evening air.

"Ms. Rey! Ms. Rey!" Mairead calls out in what is too loud to be called a whisper while rushing down the corridor as Amiria arrives back to her bed chamber in her team's private wing of the castle. "I tried to tell him to leave, saying you weren't here, but he insisted on waiting inside." She says without taking a breath and plants herself in front of Amiria.

"Names, you need to tell me names. I don't know who *he* is." Amiria says without stopping and walks around her handmaiden.

Mairead turns and follows jogging slightly to catch up to Amiria's pace.

"Calix," she hisses into Amiria's ear.

Amiria halts, her dropping stomach nailing her to the corridor floor. Squeezing her eyes shut she takes tentative steps forward until her feet place her in front of her door, a layered stone frame with a tapestry of her name and coat of arms. She lingers twirling a lock of hair around her fingers.

"I can tell him you won't be home because you were eaten by bees," Mairead chimes.

Amiria shakes her head. "No, no I-I need to do this." She smiles at her handmaiden. "Go rest up. I'll be fine."

Mairead gives Amiria an encouraging squeeze of the hand. Then Amiria is alone facing what lies behind her door.

"You can do this," she encourages herself. "You just need to tell him to leave. It's Calix. You tell him to get lost every day. This won't be any different." She lets out a groan. "Who am I kidding? This is way different."

She doesn't want to talk to him. She doesn't even want to see him. What she is in need of, is time for her to process. Time alone with no one but her thoughts before she is locked into a binding agreement she didn't sign. With a deep breath, she pushes open her door and steps inside.

There, facing the lit fire, sits a man slouched in a plush chair. *Calix?* She closes the door softly and tiptoes a circle around the slumped man.

Standing a step in front of him, she stares down at Calix's slumbering face. His thick eyelashes rest on high cheekbones as his head hangs to the side giving him a second chin. She follows his lean figure that has slipped in the chair with his hips barely hanging onto the edge of the cushion down to tan hands cradling an oblong object wrapped in cloth on his lap.

"Calix?" Her voice squeaks.

"Calix?" She says with more confidence. She taps his foot with hers, "Calix."

Calix startles awake, almost dropping the item from his lap. He straightens up in his chair and runs his hand down his face, whipping away the evidence of sleep. His crystal eyes blink up at her.

"Why are you here?" She asks, crossing her arms.

"I was waiting for you." He responds.

"I can see that." She motions to him in the chair. "I want to know why?"

"I wanted to talk to you. At practice, it was too public and no one knew where you went afterward. This was the next best option," he answers, his voice steady.

Tell him to get out. Tell him I'll have to burn that chair now, or that I'll never get his stench out of my room. She breathes in. *Chamomile and mint. Why is this so hard?"*

"Well, Sir Calix Gautier, as always, I don't want to talk to you." *I did it. Back to normal.* She conceals her smile, pleased with herself.

"Wait, hold on, please hear me out!" he insists.

"Well, apparently, I have the rest of forever to *hear* you out. So, before that happens, I want to be left alone."

"I didn't want it to happen this way either Amiria. I have strong feelings for you. I've liked you since the day I saw you during your qualifications. The way you flew. I knew you were special on and off the field. You don't know how happy I was to learn you were going to be on my team. I—I didn't know how to convey my feelings toward you properly. I would have preferred to take it slow and get close to you before I asked for your hand. But your father, he's the field marshal. I can't deny his requests. I'm so sorry," he pleads.

Amiria takes a step back. He's doing it again. The Calix she danced with in the courtyard was not a one-time fluke. He has laid down his weapons and opened the doors to his fortress. She reads the sincerity painted thick on his face. Is this the real him? Would he still expose his true feelings to her if he knew the real her? Is anyone real?

Continuing to back up, her thighs hit the goose-feather mattress of her bed. Her knees give and she drops back on the soft cushion.

She crosses her legs, "No one ever asked me if I was okay with this."

He leans forward, "I know that's why I came here. I—I brought you this gift. I want to start over. Let's forget the past years and start from the beginning." He lifts the wrapped object from his lap holding it out to her.

Uncrossing her legs, she leans forward accepting it. It is heavier than she initially assumed. Fixing herself on her bed she removes the cloth revealing two scabbards that fully enclose the double-edged short swords with matching froggers to attach to her belt.

The black leather is as hard and smooth as a river rock with golden grommets. The handles of the matching swords are simple and pure. The smokey metal of the guard is not heavy with niello ornamental engravings, the dark metal simply twists at the ends.

She stares down at the matching pommel on the bottom of the handle. Tilting the swords she watches the perpetual flame glisten inside the dark obsidian-like crystal of the wyvernite embedded into the pommel. She slips her hand around the hilt made of polished dragon horn, a white so pure, snow is not good a comparison.

She slides one of the swords free with a satisfying *chhhhhst.*

The site of the rippling effect in the steel leaves her breathless. Dark and light layers swirl and dance together as if the sword is a breathing life force.

"Calix." Amiria gasps, astounded. Her eyes are glued to the sword. "She's beautiful."

Calix watches the usual sharp features of her face soften as she takes in the glory of the steel, "Yeah, she really is."

The riders of the Winged Cavalry are all assigned long swords. Light enough to swing with one hand, but long enough to strike an opponent from a dragon's back. Lumierna's guards are equipped with cheaper quality broadswords. Amiria never cared for the long sword or any of the other lengthy blades.

"I knew you preferred double-wielding short swords over our longswords or the short sword and shield. To you, a shield is no more than a clunky object in your way."

Amiria's eyes shoot up from the swords to Calix. "How do you know that? I've always used the assigned weaponry."

"Like you said, we need to know our teammates. You can recognize my footsteps, so what's so odd about knowing your teammates' weapon preference." Calix shrugs.

Reaching into a small pouch strung to his belt, he remembers something. "Oh, I got one more gift for you."

Amiria sheaths the short sword back into the scabbard and sets it to the side.

Calix holds his hand out clutching a mysterious item inside. Unable to see anything encased in his grip, Amiria holds her hand out meeting his in the space between them. Fingers uncurling a gold and lilac braided ribbon drops into her palm.

"I knew you liked any shade of purple, and I thought gold suited you. It stands out nicely in your dark hair," Calix explains.

"Calix, these gifts are wonderful." Her voice is soft.

"Here, let's see how it looks," Calix offers, motioning to Amiria to turn around.

Amiria crisscrosses her legs on her bed and stiffly scoots herself to face away from him. She hands him the ribbon over her shoulder.

Calix steps up behind her and tenderly pulls her hair back so it all hangs evenly down her shoulder blades. The hair on the back of her neck stands as a shiver runs down her spine.

He runs the ribbon under her hair and lifts it off the nape of her neck. Gently, he ties the ribbon around her hair centered on the back of her head. Checking to be clear there are no strands caught in the knot he tightens it. Once secure he twists the ribbon around letting the long tails hang down beneath her ponytail.

Amiria tilts her head side to side making her hair sway, testing the ribbon's hold.

She leaps from her bed over to a neatly organized desk. Her heart skips a beat, Stirling's goggles lay exposed on top of the desk beside an old pair of her riding gloves.

Positioning her body between the desk and Calix she opens the drawer sliding the goggles in and pulls out a hand mirror in one motion. Blowing off the dust she holds it up to examine herself.

"It looks good, doesn't it?" Calix says, remaining by the bed.

"Yeah." She replies, trying to turn her head enough to see the beautiful contrast of colors in her hair.

"I want to get to know you." Calix offers.

Amiria turns back around, "You do know me."

"I know you when it comes to the Calvary. I know the soldier, but I want to know the girl in the armor."

She sets the mirror face down on the desk. She doesn't say anything. Calix watches as she steps back across the room and passes him. She finally stops in front of the fireplace, her toes curling on the bear skin rug.

Crossing her legs, she plops down and pats the ground beside her.

His heart tumbles, he nearly misses catching it, preventing it from being splayed across her floor. Tucking his palpitating heart back into his chest, he poorly hides his excitement to be close to her as he takes his seat facing her on the rug.

"Go ahead, ask me whatever you desire to know."

Calix grins, the dimples in his cheek prominent.

"Okay, simple question. I know your favorite color is purple, but what is your favorite food?"

"Pretzels."

"Pretzels?"

"Pretzels," she confirms with a nod.

"Not baked mote royalle? Ember day tart? Roasted quail? Dushell? But pretzels." Calix chuckles.

"Why is it so funny? You asked what I liked and I answered." She says trying to not catch the contagious laugh. "All right, Sir Princely. What's your favorite food? Lamb?"

Calix nods. "Lamb anything, especially the ribs with a good herbal rub."

Amiria fake scoffs. "Well, aren't you all high classed?"

"At least now I know traveling with you will be cheap and easy. I can just pack a bag full of pretzels to keep you happy," he jokes.

"Oh, shut up." Amiria leans forward, lightly slapping him on the shoulder. Their eyes catch in the fire's glow. Amiria blushes and sits back straight. "Next question."

Twenty-Four

The crescent moon hovers in the sky. The same star formations as the Isles of Wyverna puncture the curtain of night.

Gravel rolls beneath Stirling's shuffling feet as he crosses the property to the old stables. He has added another first place to his streak in an intermediate race. A unanimous decision was made and the judges have agreed, Stirling of Patu was participating in a ranking far below his skill level and has been bumped up to the advanced level starting tomorrow morning.

He is worn out, physically and mentally, with the number of new fans wanting to come up and converse with him. Bernard and Eve are unable to save him every time. He has exhausted himself by taking roundabout paths in an attempt to avoid everyone, unsure if he will ever get used to the overwhelming amount of attention.

It's not only the fans he wants to avoid. It's also the other competitors. They don't hide their disdain and hostile opinions about his second advancement during his first Skylit Endeavor. How could someone from the fields outpace them when it takes other racers several years to advance to the next rank? For many, they remain dormant in their current rank for their entire career.

He worries his heart is one panicked beat from giving out under the stress. Ignis' presence is only able to help to a certain extent, often finding solace in Eve and Bernard.

Tugging at his tunic, he examines the sauce stain still faintly there after scrubbing for an hour. He hasn't found the courage to go into the market. Closing his eyes he pictures stepping foot inside the city limits and being bombarded by people. He drops the fabric letting it fall back into place.

He has never bought anything in his life. He doesn't know the first step to buying a new tunic. Maybe tomorrow he can ask Eve to come with him.

Listening to the crickets chirp, he kicks at a few of the larger pieces of gravel as he relishes the cool night air on his skin.

"Hey, farm boy!" He hears someone call from behind him.

A pit forms in his stomach as his skin clams up, *Oh, no.* Without checking to see who is calling, he picks up his speed.

"Where are you going in such a hurry? Can't wait to sleep in the barn like a pig?"

The sound of shifting gravel fills his eardrums. There is more than one set of footsteps behind him.

He needs to run.

His chest lurches forward, whipping his head back. Staggering, he barely keeps hold of his balance. He wheels around with a spray of pebbles to look his perpetrators in the eye.

Merek, the man with the red and white cape from the dining hall, and two of his personal friends who are not professionals in the games.

"I told you, if you were in the advanced level you wouldn't be laughing." His voice is cold, "You don't belong here. You've tainted our profession. You should have stayed in the slums."

Stirling's fingers tap nervously at his side. Forcing himself to act brave he defends, "You're just scared you're going to lose to me. I have as much right to compete as you do." The words fall flat, his windpipe is already beginning to constrict as the panic seizes control of his body.

"I'm so *scawred*" Merek says with Stirling's accent "I can see through you. It seems to me like you're the one who is scared." Merek points out with a devilish grin. Using his thumbs, he cracks each of his fingers on his hands, "Remember, no marks to the face and nothing broken. We don't want the judges to see. All we need is to hinder his performance."

Stirling spins to run, his feet skidding on the loose turf. The second it takes for him to turn they are already on him. The two friends immediately leap forward, seizing him. They gain control of his arms by holding on to his wrists with one hand and the other used to push forward on his shoulders. His arms are forced to lock out back and away from his body.

He struggles in their grasp, pulling feebly against their restraining hold hoping to tuck his arms into his chest. He can't out-muscle them, not while they have his arms out straight behind him

Merek steps in front of Stirling, "I'm going to enjoy this."

The veins bulge from his hand as it curls into a fist hanging down by his side. Slow and menacingly he pulls it back like a battering ram.

Lights flash across Stirling's vision as the fist lodges into his stomach. He heaves forward from the impact, his toes scraping back through the gravel as they slip out from under him.

His body hangs above the ground like a fly caught in a spider web.

Merek clutches Stirling by the curls and forces him to look up at him, "Aw, you tapping out already? Or was there no fight in you to begin with?"

Stirling spits.

With his hand still gripping firmly in Stirling's hair, he rears his face back. Merek's nostrils flare as he sucks in air furiously. Placidly, he wipes the wad of spit from his face with the back of his sleeve.

In a burst of furious rage, Merek rips Stirling free of the human shackles forcing his face down into the gravel.

Before he can blink the dirt from his eyes, a second blow strikes him in the side. The toe of a shoe digs a path between his ribs.

He instantly fetals up, curling his knees into his chest. His fingers interlaced behind his neck covering his face with his elbows. Another stomping impact lands in the soft area between his hip and rib cage. His intestines move as the heel crashes into them.

"*IGNIS!*" he cries out.

The salvo begins. He is the fort and they are the catapults slinging boulders at his walls with each hammering kick. He desperately wants to call out for help, but he can't with each jarring blow sending his mind off track.

He is helpless.

He is nothing.

The attack subsides. The eye of the storm. All is calm.

He doesn't move, he can't move. His body is stiff as if still ensnared by the spider's silk. Amiria's image fills the back of his eyelids. She is sitting beside him. Her strong yet caring touch on his shoulder.

"Stirling," she says.

"Stirling."

"Amiria." He replies, his voice sluggish. His body locked in place with her hovering above him. Her loose strands of hair tickle her face in the breeze. "I nee—" he begins.

"*STIRLING!*" Ignis yells, his head laying on the ground so his golden eyes can investigate Stirling's.

Stirling's cheek resting on the gritty walkway, he opens his eyes lethargically as he regains consciousness. He coughs as he remembers how to breathe adequately.

"*Where did they go?*" He asks, unable to form words out loud.

"*They took off as soon as I started barreling over here from the stable. You called once but weren't replying to me. Guess they only like fighting when they have the upper hand,*" Ignis draws out.

Stirling's eyes glaze over as he curls into himself hugging his knees. "*Please, leave me alone.*" His body is a numb casing around his aching soul.

"*Leave you alone?*"

Stirling's eyes are focused on the haunting shadows past Ignis. "*Just leave me al...*" The word falls away as he turns his face into the dirt.

"*Stirling? Hey, Stirling?*"

He knows Ignis is talking to him, but he can't respond. He is no more than a third party watching through his eyes. He stares at the pebbles. A drop of blood drips from his lip, his tongue already beginning to swell in his mouth.

"*You leave me no choice,*" Ignis says, lightly pinching the back of Stirling's tunic in his front teeth.

Walking backward, Ignis drags Stirling's empty shell to the stables.

Why?

His head bobs with the uneven path.

Why?

His chin resting on his chest, his eyes strain to find peace in the stars. The same stars that once capped the lid closed over Wyverna. Always vigil, but never alleviating.

The stars won't help him.

196

Twenty-Five

Standing in the thin rays of the open windows of her bed chamber, Amiria shakes her head laughing, "I can't believe you convinced me to go to this stupid banquet. They must have one every month." She adjusts the last sleeve button on her barely worn orchid purple cotehardie.

Calix, modeling a smokey gray-sleeved jerkin lined with sky blue, drops his feet from the desk he was resting them on and sits up correctly in the chair. "Well, I don't want to suffer alone."

"Thanks for expanding your misery onto me." She steps over to him, their toes almost touching.

Calix lifts himself from the chair. "It's easier to handle pain as a team," he teases with a flashy smile.

Amiria gives him an exaggerated grin. "Aren't you sweet? Handing him the lilac and gold ribbon, she turns her back to him. Talking over her shoulder, she questions, "Why don't you skip them like I always do? I've been to a total of one event my entire life, not including graduation and it was that ball."

"My father." Calix scoops Amiria's hair up, tying it with the ribbon as he stumbles through his explanation, "He's not someone you say no to."

Amiria's face falls flat as she revisits the memory of how her captain, Calix's father, struck him out in the open corridor. He belittled him where anyone could have witnessed, "And your mother?"

Calix's hand falls to her upper arm holding on lightly. "You mean the general? Because I have a general, not a mother."

Amiria turns slowly letting his hand slide down her arm to her wrist where he spins her leather bracelet around with his thumb. "I see, I'd rather have a field marshal too busy to keep track of my movements."

With a sigh, he holds his elbow out. "Me, too."

Amiria jumps to his side, linking her arm in his. "Well, let's get this over with."

"If we must." Calix smiles, leading them out of her room.

A castle servant pulls open one of the double doors leading into a secondary hall half the size of the grand hall for Calix and Amiria. The smaller hall is a colorfully decorated room emphasized by the midday light pouring in through the two-story windows. The walls are painted with sceneries; of the mountains, wild dragons flying around their island to the southeast, men in armor riding on horseback, and women in beautiful gowns holding the hands of children. Gold trims the pillars and the arches supporting the ceilings and, in Amiria's eyes, clashes with the red rugs layering the usually cold castle flooring.

Tables are set up in a box frame for the banquet allowing servants to set and change out the courses periodically without having to reach over those who are in charge of them. Entertainment will also conduct their acts, dances, and jokes in the center to please the top brass of the Calvary and their immediate families.

"Amiria Rey, I haven't seen you at one of these banquets before." Captain Gautier twirls his lunch wine inside his silver chalice.

"Captain Gautier." Amiria nods, bowing her head in respect to her captain. "I have always been too preoccupied with training and work to set assigned time for such…lavish events."

Captain Gautier smiles with approval. "If only my children saw to their responsibilities with such dedication." Still speaking to Amiria, he glares down his nose at Calix. "Instead of wasting their youth with frivolous acts." He doesn't unlatch his matching diamond eyes as he stabs into Calix. "But, It appears he isn't useless after all."

Amiria refrains from stepping between them, her eyes flipping from her captain over to her newly assigned betrothed. She tilts her head at the muscle twitching in Calix's cheek. Shifting eagerly on her feet she holds back the question resting on the tip of her tongue, *what does he mean, isn't useless after all?*

Feeling Amiria's impatient movements, Calix's face turns before his eyes break their contact with his father's. He answers as if he could read her mind, "It's nothing, don't mind him. Let's go wait for lunch to start by the window."

Amiria bows her head at her captain once more. "I'll see you around, Captain," she manages to say before she is dragged away by Calix.

Reaching the skinny and elongated windows, Calix's shoulders relax as he slumps down on the window sill. Amiria remains standing, slowly inching closer for the social security of the boy she arrived with. The one person she would have purposefully avoided in this situation is now her safety blanket from awkward social encounters with these Calvary executives. Why did she agree to this again?

She looks over at the boy with his head resting back on the window, dark stubble lining his square jaw, and thick eyelashes brushing his cheeks on either side of his straight nose.

He opens his eyes, smirking. "Something on your mind?"

"Nope," she says quickly, shifting her gaze to scan the room. "Just wondering if you were going to play dead and leave me alone to these vicious creatures."

Her eyes fall to the head table of the room, her father already seated, mingles with the Major. Beside him, General Gautier with her light brown hair pulled back into a tight knot sits painfully straight. Her eyelids hang low on her eyes as if the conversation being spoken beside her isn't worth her oxygen to join. Amiria's father breaks away from his discussion long enough to give Amiria a nod of approval before carrying on with the Major.

General Gautier's eyes slither across the room to find who had caught the Field Marshal's brief attention. Her caramel eyes strike like a coiled snake as they stop on her second eldest son gazing longingly at the girl whom he is only betrothed to for the sake of her name. What a vulgar girl. General Gautier's mouth is no more than a crease on her face as Amiria finishes scanning the room and meets her son's eyes.

She should be grateful for who her father is. If she wasn't the next Field Marshal, she would never let one of her own offsprings even converse with someone who carries themselves in such an aloof and heedless manner. A leader does not hide from her people. A leader represents them and makes a display of how one should conduct themselves, not punch a lord at a ball.

Amiria's eyes flit to General Guatier then back to Calix. "Your mother looks enthused."

Calix scoots on the windowsill to peer out the glass refusing to acknowledge his mother. "General."

"Sorry. The *general* looks enthused."

Calix doesn't remove his eyes from the clouds gathering outside for a light shower, "That is her happy face, trust me." He blinks, flicking his eyes up to her. "No emotion is the better option."

"Oh," Amiria learns, understanding quickly. She has never had to deal with the general herself. She has been lucky enough to skip the ranking ladder and speak to the field marshal on every occasion. The field marshal. In a short amount of years, her father will retire and she will occupy the seat at the head table. Will Calix sit beside her in the general's chair or will—"

"Hello." A young girl about the same height as Amiria and around eighteen leans one shoulder against the wall. Her dark hair matching Calix's is french braided on either side of her head down into two long braids. Her caramel eyes, the same as her mother's, crinkle as she smiles at Amiria. Her olive skin and tanned from years exposed to the sun, the same as the majority of the Winged Riders, glows against her rose pink bliaut gown slit down the sides over a pair of tights for better mobility.

"Go away, Kinsey," Calix groans.

If Kinsey heard Calix, she doesn't show it. Her eyes and ears fixated on Amiria and know nothing past her. Her face remains neutral as she speaks, "Surprised to see you show your face after the fiasco you caused at the ball." Kinsey playing the role of a sympathetic younger sister pouts her lower lip, "Sorry you are forced into marriage with my brother. You can only hope he doesn't fail like our eldest brother. He will never make it past a sergeant now. Not like you and I though." Kinsey shows her teeth, "We will be in charge of the Calvary soon enough." She finally focuses past Amiria to Calix whose eyes roll to the back of his head, "Then everyone will be under our command."

Amiria's voice lowers an octave as authority ripples from her like heat from a flame, "You look at me when you speak to me." Kinsey's eyes shoot back to Amiria. "There isn't a we, there is a me. I will be the field marshal, you will be only second in command, my subordinate *if* you do become general. You will take orders from me like your mother takes orders from my father. Learn your place and learn it quickly or we will have another one of those *fiascos*."

Calix lets out a low and long whistle.

A guttural sound emanates deep inside Kinsey as a growl slips past her deceiving smile. She talks through her gritted teeth. "It was a pleasure to officially meet you, Amiria Rey."

"I wish I could say the same." Amiria stiffens her posture.

Kinsey's artificial smile flashes into a sneer. Correcting her mask she smiles with a curtsey before sauntering off.

"Here, I thought you couldn't get any more attractive. That was beautiful, absolutely stunning," Calix flirts.

Bashful, Amiria playfully hits Calix on the shoulder. "Shut up," she says, joining him on the window sill, "I'm not going to lie, your sister is awful."

Calix's head bobs between a yes and no, "Yeah, I agree, but out of my three siblings she's probably the best. She is the only one who acknowledges me—Well, maybe that's not a good thing. But, my older brother resents us all. He hasn't spoken to us since I was twelve and before that, he caused—" Calix stops skipping over the details. Taking a deep breath, he starts again. "His scores didn't meet my parents' expectations."

Amiria shrugs. "So they told him he won't be captain or general?"

"Disowned him," Calix says blatantly.

Amiria leans away to get a better view of Calix. "Disowned! Like disowned, disowned?"

"Well, yeah, he isn't inheriting any of the leadership positions so they had no need for him," Calix states with a detached demeanor.

"Isn't that a bit on the harsh side?" Amiria points out.

"Is that not normal?" Calix asks, honestly confused.

Amiria looks Calix over, "No. I don't believe so."

She thinks of her childhood. Her real mother is only the faintest of memories, but she remembers the warmth of her love. She can always recall the kisses goodnight. After her passing, nannies raised her until she started officially training at the age of ten.

Busy with training, she finished raising herself from there on out. She rarely saw her father, but she never thought he would discard her like a broken tool no longer fit for its designed intentions. He has never shown it, but she knows her father loves her in some form or another. She touches the bracelet on her wrist. It belonged to Stirling's mother, he saved Stirling nearly a decade ago. He saved Stirling because he would want someone to save her if the roles were reversed.

Hanging his head, Calix watches the waves of emotions crossover Amiria's face. She steadies her expressions scooting closer to Calix till their hips touch.

Calix's breath hitches. He holds himself still as she reaches over as if she was a small bird landing on him that he doesn't want to scare away. She slips her hand into his, giving him a comforting squeeze. She doesn't know what to say in response. She has no words to mend what she doesn't understand. She can't fathom what kind of childhood he endured. Calix squeezes her hand back.

"You said the only one out of three siblings," Amiria brings back the sensitive topic, unsure of why she wants to know more. "Who is the third?"

"My younger brother Keaton, he's fifteen getting close to graduation and has been cursing me to fail since he could talk. He desperately wishes to become captain, but I'm currently the only thing standing in his way. That's him over there," Calix points to a boy who is almost a male replica of the general.

Keaton feels eyes on him, and with his instinct correct his eyes snap to Calix who merely lowers his hand back to his lap. Amiria tenses. With his face turned to them she can see the yellowing bruise healing on the side of his face. That's the kind of childhood Calix grew up with.

Narrowing, Keaton's eyes are blades; they are unsheathed, ready to tear down their opponent. Calix sucks in a deep breath dropping his gaze. He lets it sit in his lungs, waiting until they begin to burn before releasing it.

Sitting back he removes his hand from Amiria's to sling his arm around her shoulders already exasperated with the banquette, "When are they going to start serving food so we can get this over with?"

Amiria clues into the change of topic, but her mind does not. "Not soon enough. Watching people mingle is kind of entertaining though, like what do you think floppy hat Colonel and is talking to bird beak hat Brigadier about?"

"I think it goes a bit like this," Calix holds up his nose putting himself in character. "Say, Sir Terrowin, may I ask? Have you come upon the solution to that of removing a stick from one's bottom? No, Sir Aimar, I'm afraid I have not. But do not fret, I have my most reliable scholars researching at this very moment."

Amiria slaps her hand to her mouth, her ugly laugh seeping through the gaps in her fingers as she fails to hold it back.

"Yeah, you find that funny?" Calix laughs.

Amiria keeps her hand over her mouth turning red as she nods her head. "I do," she manages to say through her giggles.

He can't stop another piece of his heart from falling for her. Each time she laughs she takes another part of him. If she keeps up this pace she will own all of him and he is more than willing to give it up. He finally takes his eyes off of her as platters of divine dishes come pouring through the doors and lunch is to be served.

Twenty-Six

"*How did I get here?*" Stirling wonders. The few sunspots streaming down through the patchy roof of the stable come into focus as he wakes.

"*I dragged you here,*" Ignis informs.

Stirling lays in the bed of straw beside Ignis who is protectively curled around him. Placing his hand on Ignis' front leg he sits up.

"AHH!" he cries out, hugging his torso. A sharp pain shoots up his abdomen and around his rib cage. He smacks his lips, tasting iron in his mouth.

With pain-shaking hands, he lifts his tunic to peek at his stomach. Only lifting the hem of his tunic he exposes up to his belly button. He can already see the vibrant purple splotches on his skin.

Pushing his tunic back down hiding the evidence, he moves his tongue around as he inspects the gash on one side.

"Damn," he mutters, lying back down. "*What happened? I remember that guy Merek attacking me, but that's it,*" Stirling questions, his memory running blank.

"*After I chased them off, you were unconscious. You started to wake, but you still weren't responding so I dragged you back here.*"

"*I don't remember any of that last part,*" Stirling admits, unsure of what had happened to him.

Pushing through the pain Stirling sits up. "I'm going to need some help walking to the match today."

"*You're still going to compete? Aren't you injured?*" Ignis points out.

"I can't let them stop me." He grimaces as he crawls out of Ignis' nest. "I can't let them have power over me."

Grabbing hold of the stable's wall he rises, each breath sending sharp stabs through him.

"*You're crazy, you know that right?*" Ignis states.

"I'm aware."

He holds onto Ignis' saddle for assistance, desperately wishing he was able to walk without moving his torso. Each excruciating step brings him closer to his match of the day. He grinds his teeth, already perspiring across his forehead.

As they approach the competition grounds, Stirling analyzes the course. They had altered the racing track into an agility run. With the help of dragons, the crew was able to set up large wooden structures over the night. Hoops with a circumference only wide enough to fit Ignis' body through so you need to time the beat of your wings perfectly to lower the chances of clipping them on the rings and receiving penalties.

A long downwards sloping tunnel constructed of canvas stretched around a ringlet spine, even the smallest mistake is unforgivable. The only possible execution is with a calculated dive.

Tight-knit poles protrude from the water in a single file line. Shouldn't be any harder to weave through than dodging Taika's fire.

The finale is a single shot with a bow and arrow. A haystack has been lifted into the air on a platform with a target painted on it.

A horde of fans surrounds the entrance to the fenced-off area reserved for racers only, allowing them privacy to prepare themselves for their meet. Several of the racers have stopped outside the fence to mingle with their adoring fans. Shaking hands and offering hugs they do what they must to hold the hearts of the people, and to convince the people to purchase the merchandise with their color and number.

Several girls with orange ribbons in their hair and boys with orange bandanas around their necks or tied around their wrists turn their attention to the arriving Stirling and Ignis.

Stirling and Ignis stop short as their fans rush over to them.

"STIRLING! STIRLING!" A clatter of mixed voices shout excitedly.

Their overlapping bodies create a solid wall blocking him from his escape.

"What's it like out there?"

"Do you have a girlfriend?"

"How long have you been flying?"

"Will you marry me?"

"Did you really come from a small village like me?"

So many questions. Too many questions. His body sways light-headed. The overwhelming amount of voices sucking the oxygen out from around him. Perspiration forms on his palms and underarms. Each beat of his heart is faster than before. His mind commands him to run, it begs him to flee.

He takes a panicked step back, his body pressing into Ignis. The circling fans close the wall around him trapping him inside. Ignis needs to move, he has no room to escape. He can't even tell what they are even asking anymore. A new question is asked before the other one is finished.

Gripping the saddle he buries his face into his arms. "I-I-I—" he stammers into his sleeve, his swollen tongue unable to form words.

A female voice calls out over the crowd. "Okay, move it along, move it along. You guys are scaring the boy. He's new, he isn't used to the attention yet." Eve pushes her way through the wall to Stirling.

"And you are?" one of the girls asks, eyeing Eve.

Bernard's voice washes over them drowning out everyone else, "We're his family. So if you don't mind we would like a moment with him."

They peer up at Bernard's mountainous size and shrink into themselves.

"Excuse us," they mumble while filing away.

"Vultures." Eve scowls.

"It's whatever," Stirling says quietly emerging from his hiding place. The wound on his tongue hits his teeth with each syllable.

Look who's getting popular," Bernard says with a chuckle.

"I guess." Stirling's voice is still a whisper.

Are you okay?"

His words come out rushed. "I'm fine."

Eve lifts her chin examining the small scratches on Stirling's cheek and jaw. "What happened there?"

"Nothing!" Stirling lies, pulling his head away.

Bernard's eyes narrow. "Stirling, what are you not telling us?"

Eve reaches out with nurturing intent, her fingertips grazing his side.

Batting her hand away, Stirling jerks away, snapping, "I said I'm fine!"

Eve retracts her hand frightened, her loving eyes watering.

Stirling's shoulders soften. "I'm sorry, Eve. I shouldn't have snapped at you like that…I'm under a lot of stress, but I should never take it out on you." He looks pleadingly into her eyes. "How about after my match we go to the market together? I need a new tunic since I stained this one."

Eve holds the tears back from forming in the corner of her eyes, putting on a delighted smile, "I would love to."

"Thanks for helping me with the crowd, I do need to warm up though. I'll see you after." Stirling insists with a light wave. Holding his composure he pushes the pain down deep as he makes his way into the restricted area.

"You sure you don't want to tell them?" Ignis asks.

"I don't want sympathy. I want to compete," Stirling expresses.

He nods to the guards standing post at the gate and Ignis guides Stirling over to an open bench in the shade of a tent. Using Ignis' saddle, Stirling clenches his jaw as he cautiously lowers himself onto the seat.

"Look who still showed up," Merek says, stepping away from a mossy green lung dragon, "You should have gone home. Your winning streak ends today. My dragon is made for this. Anyone who flies any other species is a fool."

His eyes run across Ignis. "Especially people who ride pets."

"I am not a pet," Ignis grumbles.

"Why don't you do us all a favor and get out of our sight," Merek barks.

Stirling's voice is no more than a wheeze as he uses his injured muscles to push out air and form words, "Trust me. I don't want to see any of you after these games are over." He forces a smile. "Well, not until next year." Stirling attempts a laugh but ends up grabbing his stomach grimacing.

"We'll see how you feel after this loss." Merek sneers.

Stirling holds his head up until Merek has disappeared, becoming engrossed in checking his own dragon's gear. "Agh." He moans, tipping over to his side.

Holding his breath Stirling slings the quiver containing a single arrow with an orange ribbon over his back. One chance to hit the closest to the center as he can for the highest score added to his time.

He accepts the competition bow from the Bowyer. For equality and to thwart possible cheating everyone is required to use the game-provided bows.

Remembering what Amiria had taught him all those years ago, Stirling examines the yule bow. Weighing the wood in his hand he runs his finger down the length of the string searching for any nicks or frays. Hooking his fingers around the string he plucks. It vibrates with a low hum.

It is low quality, quickly made in bulk to supply the games massive order to have back stock in case any damage occurs. Seeing the drastic difference in quality compared to his old one he curses at himself for letting it break.

"Do you want to try it out first?" the Bowyer asks.

Not wanting him to observe his injuries, Stirling denies the offer. "No, this is suitable. I'll be fine."

The Bowyer raises an eyebrow. "All right, your choice."

"Stirling of Patu, get ready, you're up next," the coordinator calls out.

"Let's get this over with," Stirling calls out to Ignis.

Twenty-Seven

Exhaling out his nose Stirling pulls himself onto Ignis. With a quivering jaw, he steadies his breathing.

Push it down. Don't let them see.

Ignis stands ready at the coastal starting line. The calm waters rise and lower gently around the rocks beneath his claws.

The muscles in Stirling's face barely flinch as the horn blares, his fear contained inside, but not eradicated.

Unfazed by the sound, Ignis responds in an instant knowing their timer has begun. He vaults from the harbor's edge and rockets into the air. Banking he turns them in the direction of the first obstacle. Each beat of Ignis' wings is a kick to Stirling's ribs.

Grunting, Stirling instructs, *"All right, there are six rings."* He reaches down the nape of Ignis' neck and drums a steady slow beat. *"If you flap your wings and curl them in to fit through the rings to this beat we shouldn't have any issues. Keep the pace we are at."*

They reach the first ring. Ignis tucks in his wings pulling them tightly into his body. To keep from clipping his head, Stirling presses his cheek to Ignis as they barely fit through the ring. Gravity begins to take over before Ignis pumps his wings and they leap through the next hoop as if they are a horse jumping hurdles.

Completing the rings with ease they move on to the next obstacle.

"Okay, now the tunnel. Remember, same as the rings. You can't stretch out your wings. It's a glide." Stirling informs.

"Yeah, yeah. I know." Ignis gives one final burst then folds his wings leaving them only open enough to allow airflow to slip through and control their descent.

They are swallowed by the tunnel. The light dims to a clay red as the sun's rays force their way through the thick canvas. Stirling tilts his head back watching the white burst of light follow above them. The tunnel's rings pass overhead, breaking the light as if they are the ones moving and he is hovering there stagnant.

Blind.

His eyes shut close from the sudden contrast of light blinds him as they emerge free from the tunnel. This is a deliberate side effect. The inventors, well aware of the hindrance, kept it in the races to add more stakes to the competition as racers struggled to regain their bearrings.

Finally, Stirling has luck on his side. Ignis is unaffected by the change in light. His pupils constrict automatically as he aims for the weave poles.

"Last stretch, then it's the bow and arrow," Stirling states.

"Don't touch any or we get penalties," Ignis adds.

"Pretend we're running from Amiria. Sharp abrupt weaves."

"Got it."

Turning himself sideways with his back facing the poles he thrust his wings sending a strong gust to shoot himself through the first gap. Before he extends his wings back out he contorts his body keeping his back facing the poles. After another quick burst, he sends himself to the other side.

Stirling can't imagine how difficult this must be to perform these obstacles with reins; unable to directly communicate. He can truly appreciate their skill, but he does not feel guilty or feel he is cheating by talking through the steps with Ignis. It is his gift and he is only using his skills to his advantage. It is no different than how they use money, selective breeding, and professional training to increase their probability of winning.

He hunches forward in the saddle. Holding in an agonizing cry of pain as they move back and forth.

He's going to pass out.

He's going to puke then he's going to pass out.

The fibers of the muscles in his abdomen are tearing apart.

It's almost over.

He removes the bow clipped to his waist as Ignis clears the last pole. He has practiced archery every day since he made that promise to Amiria three years ago. It is one of the factors that kept him alive in the forest for so long.

He could never properly swing a sword, but he can shoot an arrow. Gritting his teeth he reaches over his shoulder and removes the perfectly balanced projectile. Ignis levels himself out.

Sitting up straight Stirling takes in a deep breath and holds it. He lifts up the bow and pulls the arrow back aiming for the center of the target.

It doesn't matter the distance you shoot from, but your time doesn't stop until your arrow hits the target. Waiting until you get closer ups your probability of hitting the center but extends your time. Shooting from a distance lowers your chance of a bull's eye, but your time is stopped sooner.

All but four people have embedded their arrows in the
third ring of the painted target. There's three in ring two
and only one that has succeeded in landing their arrow in
the direct center of the circle. A red and white ribbon
flutters taunting anyone trying to hit a better shot.

Stirling makes his split-second decision on the latter
and saves time by shooting from a distance. If it wasn't
for the pain emanating from his sides this would be no
different from shooting a wild boar in the place right near
the armpit allowing the arrow to slide through the soft
lung tissue with ease and strike the heart.

"AHH!" Stirling cries out. Succumbing to the pain, he
releases the arrow before he is able to properly align.

The orange ribbon flies through the air and with a soft
thunk it embeds in the third ring grazing the inner line
bordering the second.

He should have hit the center. He *would* have hit the
center. If he was part of the Winged Cavalry he would
have been able to shoot through the pain and land
perfectly. Amiria wouldn't have missed. She would have
won with rage filled energy.

Amiria wouldn't be injured to begin with.

Stirling is not Amiria or a Winged Rider. He isn't even
angry about what they did to him. What he is, is
disappointed. Name-calling and ridiculing him wasn't
satisfying enough to them. They believed it was necessary
to take it one step further. Their plan has failed. It has
only given him more of an incentive to keep going.

He's grown accustomed to the exiled feeling. Being an
outcast is all he's ever known. He doesn't care about
making new friends. He has already made more than he
has ever had in his life. At this point, he would be content
if the other participants ignored him for the rest of his
career.

Ignis lands in the finish zone and they watch the
scoreboard as the judges tally up their time and score.

The employee is shown a note from the judges, and he shuffles the wooden slats painted with their color and number.

Fourth.

Fourth place.

He is accepting of losing his first-place streak with second or third. But he didn't place at all. Now he can only hope no one pushes him further down the list.

"No," Stirling tells himself. "*Remember why you joined. It's for the love of flying.*"

Stirling pats Ignis on the side of the neck. "*Maybe next time.*"

Past his feet propped up on the railing, Quilan watches the orange slate representing Stirling slide into fourth place in the agility competition. Fourth, third, second, *first*. First place, painted red and white checkered, is Merek. Pulling his lips in tight, they disappear into the crease of a scowl.

Stirling was able to pull off fourth place, but even from here in the Elite's private box, Quilan could see hesitancy in his movements as if it pained him to move with his usual fluidity.

Wearing his quartered sea green and yellow cape with a number two, Peyton with brown waves and dusky skin, talks with his mouth full of roasted almonds, "Guess he finally lost his luck."

Lucan, sitting with the other two elite racers in a purple and white striped cape with a number four, doesn't look up from his strategy game consisting of moving small stones on a leather mat carved with three squares one inside of the other. Firmin, the second oldest in the division sits directly across as Lucan's opponent with Aylmar, the most senior, sitting beside them. Barely more interested in their game than the competition, Aylmar's head bobs down to his number three cape in solid yellow with the beginnings of nodding off.

"Luck? He's a cheat. Just don't know how though." Lucan moves one of his stones. Quilan pops his jaw, his eyes locked forward.

Peyton turns in his seat to respond to Lucan. "Well, however he's been winning, it's ended. He messed up this round and there goes his streak."

Eyes focused on his move, Firmin joins the conversation. "Maybe after this loss, he'll finally get the clue to stay out of our games."

Heavy eyelids take their time blinking as the next racer readies himself to take off. Quilan drops his feet from the railing with an intentional arrogant thud and stands up without warning.

"Where are you off to?" Peyton reaches his hand into the wooden bowl set on a table between them and grabs another handful of almonds.

Firmin laughs, "Probably to get another drink."

"Or a quick one before the race. A different one each day? Am I right?" Lucan nudges Aylmar with his elbow.

Quilan ignores them all.

Aylmar huffs, "Not like it's any different if he is here or not, he's too vain to talk to us." Aylmar's gruff eyes follow the aloof boy in the robin's egg blue cape across their private box to the exit, "Maybe if we showered him in compliments we can at least get a good morning."

As if he didn't hear a single word, the number one racer slips out of the room.

The last participant has finished. Stirling sits in a waiting area staring up at the scoreboard. Somehow he has managed to hold his fourth place standing.

"Stirling?" a coordinator says, stepping up behind him.

"Yes?" he asks, turning stiffly to see who is speaking.

"I need you to come with me."

"Shhh."

"Hush."

"Stop talking."

The audience hushes as the crier steps in front of the crowd, "A last-moment change to the scores will occur. The racer by the name of Merek is being disqualified for conspiring to and then committing violence on another games participant. The racer who was harmed will not be named. The scoreboard will now be updated."

Bernard and Eve sit confused. Shifting their bodies, they peer up at the board. There for everyone to witness is Merek's slate being removed from first place, bumping everyone up a spot.

"Look! Look! Stirling still placed! He's in third!" Eve shouts, pointing out what Bernard can see for himself. He doesn't join in on her enthusiasm. His jaw pops beneath his burly beard as he contemplates.

With arms and legs crossed, Quilan leans against the exit of the restricted area. He rests his head against the fence, his eyelids sliding to half closed. His barely awake dark blue eyes follow Merek as he is escorted off the grounds by the guards. He holds a single hand up, halting the guards as they reach the exit beside him.

Merek hisses, "So the boy wasn't the one who squealed, and to think someone as highly ranked as you would side with someone who sleeps in the stables." Quilan lifts his head from the wall narrowing down on Merek. Merek barks, "You got something to say, then say it!"

Quilan doesn't break eye contact. "Ticks need to be removed." The guards shove Merek forward to continue their escort.

Twisting in the guard's grasp, Merek strains to look over his shoulder at Quilan, "How? How did you know?"

With apathetic eyes Quilan smiles.

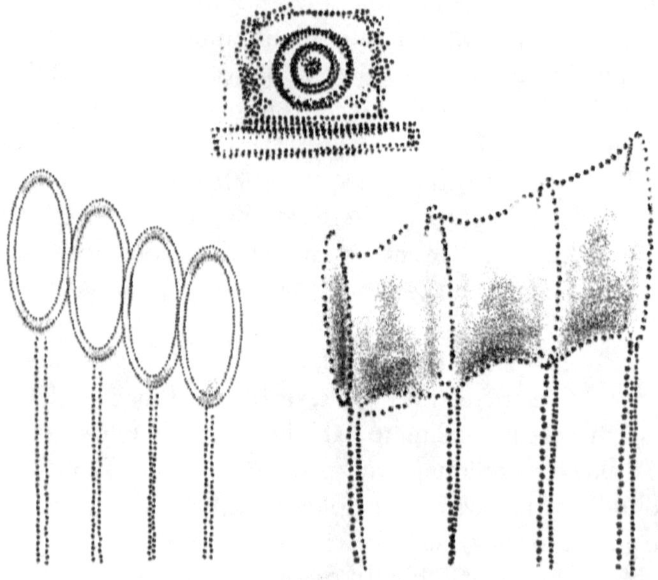

Twenty-Eight

Stirling!" Eve shouts running up to him and Ignis after they've exited the restricted area.

Bernard strolls behind her, remaining at his casual pace. A wide grin showing teeth through his beard.

She contains her excitement, stopping just before tackling him. "You ended up still being able to place! And at the advanced level, too!"

Crossing one arm over his center, Stirling holds onto his elbow and kicks at the pebbles by his toes. "Yeah. I guess I did."

Bernard gently clasps Stirling on the shoulder.

"Congratulations, third is still wildly impressive considering a month ago you had never even heard of the sport."

"Yeah, but I don't feel as if I earned it. I would rather have accepted fourth place." Stirling shrugs.

"Well, that man got what he deserved for hurting a fellow racer," Eve inputs, putting her hands on her hips.

Suspicious, Bernard raises a bristly eyebrow at Stirling. "Do you know who it was?"

Stirling's hazel eyes quickly find a tuft of grass to stare at. "I don't know." A large hand on his shoulder pulls his attention back.

"Don't let them put you down. You are the better racer. Fly higher than them so they have no choice but to look up at you."

"Thanks, Bernard," Stirling says with a weak smile.

Bernard releases his shoulder as Stirling offers his arm out to Eve. "Ready to go to the market?"

Elated Eve wraps herself around his arm. Stirling ignores the pang in his ribs as she accidentally grazes his side.

He glances over at Ignis. *"I'll see you after, all right?"*

"Sure thing, lover boy." Ignis chuckles before trotting off to find a nice napping location.

Groups of girls cluster like small packs of hyenas as they wait to meet the racers. Their ears perk as they sense Stirling. Silently snarling they nip at their pack members as they point at Eve. Eve makes eye contact with her hunters and sticks out her tongue. Facing forward she nuzzles her cheek against Stirling's shoulder as they head toward Leucasia.

Eve has always loved the natural white sand-colored buildings and their red shingled roofs. She tilts her head to observe their illusions. The buildings sit on top of one another in an acrobatic balancing act.

She barely comprehends Stirling nodding to the city guards as they pass through the gates at the edge of the bay. Her full attention is on the plaza just inside the gate ahead. Her shoulder collides with the back of Stirling's arm as he stops in place. She gazes up at him confused. She smiles at his dropped jaw.

Breathing in slowly she takes in the sight with him. The gate's plaza is paved with cut stones varying between light and dark shades of grey laid in a spiraling pattern connecting to a marble fountain of a victorious man riding a quetzalcoatl.

Shops line the circumference with brightly colored tents and tables overflowing with products. The smell of herbal remedies and incense waft through the market masking the aroma Stirling has associated with cities.

That isn't the only factor. Stirling takes this into account as they cross the plaza.

The cleanliness of the city is baffling. Beneath the city is a complex system of channels attached to public latrines and shoots allowing people to dispose of their trash. A constant supply of water flows through the city from cleverly designed aqueducts, cleaning the channels, and providing fresh water to the people.

Heads turn, eyes widen, and fingers point.

Stirling's face grows red hot.

"LOOK!"

"Is that the racer Stirling?"

"I can't believe it's him."

"Stirling."

"Stirling."

"Stirling."

He enjoyed his invisibility in his old market streets. Always able to slip through the town unnoticed. He was nothing more than the baker's son.

So many faces. So many eyes.

Every single movement he makes is being analyzed.

Who is friend and who is foe?

Watching.

Watching.

Everyone is always watching. Each eye latching onto him like small hooks clinging to his skin. He can feel the pull of the strings adding up and slowing him down. He wishes he can fly away to the world in the clouds where they can no longer reach him.

Eve can feel Stirling's body tense as they stroll across the plaza. At first, she thinks she is imagining it, but without Stirling realizing it, she trails her eyes down to examine his hand held up at chest height. There is a significant tremble.

She glances at the people around them. How the city folk hang on to his every breath as if he is a deity walking amongst them. Growing up near the capital she is well aware this is how they always behave toward professionals. Especially those who win; and Stirling coming from a small village is only amplifying the attention.

She has never put much thought into what it must be like under all those eyes. Here and now she finally understands the unnerving effect.

"Hey," she whispers, placing the palm of her hand gently just below his shoulder. "It's okay. They'll stare, but they won't crowd you since you aren't alone. They might act like idiots to get the racer's attention, but they aren't heathens. There are unwritten boundaries most won't cross. A racer with his family or friends is one of them."

Smiling, Stirling's body relaxes.

"If I remember correctly the tailor is up this way," Eve informs, pointing at a staircase leading up to the next layer.

She watches from the corner of her eye as they ascend the stairs as if each step is a troublesome hurdle to him. His teeth grinding, he clenches his jaw and clings to the railing.

He stares at his hand on the railing refusing to meet her eye, "I'm just tired, all right."

They reach the top of the steps and Eve gently nudges Stirling to take a left. "Here it is." She directs, slowing to a stop several shops down the paved path.

A needle and thread sign hangs above the propped open door allowing the ocean breeze to fill the shop with cool air. On each side of the entrance and lining the windowsills are potted flowers filling the salty air with a mixture of perfumes.

Eve can sense Stirling's uncertainty, letting him stay back she enters the shop first.

"How may I help you, miss?" the tailor, an eccentric dark brown skinned man folding a sheet of cotton cloth, asks.

"My friend needs a new tunic, nothing specially tailored. Any waist-length tunic, preferably with long sleeves will do. Actually, do you have any with ties in the sleeves? He has to deal with a lot of wind," Eve explains as Stirling slips in behind her.

"The new racer!" the tailor says, clapping his hands together then bangles around his wrists chiming, "I am honored you have chosen my shop in the lower level of the city. My name is Tobias and I do apologize ahead of time for the poorer quality of fabrics than those above. It is what it is and it is what I can afford."

Stirling blushes, embarrassed, and mumbles at the ground, "Don't apologize. I've only ever worn linen and wool. I don't even know what other fabrics are. Except for whatever this tunic is made of." Stirling holds the hem of his tunic out and looks up at Tobias, "I do like this fabric."

"Oh! You are too humble." Tobias smiles, waving off Stirling. "Also the tunic you are wearing is cotton. Soft isn't it?"

"Cotton?" he repeats.

"I've got those in all sorts of colors! Did you want a long sleeve for the under-tunic or did you want the top long sleeve? Do you want to stay with this style you have there or did you want to change it up a bit? Maybe a nice jopula and a pair of tights?" Tobias starts to ramble as he steps uncomfortably close to Stirling visually measuring him out.

"I—uh—what do you think?" Stirling asks, unsure. His body naturally pulls back to create some personal space.

Tobias snaps his fingers. "I've got the perfect idea! Your lady will love it.".

"Uh-okay," Stirling answers, only growing more embarrassed.

Tobias turns to Eve. "What color do you want to see him in?"

Eve wastes no time answering, "Green! To bring out his eyes."

Skipping over to a stack of clothing, Tobias skims through the folded fabric. He spins around, hugging three articles of clothing. "You can try these on behind this divider here."

Stirling steps over the wooden divider with one end pressed against the wall segmenting a small changing room. Tobias giddily presses the clothing into Stirling's arms and ushers him behind the wall.

Stirling checks behind him. He's alone. With a long drawn-out breath he hangs the new clothing over the wall and unties his orange cape dropping it to the ground. He hesitantly reaches over grabbing the back of his tunic and under-tunic tenderly tugging them off together. He drops them into a heap on top of his cape. This is the first time he has evaluated his injuries.

He had hoped if he ignored the pain it would all go away. Pretend they never happened.

Somehow the games director had found out. He was brought into the privacy of the director's booth along with several other employees and was instructed to lift his shirt exposing his injuries as evidence. He had stared up at the canvas ceiling refusing to look at himself even in the reflection of their eyes.

His ribs, stomach, and back are blotched in deep purple bruises like dye splattered on white linen. Rich in the center and faded as it blends into the cloth, seeping outwards until it is greeted by another blotch. He can see a few of the bruises extending past his pant line onto his hips and several on his arms where they had missed his midsection.

He pulls a cream-colored tunic down from the wall. He freezes.

Eve stands there, her body partially leaning around the divider as if she had come to check on what was taking him so long. Her eyes shine with the glaze of forming tears.

"I knew it." Her breath hitches covering her mouth with both hands. "Oh, Stirling."

"I'm fine," he mumbles, quickly shrugging on the new tunic.

His face growing hot he turns away from her.

Eve opens her mouth to question further but slowly shrinks backs away giving him privacy.

Stirling tentatively steps out from behind the wall. Halting their conversation mid-word Eve and Tobias stand up from the table they were sitting on. Above the new cream tunic, Stirling wears a forest green sleeveless jerkin, a cotton vest laced closed up to his collar bone with gold twine. Tobias has given him his preferred drawstring trousers with the cinched tie at the ankles but more form-fitting dark brown fabric.

Tobias whistles long and deep.

"It fits," Stirling states, refusing to make eye contact with Eve. "How long will it take you to add some ties to the tunics sleeves?"

"It won't take long at all. You can either wait here or you and your lady can grab a bite to eat at the bakery across the path. She makes the best gingerbread," Tobias suggests.

"Gingerbread?"

"Oh, that's your favorite. Come on, let's go try some," Eve says politely, tugging on his sleeve.

Stirling smiles warmly at her, "Sure. Let me change back into my old tunic."

Eve practically leaps from threshold to threshold over the pathway made of crushed and layered stone. Stirling follows stepping around the grass sprouting up between the stones.

Stopping at the entrance, she takes in a big huff of the sweet dough aroma. She snatches Stirling's hand and practically pulls him inside.

"Oh! Look at all the pastries!" Eve drools, scanning the bakery's spread displayed on a table.

Each delectable item is garnished with a variety of honey, shaved almonds, fruits, nutmeg and cinnamon.

"Anything look appetizing to you?" Amata, an elderly woman with gray curls springing loose from her bun the same way Jannell's used to, asks.

"All of it." Eve's eyes are glued to the sweet treats.

"How about you, young man?" she asks Stirling.

"Ging-gingerbread," he stutters. "And whatever she wants."

"Really!" Eve exclaims, "I'll have a frutella from apples please!"

Stirling breathes in the scent of rising yeast while he watches the elderly woman wrap a loaf of gingerbread and a cheese dough fried with apples. The tickle forms in the back of his throat. The feeling of mourning. The feeling of missing something or someone you will never see again.

Pulling a coin from his recent win bag, Stirling pays Amata.

"Thank you for stopping by." She drops Stirling's change into his palm. "I hope you enjoy."

Her smile is as warm as a hug and he can't help but smile back. "Thank you, we will."

Eve hops out the front door with Stirling in tow. She leaps and slides across the bench beside the bakery stopping just before the end. Stirling places his hand on the bench and slowly lowers himself beside her. He hands her the frutella and she accepts it graciously.

Barely waiting until it was in her hands, Eve unwraps her pastry and tears into it covering her lap in crumbs. Stirling breaks off a piece of gingerbread and nibbles on it. It *is* delicious. The quality of a true master compared to the loaves he made for the village.

The taste of cinnamon and nutmeg fills his mouth. He is back home, lying on the worn floorboards of his shanty bakery. His mother standing over him threatening to tickle him if he doesn't get up and help.

He looks down at his scarred hands, the pink and white webs stretching across his entire knuckles and down the back of his hands. "Should I get gloves?"

Eve stops mid-bite, her eyes gliding over to stop at the corner of his. She lowers the frutella setting it next to her without taking her eyes off him.

"Can I see your arm?"

"Um, sure," he answers.

Eve scoots closer until their hips are touching. Taking his arm, she pulls it over into her lap and tugs up his sleeve revealing his insignia. Stirling swallows a lump in his throat as a fluttering feeling begins to tickle his stomach. Her eyes turning soft she runs her fingers along the length of his insignia. Stirling shivers. Goosebumps form raising the hair on his arms from the sensation of her fingers coming and going as she crosses over the numb scar tissue.

"I can't imagine what it's like to grow up in a place where they permanently mark children. A world where you're told who to be." She says resting her hand over his insignia, "Let the people see. Let the people think what they want. You shouldn't hide something that made you, you. This mark, these scars. They are your story and it's an incredible one."

He is speechless. Eve the girl who rolled her eyes the first time they met. The girl who had given him a copious amount of attitude while he worked beside her. This problematic girl is also the girl who has also been supporting him at every single one of his matches. The one who has become a safe haven these past weeks.

Pulling her hand away she picks up her frutella and continues eating. Stirling can still feel the ghost of her fingertips on his skin.

Bernard's voice replays in his head. *"She cares about us and she cares about you."*

"Is Eve short for anything?" Stirling asks unannounced.

With a mouth full of pastry, she answers, "Evelina, but I don't really like it."

"I think it's really pretty." Silence suddenly falls beside him. He follows it to Eve, finding her mid-bite in her frutella with cheeks as pink as a tulip.

Regaining herself, Eve stuffs the rest of the pastry into her mouth. Chewing she tucks a loose strand of hair behind her ear. "I'm guessing." Her honey eyes fall to his tunic. "You don't want to talk about what happened."

Stirling pulls his sleeve back down, "No, but this—" He motions to his ribs. "—won't stop me. Then when this is over. I'm going to build a home and settle down in Patu."

Tobias pokes his head out of the shop. "Oh, good, you didn't go far. I have your tunic ready."

Standing up, Stirling offers his hand out to Eve. "And that is a promise."

Twenty-Nine

"A miiiirrriaa," the voice sings. "Oh, Amiiiria."

In search of the mysterious disembodied voice, Amiria comes to a slow stop beneath the arching red and gold posts attached to the decorative fence surrounding the courtyard.

"Hello, Amiria," the voice purrs.

Tilting her head up the owner of the voice comes into view. Kinsey paws at a morning glory, her body tangled in the curving wood like the crawling vines.

"Kinsey?"

Without disturbing a single flower, Kinsey swings down from her perch, "The one and only. Well, I might not be the only Kinsey, but I am in fact the only Kinsey Gautier. Sister of Calix Gautier, your very own betrothed." Kinsey wraps her arms around Amiria's arm hugging it to her chest. The same in height she rests her head on Amiria's shoulder. "And your future sister-in-law."

"Umm..." Amiria is taken aback. "Yeah. I guess we will be sisters."

"Yay!" Kinsey squeals with a giddy bounce. "I've always wanted a sister, we can get ready for the balls together, and braid each other's hair." Keeping her arms wrapped around Amiria's, she begins tugging her along the courtyard with her pep-filled step.

"Wait, I'm supposed to be meeting—" Amiria's words are drowned out as Kinsey talks over her.

"We can do everything together. My brothers never wanted to spend time with me, well there was—" The words fall away from her lips, her eyes traveling back to her past. Shaking it away Kinsey slaps the smile back onto her face. "But that's not important anymore."

Amiria tilts her head away, her body held in place by the constricting arms of the effervescent girl in pink. "Ookaaaay," she drags out the word, uncertain.

"What's important is you—" She pokes Amiria's nose. "—and me and how we will run this place soon enough. I want to have girl talk, I've never had girl talk before." Kinsey's light brown eyes shine with fanaticism. Her body leans forward with expectancy.

Amiria scans the courtyard in search of someone before raising an eyebrow at Kinsey, "Girl talk?"

"Yeah!" She says with more enthusiasm than necessary cutting her off. She takes Amiria's hands in hers. "Tell me, tell me." She lowers her voice as if for only Amiria to hear. "How do you *really* feel about my brother?"

"Calix?" Amiria is yanked abruptly by Kinsey guiding her to the marble bench. With a twirl under Amiria's arm, Kinsey slides onto the bench pulling Amiria down next to her.

"No Keaton–Of course, Calix."

"He's um, he's all right I guess."

"Hmm." Kinsey dips her chin and looks up at Amiria through her eyelashes. "Well, he's head over heels for you."

Amiria rolls her eyes. "Yeah, sure. Just like he is for every woman who passes him by. This was an arranged marriage."

"Oh, if only my father would find me a sutor." She cups her hands together at her chest fantasizing. "I would love nothing more than to be a wife. Especially to a husband that adores me as my brother does you."

"I wouldn't say *adores*." Amiria bashfully tucks a loose strand of hair behind her ear, "Is it not more for the sake of my name?"

"You think a Gautier courting a Rey would all be for gain." Her voice projects like an actor on stage. "But it is not. For this unity, it'll be for true love."

Heat races to Amiria's cheeks. "L-love."

Kinsey throws her arm around Amiria's shoulder pulling her in close. Tracing Amiria's cheek down to her jawline she whispers in a low voice, "He's been madly in love with you for years." Her fingers stop at Amiria's chin cupping it. "His precious, little—" Kinsey brings her lips close to Amiria's ear. "—bird."

Curling her fingers into the shape of a paw, Amiria strikes the heel of her hand into Kinsey's chest, sending her backward off the bench. As if she wasn't suddenly accosted, Kinsey rolls perfectly like a wheel into a kneeling stance facing Amiria with a wide-eyed grin.

Panting with the spike in heart rate, Amiria leaps up from the bench keeping her eyes trained on the unsettling girl that rises to meet her.

"Aw now don't be like that." Kinsey pouts, her voice eerily sweet. "Aren't we chatting like friends?"

"No." Amiria points accusatively, "No, we're not."

"Oh." Kinsey prowls with silent footfalls around the bench, "But why not?"

Amiria takes guarded steps back, "What do you want from me, Kinsey?"

With the bench no longer between them, Kinsey's sharp smile flickers. Then with a bat of her eyes, her lips soften. Her voice turns childlike. "I just want to talk, sister to sister."

Words wavering, Amiria takes tentative paces backward shaking her head, "What? No."

"Oh, come on, Amiria." Kinsey hops forward playfully causing Amiria to stagger several strides back. "Let's spend—" Her eyes narrow into spears that nearly miss Amiria's head, puncturing the object behind her. "Oh."

"And you wonder why no one wants to be around you," Calix speaks over Amiria's shoulder.

Kinsey's top lip curls in response. "Why are you *still* stalking her?"

"We have plans today, this is our meeting spot." He touches the tips of his fingers to Amiria's arm. "Come on, let's go."

With her eyes still fixated on the girl and her constantly changing facade, Amiria reaches back, finding the security of Calix's hand. "Yes, *please*. Let's go." She whips around tucking herself in close to his body, "*Now.*"

As if evading a predator, Calix hugs Amiria close to his side and walks backward removing them both from Kinsey's range. His feet shuffle onto the cut stone walkway surrounding the courtyard.

"Never turn your back on a wild animal," he mutters under his breath, still watching Kinsey stand statuesque with her deadpan eyes locked on him, a devious smile creeping onto her face.

Thirty

After escorting Eve back to Bernard, Stirling crashes next to Ignis in the pile of straw tucked away in the old stables. His new cotton attire folded neatly on a crate, not wanting to ruin them already by sleeping in it.

"*So?*" Ignis initiates.

"So what?" Stirling replies with closed eyes and intertwined fingers resting on his chest.

"*So, how did your date go?*" Ignis probes.

"It wasn't a date. Eve is a friend and I needed help with shopping."

"*Yeah, like how you and Amiria were just friends?*"

Stirling's eyes pop open. Ignoring the pain in his sides he twists to look up at Ignis, "It wasn't—we weren't like that."

Ignis moves his head imitating an eye roll, "*Sure.*"

"Shut up, Ignis," Stirling mumbles.

There's the knot forming in Stirling's chest again. A sensation that has become exclusive to when he thinks of Amiria. It is as if there is an empty hole inside his ribcage.

A sinkhole pulling and tearing his heart in two. As if he has lost part of himself somewhere along the way.

Stirling drags his hands down his face in frustration, "I sometimes forget it's been almost two months since we've last seen her. I keep thinking she's going to walk through the stable entrance any minute now and tease me about my mistakes during the races like how I missed the target. Then I remember she's on the other side of the world. I guess I'm just wishing that I'm going to see her again. I keep hoping one day I'm going to hear someone shout *baker boy*. Then I will turn around and she'll be standing there. But with each passing day, it becomes more apparent that it will only ever be a dream."

"Do you know what I would do if I was Amiria?"

"What?"

"Kick my feet up and enjoy that sweet castle life now that I don't have to worry about your butt hiding in a cave. Maybe find myself a nobleman, what was that one's name, Calix? Yeah, Calix." Ignis answers bluntly.

Stirling crosses his arms, pouting, "I really need to find someone else to talk to."

"You're expressing your worries to a dragon. This is all on you." Ignis jokes blowing warm air down on Stirling sending his curls dancing.

He fakes a laugh, his mind detaching as he thinks of what Ignis had said. It is true. Amiria and he were never a couple. They were close friends and she chose to stay in Wyverna. There is nothing stopping her from forming a relationship with someone.

Isn't that what he wanted? Isn't that why he left her behind instead of forcing her to come with him? So she can successfully live her life without him holding her back?

So why in the end, does it still hurt so much?

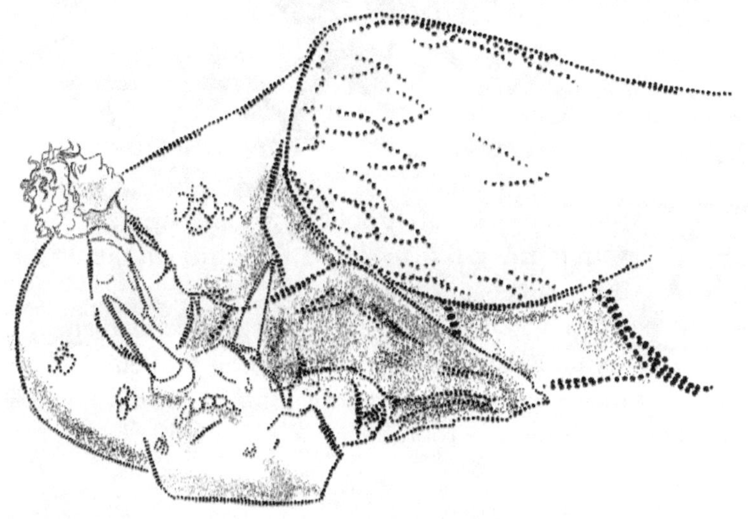

Thirty-One

Worn-out shoes barely holding on and bare feet with more scab than skin, march through the dusty streets in a single file line.

Toes drag through the dirt barely lifted by their owners. They periodically stagger and stumble as their person with bounded hands is yanked off balance by a scratchy rope displayed around their neck tethering the line together.

The blood drained from their sunken faces coats the ropes sawing away at their wrists.

The city of Lumierna watches in eerie silence. Hundreds of minds watching, but not a thought to be said aloud. The only sound comes from the clinking of the guard's armor. The townspeople watch the dragging feet, refusing to make eye contact as their neighbors, friends, and family march past them.

Clyde, sitting on horseback and flanked by two guards Robert and William, barks orders for the bound souls to pick up speed. The line remains at its current pace, physically unable to maneuver quicker. Their blistered toes are already stabbing at the heels of the person in front of them.

Amiria doesn't know why she agreed to come. She sits beside Calix on a set of raised seating to separate the classes while they gather to watch the public hanging in the town square.

A new set of gallows now with the capacity to hang up to six people at the same time has been erected to accommodate the surplus of sentences. The myth about Stirling and his dragon, how he decided living a life on his own accord even if it's short, was more important than living a long-dictated life, had spread across the kingdom like a plague.

Citizens following in Stirling's path have been shipped into Lumierna in overflowing carts. People only trying to fulfill dreams and aspirations. Discovering untapped talents lying dormant, snuffed out before they got a chance to breathe. Individuals discover it's better to try flying and fall than to never leave the nest.

For that short brief moment. You had free will.

They make Stirling out as a martyr. He did the impossible. He rose up to the clouds. He touched the forbidden sky before he was shot down by those who wish to keep everyone grounded.

Would they still look up at him if they knew the truth? If they knew he did it solely for himself? If they knew he escaped alive and is out there living free? Or is it, Stirling is only an excuse for everyone to act upon desires they already planned on?

She doesn't want to watch this. Her eyes leave the marching souls whose faces remain uncovered. Everyone here will be able to watch the light die in the eyes of those who tried to guide their own path. She scans the crowd so tightly packed in the square their faces are nothing more than a blur of tan and beige. Cobblestones forming a decorated road of the square leading out into the streets around it.

She watches the two young guards flanking a version of Clyde she doesn't recognize. The pair seem vaguely familiar to her, but she can't place it. She watches as the taller dark haired one walks close enough to brush his fingers against the other guards. The auburn-haired guard's fingers reflectively twitch as if to intertwine but then immediately curl into his palm. His dark green eyes cast up to her as if he could feel her watching. Amiria turns her head, pretending she didn't notice.

She continues her visual sweep to the men and women sitting with her. Their facial expressions muddied in a variety of emotions from bored and disconnected to uncomfortable and disturbed. Mixed in with the clean faces is Kinsey. Amiria snaps forward, locking her sights back on the gallows. She is now in an internal argument with herself, what is more unsettling? Witnessing these innocent people being hung or Kinsey's tilted head and a slight smile as if she is watching a maypole celebration.

A shiver runs down Amiria's spine.

A woman's chin is forced up by the rope around her neck. The person ascending the stairs before her tries to suppress a choking sound as the rope pulls back on his own throat. Their feet fall soundlessly as they carry themselves up the steps of the gallows.

The guards line them up. The six nooses hanging tauntingly in front of them, the rope framing their faces like a portrait. They clamp their jaws and hold their chins up as the guards remove the tether around their necks. They are unvoiced, but their act is thunderous.

A muffled sob escapes from somewhere in the crowd.

Tears clean tracks on the woman's face as the executioner stands behind her. She lifts her chin higher allowing him to tighten the noose around her neck.

Why are any of us here? Amiria wonders. *What do we gain?*

She touches her own neck thinking about what it must be like to be on that stage. To feel that rope burning against the thin tender skin of your neck. Knowing these are your last breaths, your last thoughts, the last time to look up and feel the warmth of the sun on your face. Would she stand strong for her peers, or would she break down while she counts the seconds until the floor beneath her drops? She shudders at the throbbing pulse beneath her fingertips.

Calix places a comforting hand on her knee. Setting her hand over his she gives it a squeeze. Keeping her breath steady she closes her eyes as the executioner takes hold of the lever. Her face flinches at the clunking sound of the dropping floorboards.

Death has never bothered her. Not until she saw the man get run through with a broadsword in the street. Murdered over the crime of learning how to act. It has poisoned her. The image of his begging eyes for her to help stains the back of her eyelids, but all she had done was run away.

Her stomach churns. "I need to take a walk," Amiria tells Calix, releasing the tight grip on his hand, still refusing to look at the bodies being pulled down as the next in line wait at the bottom of the steps.

"Do you want me to come with you?" he offers.

"No, no. I just need a moment to myself," she says, touching his shoulder, her eyes slip back to Kinsey. She stares at Amiria with the same crooked smile and flat eyes. Disgruntled, Amiria hides it behind a fake cough.

"Okay. I'll see you back at the castle for lunch?" he asks.

"Uh Yeah, yes, I'll be back by then." Amiria quickly excuses herself from the stands as the next group is forced up the stage.

Giles stands in the back of the crowd. He shuts his eyes, breathing heavily through his nostrils. The sight of the first group already burned into the back of his mind. The image, a scar like the tattoo on his arm, permanently altering him for the rest of his life.

The way they seemed to float above the crowd as they stood high on the stage with the noose around their necks. They held strong until they vanished from his sight and vanished from existence. Their support ripped away from them.

He can feel a shift in the crowds dynamic. He opens his eyes. The movement is minuscule with their shoulders pulled back, everyone lowering their chins to their collarbones, their eyes staring at the person in front of them's back.

They are bowing.

Amiria didn't wear anything belonging to the Calvary, not even a weapon on her hip. Nothing but her mauve cotehardie and tights with a gold and lilac ribbon tied in her hair. The citizens recognized her undoubtedly, her face amongst the list of regulars in the market. Even as condensed as they are, the people still find ways to part for her. Stepping back like dozens of opening doors.

She actually misses when she wears her hood up and she has to push her way through just like anyone else.

A face catches the corner of her eye. Her eyes dart locking in on a man who has begun disappearing into the thicket of bodies. It's her father, this she knows for sure. He is out of his regular Cavalry uniform and is wearing a simple tunic. If it wasn't for his well-groomed hair he wouldn't look any different than the folk around him. No one recognizes him as they do Amiria and they don't part for him as he slowly picks his way through the crowd.

Picking up her speed she follows her father through the packed streets. Losing full sight of him, she tracks the glimpses through the gaps in the flood of flesh and blood, like the enemy's mass popping in and out of view in the rough sea.

They've turned twice and traveled several blocks. The crowd has thinned out, evaporating into small clusters. Slowing her steps she hangs back to stay undetected. When the distance between them begins to close she hangs back clinging to the shops to inspect the product.

Only a few blocks away from the bakery, she follows the man who has casted a shadow over her life.

Where is he going? She ponders.

He stops.

Amiria halts in her tracks. Panicked, she leaps behind a grocer's stand. The grocer cocks his head as she peeks around a crate of potatoes.

Her father runs his hands through his hair smoothing it back and straightens his tunic. With a wild grin, he steps inside a shop.

Ignoring the bystanders' nervous glances, Amiria sneaks up to the side of the window pressing her back against the wall. Her thin stature is barely visible as she peeks around the edge of the window frame.

There he is. Her father, the Field Marshal of the Winged Cavalry, is standing in the middle of a spinster' home with his arms wrapped around a woman with long dark hair. She pulls back from their embrace. Her face is in full view of Amiria.

Amiria's heart drops. She has met this woman before. She held the door for her the first time she had visited Giles three years ago. The memory is still so vivid because of the way the woman behaved. The way she looked at her was as if she was afraid of her and not because she was in the Calvary.

With her heart thumping, she glances at the nosey onlookers. She can recognize most of their faces from the countless times she strolled these streets.

"No one is in trouble, go away," she hisses, waving them off.

They nod with earned respect and carry on with their own personal business.

She peeks back around the window frame. Immediately she regrets her decision. With her face on fire, she practically trips over her own feet as she walks quickly away from the spinsters' home.

Her father was kissing her. His lips were interlocked with a spinster.

A marine layer hangs heavy over the Winged Cavalry's base the next morning. Field Marshal Rey whistles a low tune as he walks up the steady hill to his office. Still whistling he pauses between two waist-high wooden posts. He opens the door to the lanterns mounted on top and carefully snuffs out the flame.

He takes several more paces up the path to his office door and stops. His whistle cut off mid-tune. His senses heightened, listening to his surroundings as his eyes lock on the office door already ajar.

He holds his scabbard with his left hand and takes hold of the gold handle of his arming sword, a one-handed double-edge straight blade.

Pulling the blade halfway out of the hilt he prepares himself for an ambush. Using his toe he taps open the door stealthily stepping through the threshold.

His eyes, slowly adjusting to the light, scan the room for threats.

"AMIRIA!" He shouts surprised to see her, his eyes still darting back and forth unsure if she is alone.

She stands with her arms crossed behind her back unmoving. She watches as the rising sun breaks through the low clouds lighting the training fields below. The next classes of riders are training for graduation, warming up with sprints across the field. Some veteran riders amongst them are preparing for their busy day with a workout.

Her father secures his sword back in the hilt with a significant *click*, "Amiria, what in the world are you doing in my office." His voice is harsh and demanding.

She doesn't turn around, "The spinster you visited yesterday, who is she?"

"I don't know what you are talking about?" His words are steady and firm.

Amiria spins around, "Don't lie to me!" Her face is as pained as the quiver in her voice, "I'm obviously aware of where you were. I saw you with a spinster, and if you need a reference to jog your memory. She looks a lot like that picture on your shelf." She stabs her finger in the direction of the charcoal sketch.

She closes the gap between her and her father by a few steps, "So tell me, Father—Who. Is. She."

They lock eyes, two predators squaring off, their lungs the only thing moving in their static state.

Her father sighs, breaking eye contact first. "Sit."

Amiria doesn't budge.

"I SAID SIT!" he orders, pointing at his chair directly in front of her.

Amiria clamps her mouth shut. With exaggerated movements, she pulls the chair back and sits with her legs crossed.

Breathing through flared nostrils he sits across from her.

Amiria immediately picks up from where she had left off by hounding him with questions, "So? Who is she? Some mistress? Did you sneak off to see her when mother was alive too? Or is she a new fling? How long did you commit adultery?"

"Amiria stop. Stop. Stop talking." He says pinching the brim of his nose and struggling to remain calm despite the vein popping from his temple. "You're jumping to conclusions when you know absolutely nothing."

"I know nothing because you've told me nothing." She throws her hands exasperated, "Tell me, Father, who *is* she?" Amiria leans forward, her eyes never deviating from his.

"That woman is your mother," he says locking her dead in the eyes.

"…what?" Amiria says her heart plummeting as if the floors of the gallows dropped beneath her.

"That is what you wanted to know, is it not?" he says, unblinking.

"What do you mean?" Amiria falters, searching for her bearings. She has lost track of her argument. Her eyes search the room.

Her father sighs as if she has soiled his morning, "The woman who raised you isn't your birth mother. Corliss was my best friend from childhood until the day she was stolen from us. But that was it, we were only best friends. I fell in love with a spinster named Arietta. We kept our relationship a secret from everyone except Corliss. The next in line field marshal can not be having a romantic relationship with someone in the lower class."

With each word spoken by her father, Amiria sinks deeper into her chair.

"Then we discovered we had conceived a child out of wedlock. For everyone's sake including *yours*," he pauses letting the weight drop into Amiria's lap. "Corliss offered to marry me as a way to protect *us* and she raised you as her own. She told me nothing would make her happier than to help me."

He sits back in his chair remembering his old friend, "She always wanted a family, but she couldn't find herself attracted to men. This was her way to finally be a mother. She loved you as if you were her own."

Amiria stares, her mind wiped of all cognitive thought. How does one comprehend the news, your mother is not your mother? She has gone fourteen years without a mother and now the fact she has one alive whom she never knew is being thrown upon her.

Her birth mother is a spinster? A commoner he sneaks out to visit?

Rage begins to boil beneath her skin. He lectures her about whom she needs to marry and how to maintain her status. He is a fraud. Her parents are not the field marshal and captain. Its field marshal and his lower-class love affair.

Amiria leaps up from the chair causing it to crash to the ground behind her, "You've been smitten with a peasant woman, but you have the audacity to give my hand away to the first nobleman who offers!"

"Do not raise your voice at me! Fix that chair and sit back down. If we are to further discuss this, it will be under civilized terms," he demands.

Her mind breaking, Amiria cries out, "NO! We're past that father! You've lied to me my entire life!" She hugs herself, her voice lowering to a whine. "If you can casually lie to me about who my mother is, what else have you lied to me about!"

"You are being ridiculous. Compose yourself now. You are my daughter, the next field marshal," he instructs, rising to his feet.

"Compose myself! I just found out that who I am is a lie! I will not compose myself!" She throws her arms into the air.

Her father rumbles, "Lower your voice or people will hear."

"LET THEM! Let them know! Let them know the truth! Let them know the hypocrite you are!" she screams pointing her finger at him.

"You ungrateful child. Every choice I've made was for your benefit. I saved—"His voice rising, "I preserved your reputation from constructing this lie. I'm laying down a successful path for your future."

"My reputation? This isn't about my reputation! This is about yours! If this wasn't about you then you would have married her before I was conceived and still made sure I was assigned to the Calvary. I don't need a special title. I know I'm good at what I do no matter who my mother is, so now I know you've ruined both our lives because I loved someone, but I had to tell them, no, to protect your dignity!" Amiria bites her tongue. She had said her internal thoughts out loud.

She lets a small breath of relief out as her father passes over the last part of what she said, "This doesn't change anything. You are still scheduled to marry Calix when you return from your deployment, and I will see to it."

He doesn't see it, or worse, he does but doesn't care. Her body sags defeated; arguing is useless. She hands her head. "I'm done."

"What do you mean, done?" he says, turning in place as his eyes follow her walking past him.

She pivots halfway to face him, her eyes lowered. "With you."

"Amiria?" he says.

She bows appropriately. "I will see you at the assembly, Field Marshal Rey."

"Amiria!" he calls out as she excuses herself out the office door. "AMIRIA REY!" he shouts through the closed door.

Struggling to maintain her composure she storms down the path away from his office ignoring his calls. Growing purple in the face she releases her anger by driving the heel of her boot into the wooden post uprooting it from the ground. Tipping over, the glass lantern cracks as it hits the ground.

She doesn't look back. With hands balled into fists, she stomps down the hill, a group of riders on their way to training jump to the sides of the path splitting their pack for Amiria to pass through.

Thirty-Two

In the dead of night, three tip-toeing girls stifle their giggles as they peek over each other into the dilapidated stables. Their heads layered like a totem pole, one a top of the other.

From the entrance, they can see directly into Stirling's stall.

"Look, there he is," one says in a hushed tone.

"He's so cute!"

"You don't see any other professionals having such a close relationship with their dragons like he does. It's like they're brothers."

"He's no Quilan though, that man made racing an art form."

Wearing his old tunic as a nightshirt, Stirling lies nestled with his head propped up on Ignis' curled neck, his long legs stretching up and over the scaly front leg. Bundled in his blankets a soft snore can be heard.

With an uneasy feeling of being watched, Stirling stirs awake. His vision is fuzzy as his exhausted eyes crack open. He can hear the sounds of laughter running off into the night.

Pulling the blanket over his head Stirling hides himself. Longing for a day of solidarity.

"Okay, I think I understand the rules of the game," Stirling says to Ignis as they prepare themselves in position above the stadium,

"I hope you do because it's about to start," Ignis replies looking down at the rowdy crown.

The eleven advanced racers are spread evenly across a catwalk designed to hold the weight of a dragon that encircles the stadium.

"Yeah, don't get hit by the balls filled with colored chalk. Easy." Stirling bounces with excitement ignoring his tender ribs, *"This is going to be so much fun."*

A referee steps out into the middle of the arena where Stirling stood on his first day almost a month ago. Now they are rounding to the last few matches of the Skylit Endeavor.

The third place he had received in the agility course had stunted his advancements holding him steady at the advanced level. To move up he needed to be undefeated, proving to the judges he is prepared and deserves to be in a higher rank. Even if he won the rest of the matches he will still not be bumped up to the elite level until he proves himself next year.

Sitting at the bottom of the stands Eve and Bernard look up at Ignis and Stirling ready to go.

"This is my favorite game!" Eve announces, filled with static from the energized crowd.

She leans forward as the referee raises the horn to his lips. Her eyes dart to the ballistas, large crossbows as long

as a man is tall, mounted sporadically around the stadium
from up in the catwalk to down in the arena.

The artillerymen place their first colored chalk ball the
size of a head into the ballista. Using a winch, they crank
it back preparing to fire. Each ball is crafted from paper
derived from pressed linen. It is set and dried in a
spherical shape and filled with colored chalk then glued
shut. Resulting in a ball that can be easily launched but
will explode on impact causing minimal harm.

The horn blares. Dragons of all shapes and colors leap
from their posts. The clunking and sliding of the ballistas
can be heard as they launch their first balls in a
randomized sequence.

Ignis twists and somersaults, careening through the air
and dodging the array of projectiles that fall into the
crowd dowsing them in blues, yellows, reds, and purples.

"WOOO!!!" Stirling cheers out in glee.

He ducks as a ball whizzes past his head striking a
racer flying past him in the opposite direction. A green
cloud erupts into the air. The crowd goes ballistic as the
wind carries the chalk to rain down on them from the
first strikeout.

Yellow and pink burst to life like April tulips as they
simultaneously strike another racer. Ignis banks hard
dodging another ball. Each plume of color means another
competitor down. Each plume of color means fewer
competitors to aim at and use as a shield.

Three people are already down for the count, leaving
seven not including Stirling. Ignis barrel rolls missing a
slew of several projectiles aimed directly at them. Sweat
wets his curls and beneath his dampened tunic his bruised
body aches.

Ignis flies up and over two chalk balls that were aimed
to side-swipe them on both sides. Stirling's muscles strain
to hold his balance as Ignis rodeos through the air.

"Why is Stirling having to dodge more than one at a time, but no one else does?" Eve points out.

Bernard squints at the dragons tumbling above them. Eve is correct in her analysis. It appears they are targeting Stirling over the other competitors. He watches attentively as Ignis flies close to another racer. A ball is launched from a bastilla above them in the stands aiming directly for them. Waiting till the last moment Ignis dives, the ball missing its intended target and explodes on the racer behind them in a sunburst of color

"Looks like our boy caught onto that, too," Bernard shares.

"I wish I could single out their friends and see how they like it." Eve pouts, crossing her arms.

"It'll be fine. He's a stubborn kid. He won't give up easily," Bernard tells her.

"*Stay below that yellow dragon,*" Stirling instructs.

"*Got it,*" Ignis answers, flying into position.

"*They want to play like this, then we will play.*" Stirling smirks.

The racer on the yellow draco observes Stirling hovering below him.

"*What is he doing?*" the racer ponders, taking a sharp turn to create distance.

Ignis follows as if they are magnetized.

"GET AWAY!" he chides. Pulling on his reins, he zigzags his dragon in a desperate attempt to shake Stirling off.

With all his efforts the racer accomplishes only two things, becoming frustrated and distracted. Stirling braces himself preparing to keep himself from slamming forward as Ignis tilts his body vertically. Catching the wind, they stop in place as if they hit an invisible wall.

"Finally." The racer grumbles.

Green and orange suddenly clouds his vision as the balls strike his dragon's belly one after the other. Enraged, the racer spits out the chalk in his mouth cursing Stirling's name.

There isn't time for Stirling and Ignis to celebrate the fact another racer is out of the game as several more projectiles are sent out with them as their designated target. Ignis weaves around the remaining racers like a buzzing house fly.

The racers catch onto Stirling's plan and spread out across the playing field. He won't be able to hide behind a group and is left to pick and choose one at a time. They have inadvertently revealed their weakness.

Stirling chuckles to himself. This display of knowledge will be their downfall. They have revealed they are more concentrated on Stirling than they are on the chalk balls.

Both Stirling and Ignis keep their priority focused on the ballistas. Ignis pays attention to the field before him and the flight path while Stirling watches their blind spots. Bernard was correct when he told Stirling to keep his ability a secret, but for the wrong reason. Stirling has still ended up continuously being bullied whether they knew he talked to Ignis or not. But them not knowing has become his weapon. Two minds against one, teamwork against solo players.

Their tactics knock out two more racers. Stirling remains on the field with only one other competitor on a lime-colored lung dragon. Its snake-like body weaving and slithering out of the way of the chalk balls being aimed at them.

Both heaving with exhaustion, Ignis spots three balls coming from the front and Stirling turns back in time to see three more sneaking up. They are surrounded as their opponent dodges poorly aimed and spread apart projectiles. Ignis folds in his wings letting his body drop. The balls miss and pass them overhead. Two collide with each other in an explosion of pink and blue.

"*STOP!*" Stirling commands as they plummet.

Ignis's wings shoot out, catching them. Stirling is barely able to stop his chin from hitting Ignis as they stop in midair, his injuries screaming in protest. A ball sails untouched beneath them.

"AHEAD!"

"BEHIND!"

"RIGHT!"

They warn each other, shouting the directions in the order of the impending impact. Stirling grits his teeth as his sore body whiplashes in every direction as Ignis, flips, spins, and dodges the beautifully colored paper cannon balls striving to take their ship down.

"We need to bring the ambush to the other guy," Stirling explains as Ignis spins a tight corkscrew.

Stirling's curls fling to one side as he thanks the harness keeping him fastened to Ignis. Ignis stops abruptly, altering his direction to miss a collision with a purple ball. Stirling falls sideways sending agonizing pain through his ribcage.

He shakes off the dizziness. He needs to keep a grip on which way is up and which way is down.

"I don't think he will fall for it. He's avoided our act so far." Ignis points out.

"We're not going to trick him into it. We're going to force him into it. Circle him, and don't stop until I say so," Stirling instructs.

Aiming himself, Ignis b-lines for the green dragon. With only so much space to fly in the arena, Ignis has no trouble catching up to the last racer. Flying up and over, Ignis begins to spiral around them. The racer viciously yanks on his reins pivoting his dragon in sporadic directions in the hope to dislodge Ignis. This tactic fails the same as the racer before him as Ignis remains in sync.

Changing his game plan, the racer begins to match Ignis. Stirling looks up at the racer who peers down at them as they are held frozen in the center of a scaly tornado. They orbit each other like two suns caught in the other's gravitational pull. They are close enough that Stirling can almost reach up and snag the goggles off the other man.

The lung's long body trails behind them wrapping around Ignis like a ribbon around a pole, making it nearly impossible for the artillery shooters to aim and hit Ignis without also hitting the lung.

Stirling waves his hands catching the racer's attention. The racer glances up at Stirling for a brief moment before turning his attention back to his surroundings. Stirling waves his hands in the air again. The racer's temple pulses under the tension, he refuses to give into Stirling's antics and refrains from looking anywhere but forward.

Stirling shrugs and Ignis quickly secedes from their tangled dance and veers off to the side.

Purple, yellow, red, green, and blue explode one after another as they strike the lung.

"Tried to warn him," Stirling laughs with Ignis.

Rippling from the bottom of the stands to the top in a wave the audience goes ballistic. They leap up with rainbow hands shooting to the sky. The stadium is filled with a roar of overly animated cheers.

"YEAH! TAKE THAT!" Eve hollers pumping her pink and orange fist into the air.

Bernard lets out a long, slow breath. "He did it. I knew he wouldn't let a little foul play stop him."

The sand of the arena has turned into a mosaic of abstract colors. Ignis lands in the middle upturning the rainbowed sand. He raises his head up triumphantly, his orange scales completely clean as the painted lung lands beside them. Stirling slides off Ignis as the third-place racer emerges from the ground entrance.

Catching his toe in the sand pit Stirling trips, he catches himself before falling forward as he awkwardly finds his footing. The world refuses to stop spinning even though the game is over. Stirling stares down at his feet as he waves, unable to raise his head to meet the audience.

Bernard wipes a proud tear from his eye.

"Are you crying?" Eve asks, putting her face in Bernard's personal space.

"No, I've got some of the chalk in my eye," Bernard fibs.

Eve playfully pushes his shoulder then leaps onto her seat. "STIRLING IS UNSTOPPABLE!"

His voice choking on the dust still in the air, Bernard agrees. "Their petty antics aren't going to scare a boy who nearly escaped death to get here."

Standing as a single face amongst thousands, Eve watches in a state of euphoria as Stirling accepts his first-place prize. She hones in on what is now obvious to her, but invisible to the rest of the crowd. Stirling's nervous trembles in his hands, or how he forces his head up to smile at his fans, but his eyes still fall low to the blank wall. He is the bravest person she has ever met. He has developed a fear, a paranoia of the crowds around him, but he gets up every day and faces it head-on. Nothing will stop him from fulfilling his dreams.

The people don't know the struggles he has gone through, and how many walls he had to climb to get here. The nightmares of his past that mark his skin as a constant reminder he shouldn't be here. They see him as an unstoppable superhuman, a demigod that was mistakenly placed in the farming fields instead of the leading household as they did with Sir Quilan. What she loves and what inspires her is the fact he is *only* human. He could be another one of these faces in the stands. He bleeds the same as everyone else.

Her eyes sparkle. *He's amazing.*

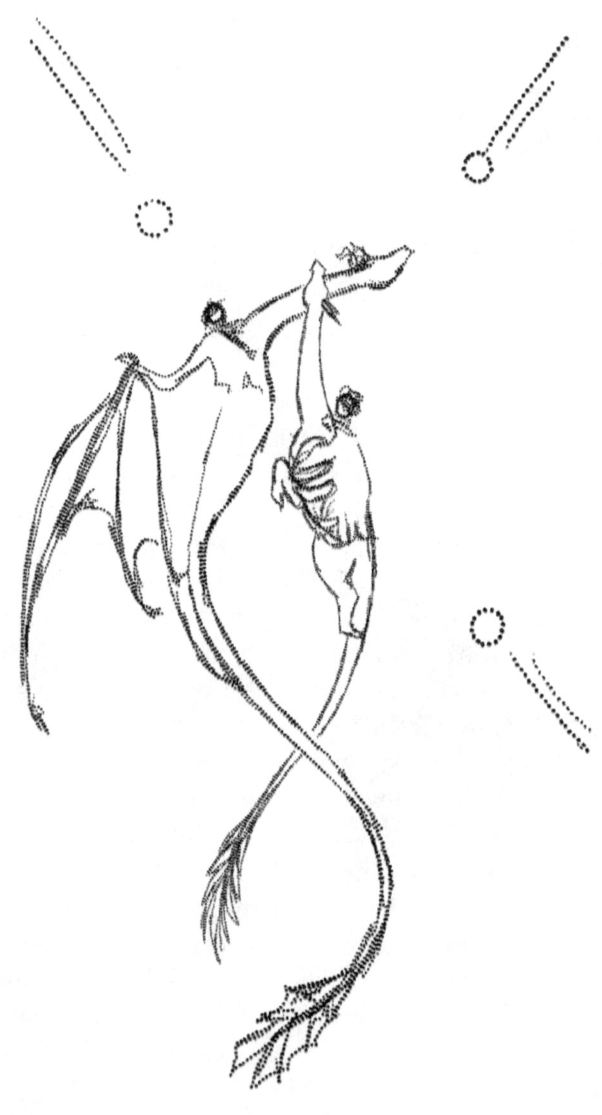

Thirty-Three

The once-packed tavern is on a slippery slope to becoming a desolate wasteland. Each citizen is too afraid to step foot out of the establishments. Afraid of being accused of diverting away from their trade. Afraid for their lives.

Standing shyly by the tavern's stage Giles shifts his weight back and forth on his feet. "Excuse me?" He mumbles as the red-headed woman steps down from the stage.

"Yes?" She asks with a tilt of her head.

Giles bites his lip, his words a sputter, "I really enjoyed your performance. The citole is my favorite instrument. You have such a beautiful melody when you play."

"Thank you!" The woman replies immediately perking up, "I love the citole too. Luckily as a musician, we are given the liberty to choose our instrument. At a young age, I was just drawn to it over the others."

"Are you, uh, hungry or anything? I can treat you to something to eat…or maybe at least a drink and we can sit and talk?" Giles offers.

The woman hums to herself as she thinks it over, "You know what, I'll accept your offer. I am parched." She holds out her hand with a bright smile, "I'm Grace Fitzsinger."

Giles blushes beneath his recently trimmed beard, "Giles Bakere."

Grace's expression brightens as she recognizes him, "Oh! You own the bakery around the block, don't you?"

Here it comes. Giles thinks, his voice turning defensive, "Yes, I do own the bakery."

"Oh good, I'm just making sure my memory isn't failing me. So, I have seen you around. I live in the opposite direction, so I tend to go to the bakery over there." She answers making small talk as they sit at the table closest to them.

Giles releases his breath and raises two fingers signaling his order to the maid.

"What's it like being a baker?" Her voice is a song of its own.

"Probably nowhere near as interesting as being a musician," Giles says humbly.

Grace shakes her head, "I don't think so."

"Why is that?"

"From my point of view, it seems fascinating. All I know are notes, but if I stop playing life will go on. Think about it, if you stop baking it will affect your entire neighborhood. So many families depend on you."

"They can't be that dependent, people won't die of starvation if they no longer have bread," Giles states suddenly unsure.

"Yes and no, bread is filling." She leans in. "Here's an observation. How often do you eat some sort of bread product?"

"Well, I'm a baker, so every meal."

"You're not alone." She says pointing her index finger as if it helps put her statement into perspective, "It's affordable and accessible to us common folk. It's essential to our diet."

"Huh." Giles says scratching his beard, "I guess you have a strong point." The tavern maiden sets two tankards down in front of him and Grace. "Thank you." He tells her. Taking a sip of the brewed liquid sitting level with the brim, he asks Grace, "Do you have a family?"

"Two daughters and a son. The youngest just left the nest. My daughters are wonderful lute players, and my son took over his father's position as the neighborhood's bard after his passing." Grace says in a proud tone.

"Sorry to hear about your husband." Giles's mind brings up old memories of Jannell.

"No need to be sorry, people get sick. It's a sad fact of life. But no need to dwell on it, it had to be, three, almost four years now. Time sure flies." She says with her eyes on the cobweb-filled rafters. She returns back to Giles, "How about you? Any little ones? A Mrs back home?"

"N-no, not anymore…both are gone… I run the bakery alone now." Giles says his words truthful but insinuating half a lie.

Grace is struck hard by the news. "Oh, now I am the one who is sorry." She reaches over, placing her hand on his. "I can't imagine the devastation I would feel losing one of my children." Giles stares down at her hand not wanting to make eye contact as liquid forms in the corners of his eyes. "What was your child like?" she says, curling her fingers around his.

A quivering smile peeks into the corner of Giles' mouth, "He was a goofy kid with this wild curly hair. It was impossible to tame, both the hair and him." Giles chokes out a laugh, "He looked just like his mother, he was a dreamer like her too."

Giles pulls his hand back with a fake cough. Forcing his emotions back down, he taps his tankard on the table as a personal distraction. "Despite his head always in the clouds, he was a good kid." He raises his drink to his lips taking a long-deserved swig.

"Dreamers are the best kinds of people." She tells him her porcelain face glowing.

"Why do you say that?" He asks, setting his drink back down.

"Because they found the one true escape. No one can stop you from dreaming." Her emerald green eyes skip back and forth at Giles' brown ones.

Giles's heart drums in his chest as he watches her red hair fall loose from its tie and frame her face. She tilts her head down and looks up at him with shimmering eyes.

The candles spend half their life span listening to Giles and Grace talk about what they love and what they dislike. Learning what is important and what is trivial. He learns her daughters are sixteen and eighteen years, and her son being a little over a year older than Stirling. Both of her parents were musicians. She loves her job and doesn't wish to do anything else. What she does wish is to have more essential qualities to be self-sufficient around the home.

Giles admits to Grace how Jannell always dreamed of having a large family but was only blessed to be with child once. She was a wonderful mother who provided Stirling with all the love a child needed growing up. Then with tears in his eyes to tells how he wishes he had told Stirling that he loved him while he was still around.

She comforts him by retaking his hand and explaining to him that it is only something one can know in hindsight. As a parent, you're only doing what you believe is the best to guide your children in life.

Thirty-Four

"Mr. Bakere? Mr. Bakere!" Amiria's voice frantic voice travels up the staircase.

Giles rolls over in bed. "Huh? What?" he says drowsily. He can hear the light footsteps of an athletic girl tapping up the staircase.

"Mr. Bakere?"

Groggy, he sits up in bed. After talking with Grace until the tavern closed he walked her home in the opposite direction of his own to keep his mind at ease that she would make it home safely. He hasn't slept in this late since he was a child.

What time is it?

"Mr. Bakere?" Her voice is now concerned. She is on the other side of the door.

She taps her knuckles on the old wood, "Mr. Bakere?"

"I'm here. I'm here," he tells her. "I had a late night. Give me a moment to get dressed."

Waiting patiently, Amiria sits at the dining table resting her clasped hands on the wood stained from years of

266

meals spilt by a growing boy. Her gaze slips towards the window longingly, her breath breaks into uneven steps as she sighs. She is wearing her usual mauve cotehardie, but her hair falls in dark waves, flowing down the front of her shoulders and her back.

She snaps back to attention as Giles exits his room, he stops short. At first, her clasped hands appear composed and professional, now he sees their color fading to white. Her face shows years of practice holding it together, but deep beneath her dark irises, there is the now apparent strain. A girl who was never allowed to let her emotions be her own is starting to slip. The sight of her is unnerving and unstable like the lake's ice spider webbing beneath your feet.

Her eyes fidget, unable to settle on a single object, constantly looking back out the window. "I don't think I can go through with it. I can't marry Calix," she blurts.

"Good morning to you, too." Giles rubs the sleep from his eyes.

"Mr. Bakere!" Her eyes plead with desperation. "I don't know what to do." She flattens her hands on the table.

Giles scratches his newly trimmed beard. "I thought you were starting to like the guy, what changed?"

Amiria dips her head concealing her face with her hair. "It's not because of him. Well, maybe it's a little because of him or—" Biting her lip before she can say more, she folds her arms on the table and buries her face. Talking into the crook of her arm she reveals. "I found out I have a birth mother who is still alive. She's the spinster a few blocks from here."

"Oh." Giles frowns halfway to understanding what the young girl is insinuating. He sits down across from her, "Is *that* the reason you can't marry this Calix guy?"

"Nooo. It's not *that*." Amiria rolls her head to peek up at him from her arms. "It's, well, it's that my father is still with her secretly. He gets to be with someone he loves. It's not fair."

"Can you not see yourself in love with Calix?" Giles questions.

"I don't know, maybe one day, but that's not the point. He had a choice on whom he fell in love with. I had to suppress—let go on the idea…" Amiria trails off.

"It sounds to me like you and your father have a lot in common," Giles suggests smiling down at her.

Amiria sits up straight, "We are nothing alike!"

"I don't know." Giles teases and brings into light, "What I heard was Stirling is the one you want to be with."

Amiria scoffs, "I said no such thing."

"Sure." Giles smirks, "Are you hungry? I've got pretzels? Or I was going to heat up some oats, maybe throw a little cinnamon in it."

"The oats sound good." Amiria pushes her hair back over her shoulders.

She watches in silence as Giles gets up from the table and steps over to the small pit of coals only big enough to fit a single pot.

Her fingernail traces down the length of the table's wood grain, it stops at a dark knot and circles it. The three of them, Team Perimo, will deploy before the break of dawn tomorrow. She and Calix will travel to another kingdom together, and when they return. Her eyes fall back to Stirling's old bed and his footprints warn into the flooring. Her forehead drops to the table with an audible *thump*. Her hair blankets around her.

He is *everywhere*. His shadow still walks this room and these city streets. She hasn't been able to return to the forest, the image of him just out of view through the trees. His memory haunts her mind, his smile fills her dreams, and his voice speaks her thoughts.

She imagines him sitting across the table from her. He would tell her some pointless story and she wouldn't be able to refrain herself from smiling as he laughs at his own jokes. Giles would shake his head at their childish banter and join them for a simple breakfast before they begin their day.

She would give up everything. She's learned her seat as the next field marshal means nothing to her. She would launch catapults at her castle life. Tear it all down until only rubble is left. She would give it all up to live in a quaint and cozy home filled with the sound of Stirling's laughter. Her eyes slide shut and Calix is there to greet her. His dimpled smile as they mock Cavalry brass at the banquet. The security he granted her when she encountered his sister in the courtyard.

Would I give it all up if he asked me again?

Giles sets a wooden bowl in front of Amiria, "Here you go." Her eyes are slow to open as he sits back down across from her, "You look deep in thought."

"Yeah." She mumbles barely opening her mouth.

"Do you want to tell me?" He watches her stir the oats, her face revealing a state of uncertainty. A traveler stuck at a fork in the road with no inclination of which path to take.

The cooling oats move about her bowl guided by her spoon. She will be leaving in the morning to do the King's bidding. A platoon of trained killers on a hunt for her best friend, everyone including her fiancé itching to put a blade through his heart. Then what? Then would King Dietrich lay rest to this madness when Stirling's body is laid at his feet?

No, he won't, because it's too late.

"I hate Stirling."

"No, you don't."

"I do." She huffs.

Sighing Giles runs his fingers through his hair pushing it back, "Amiria." She meets his eye. "Have you spoken to this woman, your mother yet?"

"No. I don't wa—"

Raising his hand to stop, "Talk to her. You don't know what the future entails, or what will happen after tomorrow. Before you make any decision at least find out what made your father and her choose what they did."

She drops her gaze back to her bowl of oats, "I'm scared Mr. Bakere."

"Of what?"

Irises so dark they appear pupilless, rise to the window, skate across the room, and land back on Giles, "I don't know."

The sting in her eyes, the itch in her throat, all the familiar symptoms of oncoming tears. Tears that haven't been able to reach past her eyelashes since she was a child. The tears that she was told Winged Riders don't let fall. Winged Riders don't cry.

She wanted to cry as she hugged Giles goodbye for what could be the last, but her body failed her. After all these years of reprimands and holding it back maybe she finally lost the ability. She will return, and even though Stirling is gone, she had made a promise to check in on Giles' well-being. She will return to protect the only person who felt like a father to her.

Boots stop at the door to the spinsters' home. With her hair tied back with a gold and lavender ribbon, Amiria takes in a deep breath to ease her nerves. Bringing the Winged Rider in her to the surface Amiria raps her knuckles on the door.

"One moment," Arietta calls out, not expecting any visitors.

The joyful woman opens the door humming and pops her head out. Her smile immediately vanishes as she stares at the young rider, even without the Cavalry's emblem the folk in the market know who Amiria is.

"I'm sorry miss, this isn't a shop. It's a personal residence. Is there an issue?" Her voice wavers. It is like looking into a mirror of the past, their faces identical.

"Drop the act. I already know," Amiria says unrelentingly.

Arietta flashes back into a smile and steps back into the house. With a quick movement, she forces the door closed. Amiria kicks out her foot, placing it down as a door jam. The door strikes her solid boot, pinching it in the frame.

Pressing her forearm against the door, Amiria recites the lines. "As a Winged Rider, I have the authority to access any home I suspect has any ulterior motives." She leans in more adamantly. "Now, I have some questions and you're going to open this door and answer them."

"If that's the law," she parodies, slowly opening the door as if it is dragging through the mud, begrudgingly granting permission for Amiria to step inside.

Shuffling backward and away from the door, Arietta lands in the center of the room. Her hands fidget with her surcoat curling the soft fabric around her fingers. She bites her lip searching for something to occupy herself with.

Amiria timidly closes the door behind her. The woman, her mother, begins picking up random items around the home. Restlessly she scoops up spools of wool that already have an organized location into her thin arms and settles them into a new spot. Amiria scans the small room no more than half the size of the bakery with a ladder leading to a loft just big enough to sleep in. A spinning wheel sits off to one side of the room with baskets of unwoven wool beside it.

"Will you put those down?" Amiria crosses her arms.

Arietta jumps, nearly dropping the spools she is carrying. Keeping her head down, she sets the pile down on a small counter in the kitchen area at the back of the room. Motioning to a small stool positioned at a single-person table Arietta offers Amiria a seat. Amiria raises an eyebrow, her focus zoning in on Arietta's shifty expression.

Dismissing the offer, Amiria holds her voice steady. "I'm going to get straight to the point, I want to know why?"

"Why what?" She plays ignorant.

"Why everything?" Amiria expands her arms. "Why did you—why did you choose to give me up? Tell me why you stayed away?"

Arietta hugs herself as she stares at the ground. Watching carefully Amiria waits for a reply, but the woman makes no effort to make eye contact or speak.

"Please, I need to know. Why did you choose to keep your relationship a secret? It is not illegal to marry someone in another class, it's merely frowned upon to reserve bloodlines." Amiria puts up a finger as if to stop Arietta from answering, but her lips remain sealed. "And don't give me the same lie that it was all for my sake, because we all know the field marshal could have ensured my placement in the Calvary."

Amiria pauses, her eyes shaking back and forth, searching, hoping for some explanation. After a long drag of silence, she continues, "My mother, the woman who *actually* wanted to raise me died when I was only five. You could have reached out then, you could have reached out and been my mother while my name stayed *pure.*"

Arietta shifts on the balls of her feet, staring at nothing but the hem of her dress.

"Say Something!" Amiria snaps with clenched fists, making her jump.

"Your father and I love each other." She stops. "Okay?"

"W-we couldn't ruin his reputation, they were already talking. Then—when I got pregnant out of wedlock," she says, stopping again and turning her back to Amiria.

Frustrated, Amiria pushes farther, closing the gap. "I'm still not seeing your point."

"I couldn't face them," she mumbles, barely coherent.

"What? Who?" Amiria says circling her to see her face.

"The townspeople," she says with a broad sweeping motion directed at the window, "My friends and family. I would have been shamed."

"Family?" Amiria raises a lip. "Yeah, you're really family-oriented, you abandoned your own daughter." She takes a disgusted step back. "It's all clear now, you really did cast me aside to save face."

Suddenly full of energy Arietta turns to Amiria defensive, "We weren't only saving ourselves, we were saving you too!"

"I DIDN'T NEED SAVING! I NEEDED A MOTHER!" Amiria cries out hurt, "I didn't need a title! I needed a mother to go to! A mother to hold me! To raise me!"

"BUT I DIDN'T WANT YOU!" She snaps back.

The words sting Amiria as if they've been slapped across her face drawing blood. They stare eye to eye. The room is thick with tension that absorbs the chatter from the townsfolk outside. Amiria swallows, the sound like a rock dropping in a well.

Arietta speaks up again on the verge of tears, "Your father, he wouldn't let you live the life of a spinster. I couldn't, I just couldn't do it. I didn't want to raise a child I knew had a chance of being slaughtered!" Her face turns ashen as the realization hits her. If Amiria stands here alive then– "How much blood is on *your* hands?" Amiria curls in her fingers as Arietta's face warps with revulsion.

Stepping back Amiria's face twists in agony from the wound in her chest. Her father's hands must have more blood than hers, so why is she the only monster in her mother's eyes.

Arietta, realizing the extent of what she had said and done, steps forward with forced sympathy to hide the obvious aversion, "Wait, it's not too late, we can start now…if you want?"

Her features turned down with loury, Amiria shakes her head. "No-No. It's too late for that. I don't need a mother anymore." She crosses her arms trying to hold her breaking heart inside her chest. "I don't need *you*, the field marshal, or this place."

"Then why did you even come here?" Arietta asks in an icy voice.

"I needed to know," Amiria says, thinking it over, "if I am making my own right choices, and I guess I wanted you to acknowledge me. Acknowledge my existence."

Amiria inspects the room around her with a new perspective. The crates overflowing with supplies, more than a single spinster can afford. The fine surcoat and clean appearance. All are mostly funded by a high-ranking official.

This is reality. Her birth mother doesn't regret giving her away, she only regrets being discovered.

She is thankful Giles told her to come here. Glad she met Arietta and now knows the whole truth. This woman is not her mother, never was, and never will be. Her real mother died a hero, saving countless lives. That is the woman she aspires to be. She's received her closure. When she deploys tomorrow there will be no mysteries lingering in her thoughts. She can make her decision based on her own desires now.

A smile cracks, slowly forming across her face. Her voice is an uneasy calm, "I hope you and the field marshal stay together. If you make each other happy then you shouldn't hide it anymore. I'll be going now, I'm sorry to have intruded on your quiet life."

"I'm sorry, I'm sorry, I'm sorry." Arietta begins to string the apologies into a never-ending murmur.

Shrugging her off, Amiria turns for the door, "Do what you do best and forget about me, because who knows. I might die tomorrow." She turns back to Arietta now walking backward, "Thank you for telling me the truth. I wish you well."

"I'm sorry Amiria." Her mother says hollowly.

Her smile only widens. Spinning she faces the door before bumping into it. Pulling the handle her steps are light as she leaves the spinster's home. No number of apologies can mend a torn seam that never existed.

Thirty-Five

Amiria uselessly pulls at the hair stuck to her lips, a wall of wind sending the rest of her hair to slap across her face. She doesn't look behind her as the wyvern's talons crack the tiles. Lit by the setting sun, the golden rooftops of the city reflect in her unfocused eyes. Up here, on top of the castle's roof, Lumierna is beautiful. A sprawling city at the foot of the mountains leads out to endless fields. From here you can forget the misfortune and the genocide inflicted upon the people who call this home.

"Quite the view from here." Calix lowers himself next to her halfway down the slope of the roof.

"Yeah." She pulls in her knees tight and wraps her arms around them.

Leaning back on his hands, Calix closes his eyes letting the distant sounds of the people living below fill the space. He opens his eyes, the striking pale blue softened by the rich orange light, "It's not about the deployment is it?"

Her heart stops at the accusation, but her muscles relax. Calix's voice isn't critical. He's sympathetic. She keeps her eyes on the homes filled with families settling down for the evening. Holding her tongue she will let him speak the words for her, let him answer what he believes it to be so she doesn't have to say the truth.

"You're worried about them, aren't you?"

At this, she turns her head. Her pupils dilate with the unexpected proximity. He had sat up, their shoulders nearly touching. His eyes search hers, hoping to help settle what is eating away at her mind.

"I get it." He breaks the gaze, dropping it to his lap.

"Get what?"

"We're born to protect them, but it is us whom they fear. You're worried about what else will happen to them at the end of this."

"How did you…" The question fades.

Calix picks up a piece of broken tile and throws it from the roof, "Because I worry the same thing."

"Really?" Amiria raises an eyebrow skeptically, "And here I thought you only worried about your hair."

He lets out a single breathy laugh at her quip, "I don't have to worry. It's always perfect." He runs his fingers through his hair brushing the stray locks from his recent flight back into place.

Biting her lip, Amiria reaches over and tousles the dark brown locks. He blows a single puff of air up at the chunk of hair hanging over his eye and smiles, "See still perfect."

Amiria sucks in her lips, struggling to contain her smile as she rolls her eyes, "You're ridiculous."

"Many have called me that." The genuine smile falters and collapses, "No, really though. I do worry about them." He nods his chin at the city. "I worry that this will never stop. Can you answer this, Amiria?"

"What?"

"When did we stop being the heroes and become the monsters?"

Orange light fills the clouds in a fiery storm above Wyverna. A night that changed everyone's life. Everything unraveled by a single boy. "When we turned on them." She whispers.

A tan hand is offered to her palm up, a hand she has seen covered in the blood of invaders from Uviktiland. A deadly hand that she has found security while holding. She takes it, intertwining her fingers with his.

He shifts, their shoulders brushing as he leans in close, sending wafts of chamomile and mint. Amiria freezes, her mind spasming unable to respond. Slender fingers, strong from years of wielding a blade, pinch her chin tipping it up to him. Her heart rate begins to elevate, she doesn't know where to look, but she can see his eyes on her lips. They close resting thick lashes on high cheekbones. She stiffens as his skin brushes hers, but his lips stop short before touching. She strains to breathe, her lungs unable to function as her body is overtaken with a new sensation.

Then she closes the gap, and her lips are on his and her fingers run through his wavy hair.

Winter berries. She thinks. He is winter berries, a sweet relief from its cold surroundings.

Calix pulls back first his hand still cupping her face. The kiss was as short and sweet as it tasted. Her dark eyes find his light ones. She waits for him to speak, to say something, to say *anything* about what had just happened. He doesn't need to. His fingers slide to the back of her head and he presses his lips to her forehead.

She doesn't resist as he lays them back on the tiles. She doesn't argue when he rests her head on his chest. There is no excuse made so she can leave because she doesn't want to. Watching this final sunset over Lumierna with him is exactly what she needed.

Thirty-Six

reathe. Breathe," Stirling repeats to himself. Sitting on the bench he doubles over with a groan, "Public speaking. Why does it have to be public speaking?"

"Hey, you'll be great," Eve comforts, her hand soothingly rubbing his back.

Her hand on his bouncing thigh gives a gentle squeeze as she rubs circles between his shoulder blades. Through the cotton fabric of the jerkin she can feel his muscles twitching as his body shudders from the idea of standing on stage.

All of the elite riders are here in this simple room designed to hold actors backstage or in this case, interviewees. A place where they can talk and prepare without being heard by the audience.

"Just be yourself," she soothes.

"That's the problem. Most of myself is a secret," he whispers to her.

His hands fiddle nervously tapping fingers to his thumb as he reads the other five racers in the room. Each one of the men with their allotted single family member or friend they are allowed to bring backstage with them. Four of them have brought their spouses except… his eyes land on Quilan. The only one who is sitting alone. His arms are crossed and his fair hair falls over his eyes as his tired head lolls forward. His chest rising and falling in a steady pattern. Even with his eyes closed and possibly sleeping, Stirling can see on his face that he is already finished with being here.

Quilan's eyes open halfway as if he can sense Stirling staring. Dark lethargic eyes glide across the room and lock with Stirling's. Spooked, Stirling quickly averts his gaze to the third youngest elite racer named Peyton. He coo's at a swaddled baby in his arms beside his wife. Who strikingly looks exactly like Quilan with long pale hair twisted into an intricate braid. This woman will never worry if her husband will return home each time he takes off. *Is this our last goodbye*, will never cross her mind.

It wasn't Amiria who never returned in the end, it was him. He was the one broke the promise of *See you next week.*

Lowering his eyes to the ground, he brings them back up to Eve who is still rubbing his back. She's humming a sweet melody he has never heard before. He begins to relax, the sound of her song is a drug instantly nullifying his fear.

His mind drifts off wondering what Amiria is doing at this moment. Is she okay? Has she been able to return to focusing on her duty since he has left? Does she think of him as often as he thinks of her? Or has she moved on? They *were* only friends.

"Stirling," a man announces into the room. Eve's cheeks burn as Stirling instinctively grabs her hand. "You're up first."

His face turns gray. "I'm going to be sick."

She squeezes his hand back. "Don't worry, I will be right off to the side watching. Just look at me when it starts to get overwhelming."

With wobbling knees Stirling stands with Eve's assistance, their hands still interlocked. He steals a glance back at Quilan whose gaze remains latched on him through the slitted eyelids. For the first time since he's met Quilan, Stirling holds his inscrutable gaze. There is something alluring about the number one racer. What does the famous Quilan of Leucasia think about when his blue deadpan eyes stalk you across the room?

Chewing on his lip and a whirl in his chest, Stirling turns away from Quilan and follows the coordinator out of the room.

His feet nail to the entrance of the stage just out of view of the audience. *Oh no. Oh no oh no no no no no.* He thinks, suddenly faint as he sees the two chairs positioned in the center of the stage a few steps back from the edge. One chair for the interviewer and one for him.

The audience sits in a half circle around the stage rising in segregated layers. The theater is specifically designed to amplify the voices on the stage using natural acoustics making it possible for whispers to be able to be heard from the top row.

"For our first interview, we have our rookie who climbed the ranks faster than anyone would ever believe. He has put his name in the record books as the third quickest ascent to the elite level and straight into our hearts. We have our new favorite amongst the ladies, Stirling of Patu!" The interviewer with a bronze complexion and slick dark hair announces his introduction from the center of the stage, his hand extending out to where Stirling is set to appear from. His flamboyant attire adds an exaggerated appearance to his simplest movements.

The girls squeal wildly in the crowd at the mention of Stirling's name.

Boom, boom, boom. His heart pounds in his chest. He finds Eve with desperate eyes. Flinching, Stirling is startled at the coordinator who taps him on the shoulder and points out to the stage, Stirling shakes his head. The coordinator nudges him forward. Stirling staggers one step forward, his head still shaking. Refusing to let go, Stirling stretches Eve's arm out as the coordinator pushes him farther out onto the stage.

He is still half a step out of view.

Fed up with Stirling's behavior the coordinator gives him a final shove. Stirling's fingers slip from Eve's as he is forced out into view of the people. They cheer and holler his name. He turns over his shoulder silently calling Eve for help. With a gentle smile, she motions with her hands for him to keep going.

Swallowing the lump in his throat he takes rigid steps forward, his eyes straining to focus only on the chair and nothing beyond it.

"Don't be nervous, come on, sit, sit," the interviewer insists. Stirling treks across the stage with quaking legs. The interviewer holds out his hand, "My name is Heath, It's nice to finally meet you."

Accepting with a clammy hand Stirling gives a clumsy handshake, his eyes never leaving Heath's pointed shoes. The well-groomed man touches Stirling's shoulder and motions with his other hand to the interview chair.

The chair, placed to put him on display like the stocks and pillory in Lumierna's town square, heckles him. Each splinter waiting to pierce him for his treasonous crimes. Numbing hands grip the backrest to steady himself as he commands his stubborn body to move around to the front and take a seat. Barely able to take a breath of relief through his nerves he sees Eve is barely a head tilt away.

"From my understanding, you're not a fan of public speaking?" Heath clarifies.

With a dry mouth, Stirling answers, "No—no, not really." Heel bouncing rapidly he coughs nervously into his shoulder earning a few sympathetic awes from the audience.

"It's okay, Stirling, it gets easier over time," Heath ensures.

Stirling manages a nod. "Tell us a little about yourself. We know all the other racers. We've watched many of them grow up. But we don't know anything about you." Heath sits back in his chair and crosses his legs.

Oh, no. Stirling searches his past for the threads to spin his lie with. His voice quivering, he says, "I'm from the small village just over the pass."

"Yes, we are aware of that. That is the only thing we know about you, but is that where you're *from?* We know the ladies adore your accent and have started to adopt some of it. So, tell us where did you grow up and how did you end up here in the annual games," Heath pressures.

"Um, uh." Stirling tugs at the cuff of his sleeves, his eyes dart to the audience then immediately retracts his line of sight back to Heath. He can't tell them–he won't tell them. Maybe he can just say the direction and it'll be fine enough and they will move on. "Its-ts far w-west. I was raised to be a baker, b-before I obtained my dragon– –I am self-taught—m-my dragon is my best friend, we— um—needed each other, I guess."

"Impressive, you went from beating eggs to beating the competition." Heath turns to the crowd, "Did you hear that ladies, he's handsome and he can cook." Stirling mentally sighs with relief he didn't press how far west.

The girls giggle and cheer in response. Stirling's cheeks turn pink, he stares down at his lap letting his loose curls obstruct his face. In the back of the stage, Eve rolls her eyes.

"Your parents must be very proud of you," Heath points out.

Stirling mumbles a half-truth. "They aren't around anymore."

"I'm sorry to hear that," Heath consoles in his best apologetic voice.

The crowd watches silently.

"It's—its fine," Stirling says, choking up, subconsciously touching his scar through his sleeve. "My mother…she still believed…in me. That I would be more than a baker."

"I'm sure you've surpassed her expectations. She would be very proud of you. Any mother would." Heath plasters on a smile and moves onto the next question. "Stirling, us as spectators have noticed the other competitors treating you unfairly. Is this true? Do you have any comment on the fact?"

Stirling's stomach flips. He shakes his head, refusing to make eye contact. "Next question."

"Hmmm, I see." Heath's eyes narrow for a brief moment before returning to his usual dazzle. "Let's go on to a lighter topic. I know plenty of girls out there are wondering this question. Is there anyone special in your life?"

The girls in the audience wait eagerly on the edges of their seats for Stirling's next words.

"Wha-what do you mean?" Stirling stutters.

"You know." Heath winks at the audience. "Is there a girl in your life? Someone special?"

His heart flutters, his eyes bounce from the audience to Eve, she jumps as their eyes meet. His gaze lingers before slowly returning to Heath who has turned around to see who he was looking at.

Heath smirks. "I see."

Stirling shifts uncomfortably. "Next question."

"I hope this doesn't offend you, but we noticed you have some pretty intense scars on your hands. Are you all right with telling us what happened?" Heath inquires motioning to Stirling's trembling hands in his lap.

Pulling at his sleeves Stirling tugs them down over his hands. "A fire accident, next question."

"Aren't you just a secretive one? Let's move away from your personal life. We've learned you are a jumpy fella, so during your first race you froze at the starting line. Why was that?"

"I was scared," Stirling answers distantly, his eyes staring off at nothing.

"Scared? Scared of what?"

He shrugs. "Just scared."

The audience gives him another unanimous *awe*.

"You're amazing!"

"You're doing great!"

"We love you."

The nameless people in the stands call out their reassurance. Praises are thrown upon the stage hitting the timid boy. They don't see him, they see an image they've conjured up. To each one of them in the stands he is a representation of themselves.

His fingers curl into fists around his thumbs, the urge to tap his fingers gnawing at him. He can't control the rapid bouncing of his left knee. His legs urging him to run as he wonders, what would they be shouting if they knew the truth about his scars.

"Look at that support." Heath grins. "They want to hear from *you*. They want to know, from being scared during your first race to now making it all the way to the elites just in time for the final race, how do you feel? What is it like?"

Stirling steals another glance out at the crowd. His hazel eyes widen in panic, immediately regretting his decision. Everyone is glued to him. Everyone is leaning in, their ears straining to hear the vibrations formed in his throat turn into sound waves for them to interpret into words. They cling to his every syllable as if he is a lifeline and they are lost at sea.

"I—uh—I don't feel like I deserve it." Stirling drops his gaze back to Heath's pointed shoes.

"No? Explain to us why you feel as if you don't deserve it?" Heath repeats louder for the audience. He leans forward resting his elbows on his crossed leg. Steeple fingers touch his lips.

"I got promoted on a recommendation and not because I scored high enough," Stirling expands.

"The person who recommended you believed you are. Despite your injuries you still accomplished placing in the advanced level," Heath points out. Stirling pulls his shoulders in with a hunch. "One last thing before we wrap this up, Stirling." Heath sits back properly in his chair.

Stirling nods wishing he never had to get on the stage in the first place.

Heath waves his hand out across the audience. "You are giving a lot of kids hope for their futures. You beat the odds, you refused to take no for an answer. Do you have any advice for the next generation? Or any words of encouragement?"

Hope? Advice? Encouragement? From him? Does he have the right to give that? What would he say to them if he told them his guilt-riddled truth? To disregard laws. Steal from the innocent. Runaway from home. Abandon your friend. Disregard everyone else for your own selfish desires. How does one sum this up into words?

He can't make eye contact with the crowd, not with a lump of lies stuck in his throat. He wants to throw up. No, *needs* to throw up. He focuses on his knee bouncing rapidly. Finally, he brings his head up, finding Eve with her hands clasped and love in her eyes.

"You all right?" Heath questions. He leans forward again with concern for the pale twitching boy. Stirling nods, unable to open his mouth, afraid that it won't be words coming out. "Take your time, it's not an easy question to answer knowing it can impact a lot of futures."

Not helping.

Stirling inhales slowly through his nose. Focusing on steading his breaths, he tries to come up with something, anything to say so he can finally leave this stage. "Sometimes—" His voice croaks. Coughing, he clears his throat, "Sometimes you need to put yourself first. The most important choices are also the most difficult."

Heath rises to his feet laying his hand on the distraught boy's hunching shoulders, "It seems as if you've made some difficult choices in your life. Thank you for coming up here despite your obvious discomfort." He turns to the crowd, "Let's get a round of applause for Stirling of Patu!"

Stirling forces a smile as the crowd cheers his name. Giving a stiff wave goodbye he refrains his legs from running off the stage. He returns to Eve's side and out of sight of the crowd as Heath announces the next racer, Peyton.

His body going limp he tilts sideways into Eve who puts her arm around him to help stabilize, "That was awful, I never want to do that again. I was terrible."

"Nooo…You weren't terrible…more like inexperienced." Eve fibs patting him on the shoulder. Resting her hand on him she thinks it over for a moment, "Your shyness is a quirk that people are finding charming. Most racers are overly confident and narcissistic. It's a nice change of pace to see this new, well, normal personality. Someone actually behaving how most of us would if we were placed center stage. When we see the other racers, we think to ourselves that can never be me. I can't do what they do. Then we see you, and like what the interviewer said, you inspire us. We think, hey, maybe I can be someone, too."

Jaw slack, Stirling stares down at her in astonishment. There she goes again. These words when said by strangers come out sounding fabricated, but when they come from her lips they don't only calm him down but also boost his confidence in himself. She knows his truths and accepts him, and maybe so will these people if he lets them. He isn't blind to the progress he has made with them. The alterations in the way they react to him are apparent. There are more people cheering his name each time he wins a match. How his weak and underdog personality tugs at their hearts. He never knew what famous was. He only wanted to race. What he is experiencing now is an unexpected lifestyle he has no clue how to cope with.

Eve catches him staring and blushes. "Sorry, I started rambling again. It's just, even if you didn't intend for this, you became a true idol."

"Thank you, for being here for me," Stirling says sincerely.

"It's my honor, Elite Racer Stirling of Patu," she jokes, poking him in the sides.

Stirling jerks involuntarily, the tip of her finger reminding him of his injuries. Slowly returning to himself, he lets out a small laugh as he follows through to the back of the theater.

"I don't know how to be famous."

"No one knows *how* to be famous," she says, stepping in front of him. "That's the great part about it, you can do whatever you want. Famous means people know who you are, but they don't define who you are." She places her hand over his heart. "They love this Stirling, so keep being you and never change."

Stirling's body flutters, the skin beneath her palm growing warm until it feels as if it's burning. An urge to pull her into him, to hold her close rises from his core. She blinks up at him with her honey-colored eyes.

Before he can act upon it, Eve takes his hand in hers and steps back. "Come on, let's go watch the rest of the interviews."

She walks backward not wanting to break their gaze while he allows her to pull him along. His long stride catches up in several steps and still holding hands she turns to join his side as they exit backstage together.

"You know we did this on purpose." Heath teases the audience with the last interview of the day, "The man you're all eager to see, year after year he never fails us, the ladies love him, the fellas want to be him. Your very own Quilan of Leucasia!"

The audience roars with excitement. A rumbling sound emanates from the stone and wooden layers of the audience's seating as they stomp their feet. Stirling can feel the structure holding them up high in the back of the crowd quake beneath him.

Quilan appears from the side of the stage with both hands raised into the air taking in the applause as if he needs to absorb their love and affection to live. He is a plant and they are the sun. This is the first time Stirling has seen him smile. Quilan's grin is a perfect stretch from ear to ear with the practiced amount of teeth showing. Deep dimples rivet the middle of his cheeks only adding to his delicate features. The girls cry out his name declaring their devotion to him.

Stirling doesn't cheer, he leans forward observing. What he sees past the sparkling smile is Quilan's unchanging eyes. How they are dark and dull like a marionette's puppet. He is displaying the emotions he is directed to. He is a performance artist, his true self locked deep inside. Stirling feels a sense of pity towards Quilan as he caters to the crowd, he is no longer human, but merely a doll to entertain the masses.

"Unlike our new boy Stirling, you should feel very comfortable up here." Heath chuckles, motioning to the chair for Quilan to sit in.

"It's like my second home," he answers, waving to a few girls in the front row who act as if they are going to faint.

"Yes, and that is the exact problem I am experiencing as the host. I'm running out of questions to ask you." Heath laughs; he sits back crossing his legs. "Though these games have been quite different than normal. So I'm going to skip the small talk and get straight to the big question. Tell us Quilan. Why did you recruit Stirling into the elite division? There is only one race left. Why now instead of waiting until next year?"

The sound of his name slams Stirling through the floorboards, *Quilan…...it was Quilan?*

Quilan puts his hands up, his face unfazed. "I was bored."

"Bored?"

"Bored." He haphazardly shrugs. "Thought it would be interesting." His eyes shoot to Stirling, "Let's hope he doesn't disappoint me."

The entire audience turns, all eyes scanning the seating to see who he is directing his line of sight at. Pointing at Stirling they lean in whispering amongst their friends. Stirling sinks further into his chair.

Eve grabs Stirling's arm in shock. "Quilan is talking about you! He's looking right at us!"

Quilan's slow-to-shift gaze lingers on Stirling before sliding methodically back to Heath.

"What do you take on his style?" Heath points his chin up at Stirling. "You must be observing since you want to race him."

"There's a wayward way about it." Quilan's body is as calm as an undisturbed pond. "I enjoy it."

Stirling is baffled. This is the most words in a row he's heard from Quilan of Leaucasia. Even witnessing it he cannot wrap his mind around how a person can string along a sentence, while still lacking any emphasis on syllables at the same time.

Eve, still giddy, says, "I can't believe it. Quilan wants to race you! YOU!"

Stirling grimaces at her squeaks, but he is on the same page as her. He is in disbelief. He has risen from an absconder to a celebrity. Someone who is seen as an equal opponent to their top racer.

Heath changes subjects, "On the topic of coaches, I know you are still young, but do you plan on coaching like your father when you retire?"

"Who says I'll retire." The corners of Quilan's mouth twitch.

The audience cheers at the idea of watching him for years to come. Stirling rolls his eyes. Of course, he isn't thinking of retiring. He is the number one racer, he single-handedly holds everyone in the kingdom's heart. His word is gospel, what he says is set in law and the people follow.

"Stirling! Stirling!"

He can hear his name being repeated in a hushed shout. Turning to Eve with a raised eyebrow he receives only a shrug in response. He timidly leans forward and peeks over the railing to the seating below him. Several girls peer up at him waving wildly.

"Hi, Stirling! Hi!"

Stirling manages to uncurl his fingers enough to acknowledge their wave before quickly retreating back into his seat.

Nope, he will never get used to this.

Thirty-Seven

The extensive harbor town of Vistjaldenne is over half a day's flight behind them. Like a storm rolling in from the ocean, Amiria, Calix, and Dicun lead a small platoon of Winged Riders from various squads across Uviktiland. Each Rider was specially hand-picked by their captains to tailor the best possible team. When the platoon finally reaches the rendezvous point they are instructed to break into three squads of ten and set off in their assigned directions to cover more ground.

Amiria checks over her shoulder at the steady group of trailing dragons. She hasn't seen Nellie, Garret, and Warrick since their graduation. The three childhood friends flying grouped together appear to still be young and eager riders ready to follow their orders in serving Wyverna they were never her friends, only her classmates. She had no reason to send letters to keep in touch.

Before the sun broke on the morning of their deployment the platoon had gathered in the coat of arms luggage in hand. From their reaction to seeing each other Amiria could tell they frequently wrote to one another. They embraced in a group hug Amiria wasn't invited to. After three years spread out across Wyverna, they are back in the same squad, but instead of Amiria being the one they didn't want to partner with, she is their Staff Sergeant.

The only one that isn't here is Clyde, but he has become someone new entirely.

Switching to peer over her other shoulder a bone-white dragon with two horns projecting out from the top of the skull and two more from the back of the jaw flies on the far side of the formation. Fortunately for her and Calix, Kinsey is assigned to Dicun's squad.

The formation of dragons ventures over the mountain range northeast following along the map established by Team Requaero's surveying. Their designated runner had delivered it to King Dietrich several days ago and after his extensive review, their plan was set forth. Team Requaero had found no leads, but was able to map out a detailed depiction of the surrounding landscape with the intel they have cataloged.

According to the map, Team Requaero is a three day straight flight. They have marked and coordinated safe landing zones suitable for a camp to fit thirty dragons. Checking the notes over, there was important information left off the map, leaving them blind. Nowhere on the map is there a warning for thick fog.

A white blanket is rolling over the mountains consolidating in the deep pockets between them. With each passing moment, the fog rises like water filling up a bucket. Dicun squints in the dying light and checks the map. His frustrated eyes scan the area, none of it matching. He holds his thumb up to measure the quickly diving sun.

"We should have reached the camp by now," Dicun gripes.

Calix calls over to him, "We probably passed it. We can't see anything in this fog and it's only getting worse. We'll be flying blind if we don't land." He waves his hand at the platoon behind them, "Their dragons cannot breathe fire to signal like ours can."

Dicun runs the options through his head. They can keep traveling through the night, but risk the fog rising into cloud coverage and they will end up farther off course with an overly exhausted team. The other option is to rally his troops to land and make camp here, the risk is the unknown quality and safety of the area.

Making his decision, Dicun picks up the signal horn strung around his neck. Trumpeting two notes he informs the troop they are off course and need to muster up. He raises his hand held straight like a blade pointing to the sky. Moving his hand counter clockwise he points down signaling a new waypoint.

Amiria follows along as they gradually descend into the thicket of ground-level clouds. Even one dragon ahead of her, Amiria struggles to see the dark reflective surface of Calix's armor. Their platoon was wiped from existence behind them.

Silence. The same silence after a snowstorm. The sound of the living is muffled by the natural insulation of the inanimate. She can see the burst of fire light like a small sun deep in the fog.

"That way." She tells herself following the guide.

Following the consistent pattern of fire like Morse code, Taika's claws clip the tops of the trees as they protrude from the abyss like punji sticks. She blinks as a long stream of light comes to view.

He found a clearing.

Amiria comes upon a small glade sizable enough to fit ten dragons comfortably but any more will start to feel cramped. Landing beside Calix and Dicun, she follows suit with Calix and dismounts her dragon with the removal of her helm. Turning back to the sky she strains her ears to listen for the rest of the troop.

Dicun, still mounted on his dragon, commands it to shoot another steam of fire into the sky.

They wait.

Another stream of fire.

They wait.

Nothing.

"Useless fools. They must have gotten separated in the fog. Just useless." Dicun spits on the ground, "King Dietrich should have sent us alone, so we aren't babysitting these incompetent troopers instead of focusing on our mission."

Calix rubs the forehead of his dragon, "No point in looking for them now in this fog. Better if we just set up camp here and find them when the sun breaks in the morning."

"You two start working on a fire. Gather up as much firewood as you can so we won't need to search in the middle of the night. I am going to scout the area. One of you, count, and have your dragon send up a signal each time you reach sixty so I can have a reference point to where I am." Dicun instructs

"Understood." Amiria and Calix say in unison.

With a nod, Dicun takes off disappearing through the slowly darkening curtain.

Calix turns to Amiria, "I'll focus on gathering the wood if you want to keep track of the time."

"Why? You can't count to sixty?" Amiria jabs.

"Does it come right after fivety?" Calix says with a sly smile.

"Yep, got it. I'll keep track of the time because I know we are already at forty seconds." Amiria plucks her metal clicker strung around her neck alongside her whistle and horn.

She bobs her head as she counts. Looking Calix directly in the eyes she clicks twice. Taika raises her head and lets out a short jet of flames into the air. Calix can't resist smiling. He loves her witty comments. She might come off as uptight and standoffish to people who look at her from a distance. But he's gotten the chance to spend time with the real her. She is devoted, compassionate, and frolicsome. She is not showing off when she is on the back of Taika or wielding a blade. She is herself, and that person is amazing.

Amiria pushes him teasingly. "Go, do your part of the deal and get the firewood. You know before the day is over."

"Yes, Your Highness. Whatever it is you desire." Calix mockingly bows.

Laughing Amiria shoves him, her gauntlets clashing against his breastplate. "You are so annoying. GO!"

Jogging backward, Calix's grin takes up his entire face before he spins to face the tree line. Amiria clicks the clicker twice. Taika responds by sending another jet of fire.

Squatting down Amiria picks up an old dried branch from the ground just outside the clearing. She pauses, her fingertips resting on the dead wood. The cooing of pheasants ripples through the fog. She waits, counting in her head.

Clicking twice, Taika sets off a jet.

Two pheasants fly startled at the fire. Not sensing they are in immediate danger they land only three trees over. Smiling devilishly Amiria keeps her eyes stationed on the birds camouflaging with the leaves. She reaches back methodically, refraining from making any noise with her armor. Removing her bow clipped to a strap across her back, she slips an arrow from the quiver. Pulling back, she takes aim. With no more than the low whistle of the arrow, a large bird drops from the tree. Its partner takes off scampering through the air. Amiria was already prepared.

Another arrow zips through the fog.

With a soft thud, the bird hits the pine floor.

Calix sits on the ground poking at the campfire. The smoke climbing up and merging with the fog. He takes in Amiria as Taika sends another jet of flames into the air. "What do you have there?"

"Dinner." Two pheasants are tossed down by his feet.

Calix picks up one of the birds by the tail, "Do you even know how to clean and cook it? We have provisions, you know."

Amiria shrugs, "How hard can it be, get rid of the feathers and the insides then cook it over the fire. Come on, fresh poultry over hard meat pies?"

She has watched Stirling dress and clean a variety of animals. If she really focuses, she is sure she can recall each step from memory. Calix tilts his head thinking over what she has said.

"Yeah, you're right." He agrees with her point about fresh meat.

"Teamwork, we'll each do one. Follow my lead." Amiria instructs.

"Sure." Calix picks up one of the birds as Amiria sits on the grass beside him.

She shows him how to dress the birds in only a matter of minutes by removing the legs, wings and head then skinning the bird instead of plucking the feathers.

"This is actually really hard," Calix admits.

With her completed bird, Amiria skewers a long branch through the length of it, she pauses to hit her clicker twice, "Yeah, I give props to the chefs at the castle."

Staring down at her blood and feather-covered hands she recalls the quick and fluent speed Stirling was able to complete the tasks. After several years of practice, he didn't even break a sweat, as if it was no different than cracking open an egg. Here and now trying it herself, she has discovered a new appreciation for Stirling and those who must prepare meals that she takes for granted to be served to her on a silver plate.

"DAMN!" Calix curses.

The fire Calix tenderly kept ablaze blows in the cyclone created by Dicun's landing wyvern. Leaping to his feet in a clanging of metal, Calix rushes to the other side of the fire pit in an attempt to use his body to shield the fire from the wind.

Dicun dismounts from his dragon, "I had no visuals on the troop. On another hand, I luckily had no visuals on anyone else out there. Did you guys miss me? Or were you just enjoying this little peasant date you two are on?"

"They're pheasants," Calix states.

"I didn't mispronounce. Why are you two playing farm hand when we have packs of provisions, and items to barter with the locals," Dicun criticizes.

Amiria speaks up, "You can eat your cold supplies, we're going to have a warm meal in this damp weather."

"Fine. You guys do as you deem fit. But don't look at me for help when the bird catches on fire," Dicun grumbles, the moisture of the air seeping through to his bones.

Calix shrugs and turns the cooking bird over. "Suit yourself. But we both know the truth."

With the poultry charred on one side, the three of them sit around the campfire picking at the meat. None of them have removed their armor, there is no changing into more comfortable clothing when you sleep on guard.

Calix and Amiria sit with their hips touching on a shared log they had pulled over for seating. Talking over the tips of the flames on the opposing side of the fire Dicun had planted himself on a large rock.

Even if the job was poorly executed there is something immensely satisfying about the whole occasion. We did this. We made this.

Amiria wonders if Stirling felt as proud about any of his possessions that he made himself in his cave or how he figured out how to clean an entire deer and turn the pelt into a leather cloak. Maybe not, maybe to him it was just part of life and not some camping experiment. Amiria sneaks a peek at Calix from the corner of her eye. He seems as proud of himself as she is about herself.

Dicun wipes the grease from his face with exposed fabric in the crook of his arm, "You know I believe that boy has to be dead by now. It has been what? Almost two months? He's been hiding in an empire that for one speaks another dialect and two is our personal enemy. As soon as he landed and tried conversing with any of them, he would have been apprehended for trespassing on their land. If the officials didn't get him, living out here in the woods sure would have, if not by the elements, then surely by bandits."

Amiria's chewing slows, the food suddenly tastes like bile in her mouth. She knows Stirling has no issues with surviving the elements, for three years he has proved that. What're two more months? On the other hand, bandits. Stirling is not a fighter. If Ignis is unable to protect him, bandits can easily overpower him in a matter of seconds.

"You okay?" Calix asks, nudging Amiria with his shoulder.

She stares absentmindedly at the flickering flames, her eyes transfixed on their elegant display, "Yeah, why?"

"It just seems as if your mind slipped and went elsewhere," Calix explains.

Dicun interrupts, "Are you two love birds even listening to me?"

"No, we're not listening to your rambling. No one ever does." Calix snaps.

"It's because you're too busy drooling over a girl you were only able to get because no one else wants her." Dicun chucks the bone he was eating from into the fire sending up embers in the direction of Calix and Amiria.

Calix is on his feet in a blink, standing off to Dicun who is slipping on his gauntlets, "You can talk trash about me all day, but you keep her out of it."

"Oh? You're going to defend your lady like a little chivalrous knight?" Dicun rises to his feet and shoves Calix in the chest, the armor plates clanging. "I liked the old you, the bitter lonely you." He shoves Calix again who accepts the blow and takes a step back to hold his stance. "Come on whipped boy, fight for her!"

Amiria steps in between them with a bladed stance. "Lay one more hand on him and I'll make sure it ends up so mangled you'll never have use of it again."

Raising his chin, Dicun peers down his nose at Amiria. He isn't a tall man, but even with his average height and fit stature he still has a physical advantage over her, "Interesting? You're protecting him now? I guess you two really are made for each other. I guess it is better than dying alone. I've got a proposition, let's see how devoted he is to you."

Dicun's hand strikes out like a snake, the fangs of his hand aiming to bite around her neck. Countering, Amiria's small hand curls around his index and middle finger, her thumb at his knuckles and her pinky at his fingertips. Naturally lower than Dicun, Amiria barely needs to drop her hand while simultaneously curling his fingers back to the point at his own forearm.

Dropping to his knees Dicun's instinct is to straighten out his hand and alleviate the pain. Amiria only lowers her hand and pushes farther until she is the one looking down at him.

"Don't, *ever*, touch me."

He can't move. His fingers locked and on the verge of breaking.

Calix peers around Amiria, bragging. "I think she can handle herself."

"You've proved your point. You foul excuse for a woman. Now let me go," Dicun growls.

Amiria releases her grip. Taking a step back she collides with Calix oblivious to the fact he had stepped closer to stand over her. He cups his hands on her shoulders, steading her. Tilting her head back she looks above her. Calix's bright smile shines down on her.

The sound of a twig snapping steals her attention. She puts her arm out protecting Calix as she scans the tree line. All three dragons lock their snake-like eyes in different directions.

"We're surrounded," Dicun warns, his voice an underground rumble.

"They won't attack melee, not with the dragons right here. They'd have to be crazy or stupid." Calix wonders out loud.

"Get out your shields," Amiria instructs. She can hear it. The sound of dozens of strings being pulled back. "GET OUT YOUR SHIELDS!" she screams.

Dicun and Calix strip the shields still mounted to their backs. Their legs react before their minds, kicking up clumps of dirt and moss they take off sprinting to their dragons. They duck in-between the beasts taking cover between the scales of steel.

Arrows rain down, each watering the field and sprouting a meadow of fletchings.

"They aren't aiming for us directly," Amiria reads, half kneeling beside Taika's flank. "They're trying to heard us."

"We should douse them in flames and take off," Calix suggests.

Dicun points out "No, this forest is too dry. The whole mountain will go up in flames. We have our own men and women out there."

"We are the Winged Cavalry, we don't run and give our possessions to bandits," Amiria says out of spite. "Plus—"

Taika hisses as a few arrows slip between the creases of her folded wings sticking into the thin membrane.

Amiria continues, "With this many archers at this close of a distance you're risking turning the dragon's wings into pin cushions,

"We can't just sit in this clearing waiting for them to run out of arrows," Calix says in desperation.

"No, we won't. That's why I am going to give them exactly what they are hoping for." The whites of Amiria's eyes glow in the fire's light making her dark iris' a bottomless pit waiting to be filled with the excitement of a fight.

"AMIRIA!" Calix calls out.

He is too late. Leaving her helm behind Amiria uses her valances and gauntlets to cover her exposed head as she charges into the daunting colorless woods.

"That girl is nuts! We don't even know how many of them are out there!" Dicun chastises.

"As Winged Riders, the amount shouldn't matter to us," Calix realizes. "Amiria is a true warrior who is upholding her promise to never back down and eliminate the enemy.

"It does matter when we have a mission to complete," Dicun snaps.

Thirty-Eight

Amiria unsheathes the two short swords from her scabbards. The sun has already reached twilight leaving little to no light to illuminate the enemy through the thick fog. She steadies her breathing. Her surroundings are no more than dark gray walls locking her in a small room. The campfire long vanished behind the closed door.

She listens.

Standing as still as a statue, she is fully aware of her surroundings like a meek mouse listening for a swooping owl. Her knees flexibly bent, she raises her blades up defensively.

From the right.

One of the twin blades reflexively slices through the air deflecting a chipped bastard sword. Moving swiftly and tight she thrust her left blade at an upwards angle through the bandit's rusting chainmail stabbing the soft flesh of his stomach and slipping under the protection of his ribcage.

Yanking the blade free she whips around splattering blood in a half circle as she traps the partial blade of a broken two-handed sword of an incoming attacker by pinching it between her double short swords in the shape of an "X".

The man's murderous leer glows through the small window of his enclosed helmet. Not retracting his blade, the bandit insists on pushing down on her crossed blades in an attempt to over power the girl before him.

Well-balanced, Amiria kicks the man's foot out from beneath him while throwing his blade out to his side. The man tips over as his body is put into momentum in two different directions. Through Amiria's calculated movements, the man's exaggerated fall moves in slow motion. Taking her sword in the hand closest to his head she lowers it closer to the ground with the tip pointing up. With the help of gravity the blade slides through the viewing slot of the enclosed helmet.

As she kicks the man's body free of her blade a set of muscular arms wrap around her thin frame lifting her from the ground.

"You should never have left your man's side," he grumbles, the whiskers of his face scratching her ear as he speaks.

A secondary bandit forms out of the fog before her with a dagger in hand. "Let's carve her pretty face before we have our fun."

Amiria kicks out in rage, the tip of her metal-covered toe connecting with the man's exposed chin snapping his head back with a crack.

"You'll pay for that!" the man holding her threatens, he slides one of his hands up to her neck. His large hand spans from her neck and up around her jaw.

With her short swords from end to end being similar in length as her arm she lines the flat of the blades against her hips and drives them backwards into the groping man. Blood drains from his mouth and showers the back of her head wetting her hair. His grip slackens and his arms fall away. The slick leaves shift beneath her as her feet touch the ground. She holds her footing with the weight of the man pressed to her back. Letting gravity pull the man free of her swords she raises them just in time to counter the next opponent.

Moving deeper and deeper into the forest, Amiria fights. Each poorly equipped bandit fell to her touch. Unable to match the steps of her dance. Understanding they are unmatched when fighting one on one, they move into a mob approach. They attack from all directions, there is no choreography, and there are no rules. These aren't wooden swords made from branches as you call time out. This is life or death.

Amiria is accustomed to these rules. The Winged Cavalry, are aware of their low numbers compared to those of the Uviktiland's army and has arranged their training accordingly, by systemically focusing on one versus a group scenario.

She twists and twirls through the ribbons of steel. This is her stage, this is her show. She will be the last to bow.

As long as she can avoid any well placed jabs where her armor does not cover like her underarms, any blades slipping beneath her brigandine, or any blunt force trauma as in a mace or war hammer she will be able to walk away.

Running up a slate, she scales a massive boulder. She vaults off the stone diving board landing with her knees striking a bull of a man in the chest. As his body leans back from the force she power drives her blades into the slots of his collar bones. She takes the ride down, the man crashing into the ground like a timbering redwood. She moves to leap up.

Stuck.

Her blades jam in the man's bones as she pulls at them from a different angle than their original entry. An overpowering weight slams down into the armor above her shoulder blade crushing her down against the gurgling man. She gags choking on the air through waves of pain, the agony of her shoulder blade screaming out through her whole body.

A bandit wielding a war hammer kicks her in the stomach, toppling her away and out of reach of her weapons. "You're lucky. I'm not going to kill you. You're way too pretty for that. But I will break your arms and legs for what you've done to my friends." He threatens.

Full of adrenaline, Amiria bites her lip and fights through the pain in her shoulder and shoots up into a crouch. She spits in the bandit's direction. Her saliva dyed pink with blood from her tooth-punctured tongue. Seething, the man's face contorts into a ghastly scowl as he bears his teeth like an enraged animal. He lifts his war hammer out behind him and with a battle cry, he swings down at her with the motion of chopping wood. Amiria dodges rolling out of the way of the slow deliberate strike. She lets out a whimper as her injured shoulder hits the ground.

Coddling her arm, she poises herself into a low crouch. She eyes the man watching for any sudden movements as she tests her stiffening shoulder in its socket. Even with both the metal and padded armor receiving a large sum of the blow, she can still feel the grinding of her shoulder blade. She needs to end this fight, now.

With the drooling man too busy fantasizing about what he is going to do to her, Amiria analyzes the long staff of the war hammer. She spits another wad of bloodied saliva near her feet. In her mind, the war hammer and mace was a weapon for those who couldn't learn the art of swordsmanship and rather rely on brute force. She will admit though, one strike to the head, and her skull will split as easily as a gourd. Any blocks with her forearms will snap the bones despite her valances and with her current injury, she's standing on the chopping block before the executioner.

A sinister smile stretches across the bandit's face. She looks into the bandit's demented eyes. Traveling through them she can see into the absence of his soul.

A rare emotion vibrates her bones. Fear is beginning to pump through her veins hindering her mind of coherent thoughts. For once her body screams flight over fight. She can't dodge him forever.

What can she use to her advantage?

Think, think.

There. She sees it. The war hammer is held on a long-staff, long-ranged weapon with a slow swing. Steading her hitching breaths, she watches. The bandit rears the war hammer back preparing himself for the next blow.

Timing it she lunges in the direction of her swords. He falls for the faint. Falls for portraying what any normal opponent will be opting to do when cornered, desperately attempting to rearm themselves.

He swings from below, with the goal to strike her in the chest at an upwards angle and knock her off her feet—and hopefully incapacitating her. A deadly pendulum aimed directly at her

She springs in the opposite direction. The head of the hammer swings up through the empty space. Tucking in her head she drives her strong shoulder into the bandit's gut. His mouth gapes open in surprise. The hammer slips free from his grasp as he stumbles backward finding it difficult to regain his footing on the pine and oak leaf-layered rug beneath him. The backs of his heels bump into an object.

Amiria careens with the bandit as he trips over his comrades' legs. Agile as a cat she rolls with the fall leaping for her blades still protruding from the giant's body. Her hand barely reaches the hilt as the war hammer bandit seizes her by the ankle.

Flipping over she stares at the man reeling her back in, at the man who wants to do more than kill her. Frantic she kicks at his fingers, her heart racing up through her throat choking her. With a helpless cry, she grabs a handful of damp earth and pebbles and flings it at the bandit's face.

His eyes are forced shut from the contamination of foreign debris. Screaming out in rage, he instinctively releases Amiria and he wildly claws at the dirt in his eyes. Barely able to open one, he searches blindly, desperately trying to find Amiria again.

She scampers past the dead man's head before the bandit is able to take hold of her again. Putting her feet on the man's shoulders she grips her swords pulling them free.

Blinking rapidly and through blurred vision the bandit refuses to give up. Rabid, he leaps at Amiria before she is able to regain herself tackling her back to the ground. He hovers over her, pinning her arms down.

He leans down close to her face. "You had to make this harder than it needed to be. Now I'm really going to enjoy this."

"HELP!" she cries. "CALIX!" She will never give up. She will never let him have her. If one person walks out of her here it will be her. She will see Stirling again.

Knowing Stirling is out there lost in this new world, she bucks her hips off centering the bandit. He casts out his hand to steady himself. She wraps her arm around his, pulling it out from under him. She frees her own legs and flips him over reversing the rolls. With her swords crossed like scissors, she raises them up above her head.

"AHHHH!" Amiria howls, sending her blades down like a guillotine.

Panting, she leans on the pommel of her swords stuck into the ground. Her shoulders and back heave with each exhausted breath. Sweat drips from her chin into the pool of blood where a head used to be.

"AMIRIA!" She hears from the dark fog surrounding her. "AMIRIA!" Calix's voice is a wolf's howl as he searches for a member of his pack. She checks in the direction of his voice and then switches to the direction of the unknown.

"AMIRIA!" Calix calls through cupped hands. "I thought I heard her. Where is she?"

Dicun lights the path with a torch as they search. "Whoa, Calix, watch your step." He warns holding the torch out farther in front. Calix can smell it before he sees it. Bloodshed. "Found where she was fighting," Dicun observes.

A dozen full-grown men lay dead in her wake. Blood gathers into small red seas in the uneven soil.

"AMIRIA!" Calix's voice frightened at the probabilities running through his mind as he scans the gruesome landscape.

Dicun nudges a corpse with his foot, "Pathetic. They got what they deserved. Don't underestimate us."

"She had to have won. Look at this carnage. There's no way she didn't win." Calix brings up, his voice beginning to quiver with uncertainty.

"What we can see is that she was able to hold her ground well, but we don't know if this was all of them," Dicun points out. "We had to fight a group of our own too."

"She can handle twice this amount. There is no way some mediocre bandits were able to beat her. That is why she was selected for our team," Calix states, trying to convince himself, his eyes trailing the perimeter of where the light reaches.

An uneasy twinge in his stomach forms, a natural intuition developed from years of fighting. With melancholy steps, Calix searches around the bodies for clues. With each step he takes the spidering crack in his heart grows.

Where is she?

He can read the scene. He can see it in his mind like a theatrical play. He can see where the curtain was drawn and the actors began. He can see each change of characters as your hero continues through the act.

The silver handle of a war hammer glints in the torch's light.

"Dicun, give me the torch," Calix asks.

Dicun raises an eyebrow and passes the torch. With an unsteady heart, Calix steps around the war hammer. His armor rattling with his quaking body. If someone was to attack at this moment he will be taken by surprise. His mind is clouded with the thoughts of Amiria.

The Winged Cavalry are raised in a way the average citizen would describe as soulless, but they aren't heartless. They are taught to keep their distance from everyone. To keep their heart enclosed and their head in the game. A heart can only handle so much loss, so lock it up and save your mind's sanity.

He steps over the giant's body stopping at the decapitated man. There it is. Where the hero bowed and the curtain was pulled. He can see it in the dirt where the two swords dug. This was the last opponent. She would only have taken the opportunity to kill him in such an exposed way if she was not worried about another approaching attacker.

But what if there was someone else? He searches the ground around the body. The ground scribbled with shuffles and drag marks. But none leading away from the body. Though Amiria is small enough if she was unconscious she can easily be carried away.

Time is frozen. He slowly drops to his knees under the crushing weight of his heart. He clenches his jaw as he scoops up a gold and lavender ribbon saturated in iron-filled liquid. He wants to scream, but he can't take in any air.

She couldn't have lost. Amiria doesn't lose.

Dicun places a hand on Calix's shoulder. "One of us can stay and secure the camp. If she is not recovered by the morning, we will send a situational report on our casualty."

Calix violently swings his arm, throwing Dicun's hand off his shoulder. "SHE'S NOT DEAD!—AMIRIA!" His eyes wide and wild, he takes off sprinting. "AMIRIA!"

Sighing, Dicun charges after him.

Amiria's hair flows wildly behind her like a flag being flown on a galloping horse. She can hear her name and the urgency in Calix's voice. She pushes away her instincts. Fights against her urge to run back to him, back to the now familiarity of his arms.

No. She needs to keep running, to keep going. Her lungs burn with exertion. She can't slow. This is her only chance.

Dicun chases after Calix, clipping at his heels. "Calix! Stop!"

"AMIRIA!" He calls ignoring the demands.

Still running, Dicun reaches out, snatching the younger man by the arm. Digging his heels into the ground he yanks back on Calix spinning him around to face him. Without hesitation, Calix chops down on Dicun's elbow, freeing him of his grip.

Furious, Dicun rears his gauntleted hand back and swings, striking Calix in the jaw. His head snaps to the side with his body falling suit as he topples to the ground from the sudden impact. Lying on his back, Calix holds his already swelling jaw.

"Have you lost your mind!" Dicun screams, foaming at the mouth. "Have you forgotten all of your training, or have you disregarded it because you let emotion take over? You won't even be able to find yourself running blindly like that!" Dicun pinches the brim of his nose as he takes a few calming breaths. "If you want to find a missing-in-action rider, you follow the dragon."

She won't call for Taika. A dragon can hear their unique rider's whistle across an entire mountain range. If she spends the next several days walking she will gain a substantial amount of distance without giving herself away. Taika will not be called. She is to remain unresponsive. If she is not called by Amiria they can only assume she is not calling for help because she has already joined the deceased. When they declare Amiria a loss, they will leave Taika behind. Then and only then will they be able to reunite.

Calix couldn't sleep. He sat leaning against a tree until dawn finally broke through the now clear skies. His red-rimmed eyes stare unblinking. Continuously watching. Still waiting. His gaze upon Taika never broke. For a creature who lacks facial expressions, it truly appeared confused when Amiria did not return.

Uncurling his hand, he stares weary-eyed down at the stained ribbon, the golden strands now lit by the rising sun. He chokes back everything as a long shadow crosses him.

Kinsey hovers over Calix. "Aww, *so* sad."

With hardening eyes, Calix glares up at the eclipsed silhouette of his sister. "Go crawl into a hole."

"Why do you say such mean things? I'm just trying to comfort my older brother.

His fingers curl around the ribbon. "We both know what you're doing."

Dropping her jaw, Kinsey places her hand over her chest, mimicking hurt. "Why can't a sister try to console her brother without being accused of something?"

"Because it's you." Calix uses the tree he was leaning on to slide up to his feet. "Don't you have some men to fool."

"None of them are as fun to torment as you are." Kinsey's fanged smile glints.

Taking the ribbon he ties it to the straps of his shoulder plates so the remembrance hangs over his heart. Returning to the soldier he is, Calix states, "The report needs to be sent back to King Dietrich and the field marshal."

Thirty-Nine

Stirling erodes a worn trail as he paces nervously back and forth in front of the racers tent.

"Calm down, you're making me anxious," Ignis says, his eyes tracking Stirling.

"I can't. I'm excited but scared at the same time. I can't sit still. My chest is going to explode. I think I'm dying. Oh no, am I dying, I think I'm dying." Stirling hunches over, putting his hands on his knees.

"Why is this race any different?" Ignis questions.

"It's the last race and it's at the elite level. Everyone will remember this performance."

Pale hair steps out of the tent, Quilan squints at Stirling jittering in place.

"Q-quilan!" Stirling stutters. "I haven't gotten the chance to thank you."

Quilan puts his hand up. "Don't."

Clamping his mouth shut, Stirling hunches his shoulders in submission. The color drained from his face. He will never understand Quilan. He supposedly instructs the games committee to place him in the last elite race, yet refuses to speak to him. What is his ploy? He acts as if he wants to be anywhere else but races anyways. Was the true reason he requested to race Stirling strictly out of boredom? Is Quilan using him for entertainment like the people of Lumierna use them, the racers?

As if Stirling is nothing more than another one of the stakes around the tent, Quilan passes him by, his face turning tranquil as his sights set on his quetzalcoatl.

"RACERS! MAKE YOUR WAY TO THE STARTING LINE!" the announcer cries towards the tent.

Pulling in a deep breath Stirling holds it in until his face turns red. With a forced exhale of the old stale air and Stirling gasps sucking in the new oxygen. Standing idle, he watches one by one as the elite racers exit the tent to fetch their dragons.

The oldest of the group, Aylmar stops. "Just because pretty boy wants to race you, doesn't mean you deserve to be up here. You're going to see you're in over your head newbie."

"I uh." Stirling shrinks as his insecurity grows around him.

"See you at the starting line." Aylmar huffs.

Stirling lowers his eyes and shuffles to Ignis. *"Are you ready?"*

"Am I ready? I'm not the one making a trench with my pacing," Ignis replies getting up.

Stirling pulls his lips into a straight line and grabs Ignis's harness. Not waiting for Ignis to pause, Stirling climbs up onto his back as Ignis walks them toward the start. They line themselves up with four of the other racers at the edge of the cliff.

Closing his eyes, Stirling mumbles encouraging words to himself ignoring Ignis who lowers his head distracted by a dragonfly hovering around his legs.

Through the stilts of his legs, he sees light blue feathers. His head immediately pops up as Quilan's quetzalcoatl slithers across the ground like a piece of falling sky. Quilan sits perched between their wings, the same dull look in his eyes.

Stirling now well familiar with Quilan's wonders, *Does he ever show any expression?*

"Hello, beautiful!" Ignis chirps, his heartbeat picking up as they slide into place beside him.

"Stirling! Stirling! Stirling! LOOK!" Ignis giddily whispers.

Stirling rolls his eyes.

Stirling! We're next to each other!" Ignis points out, being overly excited.

"I am well aware," Stirling says, annoyed.

The quetzecoatl ruffles their icy feathers and tilts their head at Ignis. Ignis' heart lurches in his ribcage. Stirling sighs, he doesn't have time for Ignis' antics. He needs to focus on the race that will be starting at any moment. Leaning, he checks down the rest of the line. Beside him is the racer he remembers named Peyton with a knuckler dragon, then the older racer on a draco, and the two whose names have slipped Stirling's mind with a draco and an amphiptere. They are all older than him, averaging in their mid to late twenties.

"May I ask you a question?" Peyton shifts on his dragon toward Stirling.

"Me?" Stirling points to himself.

"No, your dragon. Of course, you," he says sarcastically.

"It could have been me," Ignis inserts.

"Sure, I guess," Stirling replies awkwardly.

"You've won all those matches, how come you haven't updated your gear? Besides your goggles everything else looks so umm, economical," he says, trying to word the sentence so he won't offend Stirling.

Pearlescent goggles reflect rainbow light as Quilan tilts his head listening in.

"That's because I made them myself. Well, me and a close friend. This is much more valuable to me than any of the gear I can buy," Stirling answers.

"It doesn't impede your racing?" Peyton asks curiously.

Stirling shakes his head. "Not that I'm aware of, but I really don't know any different." He pauses. "I have a question for you."

"Go for it," Peyton says, now drawn in.

"Is the gear really what makes the racer?" Stirling inquiries.

Peyton's eyebrows scrunch as it dawns on him. "I guess not."

Stirling steals a quick glance at the legendary Quilan, who turns away and pretends to be inspecting his gloves. But Stirling had seen it in the split moment. The man has the personality of a bag of coal everywhere he goes, but up here. Up here when he is flying they light up in flame. Unable to stop himself, Stirling slowly returns to Quilan.

Quilan's eyes, already beginning to glow, dart back to Stirling, "Good luck."

Thrown back, Stirling replies, "Oh—uh—you, too."

Smiling on one side, a dimple creases on Quilan's cheek, he answers, "I don't need it."

The announcer steps up the metal funnel amplifying his voice, "RACERS! ARE YOU READY!"

The crowd goes wild. They holler from the stands down below, calling out their favorite racer's name and waving their colors in the air.

Stirling peers down at the audience from the top of the cliffside. He is back where he started, the same cliff from his first race. This time he will not falter at the sound of the horn, this time he will leap with the rest. *This time* he can hear his name being called out by his fans in the crowd. He can see the orange flags and banners being held above people's heads.

This is his accomplishment. He deserves to be sitting up here. Despite Quilan's recommendation, he earned his place beside them in the ranks. He was the one who refused to accept the "no" that life kept hitting him in the face with. It was drilled into him that he was nothing and should stay that way.

His mother didn't see him as nothing. Amiria, Eve, Bernard, and Ignis, with matted hair and patched-up clothing still all saw him as someone.

Raising his sleeved arm, he places his forehead against his insignia, *Even if I get last. I did this all because you believed I could. This is for you.*

Dropping his arm Stirling runs the course through his head. They will fly past each checkpoint, swooping between the building with a referee and a flagpole. As they pass, a flag with their color will be lifted signaling to the next checkpoint their current placement.

Out over the water. Around the east side of Leucasia. Fly north over the small velvet mountains. Then west following the river over Patu and finally south back to the water through a gorge carved out by man.

He grips the handles of Ignis's saddle, scrunching his lanky body down tight against his back. He can do this.

The horn sounds off.

Chunks of dirt and debris tear loose from the ledge as Ignis plunges, diving like a falcon after its prey. A cyclone of wind bursts from the six dragons as they launch themselves. Dust and sand are blown into the air storming out over the audience as they propel themselves forward and out over the water.

At this point in Stirling's first race, the large group had already started dividing, those with more experience pulling ahead and taking the lead during the first lap. Now here, racing with those who have climbed the ladder earning the right to be called an elite, they are flying neck and neck. They are a tidal wave of scales and feathers returning to the ocean.

They pass the last of the pillars and soar out towards the first checkpoint stationed on a small island that is barely larger than a cluster of boulders. A lookout tower hardly able to fit atop sits mounted to the top of the rocks. Undulating in the water sits a small rowboat tied to the bottom of a series of ladders leading up to the tower.

Standing in the rickety tower, the referee wears his own pair of goggles to protect his eyes from the wind as the racers pass through the checkpoint. The intensity of the wind rocks the weathered wood as the referee pulls strings hung above him releasing the flags in the order of the racers.

Sky blue is up on top and orange is in fifth place.

Stirling checks over his shoulder to check his official placement. He smiles. They aren't leaving him behind. He is able to hold his own and stay with the pack. This is a marathon, not a sprint.

He doesn't need to push Ignis until the last moment. Straight in front of him, the pale blue snake-like dragon's body ripples through the air as it slowly starts to pull ahead of them. Don't try to catch up. Hold your ground for now and go all out at the end.

They curve around the next watchtower heading back to the shore now on the opposite side of the capitol.

Stirling can't help but take his eyes away from the race to look down at the city as they pass by. Citizens crowd the streets and huddle at the top of buildings flying their racer's colors. Stirling can hear the faint sounds of horns and cheering.

Pulling his focus back to the race, they reach the summit of the mountain behind the city and pass the next checkpoint.

They are halfway there.

Stirling leans back over the side of Ignis.

"What are you doing?" Ignis asks, keeping his pace.

"Looking at our shadows," Stirling replies honestly.

He watches in amusement as the shadows of the six dragons distort; they shrink, enlarge, bulge, and pinch as the uneven land below them changes.

"You remember we're in a race, right?" Ignis points out.

"Yeah, but this almost feels like a casual flight at the moment. So why not enjoy it." Stirling says back.

Adjusting himself properly in the saddle, he spots Quilan abruptly turn back around as if he had been watching him.

They are now approaching the prairie checkpoint. Stirling inspects his opponents. None of them appear to be having any stamina issues. This is nothing compared to the distance he and Ignis flew to get here. This has to be an endurance race if nothing else. They must all have the same idea to wait until the last stretch.

They loop around the watchtower changing their direction west.

"Ignis look!" Stirling yells referring to Patu appearing to the southwest.

Passing over the village the other elite racers roll their eyes as Stirling energetically waves both his hands overhead. The villagers pile into a heap outside the entrance of the alehouse. They leap and root for Stirling as the six dragons soar overhead like a migrating flock of birds.

Ricocheting around the second to last checkpoint the racers around him begin to pick up their pace as they fly south. Stirling's eyes widen at the advancing gorge cutting through the small mountain that separates the plains from the coast.

Erosion from the river the villagers relied on initially created the pass, but humans with the assistance of dragons widened the walls and placed decorated pillars creating an elaborate obstacle course.

Four-fifths of the race was a leisurely glide, merely sailing over the lands with your peers. If you spend too much energy trying to gain distance from the group you will be exhausted by the time you reach the gorge and fail to make the quick maneuvers around the pillars.

Stirling smirks. His confidence spiking, he's unknowingly been training for this for years. Speeding through a dense stone forest is his specialty. It is what he does for fun.

They enter the gorge as a group and are out of sight of any referees.

Stirling yelps in surprise as Ignis is slammed to the side. Twisting his body around, he narrowly misses crashing into one of the pillars with a sloping bridge connecting to a second one.

They are more than just pillars, between them are connecting crossbeams varying in circumference, direction, lengths, and amount. It reminds Stirling more of a spider's web connecting between a wall and a fence and they are the flies.

Hugging close to the wall Stirling takes note of the new aggressive attitude of the group. Quilan, still far in the lead, slithers through the branches as if by memory. The other four racers, nip, claw, and shove at each other. Each one trying to knock out the competition by forcing them to crash.

"So that's their game," Stirling fears.

They weren't conserving energy so they could go all out in speed at the end or help with maneuvering through the web of stone. They saved energy in the public's eye so they could be prepared for the battle royal. Here, there are no rules.

Stirling has fallen into last place too afraid to try to pass the group. Keeping his distance from their vicious and relentless attacks, he watches as Quilan pulls farther into the lead, unaffected by the war going on behind him.

He's already told himself he is accepting of last place. He is satisfied he has accomplished this much. What he is not accepting of is giving up. He will still try to give it his all. There has to be a way through.

What to do? What to do? Stirling ponders.

If he attempts to pass the group they will no doubt they will team up to cast him down to the river below.

The river.

"THAT'S IT!" Stirling stretches his neck out over the side of Ignis excavating the land beneath them.

The riverbank appears to be a solid rock bed. The river itself is a quarter the size of the portion near the village. The river is no wider than Stirling is tall. Each one of the pillars is built a few jumps back from the bank. Stirling can only guess it's to keep the pillars from eroding during the flood season.

Up here with the dragon's massive wingspan, the pillars feel close and cluttered, but on the ground, following the riverbank, it's a clear sprint.

Stirling sees the racer named Peyton is trapped in the middle of the two draco racers who hover above and below him. They keep him sandwiched as he tries to unpin himself. The racer above swipes his talons, and the one below snaps its jaws.

They are aiming him directly to one of the bridges. At the last moment, they separate, one ducking beneath and the other leaping over. Peyton pulls back on his reins rearing his dragon and nearly colliding into the wall, losing his place.

"Ignis. Let's go for a run," Stirling offers.

"Yes, let's go!" Ignis agrees.

Without letting up on his speed, Ignis lowers himself to the riverbank with the occasional dodging of a pillar.

Aylmar scans the course behind him checking on Stirling's location. Nowhere in sight. *Good.* Lucan on his amphiptere rams into his side, turning Aylmar's attention back to his real opponents.

Galloping below the fighting beasts Stirling and Ignis pass undetected. Stirling throws his head back to gawk at the chaos above.

"*We can do this!*" Stirling roots as he comes to terms with his new possibility of winning the elite race. He bounces in the saddle with a surge of adrenaline as they sneak into second place.

"*We still need to catch up to Quilan,*" Ignis mentions.

Stirling squints as he searches for him through the copious amount of pillars holding up the sky above them.

"*Look, the end narrows.*" Stirling realizes this through his search.

They have almost completed their run through the gorge. Once they make it out, it's a clear path to the finish line. Stirling spots him. The blue sliver of a dragon enters the narrow pass. They aren't too far behind.

Ignis sprints into the shadows.

Tree trunks are jammed between the walls, stretching across like when Stirling would pull a lump of tacky dough apart. Some fit perfectly while others are logged at different intervals and angles.

Quilan checks behind him, he can see the small images of his regular competitors fighting in the forest. Raising an eyebrow he twists his spine to peer down below him. He scoffs at the approaching orange dragon and emerges out of the pass and over the salty bay.

Ignis leaps into the air returning to his gravity-resistant world as they pass the last checkpoint. The referee is awe-struck as the dragons rocket by. Steadying his stance in the creaking structure he pulls the ropes to release the flags.

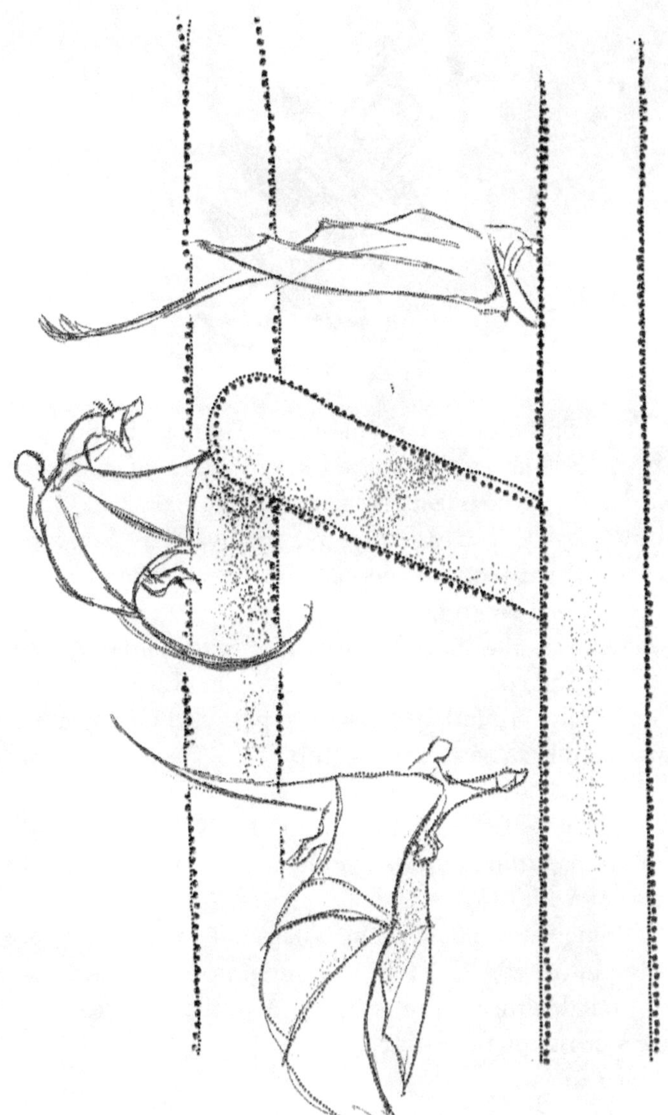

Forty

Stirling's eyes bulge. There it is. There is the finish line. They soar over the last outstretch of the ocean back to the pillars. He can hear the crowd's enthusiasm being carried out over the water as they race towards them at speeds people who haven't seen it wouldn't be able to fathom.

They pass the shoreline of eroded land bordered with rocks and the odd pink creatures. Folding his wings Ignis drops to the ground, his claws gripping and tearing in the churned dirt as he skids to a stop.

The audience leaps to their feet, the bleachers structure groaning as the people go ballistic. Horns blare and drums rattle as they wave their flags dancing and cheering with delight.

Stirling stares out at them. Their individual voices muted into a constant roar like the bottom of a flowing waterfall. He turns in his seat to watch the other four racers cross the finish line.

He can't believe it.

Is this real?

He whips his head in the other direction, his curls bouncing across his forehead. He locks eyes with Quilan who has already dismounted his dragon. Quilan slowly blinks his empty blue eyes. They linger on Stirling's disbelieving expression as he pivots and saunters towards the podium.

"Get up there." Ignis ushers, shaking his back to wake Stirling out of his euphoric daze.

Unclipping, Stirling leaps off Ignis. His feet fail him. Catching his toe on his heel he lands on his hands in the dirt. Too elated to feel any embarrassment Stirling jumps back up and shakily jogs over to the podium waiting for the first, second, and third-place winners.

He is already beaming. There's no control over himself. He has even outdone his own expectations this time. He wants to jump, he wants to scream, he wants to dance.

His body vibrates as he tries to lock up the erupting energy.

If he had listened to society he would be back in Wyverna. He would be miserable in the bakery not knowing all the options the world has to offer. All he needed was to be willing to take the risks and go for it. The only person who chooses his future is himself.

Stirling bounces up onto the podium like an excited child beside Quilan whose mouth pinches into a straight line. Dimples in both of his cheeks surface as if he is holding something back.

"In third place, we have Peyton of Leucasia!" The announcer's voice booms.

A hefty velvet drawstring is placed in Peyton's extended hands. They bow their heads, and the announcer moves on.

"In second place we have Stirling of Patu!"

Stirling bursts, throwing his arms up with a, "WOO!"

It is real. This is real. He holds his hands out and the velvet sack is dropped into them. He cradles the sack of coins not expecting the heavyweight. He runs his fingers over the velvet fabric, this has to be more than all his other winnings combined.

What will he even do with this amount?

Still stuck in his own world of amazement he doesn't even hear Quilan's name being announced for first place. He doesn't care. He is ecstatic beyond words. He placed second.

"WE PLACED SECOND!" He shouts out to Ignis.

Losing himself in the sky, Stirling hugs the coins close to his chest. Quilan hooks his winnings to his belt and steps down from the podium. The announcement of the final winners in Leucasia's Skylit Endeavor is now over. The Annual Games are over and the celebrations are beginning.

Still hugging the coins Stirling sees the audience beginning to descend from the bleachers and onto the racer track to congratulate and celebrate with the celebrity racers. The evening will kick off with a closing ceremony that leads to a party lasting the rest of the night until daylight strikes again in the morning.

Quilan stares up at Stirling.

"Eh hem." Quilan exaggeratedly clears his throat.

Stirling steps down and faces him, his dark eyes meeting Stirling's bright ones. Night looking at day. Quilan holds out his hand. Stirling gazes down at it then his eyes dart back up to Quilan's face.

"Oh. Uh." Stirling takes Quilan's hand in his. A smile stretches across Quilan's face, his perfect teeth brighter than the moon. Stirling is left speechless with an odd pulse in his chest. This is the first time he has seen a genuine smile come from Quilan. This isn't the practiced smile he had seen on stage, but a slightly offset smile with one dimple deeper than the other.

With a new spark in his eyes, Quilan shakes Stirling's hand, "Thank you."

Thank you? He's thanking *him?* Stirling tilts his head confused, "For what?"

He releases Stirling's hand as the crowd begins to flow dangerously close to them like an incoming tide. His slumping shoulders pull back as if attached to strings, his chin lifts and the fossil of the rare smile is lost to the elements. Returning to his blasé demeanor he backs away from Stirling.

"A good last race." His eyes focus on something behind Stirling, turning on his heels he welcomes his fans with raised arms.

"Oof." Stirling lets out as Eve plows into him wrapping her arms tightly around his midsection.

Bernard lopes up behind them engulfing both of them in a bear hug. "Boy, I don't even know how to begin describing how proud I am!"

The moment of ecstasy between Stirling and his friends is cut short as impatient fans surge forward all wanting their turn to congratulate him. He scans over their heads but Quilan is gone, already lost to sea.

"Stirling!"

"Stirling!"

"Stirling!"

Still stuck together by Bernard, Stirling leans close to Eve so she can hear him over the crowd. Her heart skips a beat as the warmth of his breath tickles her ear.

"I thought you said the people give competitors their space when they are with friends and family?"

Eve's eyes shoot daggers out at the fans, "Not during the closing night. They just lose their minds."

"Don't let me go, Bernard." Stirling panics as they are buried alive in the avalanche of people.

Bernard loosens his hug around Stirling and Eve but keeps his hands securely on both of their shoulders to keep Stirling from being hauled away. "Say hi to your fans, Stirling."

"Uh…hi, everyone." Stirling's lips pull back in an awkwardly forced smile. He puts his hands up in a small wave, which is rewarded by overly reactive girls. A man steps forward clasping his hands around Stirling's waving one.

He shakes it with urgency, his voice quick and rigid, star-struck, "You are incredible, really really incredible. You put a name out there for us little folk. Thank you, thank you, thank you."

"You're welcome?"

A girl takes hold of his free hand before the first man lets go of his other, "Will you keep your orange cape for next year? I want to know so I can be prepared with a new orange gown."

"Next year?" Stirling blinks.

"Yeah, I want to know that, too!"

"Same here!"

"Y-yeah, I guess," Stirling answers, pressing his back against Bernard's gut.

"Move, you're hogging him," a young girl says, pushing the woman to the side.

Fan after fan hounds him with applause and questions. His arms are being tugged in every which way. With his arms being pulled in a crisscross, he starts to see the world tilt. When is the last breath he took in? Stirling opens his mouth, but only gibberish comes out.

"Okay, everyone!" Bernard's voice rolls over the crowd. "I think the poor boy needs a break. He did just fly a marathon. We are going to go enjoy some refreshments. So, if you don't mind." Bernard squats down, throwing both Eve and Stirling over his shoulders. Dazed and confused, Stirling doesn't put up any protest. He is relieved to be leaving.

Eve looks out at the pouting girls as she is carried away. With a bragging smile, she reaches across Bernard's back and takes Stirling's hand. Feeling the comforting touch of the hand he has grown to associate with safety, he squeezes back. Eve sticks out her tongue gloating at the girls.

Once clear of the crowd Bernard drops Stirling and Eve back onto their own feet.

"Thanks, Bernard. I still don't understand why all the attention stresses me out so much," Stirling confesses.

"It would stress any normal person out. There's very few people who enjoy their life on display, but it might be because they don't know anything else. They've never had a chance to learn what personal space really means. Like your friend Quilan there," Benard advises.

Stirling peeks back at Quilan who has brought his dragon over for show. Ignis, who disregarded Stirling when the crowd showed up, watches the blue dragon with big golden doe eyes.

From here it seems Quilan is eating up the attention as if he needs it to survive, but it was the way the fire in his eyes during the race faded back into dead coals as the crowd arrived. There's something hiding beneath the calm surface of Quilan of Leaucasia and Stirling can't help but be drawn to whoever Quilan truly is. He hopes one day they can be friends.

Shaking the intrusive thoughts out of his head, Stirling shrugs, "Yeah, I prefer to stay off the stage. I just enjoy flying." His hand strokes the velvet bag, "I know you told me you won't accept any more money for the village."

Bernard raises an eyebrow. "Yeah? You've already paid us back. We're even."

"But, I am going to need a home built if I'm going to live in Patu." Stirling lifts his gaze to meet Bernards.

"Oh? You don't say? Are you going to build this home by yourself?" Bernard catches on.

"Well, I do want to put a lot of the work into it myself, but I would like some help if there is anyone looking for some work," Stirling says, beating around the bush.

"Interesting, because I know some handymen who are always willing to offer a helping hand. But they don't work for free." Bernard grins.

"I think we can negotiate a deal that your men will find suitable Sir tradesmen." The coins jingle as Stirling shakes the bag.

"Yay!" Eve cheers, hugging Stirling's arm. Licking her parched lips, she asks, "Bernard, you mentioned drinks. This whole city is going to be in celebration. Where do you have in mind?"

"This is your day Stirling, any place special you want?" Bernard says, passing the decision off.

"I have somewhere in mind." Stirling pulls his arm free of Eve and throws it around her shoulders with a goofy grin. "*Ready to head out, Ignis?*" Stirling calls over.

Ignis peels his gaze away from Quilan's quetzalcoatl and begins to trot over to Stirling. He pauses to slip in one last look. The quetzalcoatl waves the long feathers at the end of their tail in his direction. Ignis's feathers fluff as a nervous pulse runs through him. He lowers his head shyly then continues trotting to Stirling.

Stirling's arm slides free of Eve as Ignis arrives. "We're going to walk back with you." Grabbing the saddle, he hoists himself onto Ignis' back.

"Back? Like to the village?" Bernard questions.

"Yeah, I heard they have the best alehouse in the kingdom."

Eve's honey eyes blink up at him with a mixture of puzzlement and excitement. "Why not fly back?"

Stirling extends his hand down to her. "Because it's not safe if you're not strapped in."

Lost for words Eve takes Stirling's hand and looks over at Bernard, who without needing to be asked, lifts her up. He sets the giddy girl side saddle on Ignis' back behind Stirling.

"Best if you hold onto me, Evelina" Stirling suggests.

Turning pink, Eve gladly wraps her arms around Stirling and buries her face into his back. She breathes him in, the strong scent of straw bedding. Stirling holds one hand on the harness and the other onto Eve's arm wrapped across his chest to make sure she is secure as Ignis carries them away from Leucasia's Skylit Endeavor.

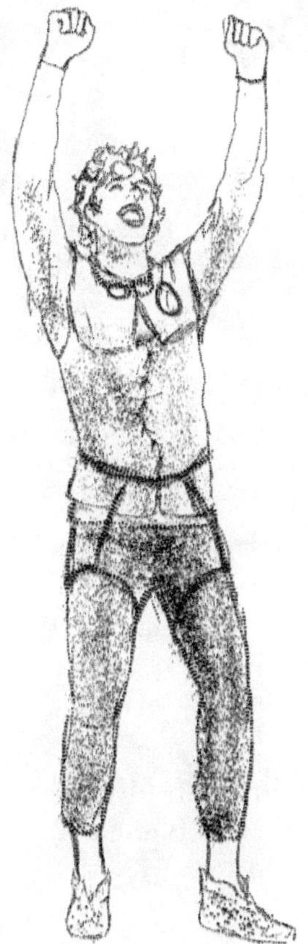

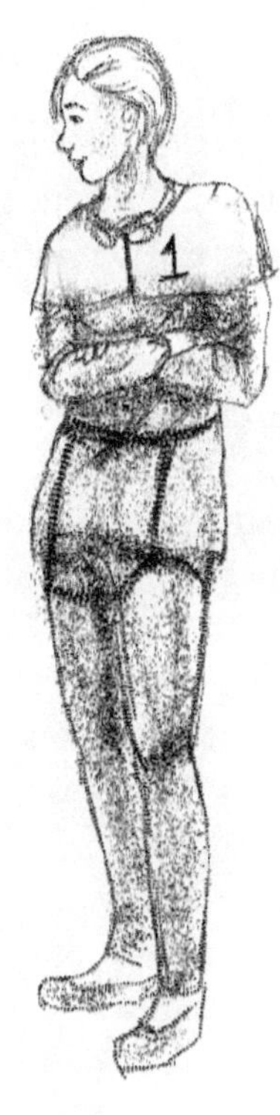

Forty-One

Small crashing waves lit by candlelight break the barriers of their containers. Ale, mead, wine, and spirits soil the alehouses floor as everyone's choice of poison is thrown into the air.

The small alehouse is vibrant and full of life. The boisterous men spill out of the windows like their drinks spill over the rim of their tankards as the entire village crams into the single room. Everyone is celebrating the spectacular turnout of this year's games.

Stirling sits on top of one of the tables laughing uncontrollably beside Eve whose black ringlets are free from their braids and are a halo around her head. Roesia leans over grabbing his face in her hands.

Pinching his cheeks, she tells him, "We are so proud of you."

"I know! You told me a hundred times already!" He says back through his smooshed face, but too polite to remove her hands.

"And I will say it another hundred times." Still holding his face she pulls him in closer and kisses the top of his forehead before disappearing back into the crowd.

He loves being surrounded by the villagers. They feel safe and warm like when his mother used to tuck his blanket around him. Their kinship is real. Win or lose they would still throw their arms around him and make him one of their own–unlike the artificial love and praise he received during the games only after he started his winning streak. The city loves the professional elite racer Stirling of Patu, not Stirling Bakere a runaway from Wyverna. Not *baker boy*.

Throwing his head back, Stirling chugs half of his ale.

"I can't believe Quilan congratulated you," one of the village men tells him.

Removing the tankard from his lips Stirling corrects the man. "No, no. He more thanked me for not disappointing him."

"In Quilan words, congratulations," another adds.

"He shook your hand!" a woman interjects. "Quilan asked to shake *your* hand. He doesn't even talk to the other racers let alone shake their hand."

Eve hugs onto Stirling's arm. "That's just how magical the whole experience was. Even Quilan was impressed by our Stirling."

"Way to show them who's boss even after they treated you how they did."

A pulsing shock runs through Stirling, he hasn't told anyone but Eve the true extent of what he experienced from the other racers. He shrugs, keeping his voice from turning hostile, "It doesn't matter to me anymore. I will forgive, but I won't forget. For Quilan–" Stirling pauses, his chest constricting as he pictures the pale haired boy with dark eyes, "he is his own mystery."

"Well, next year you're really going to give him a run for his coin."

"Yeah!" Stirling stands up on the bench seat with a new surge of energy, "YEAH! Next year, full elite games!"

The villagers around him throw their tankards up in a toast.

"You know what I say to that!" Stirling says out over the crowd of peers with all eyes on him.

"WHAT!?" they ask in unison.

"I say we DRINK! DRINK! Gather at the tavern and DRINK!" Stirling hops up onto the table still singing as everyone joins in. Their voices, unable to be contained to the alehouse, carry out across the plains.

"Place a bet and roll the dice and DRINK!"

Stirling offers out his hand to Eve. Already immersed in the frolicsome ambiance, Eve gladly accepts his hand and allows him to whisk her up to the table with him.

Still holding her hand Stirling exaggerates a bow. Eve laughs and in return, she gestures with a mocking curtsey. Stirling will admit he's never learned to dance further than the basic steps in the bakery, spinning along the floured floor with his mother. He steps forward with his left foot sliding his right across the table to meet it. His arm free sways through the air as it rides the musical notes.

"Work all day and have no coin and DRINK! Don't tell my Mrs she'll holler as I DRINK! DRINK!"

Eve follows along, her feet step in mirror of Stirling's, their curls bounce with their hopping movements. The muscles in their cheeks are starting to hurt from laughter as they sing along.

"GATHER AT THE TAVERN AND DRINK!"

Bernard leans against the wall with his arm around Roesia, "Look at those two. Eve never used to smile like that."

The small round woman nuzzles herself closer to Bernard, "Yeah, she really has changed this past month. That boy's energy is rubbing off on her."

"I'm glad, she really needed to let the light in," Bernard says, watching the twinkle in Eve's eyes as she twirls under Stirling's arm.

Forty-Two

The sounds of the active market streets drown out the notes of the muffled citole. Giles sits in Grace's home holding the citole with a string tied around the instrument's neck to dampen the sound. His sore fingertips not yet calloused press weakly down on the four strings.

"Okay, you're going to place your fingers, here, here and here," she instructs, positioning his fingers for him to produce the first cord. "Then using your thumb you're going to strum down."

Giles listens intently and performs exactly as he is told.

She claps her hands together. "Great! Now lift your index and strum again."

Grinning like a child proud of their first steps, Giles hears the tune change. He's playing, he is really playing. He repeats the two cords over and over amazed at his simple accomplishment. He believed he would never get to hold a citole. He lived a life accepting the fact and was content to only listen to the music. The music he was told he will never create.

"It's a start, your fingers will hurt at first until you toughen the skin," Grace informs, placing her hand on his arm. Her hand slips back to her lap as her smile fades. "You know what's bothering me?"

"What?" he asks, looking up at her.

"I keep thinking of that boy with the dragon." She stares up at the ceiling as if she is seeing him fly again. "People keep saying he revealed himself to make a statement."

Giles sets the citole flat on his lap. He can't look at her. He can't let her read his eyes.

She continues, "I believe he didn't do it intentionally. I think he was trying to escape for freedom. I hope his soul is free, free to fly through the clouds. But I do know his unfortunate sacrifice was a gift to this kingdom. He opened our eyes. We are not puppets. We cannot have our entire lives controlled." She removes her gaze from the rafters and looks at Giles who is staring at the citole. "What do you think?"

"I think you are right." Giles can feel the ache in his jaw from incoming tears. He blinks them back, "I like to imagine the boy made it out alive. I think he is out there making someone of himself."

Grace releases a slow breath, "I wonder who his parents are." She leans her head down trying to see Giles' face, "You know if I was his parent, I would be *so* proud of him." Giles meets her eyes. "He truly did the impossible." She states looking into his heart.

"Fly a dragon?"

Red waves bounce as she shakes her head replying, "Wrote his own story."

Blistered feet rubbed raw drag through the layers of decomposing leaves as Amiria limps through the ever-expanding forest. Too painful to remove, Amiria still wears her dark armor crusted with dried blood. Alleviating her swollen shoulder of stress she has tied her arm tight to her chest restricting its movement.

Her toe catches on a raised root and she stumbles forward. A pained whimper escapes as her armor clangs against the tree she falls into. Her good arm clings around the rough trunk holding her quitting body up. Breathing heavily, Amiria bites back a scream of frustration, her face growing red. She presses her forehead against the bark with a muffled cry.

She can go back. He will take her back. They don't know she ran. All she has to do is tell them she was captured and only regained consciousness now. Taika is a whistle away. She calls for Taika and Calix will follow. She can lie down here on the padded forest floor and wait for him. He will take care of her. He could help her remove this wretched armor and lift her into his arms. With him, she can go back home and breathe in the scent of mint chamomile, the scent of security.

"Calix," she murmurs as heavy eyelids slide shut. Her body begins to slip from her grasp on the tree. Panic shocks Amiria awake before she falls. *Stirling.* He's out there somewhere. She has to keep going.

Pushing herself away from the tree, she trudges on. She won't call Taika, not yet. She has to be certain they've left Taika behind, giving up on her guiding them to her. For now, she will continue to avoid all roads and towns. She is in a too-vulnerable state to properly defend herself.

Pushing back loose strands of sweat-matted hair, she squints up at the sun shining through the forest canopy, from what she can gather she is traveling southeast.

A rumbling sound emanates from her stomach. She needs sustenance. Coming up to a log, she collapses onto it, resting her aching legs. This land is full of running creeks so she has access to clean water, but she had left all of her provisions, and her bow attached to Taika, and at the campground. All she has are the two blades on her back. She can only hope Dicun didn't remove anything from her packs, but she would bet her coin on him taking the food.

She frowns, it's not like she can use her bow anyway.

"What would Stirling do?" she utters, hitting herself on the head with the heel of her hand. "Think, think." She pauses at the sound of a toad croaking. She raises her lip in disgust. "Next." She scans the branches above her head. "Maybe I can find some eggs, but how am I going to make a fire? Or even climb the tree…"

Covering her eyes with her hand she slides from the log to the ground. She drags her hand down her face in frustration, smearing the layer of grime stuck to her sweat-dampened skin.

She leans back against the log and watches the branches sway above.

Exhausted in the hot sun, Stirling leans on a shovel as he pulls on the collar of his tunic fanning himself. He and several of the village men have begun digging into the soft earth to give the new home a strong foundation to build on.

Using Ignis' raw strength, they have been able to move large sums of building materials quicker and in a greater quantity than compared to using a horse or ox. With his help lifting the frames, they will be able to have the home built in half the normal time.

With teams of dragons, Stirling can see how Leucasia was able to create all those elaborate designs and obstacles for the games.

Ignis stands knee-deep in the river hydrating, "*After lugging all this stuff for you, you better build me a room too.*"

Stirling had spoken to the Lord of the land who owned the property the village resides on and was able to come to an agreement to purchase his plot of land outright. It is just past the furthest house in Patu settled beside the river. The villagers helped show him the highest point the river will flood so he could build his house at a safe distance. He will have plenty of space for his own garden, goat, chickens, and maybe even a small dock to fish off while he takes in the stunning view of the prairie.

Stirling rolls his head back in response, "*Do you think I'd leave you outside? I wouldn't be able to sleep from the amount of whining I would hear.*"

Forty-Three

Newly calloused fingers wrap protectively around the doll-like hand, a hand they would climb a mountain to hold. Giles stands between Grace and the dirt road as a shield while they stroll the outer limits of the city. Both want the relief of fresh air.

An unnerving dread raises the hair on the back of his neck as he hears the sound of hoofbeats and wheels behind them. Turning around to see who is approaching he quickly pulls Grace into his chest. He coddles her head as a cage being carted by two guards, one steering and the other slumped in the seat sound asleep, rolls slowly by.

They are bringing the next group of assumed guilty into the city for the gallows. The guard steering leers down at Giles whose jaw hangs unhinged.

He watches unblinking, unable to take his eyes off what he is beholding. Several more carts pass by with rusted metal cages that cry louder than the starved faces with empty eyes staring out through the bars. Layer upon layer people ranging from those late in their lives to those who are just beginning theirs, stand on top of each other with no room to turn around. These are fathers, mothers, sons, and daughters.

As Amiria had said, *He set a fire and left us to burn.*

The news spread across the entire Wyverna like wildfire. With each village, it consumes it only grows stronger. It will stay a blaze until it runs out of fuel and everything is dead. What is a king when his kingdom is nothing but ash?

The afternoon light shines through the mosaic windows of the throne room giving a colorful display to the dreadful gloom of the attendants. Armundus, Eda, and Everard stand at attention at the bottom of the throne's steps. King Dietrich sits slouched on his throne leaning heavily to one side, his arm gripping the armrest as it is the only thing keeping him seated. With his free arm, he rubs deep into his temples, his mind bursting with contemplations.

Standing halfway up the steps Field Marshal Rey's jaw goes slack as his knees buckle. He lands in a sitting position and slides down two steps before coming to a slumping halt. His spasming hands release the parchment he is reading from.

"I don't believe it." He utters as the paper softly drifts to the red-carpet cascading down the steps. "It's not true."

Disheveled, he buries his face into his hands. A sudden burst of incoherent vocals escapes from his mouth as he slams his fists into the steps beside him. The three Winged Riders stand at ready watching their leaders breaking over a single girl.

"Get out." King Dietrich mumbles, his fingers pinching the brim of his nose. The three members of Team Requiro move only their eyes to glance at each other. King Dietrich sits up slamming his fist on the armrest, "YOU THREE GET OUT!"

"Yes, you're majesty." Eyes wide, they bow in unison. Straightening up, they quickly escort themselves out of the throne room. The closing door echoes across the granite room.

"Rey," King Dietrich, laughs in exasperation, "Field Marshal Rey."

Rey pushes back his out-of-place hair and leans his elbows on the stairs, "Dietrich."

"Look at us, Rey. Two old fools, crying over the loss of a single soldier." King Dietrich rises to his feet.

"She was my daughter," Rey growls and matches King Dietrich's posture facing him from several steps below.

"And she was my prized rider. In the end—" King Dietrich sucks his teeth making a *tsk* sound, "She has fallen." He glares down at where Amiria had once stood and imagines her there. Her freshly polished armor shone like his gems. "I've lost her. Now Rey, whose fault is that." His eyes flick back to her father, his voice growing more furious with each word. "Tell me. Whose. Fault. Is. That!"

Field Marshal Rey holds his composure. "Well, Sire. She was under your team."

With a flash of metal, King Dietrich's claymore stops at Rey's neck. Rey stands there unmoving with his arms behind his back and his chin held high. "Not even a flinch, I'm impressed, Rey," King Dietrich turns the blade and runs it up to Rey's jaw, the sharpened edge shaving the unblinking man's stubble. "But what if I did strike you down, Field Marshal? What would you do?" King Dietrich drops his blade and steps up to Rey so their chests almost touch as he leans into his ear. "You have no heir."

Rey's chest rises and falls as he thinks. Anyone else he could run them through with a sword and order a subordinate to remove the body. There is no one else in this kingdom who would challenge him, but there is one person in Wyverna with a higher rank than himself and he is breathing down his neck.

High in the rafters above the two men, Kinsey giggles. "Oh, poor Field Marshal." She pouts her bottom lip, "Whatever will you do?"

She rolls onto her back kicking her feet in the air, "I'm glad I came back to watch the reveal, everyone's favorite little bird is gone. Oh, what will they do without her pretty face on display."

Putting her hands on the beam beneath her head she throws her legs and leaps up into the air. She lands squatted on one leg and the other hanging off the beam with a pointed toe as she balances. "Oops, almost fell," she smiles. "Now," she twirls to standing, "I've got wonderful news to tell the general."

The air is warmer here. The temperature has been steadily rising as she travels out from the base of the mountain range. How long has she been walking?

Amiria trips over a rock protruding from the ground staggering into another open glade. "Ahh," She cries out as she uses her strapped arm to help catch her balance. She grips her shoulder and pushes forward with a bite of her lip.

Heavy bags hang rich in color over her sunken cheeks. Her once olive skin faded to an unnatural gray. She is barely able to lift her feet as she steps past the line of birch trees and wades out through the field of overgrown daisies leaving a distinct trail in her wake.

If heaven exists, it must look like this. Closing her eyes, she lets her tired head fall back to feel the sun on her skin. A large shadow passes overhead. She shields her eyes and opens them to the sky. Worn muscles strain to create a smile of relief, her hair whipping around in the wind's vortex shrouding her. She drops her hand ignoring the strands sticking to her mouth.

With the shadow now hovering completely over her, solace flows through her aching body and she collapses to the ground. Her knees bend at broken angles she lies buried in the daisies dancing wildly around her. A giggle bubbles up from deep within her. She can't stop as the frenzy of laughs takes over. Her eyes water as she gasps for air between her manic outbursts.

Taking choking breaths, she reaches up at the descending beige dragon.

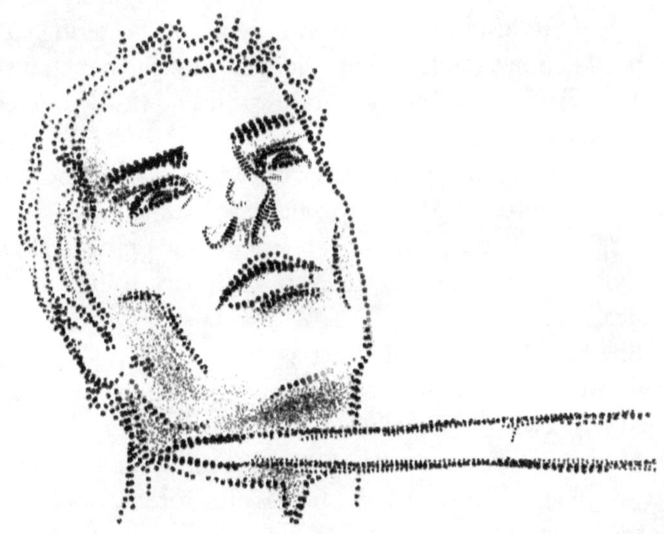

Forty-Four

With an overabundance of laughter, Stirling and Eve stumble out of the alehouse. Teetering to one side, Eve plops herself onto the bench just outside the door below the window. Stirling nearly misses the bench and falls beside her.

Checking back through the window, Eve stifles her giggles by putting her finger to her lips with a, "Shh." Stirling nods in a snickering agreement. She grabs him by the wrist and tugs him along lifting him back to his unsteady feet.

She breathes in the night air as they exit the village and begin the trek through the undulating hip-height grass filled with twinkling fireflies. "There's something refreshing about the cool air on your skin." The subtle breeze pushes Stirling's bangs across his forehead. He closes his eyes as he walks, the chill prickling his fevered skin. Eve runs her palms across the tips of the waist-high blades of grass. "I think your house is coming around nicely."

Stirling rolls his entire head before looking over at her. "It's a skeletal box. There's no actual walls yet."

Eve squints through the dark at his house. "Well, I like your stone foundation, it will be a nice porch to watch the days pass by from."

Curls flop back and forth as Stirling shakes his head, laughing. "Thanks, I guess. Don't worry you'll be rid of me soon, it shouldn't be much longer."

Eve pouts. "I've gotten so used to you being there though. It'll be so quiet without you."

Trust me, that place will *never* be quiet." Stirling pauses as they near his home to listen to the faint voices and laughter spilling from the window of the alehouse. "Also, you can literally see my house from there. I'll still be hanging out most of the days anyway. Unless I leave for a competition."

"Good," Eve states as she climbs the stairs of his porch. "You're really part of this family now." She takes hold of one of the wooden frames and spins a full circle around it to face Stirling again. Her doll eyes match the light color of the timber, "Do you ever think of them? Your family back home I mean?"

"All the time," Stirling says without hesitation.

Her face falls, the moonlight making her skin ebony. "What is it you think, exactly?" She inquires, hugging the wooden beam.

Stirling leans his shoulder against the next frame. "I wonder how they are. What they are doing. If they are okay. Sometimes I see things that remind me of my friend." Stirling pauses and smiles at the memory of Amiria. "I guess a lot of things remind me of her."

Eve purses her lips as Stirling loses his thoughts to another girl. "Do you miss them?"

"More than you can imagine."

"Do you think you would ever be able to bring them here?" She steps around the frame to be beside him.

"If I could, I would." Stirling stares off into the prairie he had traveled over to get here.

She watches him, wishing one day he will look at her like he does the horizon when he thinks of her. "Tag." Eve taps Stirling's shoulder, knocking his mind back to the present.

A goofy grin slaps across his face as if he was never thinking of his past.

"Come here!" He reaches for Eve who leaps backward just out of range.

Giggling, she takes cover by placing the wooden structure between them. Stirling bounces on his toes as he tries to guess which direction she will run in. Eve feints to run in the direction of the center of the home then changes to leaping down the patio stairs. Stirling falls for her deception, then leaps into the grass after her. Fireflies scatter into the air like shooting stars swirling around the moving planets as the two young friends run through the night.

Forty-Five

Biting her glove to keep her from screaming out in pain, Amiria was finally able to remove her armor and change into her casual cotehardie and tights. Even with her arm still resting in a sling, she has the scabbards on her hips. One-handed or not she will still put up a fight if the encounters result in it.

She passed town after town traveling at night for weeks, afraid to be seen by residents until she was certain she was out of Uviktiland and entered a new kingdom. What caught her attention about this city, in particular, is the peculiar-looking dragons with four legs loping around enormous stables built outside the city walls. The idea that any foreign nation would possess dragons had never occurred to her. She had grown up believing wyverns were the only species of dragon and they resided in the Isles. This revelation is the evidence she needed to secure the fact she had long left Uviktiland.

Was Ignis from here? she wonders as she lands Taika near the stables. Curious looks are thrown at her from the stable men when she leaps from Taika's back and ties her to the metal post held down by stone blocks.

"Pardon me? Pardon me?" She waves her good arm approaching a group of men in riding gear who appear to be on break at the city stables. "Can you understand me?"

The men's conversation dies as they take in the girl seeking their attention. One of them steps forward. "You talk kind of strange, but otherwise yes, I can understand you. I'm guessing you're not from here."

She stares blankly. They *can* understand her. How is that possible? She has to be on the other side of the world, this shouldn't be possible.

"Are you all right, sweetheart? Is that your husband's?" He points at Taika. "A woman should never be riding a dragon, it's not safe. Is that how you injured yourself?"

Husband? A woman should never—what? Amiria shakes her head confused. *What is he going on about?* "Sir, I am perfectly capable of flying a dragon."

"You don't have to be embarrassed if you fell off. That's why women don't fly."

Excuse me? Amiria bites her tongue growing impatient, she tries to remain formal. "My injuries are none of your concern. I'm here because I am requiring information. I'm looking for my friend—"

Another one of the guys in the back snickers. "I can be your friend for the night."

She continues as if she didn't hear him. "He is tall with curly blondish brown hair."

"I prefer my girls in dresses." The man beside him commentates.

She glances down at her cotehardie and tights, then eyes the men, irritated, "Are you going to give me suitable information on the whereabouts of my missing friend or are you going to continue to waste my time with useless banter about my appearance."

"Calm down. No one likes a woman who nags." The man in front looks Amiria up and down, "You have to agree, trousers are no garment for a woman."

Maybe it's the lack of food and rest that has made her irritable, but she has lost patience in trying to negotiate. Why try to be formal if it is not reciprocated, but there is a language anyone can understand.

A sly grin sneaks across his face. "I truly prefer my girls in nothing."

Her arm shoots out snagging the collar of the man's shirt and pulls him to her eye level, "Now I'm going to ask you one more time, who can help me find my missing friend?"

"Wench," the man spits, his face close enough to Amiria's she can feel the spray from his words.

This isn't Wyverna, she doesn't have to uphold her appearance anymore. What did acting properly get her anyway, pushed aside? Picked on? Used? Amiria rears her head back and slams her forehead forward, not stopping even after she crashes into the man's nose. She's not holding back as she breaks through who she used to be.

His head whips back as his hands instinctively reach up to hold his nose gushing with blood. Shocked at her actions she releases her grip on his collar dropping him to the patchy grass to ball up in agony.

"Uh." She holds her hand up at shoulder height.

The men stare horrified. Their eyes dart back and forth between her and their companion. "Y-y-you can't do that," one stammers.

"I mean…" Amiria brings back the Winged Rider in her. "Are you going to tell the guard you're scared of an injured girl?" With their friend sitting up staunching the blood from his nose they shake their head in unison. "Now if you can't help me. Tell me who can."

A trembling hand from the group points in the direction of a few cluttered buildings, "Th-the girls who hang out by the management shop seem to be in the know of the whole city. They will be your best bet."

"Thank you." Setting off, Amiria stops beside the bleeding man, "I'm sorry about your—" She waves her hand around her nose. He spits blood on the grass between her shoes in response. "Okay, I might have deserved that." She pulls her lips into a tight line. "Thanks again."

Without looking back at the man she assaulted, Amiria strolls across the stable grounds to a group of several young girls in their later teens sitting on a circle of benches. They pause mid-conversation and all turn to Amiria who desperately wants to recoil but holds herself firmly in place.

"Can we help you?" a girl with black hair says.

"I'm looking for a friend," Amiria starts. "I was told you know a lot about what is happening in this city."

"You were told right, and not just this city. We know all the racers who stop by here. So we always know who's, who," a girl with braided hair brags.

"Tell us," the girl with black hair who appears as their group leader says, "What is your friend's name? What does she look like?"

"*His* name is Stirling Bakere. He is tall with muddy blonde hair and wild curls. He would be accompanied by an orange dragon," Amiria describes.

The group of girls exchanges glances. "What are you getting at? What's your ploy?"

"What?" Amiria raises an eyebrow, confused. "I don't understand what you mean."

"We don't know a Stirling Bakere, but we do know a Stirling of Patu who matches your description. Even if we did know where he is, we wouldn't give that information out to a crazed fan."

"CRAZED FAN!" Amira blurts. "I don't know who this Stirling of Patu is. I'm looking for my friend Stirling Bakere!"

The girl with the braids rolls her eyes as if Amiria hadn't fooled her. "Stirling of Patu got second in the elite marathon during his first annual games. There is no one in Tallfallya or any of these Kingdoms who hasn't heard his name."

"I heard he's almost as handsome as Quilan," a blonde girl adds.

"You heard? You don't know what he looks like?" Amiria makes eye contact checking each one of them.

The girl with black hair flips her hair over her shoulder. "Well, I did see him once. At the race last month." She frowns, "But both him and Quilan never came to meet fans so I only saw him from afar."

Amiria blinks slowly, "Quilan? Fans?" She pinches the brim of her nose. I am so confused."

The girls lean into one another and whisper, "Is there something wrong with her like up here." One points to her head. "She talks funny."

"I talk funny? Nevermind." Amiria waves her hand not wanting to get into the discussion of her accent. "Is there someone here, who has met this Stirling of *Patu*?"

"Not that we know of. I heard he's shy and has only competed in a couple of races after the Skylit Endeavor. There is a painting of the elite team displayed inside the racer shop." The girl with the braids tells her.

Amiria nods thanks and walks up the steps to the shop. Pushing through the door she halts just inside the threshold of a store littered from wall to wall with merchandise. Half of the store is dedicated to fans with racer-themed attire from capes, tunics, ribbons, and hoods sitting folded on tables. Toy goggles for children sit by pretend riding gear made of stiffened fabric instead of leather on shelves.

The other half is where the owner of this racing shop, leans against an extravagant display of professional-grade gear for those who are serious about the sport.

"May I help you, miss? I'm Jarin. Welcome to my shop," he tells the bewildered girl standing aimlessly in his doorway.

"Uh," Amiria starts as she stares at the detailed painting hung on the opposing wall of six men with silhouettes of uniquely colored dragons behind each of them.

The placement of the six racers must be for a deliberate reason, that Amiria is sure of. A pale blond-haired boy with beautiful feminine features stands with his shoulders in front of everyone else. His emotionless eyes stare straight through her. Each racer stands with one of their shoulders behind the person in front. On the farthest right of the group stands a curly-haired boy with a goofy grin. The silhouette of an orange dragon with feathered wings painted behind him.

"You've got to be kidding me," she blurts.

"Excuse me?" Jarin cocks his head.

"That boy at the end. What's his name?" She struggles to keep her disbelief at bay as she points at the painting.

"Look, kid. I run a shop, so either purchase something or get out. This isn't a show for young girls to swoon over elite racers," he says disgruntled.

"Swoon?" she repeats with a raise of her lip. "I'm not swooning. I'm searching for my friend and I believe it might be him."

"Yeah, you and every other girl in this kingdom. Don't play this old man as a fool. Buy something or get out. I have a family to feed," Jarin tells her.

Amiria mutters under her breath about how rude the shopkeeper is then speaks up, "Fine. Do you have any maps of this, Tallfallya?"

"Over there rolled up on the shelf." He points.

Picking up one of the maps Amiria unrolls it and frowns. Her fingernails dig into the cheap canvas. Restraining herself from crumpling up the parchment she says, "Sir, I can't read this."

"That sounds like a personal problem," Jarin responds.

Anger is boiling up in Amiria as she points out, "There aren't many town names on here anyway."

"That's because it only has major cities and towns on it. Don't need to waste ink with villages. Racing cities and stable locations are what's important." He shrugs.

Amiria digs a handful of coins out of her purse hanging from her harness. "Fine, how much is the map?"

Jarin leans forward, eyeing the coins in her palm. "I don't accept foreign currency."

"Perfect," Amiria bites, tossing the map back on the shelf.

"Don't take your problems out on my merchandise." Jarin strains, fed up with this girl who will not be purchasing anything.

"My apologies sir. Do you know where the village of Patu is?" Amiria tones down her frustration.

"Nope, not a clue. Never even heard of it until Stirling. Now, I'm not answering any more questions for free. I think it's time for you to leave."

The group of girls glances over as Amiria leaps down the steps. Her only clue is the village of Patu. A village, Amiria takes from these few encounters, is a place no one knows where it is.

Spotting a new person, she puts on a friendly smile and cradles her injured arm, "Pardon me, do you know where Patu is?"

The person with sympathy in their eyes as they look at a fragile little girl shakes their head apologetically. "I'm not sure. Isn't that where the racer Stirling is from?"

"Sorry to bother you, thank you," she says sweetly before moving on to the next person.

Forty-Six

Ealdian Dietrich's broad shoulders hunch as he grips the railing of his balcony overlooking Lumierna. The purple robes pulled taught against his muscular back flow loosely forward the light silken fabric billows in the breeze that is climbing up the side of the castle.

Behind him in his private chambers, his crown lies discarded on his nightstand beside his unkempt bed. There has been no further news on his recognizance team. It was a mistake to send an entire platoon of Winged Riders to Uviktiland, too many of them now know the failure of the mission. He should have kept it small to start with. He shouldn't have sent her, should have only sent those who are disposable.

Every Winged Rider but two were ordered to return home. He can't say for sure they are his two best, but he knows they will get the job done. Out of Unit Larua, they have the most motivation. One will search until he is no longer breathing. The other is there to keep the young man's mind in check.

Knocking can be heard from his chamber door. He tenses, he is the king, why isn't he allowed a moment's peace? He should be granted a day to himself. He hasn't had any time to grieve. No one, not a single person in this kingdom understands the grief he is experiencing. Not even the field marshal.

He never appreciated Amiria, her gifts, her beauty. She was just his tool, his replacement. It's his own fault he didn't make backups. If you're a Winged Rider, you should always take the possibility of death into account. The Gautiers. The obedient Gautiers are strategic. Their entire existence is to serve this kingdom, to serve *him*. They have enough to fill their positions and the Field Marshal's. There is one positive outcome of this disastrous news. The Rey lineage has finally come to an end.

The knocking persists. King Dietrich drums his fingers on the stone railing.

"Ealdian?" Queen Oriana calls through the locked door. "Ealdian? Your children and I are going down for lunch, are you going to join us?"

A robin lands on the railing beside his hand. He watches the bird tilt its head from side to side to observe its surroundings.

"Ealdian? Are you okay?"

He doesn't respond as he remains invested in the bird. Beautiful creatures they are. That is why some deserve to be placed in cages. Their beauty and their songs need to be put on display for everyone to see, like a painting, or a theatrical act. What is a bird's song if no one is around to hear it?

"Ealdian!"

"STOP KNOCKING ON MY DOOR!" He shouts, whipping around to face the room. Spooked by the outburst, the robin flees into the air. King Dietrich turns in time to watch it disappear over the city. He grinds his teeth, that woman is nothing but a nuisance.

With his eyes back out on his city, he raises his lip in disgust. Far beneath him, the town square is filling up with citizens to watch the next scheduled hanging.

How did it come to this?

Stirling Bakere. How did one child from the lower-class market district cause this much damage to his kingdom? He is nothing but a boy, yet they follow him. He has done nothing for these people, yet they speak of him as a martyr. They hang on ropes by their necks for him. FOR HIM! A SELFISH CHILD!

Now they speak of another name. Amiria Rey. He doesn't know how her name had spread across their lips so quickly, but they whisper about her in his streets. They make up lies about her, saying she had stood up against Wyverna. A fable they are telling about the soldier who said no more, and the baker who flew.

He scoffs. Not his sweet Amiria, his perfect Amiria. It was a misunderstanding. She was defending her kingdom as she had been trained to do. If he could just have her back, he could forgive her and place her by his side indefinitely.

She was only misled. This is all *his* fault. If it wasn't for him, Amiria would still be here. She would be his loyal soldier obeying his every word. Now she is gone, lost to the menacing world outside of his reach.

Calix will bring the traitor back to the kingdom, to this castle, to *him*. She will be back and everything will be in place. He will show her to the people. He will keep her chained in a cage as a reminder to those down there who they are supposed to follow and what happens when they don't.

When life falls back into order, these events will be erased from the history notes. People will never speak of these tales again, and for those who do, the story will die along with them.

Tugging at the stained ribbon tied around his wrist, Calix sits deep in thought at a table in the corner of an alehouse across from Dicun. With their dark armor packed on their dragons, they blend into the crowd's shadows wearing black woolen jopulas.

"Hey." Dicun leans over the table, snapping his fingers directly in Calix's face. "Hey! See this, this is why King Dietrich sent me to nanny you."

Calix smacks his hand out of the way. "I don't need a nanny. I can complete this mission on my own." Picking up his mead, he takes a sip of the dry drink and scans the room.

He should be questioning every single person in here. They have a lead, Patu. The description matches the boy, curly blonde hair, and an orange dragon with the same first name. What he can't figure out is, how does not a single person they have met know where Patu is?

"Ha, you couldn't even order your drink on your own. You're just a love-sick puppy following a dead trail." Dicun lifts his empty drink and shakes it in the direction of the maiden.

Setting his tankard down, Calix's cold eyes flow back to Dicun. "If you didn't insist we leave the dragon behind and continue to the rendezvous point, we wouldn't have a dead trail now. Would we?"

"Lighten up," he says with his eyes still on the bustling room. "We're in a new land, where no one knows what the mark on our arm means."

"What is your point, Dicun?"

"My point is, we're not allowed to return to Wyvern unless we complete our mission," The maiden appears with a new tankard filled with ale and places it in front of Dicun. "So why not enjoy ourselves in the meantime." He winks at her. Blushing, she leans over and whispers into his ear. A grin breaks across his face.

Calix rolls his eyes. "I'm going to the room." He starts to get up. "Oh, and don't bring anyone back with you. You know how us riders can be quick to pull a knife when woken."

"Yeah, yeah." Dicun disregards Calix and pulls the maiden onto his lap.

Pushing past the joyous people of the alehouse, Calix takes a deep breath of fresh air as he steps out into the night. The moon shines bright lighting the inn's grounds. They had left the forested mountains behind and entered the plains of a new kingdom. This inn and alehouse sit in the nestled grasslands with only a small village nearby.

His hands tuck into his armpits, fighting the chill of the star-lit air, he starts out across the trampled dirt to the inn's rooms.

Southeast? she had said. "*This boy will not travel south or southeast.*" Why? Why had she said that, what was she keeping from everyone?

"What did you know, Amiria?" he whispers. Faded purple catches his eye. "Amiria?" He perks up. It had gone around the side of the building. "Amiria?" His footsteps are soundless as he follows the ghost. He turns the corner. "Amiria?—Oh." He stops as he sees a woman smelling of spirits leaning against the wall, her sun-faded brown dress turning purple in the moonlight.

She pushes away from the wall and faces him. "Well well, look at you."

"I'm sorry, ma'am, I thought you were someone else."

"This Amiria?" The woman takes a flirtatious step forward. "Lucky girl she is. We don't have anything like you around here." The woman places her hand on Calix's stomach and runs it up his chest. Calix's body shudders under the touch. His tense muscles relax and his eyes flutter shut, "I can be Amiria for the night."

Eyes pale as the moon, open and stare blankly over the woman's head to the meadows beyond. "Amiria."

"I'll be whoever you want me to be." Her hand trails to his shoulder and cups behind his neck.

Calix drops his eyes back to the woman and lowers his head. He brushes strands of her brown hair back from her face and follows her hairline down to her neck. She tilts her chin up, exposing the vulnerable skin to him as he draws his thumb across.

She gasps. Her eyes bulge in terror, and she stares up at the handsome man, his features as calm and serene as her backdrop. Choking, she grabs at the hand around her throat. She tries to back away, to get out of his grip, but his other hand is locked around her bicep.

He is strong, she panics, stronger than the men who work here at the inn. She is going to die here. She is going to die staring at what she presumed was the face of an angel, but even the devil was an angel once.

He leans down to her ear and breathes. "You will never be my little bird."

The hands shackled around her vanish as they drop to their place at the man's sides. Without them, she collapses to the ground in a heap of shock. Her entire body trembles as she touches her bruising throat. Breaths come out in choking hitches as she struggles to breathe.

Cowering in place, she peeks through her arms expecting more from the frigid man, but there is no one around. The sounds of the alehouse waft across the empty road to where she sits alone in the night.

Crawling to the side of the building, she shakily uses the wall to climb back to her feet. She needs to leave before the man returns. Those glowing eyes now haunt her thoughts. A sob escapes her throat, she clamps her hand over her mouth stifling it. She fears for her own safety, but that isn't what is causing the pit to grow in her stomach.

What terrifies her more is the sinking dread for the girl he speaks of. She fears for the girl she has never met. She prays for the girl Amiria.

Forty-Elven

A family of ducks quack as they follow their mother into the lazy river. Stirling sits with his legs hanging off the side of his porch listening to the summer bugs hum. It had taken him several months to complete his house. Every handyman in the village contributed to turning this pile of timber into a home.

Stirling pops an olive from his wooden bowl into his mouth, enjoying the savory taste. Still chewing, he dips his dried bread into a sauce of herb-soaked oil. His eyes close, letting the warm sun sink into his skin while the valley's breeze jogs across the plains and plays with his curls. In the yard in front of his house, the cotton clothing hanging from a line dance without a body.

He lies on his back and watches the single cloud above him fall beneath the wooden shingles of his roof. Life has been easy. Everyday he does work around his house then spends his down time with Eve or growing closer to Quilan. At the first race after the Games were over the aloof racer sat next to Stirling and has rarely left his side since.

They have competed in matches in other cities over the past several months. Stirling continued to always place behind Quilan in every race, coming out in second or third place, but it's not about winning to him. The coin he has won is nice, but even being fruitful in his spending, he doesn't need to compete until the next annual games. It's about the games themselves. Especially now that he has a close friend to compete alongside and spend time with before and after the racers.

Stirling smiles at the thought.

He has a signed contract tucked away with the King's seal declaring him as a professional racer and initiating him as a citizen. He is officially Stirling of Patu. The name Stirling Bakere is nothing more than a remnant of the past. One of the many scars that he refuses to talk about with anyone except those he holds close.

"Don't you have errands to run for Bernard before the event tonight? It's already late morning." Ignis states as he steps out from the side of the house.

"Yeah, yeah. I need to go over to the city to get the items," Stirling says without looking at him.

"Oh, that's why you're procrastinating. You hate the city."

"I don't *hate* the city," Stirling counters, sitting up. "It's obnoxious trying to get stuff done when people are constantly crowding around you. But, I did find a solution to that." He smiles, proud of himself.

"You're going to hurt yourself," Ignis chastises.

With the same worn-out leather bag he has carried since the day Amiria gave it to him in Wyverna strung across his chest, Stirling treads gracefully across the red brick shingles as silent as a cat. He isn't invisible on the city's rooftops. The city folk still wave and the girls still call out his name, but they can't corner him up there. He smiles politely with a wave in return before carrying on with his to-do list. His goal? Get in and get out of the city as quickly as possible. His finish line is to return to Patu and begin their saint's day celebration.

Sitting at the edge of a slanted roof, Stirling lowers himself, slowly letting his body dangle. His forearms press into the shingles as he stops himself from sliding. His legs kicking the open air. Releasing his grip, he lands in a crouch at the entrance of the bakery.

"Eep! It's Stirling!" An unexpected girl jumps as she is exiting the bakery.

Hiding his head in his shoulders he mumbles, "Uh, yeah, pardon me."

The girl steps aside for him. She stares up at him dazzled as he squeezes past her, "He spoke to me."

"Oh, look what the winds brought me today," Amata says, stacking rolls of sweet bread on the display table. She turns to Stirling resting the carrying basket on her hip, "It's my only customer who can bake as well as me *and* can afford the upper city level. But yet keeps flying in through my front door. You know I won't be surprised the day you fall through my ceiling. I hope it's not on my sweet bread."

"Hey, hey don't sell yourself short. You're the only person whose gingerbread is on par with my mother's." Stirling says, snatching a shortbread from the table and stuffing it into his mouth.

She pretends to frown, deepening the wrinkles on her face, "I see. You're only here for my baked goods and not to say hi to an old lady."

"You caught me." He raises his hands with his mouth still full.

"How's Eve?" She inquires.

"Good, she's good. She's busy at the alehouse a lot. The number of people passing through has risen I guess." he answers.

"That's probably because people are hoping they will run into *you*." She gently pokes him in the chest.

Rubbing where she poked him Stirling sighs, "I know, it makes hanging out there a hassle at times. But it's good for her family's business."

Amata nods to Stirling's words as she begins packing his usual order of gingerbread, shortbreads with an almond on top, and adding a turnover packed with seasonal berries and honey for Eve. Practically singing the words she asks out of nowhere, "When are you going to ask for her hand?"

Stirling coughs, spitting shortbread crumbs into the air, "W-what n-no. We're just friends…" He trails off.

"Eve is a perfect match for you. I've seen the two of you together. She lent you a hand when these harsh city folk tried to knock you down. Is there anyone here that you trust more?" Amata states.

"I trust you. I trust the whole village, especially Bernard," Stirling says, trying to downplay the accusation.

Amata places her hands on her hips. "Well, sorry, Stirling, I'm already married, and does Bernard come with a pretty face?"

He blushes, "No, he's not really my type, but Eve isn't the first person to help me through rough patches. The only reason I'm alive is because of Amiria."

"Aw yes, your little knight who will fly in on her white dragon." Amata rolls her whole head.

"It's more of an off-white." Stirling mumbles.

"Take some advice from someone who has been alive for a long time. It's no good to stay hung up on the past. The rest of the world will only leave you behind." Amata takes her hand with skin as thin and delicate as silk and squeezes his arm.

"Yeah." He sulks, "Today is a saint's day. Anything can happen."

"Do you have any special plans?" She asks, turning back to the table.

"Yeah, the whole village is celebrating. Bernard and I also came up with a special treat for everyone." Stirling taps his leather bag making a peculiar clanking sound.

"Well, it is extra special now that you are there." Amata gives him a warm smile as she hands over the baked items.

"I'll let you know how it goes the next time I stop by," Stirling assures, adding the items to the bag.

"Don't go crushing the treats now," she tells him while peeking into the bag.

"I won't." Stirling waves goodbye as he backs out of the bakery.

Smiling shyly to a few onlookers who point at him, he jumps up grabbing the brim of the roof. He hoists himself back up to the safety of his personal red-bricked road.

Forty-Eight

Malnourished and exhausted Amiria leans over the side of Taika as they pass over another small village at the foot of the mountains, *No orange dragon. Not really anywhere you can hide one either.* She never did find out where Patu was. Instead, she would hear the rumors of Stirling competing in this city or that sending her all over Tallfallya. Her next best guess was to find the capital, Lumierna, where these so-called Games are held. If anyone in this kingdom knows where Stirling is, they will be here.

Taika skips the small village with nothing note-worthy about it and sails over the low peaks of the grassy mountains. Amiria's eyes bulge out of her head at the site of the coastal city. The city has a skyline straight out of a fairy tale. The layered buildings float up the side of the cliff from the teal waters balancing carefully on top of each other like building blocks stacked by a child. The red clay roofs pop against the lime-washed white walls.

She spots the landing zones she's grown accustomed to after months of traveling from city to city.

This is definitely where the games take place, she confirms as she sees the enormous stadium that can be a city of its own and wooden bleachers following what might be a racetrack leading out into the ocean.

The people around the landing zone give her regular responses. Kids run up to the fence pointing as their parents gawk at her wyvern dragon. A breed that, she had learned, is a rare oddity. Their dropped jaws quickly start to jabber as they become aware that the owner of the fierce species of dragon is a woman.

Hating the attention she always brings to herself, Amiria ignores the skeptics whispering about her. She rubs the bags under her eyes with a yawn and slaps the color back into her sunken cheeks. Not bothering with her wind-tangled hair still loose around her shoulders she dismounts Taika.

No longer resembling the soldier she used to be in her worn-out clothing, Amiria leads Taika to the hitching post. Keeping her head down she rolls and stretches her stiff shoulder working out the old injury.

A stable boy steps up to her, "Are you all right, ma'am? Whose wyvern is this?"

Tired of answering the same questions in every city, Amiria asks her own question in return, "Is this where I can find Stirling of Patu?"

Expecting the usual answer of *no* or *why would I tell you*, Amiria's heart drops when the stable boy responds with, "Yeah, I saw him go into the city."

"*STIRLING!*" Ignis shouts in urgency.

"*What is it?*" Stirling replies with a mouth full of gingerbread as he strolls across the city's roofs.

"*I see Taika,*" Ignis informs him. His thoughts race into Stirling's mind with excitement.

"*What do you mean you see Taika?*" Stirling pauses on the roof of a cobbler's shop with a raised eyebrow.

"TAIKA! TAIKA SPIKEY SCARY FACE! She is hitched at the landing zone. Amiria must be here!"

"WHAT!" Stirling bursts out loud coughing out his gingerbread. A man sweeping his doorstep glares up at Stirling. "Sorry, bread mishap." He lies. He turns away directing his thoughts at Ignis, *"Are you positive?"*

"Who else flies a beige wyvern with that many spikes." Ignis assures, *"Amiria is here, I'm not sure if you should run to her or away."*

Stirling goes weak in the knees, he lowers himself, sitting sideways on the slanted roof. *Amiria is here.* She is not on the other side of the world. She is not never to be seen again. She is here, she is present in this very city.

Groups of girls ridicule Amiria. Their harsh words slash at her from the shadows as they whisper amongst their friends. They mock her faded woolen cotehardie with the entire sleeves torn off after her elbows wore through. She didn't mind pulling the seams apart to give her relief from the rising temperatures, but she can hear them talking about her insignia. They have never seen a person's skin marked like parchment before. Several people comment on her saddle-burned knees showing through the missing space in the fabric of her tights, but their words fall away when they see the blades on her back.

He is here, he is here. She says over in her mind to drown out the people talking around her. He is here somewhere in this city right now. It has been months of her searching, sleeping on the ground, and participating in placing bets on herself in alehouse fights to earn coin to feed herself, all to find him. He is finally within reach. Somewhere in this massive city, he is alive and well.

She stops at the city gate and takes in the view of the ocean. *To the southeast.*

Tiles clink and threaten to crack as Stirling sprints across the roofs, dragging his gaze along the shop fronts. He must find her. He can't let this opportunity disappear like a precious shell in the tide.

He leaps over a narrow alleyway. A couple holding hands looks up at Stirling's shadow cross over them.

"Was that?" the girl starts.

"I think so."

Landing on the other side of the ally the shingle beneath the weight of his foot comes loose and shoots out from under him. With his footing taken out from below, he slides landing hard onto his side with a loud, "Humph."

Palming the roof like a gecko, Stirling slows his momentum. His feet pop over the lip of the roof as he slides to a stop.

"Hey, you all right?" he hears called up to him.

Pushing himself back up he shakes off the pain from his elbow. "I'm fine, in a hurry," he says back and takes off.

Amiria's beloved boots crunch the crushed stone path along the city streets. This city is impeccable. She has noticed the cleanliness of the cities often built of this solid stone like material, bricks, they called them. This city though, makes even those appear second class.

She walks up to a man adjusting the shutter of his home's window. "Excuse me, have you seen a young man with curly blondish hair?"

The man scratches his stubbled chin. "Can't say that I have. Try asking at one of the shops."

"Which one?"

"I don't know, whatever one you think your friend frequents," the man says before turning his focus back to his window.

Amiria scans the signs hanging from the shops along the street. None of them jump out at her. None of them have a target saying check here. What would Stirling even be shopping for? He made and provided everything he needed back in the cave. Who knows what he can make now that he isn't secluded in the mountains anymore?

Maybe she doesn't know him as well as she thought. If she was really his best friend she would know the answer. Unless he has changed these past months. She clenches her fists preparing to hit herself as she passes shop after shop.

She halts mid-step and pivots back to a woman she had just passed.

"Ma'am, may I ask where you acquired that?" Amiria asks, her heart thumping as she sees the gingerbread sitting in the woman's wicker basket.

"Oh, there's a baker that specializes in sweets up that way," the woman answers, pointing Amiria in the right direction.

"Thank you!" Amiria nods and speed walks down the path.

Scanning left and right she finally spots the bakery. With the sweet aroma of fresh bread and honey overpowering the salty harbor air, she stands hesitant in the doorway. Giles suddenly crosses her mind. How he is doing all alone in Wyverna without her there to check in on him?

"May I help you?" An elderly woman who can be everyone's grandma asks as she sprinkles shaved almonds onto rolled-out dough.

"Yes, hello, do you sell gingerbread?" Amiria asks, suddenly nervous.

"Of course! It's my signature," Amata answers with a homely smile. "Do you want me to wrap some up for you?"

"Actually, I'm asking because it's my friend's favorite. He went missing almost seven months ago and I'm still searching for him."

"Oh, that's terrible news. I'm sorry to hear that hun. What does your friend look like?"

"Tall, curly blond hair, hazel eyes, and a stupid goofy grin," Amiria describes.

Amata nods as she racks her brain. Too many girls have asked her about Stirling, "That description does bring someone to mind, but those are also very generic traits."

"Well, he has scars over a tattoo, like this one on his arm." Amiria holds out her arm exposing her own insignia.

'Oh!" Shocked, Amata knocks over the sack full of almond shavings scattering them across the natural stone floor.

"Are you okay?" Extending her hand out, Amiria steps forward with concern.

"Your name isn't Amiria is it?" Amata asks with her withered skin turning white. Amiria takes a step back as if a battle ram has struck her in the chest. She smiles inward, her voice soft as if it's only for her to hear, "You are Amiria aren't you? His little knight has arrived."

Her pulse begins to race as she asks, "Do you know where he is?"

The wrinkles around Amata's eyes crinkle as she closes them, her cheek raised and rosy from her smile, "He left not long ago, you barely missed him. He's out running some errands. But he lives in that small village on the other side of the mountain. You might be able to catch him at the gate, otherwise, that's where you can find him."

A flood of relief washes over Amira like a tsunami, she sways and leans her hip against the table to brace herself. He really *is* here. Finally, finally, the search has come to an end. The compass has stopped spinning and is pointing to her destination. If she doesn't see him in this city, Patu is there, on the other side of the hill. Patu, the village he had chosen to live in over the cities is so small it isn't on any map.

Hooking his knees on the open pergola-like structure of the floral shop, Stirling can see the arching entrance of the city gates. They loom past the last layer of roofs covering the shops surrounding the gate's plaza.

He leans back flipping upside down into the shop. The florist running the stand turns around to see Stirling's floating face only a step away.

"AH!" The florist yelps, grabbing his chest. He bats playfully at Stirling. "You scared me half to death. Why can't you walk up like a normal person."

Stirling's eyes point at the group of girls shimmying their way closer in a huddled pack, "I'm not a big fan of crowds." His eyes skim over the flowers, "I need a small boutique. Preferably purple, nothing too fancy because she's probably going to destroy it anyway."

The group of girls begins to multiply. "He's buying flowers for a girl," they whisper.

"Who do you think it can be?"

"AWWW! I wish it was me!"

"Ugh, it's probably for that girl he is always with."

The florist understands. "Ah. An apology bouquet." He whips around his shop, compiling an arrangement primarily of Aster accompanied with statice flowers and myrtle for greenery. He hands the purple bouquet up to Stirling. "Here, it's on the house, I don't know what you did, but I wish you luck."

"Thanks, I really need it. This is long overdue," Stirling admits before pulling himself back up to the rooftop.

"THERE HE GOES!" a girl squeals.

"QUICK, FOLLOW HIM!" another cries pushing her friends along.

Stirling stands at the top of the last roof overlooking the gate plaza. The vibrant-colored shop stands encircle the plaza. The decorated tile starting on the outer perimeter spirals into the quetzalcoatl dragon and racer fountain in the very center. The city folk bustle from stand to stand like buzzing bees in a flower patch. Several clumps of people surround the massive fountain talking as a few kids lean over the wall and splash their hands in the clear water.

He searches the people's faces. He knows from Ignis she hasn't left yet. His best hope is to ask the guards and wait for her at the entrance. She made it this far, she must know where he lives. She's a hunter, a persistent soldier tracking him down.

What will he say to her? Dread fills him. What *will* he say to her! His fingers hanging by his leg begin to tap nervously. *No, don't overthink it. She's one of your best friends.* Shaking out his entire body, he leaps down from the roof landing with a tuck and roll. Using the momentum, he stands up to all eyes on him.

"Is that Stirling?"

"Uh." He shrinks into himself, his fingers returning to their rhythmic tapping. Staring at the ground he watches his feet as he marches forward. "Please ignore me."

The news is an electrical charge spreading out through the conductive people. The mention of his name causes a ripple in the group and it begins bringing them to him like water filling a hole.

"Excuse me, pardon me. I need to get through," he mutters, trying to cross the plaza with fans closing in on him.

"It's Stirling!"

"STIRLING!" they cry out.

The people have become erratic. They surround him. They push and shove each other trying for their chance, their opportune moment to get closer to him. They are no more than animals at feeding time. This is the very situation he wanted to avoid. He can feel the air getting thin around him. His mind, growing fuzzy.

"Please! I need to get through!" he begs, his feet tacked to the ground unable to take more than half a step forward.

Girls reach out over each other's shoulders grabbing at his sleeves and the back of his jerkin.

"STIRLING!"

"STIRLING!"

"OVER HERE STIRLING!"

Stirling holds the flowers up above his head to keep them from getting crushed. Being a head taller than the average height of the crowd he is in full view over them.

"STIRLING!"

"BAKER BOY!"

"STIRLING!"

Everyone's voice is drumming in his ears. Then the world stops. Baker boy? Did he hear that correctly, or is his mind playing a cruel trick on him?

"BAKER BOY!"

There it is again. The name he's waited for so long to hear. He looks up from the swarming faces that have melted into one, their voices now only a muted muffle. He stares over the mob to a girl standing alone above the others on the fountain's wall.

His heart skips a beat. There, above everyone else, is the one person in this world who truly knows him. The single face he's dreamed of seeing, and the voice he's wished every day to hear. His face and body go slack. It's her. He can't hear the people around him. He can't see the people crowding and waving for his attention. All he knows is Amiria.

Through Opaque Eyes

Warning:
This story contains topics including substance abuse,
depression, and thoughts of suicide.

Dark opaque eyes roll in their sockets. Strands of pale hair hang feather light as the head they grow from rests on the back of his chair. The boneless body flows down the backrest to legs sprawled out, reaching across the room.

It's the beginning of the year and as a way to start the year on an elevated note, Leucasia has prepared its city for the annual games. The privacy curtains that make up the fourth wall of the primary room in his home are pulled back exposing the room to the natural light and ambiance of the world outside his sanctuary. The faint sounds of festival music carry in along with the gentle sea breeze through the opening adding a layer to his empty space.

Barefoot and in his undershirt, Quilan stares at the ceiling with an undisclosed expression.

"Sir Quilan," a maiden sets a tray of freshly chopped fruit and cheese on a small table beside him. She eyes a nearly empty mug on the corner of the table closest to him. "I believe I saw your mother exiting the estate. The possibility she is on her way is high," she tells him while switching the placements of the mug with the plate of fruit so the drink is no longer within reach.

Quilan doesn't remove his eyes from the ceiling, the soft curve of his jaw barely opens to say, "Is—"

"The door is locked, sir." the maiden finishes for him.

"Good," Quilan reaches out blindly to the table where his mug had been. His fingertips tap the edge of the plate. They curl into his palm, surprised. Hesitantly the fingers uncurl, settling with the loss, and plucks a piece of cantaloupe from the tray. Bringing the cubed melon to his mouth, they drop it onto his tongue. He chews unfazed as the front door to his home holds firm to the attempt of someone outside trying to open it.

"Quilan dear, it appears your door is locked. It's okay, don't fetch the help. I have a key," a high-pitched female voice calls from behind it.

Exhaling sharply through his nose, Quilan pulls his mouth into a taut line. He drags out his blink, wishing his eyes wouldn't open, but they do and roll over to his maid.

"I'll look into changing the locks sir," she bows her head and removes herself from the room as the front door swings open.

"My beautiful boy!" a woman in an array of silks draped around her like the end of the rainbow holds out her arms as if to invite someone in for a hug. She drops them quickly, raising her lip to the sparsely furnished room barren of ornaments, "You still haven't decorated? You really need some color besides white and blue, at least it's a bright blue."

"Hello, Florence." Quilan slumps forward in his chair.

"Are you still in that phase of yours? I'm your mother. Call me, Mother." She puts her hands on her hips.

Quilan doesn't reply as he lazily pushes up from the chair and walks out through the open wall onto his balcony overlooking the city of Leucasia below him and out to the harbor.

"Are you just now eating breakfast?" She reaches down helping herself to several grapes, "You really shouldn't sleep in this late. Quilan? Are you listening? The festivities for the Games have begun and you're in here laying around. Quilan?"

He leans his elbows on the solid stone wall ignoring his mother talking to him from the room. He pinches the brim of his nose. Leucasia's Skylit Endeavor. The Games. The same games every year. The same outcomes every year. The excitement, the rush of the competition, had been lost long ago.

Dropping his hand to hang over the edge, he scans the homes on the lower levels filled with people living lives below his. He should be grateful for having what others see as *everything*. A lavish home mostly occupied by servants. Talent that allowed him to earn the fame he was born into with his father being the prior undefeated elite racer.

A beautiful face—he touches the soft pink lips he hates to force into the shape of a smile—he never wants to look at.

"Quilan!" A group of girls clumps together on the walkway below his balcony. They squeal and wave their hands frantically to grab his attention. He hangs his head. He doesn't need to smile. He doesn't need to wave. They will follow him regardless.

"We love you!" they shout up to him in unison. They lean into each other giggling with the high of their confession.

They don't love him. They don't even know him. No one knows him. They know and love the Quilan of Leucasia that has been hand tailored by his mother. The one smiling on the stage is the Quilan she sculpted for the masses to admire. He is her one true masterpiece.

What's the point of life if there is nothing more to live for? What do you do when you've already obtained everything?

*Maybe…I should…*He leans forward, his weight shifting dangerously over the railing. His mother's voice breaks his train of thought.

"Quilan. Stop teasing your fans." She stands in the archway with her arms crossed. He shifts his weight back onto his feet. "Did you hear anything I said?"

He sighs up at the clouds, "No."

She clicks her tongue, annoyed, "Have you even signed up yet? You shouldn't be so lazy, it's bad for your image, the Games won't wait for you." She snorts a laugh,

"Who am I kidding? Of course, they will." She turns back to the main room. "Come on, let's get you ready. I bet people are dying to see you down there."

Quilan steps back from the rail, away from the edge, and follows his mother inside the open room.

"I had your maid get it from your room while you were flirting on the balcony," she hands him the thin folded fabric of a navy blue top with tightly buttoned cuffs, flowing sleeves, and a loose swooping collar.

His eyes drop down to the fabric in her hand then back up to meet her gaze. "I hate dark blue."

"Oh, don't be foolish," she dismisses, thrusting the fabric into him. "It matches your eyes."

"I know."

She talks over his comment. "Come on, slip it on and get your shoes. Your father has already shown face, but—" Her voice turns to a sing-song. "He's not what they're waiting for. You are!"

Quilan begrudgingly tugs off his undershirt and drops it to the floor. Silently cursing in his mind, his face reveals none of his true self when he reaches out and takes the navy top from his mother's outstretched hand. Slipping it on he trails her toward the front door.

He stops at the doorway where his shoes lay. Turning over his shoulder, his eyes land back on the balcony. He will participate in one last Skylit Endeavor, then afterward, afterward, it will finally be over.

Reference to Chapter 5

"Will you be wearing your signature light blue with the number one?" the girl at the registration stand smiles, batting her eyes flirtatiously.

"Yes," Quilan continues to scribble the information on the paperwork.

The girl rests her chin on her hands, "You excited for the games?"

Quilan signs his name at the bottom, only his eyes raise up to acknowledge her. She raises one shoulder playing bashful, oblivious to the disinterest in his emotionless eyes. He pushes the paper across the table back to her cutting off the unwanted eye contact.

"Can't wait to see you at the opening ceremony!" she calls out to Quilan's back as he makes his way toward his dragon. He raises his hand as his only response.

He lets out a prolonged sigh. Bystanders crowd his quetzalcoatl, Aether, knowing their beloved Quilan of Leucasia will have to return to it when he wants to fly them home to his parent's estate.

How did their obsessed eyes not see him standing at the registration tent? He wonders to himself. They see everything he does. Every movement, every breath, is under their gaze. His first word, his first step, his first flight…his first kiss. They have witnessed it all, there's no personal life when your life is an act on stage.

He wishes he didn't come down here. Wishes his mother left him alone. Wishes everyone would please leave him alone. Let his empty shell lay isolated in his house. He can bring his chair to the balcony and watch the clouds travel over Leucasia. He'll drink the liquid he needs to make it through and let his body decay under the sky. Quilan's eyes glaze over as he stares up at the clear blue sky. *The one place I—*

His thoughts are cut off as girls squeal his name. Lowering his chin, the emptiness in his face has disappeared. Deeply riveted dimples show on his cheeks at the ends of his practiced smile, his teeth shining perfectly in the light.

His torpid eyes, darker than the ocean, remain the same.

"SIR QUILAN!"

"QUILAN."

"QUILAN, OVER HERE!"

The boundaries break and the flood rushes him. This attention, this popularity is all he's ever known. Even in his earliest memories, people climbed over each other to shake his father's hand. He was held up in front of the crowd, put on display for adoring fans that instantly fell in love with the small boy and his blueberry eyes still bright and vibrant with life.

The faces surround him. He dips his chin nodding, shakes hands, and passes out several hugs to fainting girls and boys. They all look the same to him now, over the years they all began to lose individual characteristics until they've morphed into a storm of faceless creatures reaching out to touch him. So many people have touched him...everywhere.

"Pardon me," he requests, pushing his way through the sea of flesh, slowly making his way to his dragon.

What must it be like to be no one? To peruse the festival stalls at your pleasure, to place bets that will lose, to cheer in the stands until you lose your voice. Would he gawk at the riders? Would he forget they are human too and reach out to them as if they were a deity, or would he let them be and carry on with his day?

"Excuse me," he presses forward. The people part slowly as they step on the feet behind them. The masses pulse forward like a growing entity. What must it be like to be excited to wake up to a new day? Reaching his quetzalcoatl he seeks out the comfort of their blue feathers. He shudders a sigh of relief at the soft sensation between his fingers.

"WILL YOU MARRY US!" a set of twin girls shout.

This will be his last Games. Quilan's smile quivers, for the faintest moment his smile is real. He turns to the twins and winks. This will be the last time he has to pretend.

Reference to Chapter 11

The river of people flowing between the festival tents split for him like the bow of a ship cutting through water. They part with no resistance, stepping to the side to allow him passage, but they spin and churn in eddies, all wanting a glimpse as he passes them by, leaving them in his wake. They won't stop him today, they know he is on his way to the opening ceremony.

He had nearly forgotten what day it was, but his mother never will. A yawn almost breaks through, but he holds it back. There was no company over for pre-ceremony celebrations at his estate. Every invitation to the parties across the upper tiers of the city was lost to his fire's kindling. He did what he wanted to do and sat in his chair with the privacy curtains pulled back, sipping the burning drink from his cup. He listened to the sounds of life as he counted the stars, desperately wishing exhaustion to finally take over.

Oof. He can still feel the contact on his shoulders. Did he run into someone? He never runs into someone. Especially not when they know he's in a hurry. He slows his pace.

The voice of a young man shouts at him, "Hey! You just pushed over a girl! You need to apologize!"

The weight of the watching eyes shifts. He feels a moment of relief as the weight of the faceless creatures turn their focus to the yelling man. He should continue walking, but morbid curiosity tugs on him, edging him until he's turned around to a furious blonde curly-haired boy holding onto a girl with a crown of black braids and ringlets falling free, "Then don't be in my way."

The boy's jaw drops at his insensitive reply. Quilan steps back, turning on his heel, he puts the couple behind him and returns on his track to the stadium. He knows he should apologize. It was wrong of him to knock the girl over, but he was taken aback by the anger on the boy's face. There was no recognition on his face. This guy didn't know who he was and confronted him as he would anyone else. Quilan didn't know what to say, how to react. He had no implanted phrases to recite. He was stuck without his script and diverted to an answer that was expected from him.

The self-loathing settles in, he really should have apologized.

"You know him, You love him! Our number one racer Quilan of Leucasia riding his quetzalcoatl!" the announcer hollers into the extended horn that carries his voice across the audience the size of a city.

The roar of the crowd rumbles through the mountainous stadium. Quilan steps out on a catwalk an arm's length above the top row. The lower-class viewers gasp at their proximity to their idol. He reaches down, shaking several hands before stepping to the edge of the diving board. A rope secured to a fixture at the end of the walkway stretches down across the center of the stadium to a platform connected to the top of the wall where the front-row guests sit.

With his icy blue quetzalcoatl raining down from the sky, Quilan steps one foot onto a wooden pedal and pushes off the walkway. Smooth metal slides across the rope zipping Quilan across the stadium, one hand holding firm to the rope the other extending out to the crowd.

His dragon loops around him as he passes the center. The angle of his descent softens towards the end, guiding his speed to decrease into a gradual stop. He steps off and stands on the small stage and bows, turning to face the opposite direction he bows again.

He hops down the stairs landing on the sandy ground of the arena center. Throwing his hands in the air, he spins as he walks allowing everyone a full view of him. Aether lands soundlessly in a slither. Jogging up to them, Quilan gives his audience a final bow and leaps onto the saddle. With a flick of the reins, he leaves them behind for the clouds.

Reference to Chapter 13

Clumps of dirt tumble from the ledge as Quilan nudges the tufts of grass on the cliff's edge with his toe. It's the first match of the Games, and the beginner racers are readying themselves at the starting line.

He used to love watching the beginner's races. The rookies trying their hand in the Kingdom of Tillfallya's most honored pastime. The only competition you don't have to be a professional to enter, though most are. It's rare for a novice to come out of the fields. Everyone here has been coached since childhood, dragon racing is not some hobby you stumble upon one day while on an outing with your friends.

He can still remember how they wore these awestruck and overwhelmed expressions as a door to a new world opened for them. The excitement of the festivities in their heads and the adrenaline of a race in their veins would radiate from those racing on the track as he watched starry-eyed from the elite box seats. He respected them. His naive mind longed to feel as they did, but years come and go, and the end of upcoming and new participants arrived. It's become a revolving cycle of racers. Same games, new year.

Focusing past the toe of his shoe, he narrows in on the ground far below. His body teeters. It's only a single step. That's it. In a month's time, all he has to do is take one single step.

The horns don't bother him as they blare steps away from where he is standing. He doesn't hear them anymore. From his peripheral, he can see the beginners diving toward the coastal shelf. They pull up and race out over the water. His eyes shift over to the starting line.

Someone is still there.

He turns to get a better idea of who didn't take off. An orange Per'yanny svir perched as still as a gargoyle. He squints trying to place the boy. He has no gear besides goggles and a wild head of curls. His eyes widen with recognition. It's the boy he had run into. He's a professional racer?

No. Quilan tilts his head watching the trembling boy. *Not a professional, someone, someone new.*

Finding his courage, the boy commands his dragon to leap from the starting line and takes off. Quilan finds his predictions wrong as he watches the new boy overpower the competition, passing racer after racer, pulling from last to first.

He was incredibly wrong indeed. The boy's per'yanny svir lands back at the start. Last to leave, first to arrive. This year's games will not be the same.

Great. Quilan thinks as he enters the upstairs hall to the private suites of the inn. Peyton and Lucan, two of the other elite riders, lean on opposing walls laughing. Quilan doesn't remove his sight from his door in hopes to slip by unnoticed.

"Hey!" Peyton's grinning tan face, glowing from recent sun exposure, turns to the pale-haired boy.

Nope. Quilan steps up to his door pretending he didn't hear them.

"Quilan! Hey, Quilan, did you see the new kid?" Peyton shifts his weight, sliding his shoulder along the wall, and leans in Quilan's direction. "We were just talking about him."

"Good for you," Quilan slips the key into the slot.

"Aw, pouty pouty Quilan," Lucan clicks his tongue. "Lighten up, man. It's the time of the year for you to take all the money again."

"Maybe from you, but I always secure myself in second," Peyton gloats, jabbing his thumb to his chest. He spins back to Quilan at the sound of the hinges opening, "Wait, Quilan! You didn't answer, did you see the new guy?"

Quilan's head falls back with the slump of his shoulders. His lackluster eyes roll over to Peyton, "And?"

"For one, he looks like he was living in an alley, but the funny part is that he doesn't just look like he was born in a barn, he's actually sleeping in the stables," Peyton's gaping grin returns as if he had said the punchline of a joke.

"Huh," Quilan steps inside his room uttering, "Interesting."

"Oh, come on. We're brothers now and you still don't want to talk?" Peyton plays up being upset with an exaggerated pout of his bottom lip.

"No." He doesn't even talk to his older sister, so why would he talk to the man she married?

Closing the door behind him he can hear the two men shrugging off his attitude. He is younger than them by several or more years. He's the youngest in the elite race, he has been since he started six years ago at fifteen. The next youngest is Peyton who is three years older than him and of last spring, his older sister's husband. They've known Quilan most of his life through his father, but he's not their friend. They've watched him grow, but they remain in blissful ignorance that the light in the child's eyes faded over the years until it permanently died out several years ago. They are either oblivious, or they don't care. What is he, but in their way for first place?

Finding himself in front of the window, Quilan taps the shutters with clean fingernails. *He's sleeping in the stables?* Quilan wanted to ask for more information about the rookie, but he didn't want to join their squabble in the hall. He has his own sources of finding out information on anything and anyone.

With little to no force, Quilan pushes open the shutter letting the sun in. He leans out his window towards the forgotten stables. *Who is he?*

Reference to Chapter 18

Quilan had almost fallen asleep watching the routines of the beginners he had memorized. They lack originality and creativity, their performance is merely routine tricks. The citizens don't know any better, but any racer knows the so-called tricks are simply training exercises. Except for Stirling.

Remaining slouched in his cushioned chair, Quilan misleads the four other elites that he wasn't enthralled by Stirling's performance.

His show was a grand spectacle of daring acts never displayed by anyone except him and those who have worn the title of elite. These aren't moves you learn from any mundane coach. He claims he was self-taught. How did he train his dragon to catch him without killing himself in the process? Quilan crosses his arms pleased. It was purely incredible, everything he does is extraordinary.

Like a high-pitched octave breaking glass, his flow of thoughts is shattered.

"There's no way someone from *Patu* can pull off tricks like that," Lucan spits bitterly, his feet propped up on a wooden stool in the Elite's private box.

Peyton scratches his chin. "What are you suggesting? He lied about where he's from?"

The second oldest of the elite racers, Firmin, grumbles, "Who in their right mind would claim they're from *Patu.*"

Aylmar, the oldest, nods in agreement, "They would have to admit they live in huts with dirt floors."

Why must they ruin everything? Quilan wonders to himself. They've tainted the sport with pompous attitudes, pretentious beliefs, and materialistic acts. Fans buying their capes color is more important to them than who those people are.

"What do you think, *Sir number 1?*"

Quilan ignores him, he doesn't care which of them it was who asked the question. He will never tell them what he thinks.

"Ay! Quilan! Too good to join the conversation?"

Any light starting to brighten his dark eyes is snuffed out and listlessly rolls over to the four men, "Indeed."

"You're a drag anyway," Lucan waves Quilan off. The four return to conversing.

It's easy to tune real people out. What he finds impossible is ignoring his own voice speaking to him at night. His words ring loud in his head despite his attempts to plug his ears. Here he can practically dismiss their contemptuous conversation as cicadas in the summer.

At this rank, Stirling will be advancing to the next ranking. Would he be able to prove himself worthy to slide into the elite level by the end of these games? Quilan smiles internally, it would be nice to race him. Have his final race be the last and only real thing in his life.

The pearlescent goggles are an icy rainbow around his eyes. Quilan sits upon his quetzalcoatl awaiting his cue to start. The trick competition. The races can be hard to stand out to the crowd for what separates someone in the advanced from the elites because they are not watching them race each other. They do not comprehend the differences in speed and accuracy. But here, during this round, there is no comparison. It's strikingly obvious why they are labeled the elites.

Quilan flicks his reins and the coiled-up quetzalcoatl springs into the air. Their feathered wings carry it soundlessly across the sky like an incoming storm that has yet to release its power.

Loops, figure eights, spirals. The legless dragon spins through the sky. These will not set him apart, these are warm-ups for his last hurrah.

A genuine smile slides onto Quilan's face. Up here, away from everyone, he is immersed in tranquility. He doesn't have to pretend to be someone, he doesn't have to be anyone at all. He is no one, currently living in the present, with no past and no future. Here and now, nothing else exists.

Quilan taps the trained signal onto Aether's neck and unhooks his belt. Stirling isn't the only one who is psychotic enough to risk his life for a game. He has been practicing this move for a year. Started with balancing on a water wheel at a mill, then progressed to practicing balancing while standing on his dragon with an extended harness in case he fell. A year of his life dedicated to what he is about to do now, here in front of this crowd for the first and last time.

No harness attached, his left foot slides forward into a binding. Quilan twists the reins around his wrist and cautiously rises to his feet and secures his right foot in back. With the air tugging at his loose navy blue top, he leans, surfing the back of his quetzalcoatl. The movements of his weight directing the direction they will fly in.

Up here close to the clouds, he is the angel they claim him to be.

He pushes down, riding the air current to the turquoise water. Pulling his knees up, he directs Aether to lift up before diving into the water. The crowd screams in disbelief as he flies over them. Cheering, they hold onto their caps and duck as the gales of wind rip through them.

He's back out over the water.

Squatting down, he taps the coded command and then removes his feet from the bindings. The quetzalcoatl arcs and turns their body into a wheel. Running along Aether's back, Quilan stays at the top of the dragon's roll. As their tail narrows below him, he jumps, skipping over their head to land on their neck. Completing another revolution, they've fallen too low in the sky to continue and Quilan purposefully falls back into the saddle, giving the cue for Aether to spread their wings and carry them to shore.

Landing on the churned-up soil, Quilan can hear the wood bleachers shuddering under the rowdy crowd. He kisses his hand and whips it out across the stands giving them the small gestures they long for. At least he doesn't have to worry about finding a way to top that for next year.

Feeling disgusted with his pandering movements, Quilan grimaces in the form of a fake smile. He waves his hands above his head and exaggerates throwing several more kisses. The audience who calls out their love for him will never know he despises every breath he takes.

Reference to Chapter 19

The steam from the bathhouse opens his pores as he leans his head back against the tile. Shoulder deep in the blanket of water, Quilan's mind wanders up to the passing clouds through the condensation-covered skylight.

He blinks, rewatching the rookie's races over in his mind. He was undefeated in the beginner races, there was no comparison between him and the other beginners. He was unstoppable in their ranks and had been boosted to intermediate. The corners of Qulain's lips twitch. He can see the raw talent. The hidden potential in the boy. The judges don't see it, but Quilan knows the boy is meant to race in the elite. He can feel it in his gut.

The boy, Stirling from Patu, is the most intriguing thing he has laid eyes on since—since, well, *ever*. He displays the enthusiasm and passion for racing that the others have lost. His raw emotions are painted clearly for everyone to see. He doesn't cover up his discomfort and fear. He wears it upfront.

The other racers mock him, calling him derogatory names. They call him a nobody, a zero, but he is not nothing. He is clearly something. He is truly somebody. He is remarkable.

The door to the front of the bathhouse leading into the changing room opens and closes. Quilan sits up properly and rests his arms on the bath wall. Out of all the years he's come here during supper time not a single person has disturbed him. They are a bunch of alpha pretenders too busy growling over imaginary territories. Who is here? Who has changed the order of things? The person opens the bath door and steps inside.

Quilan's heart skips.

Is this what it feels like for people to meet him, Quilan of Leucasia? Is this what it feels like to meet someone you've watched from the stands? His heart palpitates in his chest, filled with nerves.

He sat at the same dining table as the king, yet he didn't feel as wrecked with self-consciousness as he does now. Hiding the rising pulse through his veins, his half-lidded eyes follow the curly-haired boy stepping awkwardly to the edge of the bath. *Hide who you are. Be who they expect.*

His voice comes out collectively from years of pushing down his true emotions, "Tired of the feeding frenzy?"

Conservatively, as if he has never been to a public bath, Stirling steps into the water with his towel. He waits until the last minute to remove it, managing not to reveal himself with the cover of his hand. Uncomfortable, he lowers himself into the steaming water.

"In a way. You're Quilan aren't you? I didn't know the Elite also stayed here," he questions.

Accent! Where is he from? It's not Patu like he says. He really doesn't know anything, does he? Quilan holds eye contact before switching to inspect his nails, "Obviously."

From the corner of his eye, he can see the boy shift, uneasy with the dying conversation. Quilan hasn't been much for words. If he could live the rest of his ending life in silence, he would. He has felt this way since he could talk, everyone always wanting to hear his opinion, wanting him to stand on stage and eagerly listen to his scripted words. His thoughts are his, but his words never are. Away from fans, away from prying eyes and straining ears, he's granted this small gift of freedom. He can stick to his thoughts and express nothing, this is who he is, and this is all he wants – for people to stop trying to know him and leave him alone.

This is what he has convinced himself he wanted, yet, sitting here with this stranger – he wants to converse. He wants to hear him speak, to hear the story of his life, to find out who he really is.

"Tell me," the boy jumps at Quilan's voice after the prolonged silence. "Your dragon? How?" Quilan rests his arms back on the edge of the bath getting comfortable.

"How?" Stirling shakes his head with uncertainty. "How what?"

Quilan's eyes slide back to Stirling, but he says nothing. He watches the artery on the boy's neck pulse under his scrutinizing gaze. *Is he scared of me? Is that how I come off to people?*

The boy, Stirling, twitches his fingers under the water and fumbles with his words. They come out a croak, "I—" he clears his throat, "I found him as a fletchling and I taught myself."

"Hmm." Quilan's eyes narrow into slits. Stirling hasn't failed to impress him. He, himself, was guided by his father, the best racer of his generation. *Self-taught.* Where would he even start? He continues to leer at the curly-haired boy as he falls deep into thought. Catching himself staring, he cups his hands and scoops a bowl of water. Distracting himself, he watches it slip through the cracks between his fingers.

He needs to leave. This Stirling of Patu has a quality in his own self-acceptance, flaws and all, that makes Quilan want to stay, to be in the same space in hopes he can find his own acceptance. He steals another glance at Stirling. He doesn't need a reason to leave. He's Quilan of Leucasia, he can come and go as he pleases.

His eyes wander back to Stirling, a spark flickering behind their locked doors. *Did they…?* He catches Stirling's faltering eyes and holds contact. He points at his own hair in reference to Stirling's sticky bangs matted with some kind of drink.

Tugging on the mead-soaked clump, Stirling drops his gaze, "The other racers."

Quilan stands up, cutting Stirling off from venturing further into the explanation. Stirling's blushing gaze fixates on the steaming water. "They're all losers," Quilan mumbles, wading across the pool to where Stirling sits by the exit.

Reaching the underwater bench, Quilan moves to step up and out as Stirling extends his right hand up to him, "I'm Stirling by the way."

Quilan's eyes are drawn to the revolting scars covering his hand, the scars across his arm, and the ink permanently staining his skin. *What has he been through?* He peels his gaze from the ink and crawls up the boy's arm to his face. His mask falters and empathy slips through in the form of a raised lip as he envisions the pain of burning flesh. Regret hits immediately as the younger boy mistakes the expression for disgust. Stirling's anguished face stitches itself to the back of his eyelids in preparation to visit him again as he rests his head on his pillow. The voice in his head reminding him how pathetic he is.

With no apology, Quilan utters, "I know." Chastising himself internally, he forces himself to leave the embarrassed boy to cradle his marked arm in the bath alone.

Reference to Chapter 24

Groggy, Quilan rolls over in his bed with a groan. Another restless night. Another night to watch the shadows in the room take the form of demons. He reaches out to the bed stand and takes hold of a mug. It's the only way he knows how to make them stop. Before the shadows can whisper their ruthless words of truth in his ear he gulps down the burning liquid.

The tingling mind numbs to the world around it and slumps its heavy body back to bed.

"Hey, farm boy!"

Whaa? Quilan squints at the mess of stars beyond the open window. He can hear people talking outside. Irritated, Quilan pulls the pillow over his head to buffer the sound. It's the middle of the night. What are those idiots doing messing around? Other than the initial outburst, Quilan can't make out what the men are saying. *Farm boy.*

A shot of dizziness quakes Quilan's head as he sits up. His feet find the cool floor before his body is prepared to stand. He stumbles as the room tilts, sending him to the floor of his overturning ship. With his cheek pressed to the floor, his eyes struggle to focus. With exaggerated blinks, he attempts to clear his vision.

Fighting against the waves he grabs the base of his bed and drags himself from the floor. With blurred vision and swaying steps, he throws himself to the window. An exasperated, "oof," he catches himself on the windowsill with his stomach and leans his head out over the ground two stories below.

A sobering sight clears his mind.

Farm boy. It's Stirling of Patu. He's being held by two men and is facing the racer, Merek. Merek turns irate as he wipes Stirling's spit from his face, in a flash of motion Stirling is ripped from the two men's hold by his hair and thrown to the gravel path.

Quilan's voice lodges in his throat as his instincts fight his mental training. Stirling is being attacked. He needs to help him, he can stop this. He's the only one who can stop this.

His body sways as the drink catches back up to him. It's too late, the brief moment of clarity had let the voices in.

Useless. Good for nothing. Give up. You can't help him, you can't even help yourself. Give up.
Quilan pulls back from the window cupping his hand over his ears and whimpers, "Stop."

You're a sinking ship, you'll bring him down with you. Give up already. You're nothing but a shell, used up trash. You'll fade out, he'll replace you and you'll be nothing.

He lumbers back several steps, "Stop."

Give up your life. You are nothing without racing, you're a loner, no one will miss the real you. End it now. End it before they end you.

The backs of his knees buckle on the edge of the bed sending Quilan toppling to the mattress.

Soft hands lay useless at the side of his moonlight-colored hair. Wide eyes watch the swirling shapes move across the ceiling. Infiltrated ears let the taunting words run rampant through his mind. He is tool. His body his not his. He is to be used. Over and over and over again.

With the awakening of the dawn, the voice fades to the back of his mind. He counts the hours with the measurement of the stretching sun across the room's ceiling. Legs are still hang off the bed where he had tripped backward the night before. His hands, the only thing that had moved, lay at his sides.

The morning light reflects off the damp trails starting at the corner of his eyes and running back to his hairline. His throat bobs as he swallows. The end of the games can't come soon enough, as everyone celebrates the closing night he'll take that final step. The best gift he can give himself.

He squeezes his eyes shut forcing out the final drop to run down his porcelain skin. All of this will finally be over. He will finally be alone in silence. Light eyelashes flutter open with a revelation of what needs to be done. *Merek.*

Quilan has watched Stirling leap to the advanced level; he has outpaced everyone's rankings besides his own. The potential of the next number one rider resides in the boy supposedly from the meager village of Patu.

With weary bones, Quilan sits up with a slump, his body tired from a restless night and exhausted from existing. Bringing life back to his neck muscles, he lifts his head. He might have failed Stirling last night, but he will commit his last days to him. If anyone deserves to be at the top, it is someone who had to start on the bottom and not someone like him–someone who has never experienced the lower levels. You can only appreciate what you have if you have lived with less.

Merek has participated in his last Skylit Endeavor. Racers like him take this life of luxury for granted, thinking because they are above they can step on who is below. People like him do not warrant that kind of power.

Finding the will to stand, Quilan rises to his feet. He will let Merek fly his last race. Let him get the score he believed was worth assaulting someone for. Then it will be stripped of him and he will never race here again.

Stirling *will* make it to the elite level for his last race - and he will see to it.

Reference to Chapter 27

Past his feet propped up on the railing, the orange slate representing Stirling slides into fourth place in the agility competition. Fourth, third, second, *first*. First place is painted red and white checkered–Merek. Pulling them in tight, Quilan's lips disappear into the crease of a scowl.

Stirling was able to pull off fourth place, but even from here, Quilan could see hesitancy in his movements as if it pained him to move with his usual fluidity. He can feel it chewing away at him - the guilt of the fact he could have prevented this. He was not the one who placed his hands on Stirling to cause the injuries that cost him his win, but he failed to use his voice to stop the hands that did.

Wearing his quartered sea green and yellow cape with a number two, Peyton with brown waves and dusky skin, talks with his mouth full of roasted almonds, "Guess he finally lost his luck."

Luck? Quilan refuses to remove his eyes from the sky ahead of them. He has to pretend any of the comments following Peyton's does not bother him.

Lucan, sitting with the other two elite racers, doesn't look up from his strategy game consisting of moving small stones on a leather mat carved with three squares one inside of the other. Firmin, the second to oldest in the division, sits directly across as Lucan's opponent with Aylmar sitting beside them. Barely more interested in their game than the competition, Aylmar's head bobs down to his number three cape in solid yellow with the beginnings of nodding off.

"Luck? He's a cheat. Just don't know how though." Lucan moves one of his stones.

Quilan pops his jaw, his eyes locked forward, *There is no luck, and cheats only get so far before the truth is revealed. Race him and find out his talent is fueled by passion —something everyone in this room has lost.* His eyes dip down to his light blue cape, *Every one of us. Pathetic. Trash.*

Peyton turns in his seat to respond to Lucan, "Well, however he's been winning, it's ending. He messed up this round and there goes his streak."

Eyes focused on his move, Firmin joins the conversation, "Maybe after this loss, he'll finally get the clue to stay out of our games."

Heavy eyelids take their time blinking as the next racer readies himself to take off. Quilan drops his feet from the railing with a definite thud and stands up without warning, *I'm settling this.*

"Where are you off to?" Peyton reaches his hand into the wooden bowl set on a table between them and grabs another handful of almonds.

Firmin laughs, "Probably to get another drink."

"Or a quick one before the race. A different one each day? Am I right?" Lucan nudges Aylmar with his elbow.

Quilan ignores them all. It's not as if he can deny their speculations. When was the last time they've seen him without a recent drink? Then the walls at the inn are thin, there is no hiding the flow through his room. Except, there has been no one in his room this year. Only him and his voice.

Aylmar huffs. "Not like it's any different if he is here or not, he's too vain to talk to us." Aylmar's gruff eyes follow the aloof boy in the robin egg blue cape across their private box to the exit, "Maybe if we showered him in compliments we can get at least a good morning."

They want you gone. They hate you. Quilan's face remains neutral as he reaches for the canvas flap and as if he didn't hear a single word, the number one racer slips out of the room.

With arms and legs crossed, Quilan leans against the exit of the restricted area. He rests his head against the wall as his eyelids slide to half closed. Barely awake, his dark blue eyes follow Merek as he is escorted off the grounds by the guards.

While standing at the threshold to the exit of his life, if Quilan had to list his accomplishments there would be only one bullet point. He knows it won't make a difference in the grand scheme. Erasing one rodent doesn't fix the infestation, but his moment of pride is not for helping the games. He can not fix what he is a broken piece of. Instead, he can make a difference for a single person. The person he believes will be the cure.

He holds a single hand up, halting the guards as they reach the exit beside him.

Merek hisses, "So, the boy wasn't the one who squealed, and to think someone as highly ranked as you would side with someone who sleeps in the stables."

Quilan lifts his head from the wall narrowing down on Merek, who barks, "You got something to say, then say it!"

Quilan doesn't break eye contact, "Ticks need to be removed." *Remove yourself.*

The guards shove Merek forward to continue their escort.

Twisting in the guard's grasp, Merek strains to look over his shoulder at Quilan. "How? How did you know?"

With apathetic eyes, Quilan smiles.

The green projectile whizzes past his ear. With his head tilted, Quilan keeps a lookout for another ball. The crowd below, already painted rainbow from the first three games, raise their hands ready for more. When he was a kid watching his father play, he adored the decorated people. Everyone is blotched and stained with color for the rest of the day. People purposefully wear white to stain the array of colors permanently - to treasure it as games attire and brag to those in faraway cities who could not attend.

He dips his dragon, avoiding another chalk-filled cannon ball. It is popular as an audience member to be covered in color, but as a racer, you only win if you are clean.

Quilan sighs. It has been years since the chalk has touched his skin. He yanks on the reins twirling his dragon to the left. Maybe he should let one hit him. Let him feel the impact for the first time, see the color splattered against this navy blue top.

The horn sounds at the end of the game. Quilan frowns. He had won again.

It was simple in the end, when Quilan requested the game's director his desire to have Stirling of Patu compete in the last elite race. The director didn't even ask him to explain his reasoning. He's well adverse in Stirling's growing popularity. He calculated the revenue he had been bringing in each time he climbed to a new ranking. Stirling has been this year's highlight and letting him race against the number one rider will be his true test. The people of Leucasia will go mad over the opportunity of witnessing history in the making. Then the crowds will double for next year's Skylit Endeavor to see a full month of them facing off.

He leans his head against the wall of the backstage room with his arms crossed. He's enjoying the view of his eyelids when he feels the familiar sense of someone looking at him.

With half-lidded eyes, he finds Stirling. The flighty boy jumps his gaze over to Peyton holding his newborn beside his wife, Quilan's sister. Stirling and him haven't spoken since that time in the bath house. Quilan had kept to schedule and returned every day at supper, but Stirling never did, most likely finding a new time when the house was unoccupied.

As for his sister, they barely speak in passing. Being the first born and a girl, she was spoiled by their father who provided everything she asked for with the plead her dark blue eyes. She was their father's precious little girl and their mother's daughter, someone to go get newly tailored dresses and their hair washed together. Her eyes pass over him now as if he is another stranger. That is what he is to her. If it wasn't for his mother and Peyton, he wouldn't even know his nephew's name—or that he had a nephew. Peyton, who helped cause the wrost memories of his life. The feeling of their unwanted touch still stains his skin.

Quilan can only hope his nephew's upbringing is not like his own. *Because you're filth. Used up trash.*

A song catches Quilan's attention and his gaze returns to the girl with the black braids as she hums an intoxicating melody while she rubs Stirling's back. He has only had glimpses of Stirling with his family – friends? The protective way the giant man stands over them and the way the girl smiles adoringly at him. Not the way a fan does, but how someone who is in love does. She looks at him as if he is the healing sun after a troubling night, as if, as if—Quilan drops his gaze. Even if he was still a nobody in a small village, her eyes would still light up in his presence, he would still be the most remarkable person to her.

What a beautiful soul, he thinks, sneaking another peek at the girl with warm brown skin and honey-colored eyes. What must it be like to be cared for? For someone to support you through your hardships? To hold your hand when you can't stand?

"Stirling," a coordinator announces into the room.

Stirling instinctively grabs the girl's hand. Quilan watches her cheeks turn red with heat. Quilan's own hand closes over empty air. He listens as she tells Stirling, "Don't worry, I will be right off to the side watching. Just look at me when it starts to get overwhelming."

To hide his lonely heart, Quilan's eyes return to impassive slits, trailing Stirling as the girl helps him to his feet and assists him out of the room.

"Stage right, top row," the coordinator whispers into Quilan's ear. Nodding his chin, Quilan accepts the information.

"You know we did this on purpose!" Heath, the interviewer, teases the audience. The coordinator returns to control the show from the shadows as Quilan checks his shirt, pulling at the hem and adjusting his cuffs.

Shaking out his hands, he hears the words, "Your very own, Quilan of Leucasia!"

Quilan lifts his hand to his face placing the artificial smile then runs his hand through his hair. The amphitheater rumbles as the audience stomps their feet. Raising both hands into the air, Quilan steps out into the light.

They scream their devotion to him. Hands, hundreds of sets of hands, extend out over a blur of faceless beings all reaching out to him. All straining to touch him. The ghosts of their fingers dig into the fabric of his clothing. They curl around his wrists yanking on his arms, pulling him in different directions in an attempt to tear him apart. He doesn't want to be touched by anyone anymore. He is a person, not merchandise at a shop.

Refraining from going directly to him, Quilan plays it off as if he is scanning the crowd. He spots Stirling sitting beside the girl where the coordinator had directed. He and his female companion are not cheering. Two sunflowers in a field of wheat. Her hands clap, politely engaging with the crowd, but Stirling—he is leaning forward, his eyes narrowed, reading. He is reading *him*.

Quilan stops beside the chair in the center of the stage. Heath chuckles, motioning to the chair for Quilan to sit in, "Unlike our new boy Stirling, you should feel very comfortable up here."

I'm not. "It's like my second home," he answers, waving to a few girls in the front row who act as if they are about to faint.

"Yes, and that is the exact problem I am experiencing as the host. I'm running out of questions to ask you." Heath laughs, sitting back and crossing his legs, "Though these games have been quite different than normal. So, I'm going to skip the small talk and get straight to the big question. Tell us, Quilan. Why did you recruit Stirling into the elite division? There is only one race left. Why now instead of waiting until next year?"

Because there will be no next year. He puts his hands up, his face unchanging. "I was bored." *Bored with racing, bored with these games, bored with…life. End it. Waste of space.*

"Bored?"

"Bored," Quilan haphazardly shrugs, "Thought it would be interesting." His eyes travel up to Stirling already knowing where he was, "Let's hope he doesn't disappoint me."

The weight of the eyes is lifted as the audience's gaze shifts to Stirling. He slinks shyly in his seat as the girl shakes him excitedly. Quilan lets his smile rest, his lips falling into a despondent line. *I'm sorry. Ruin his life. No. You never had a life. Owned. Creation. Please don't lose yourself.*

His lingering gaze slides back to Heath. The smile etches back onto his face before the crowd turns around at the sound of the interviewer's next question. He methodically answers the questions about what he sees in Stirling giving the people the illusion they are seeing a glimpse into his mind.

A shock pulses through his body, his mask nearly slips as heat rushes his face. *Retire? Coach? Perform for them. So I can sacrifice another kid to the gluttonous public? Feed them. Dance for them. Useless.*

The corners of his mouth twitch, "Who says I will retire?"

The audience cheers at the news of watching him for years to come.

Reference to Chapter 39

The light momentarily blinds him as Quilan pulls back the curtain to the tent. He squints letting his eyes adjust. Stirling, who was nervously bouncing on his heels outside the racer's tent, stops at the sight of him.

"Q-Quilan!" he stutters. "I haven't gotten the chance to thank you."

Quilan puts his hand up stopping him, "Don't." *Don't do the thing you do that makes me want to talk to you. That makes me want to stay. Don't stop me. You'll bring him down with you.*

The boy pales under the dismissal. Holding his features stoic, Quilan turns his shoulder to him and heads toward his quetzalcoatl.

"RACERS! MAKE YOUR WAY TO THE STARTING LINE!" can be heard from the coordinator behind him.

Stepping up to his only friend, Quilan relinquishes a sigh. His fingers trailing through the Aether's feathers, "Ready for one last race my friend?" He blinks up to their sapphire eyes.

A cooing sound cries deep in the Aether's throat. Lowering their head, they blow a steady stream of air through Quilan's fine hair before nuzzling their face against him. Quilan wraps his arms around the blue feathered neck. With his face tucked away, he squeezes. In response, Aether hooks their chin around Quilan's back, embracing him. Like the petals of a lobelia flower, the feathers bloom through Quilan's gripping fingers. A shudder runs through his body as a single sob pushes itself through his walls. Still, the forsaken tears remain trapped within his fortress. He will not cry. Especially not here, not here where his emotions will become a spectacle to gawk at.

"I know," he runs his hand soothingly down the dragon's silky neck, "I know." He pulls back letting his arms drop limply to his side, "One last time?" A heartbroken smile flutters, its form wavering to hold until it falls, unable to retain its shape. Quilan bites his lip and lowers his gaze, "Please forgive me." *Failure*

Aether slides forward offering the saddle to Quilan. The corners of Quilan's mouth curl up, more somber than reassured.

Together they slide into place at the starting line; he's next to Stirling and his hyperactive dragon. The prior night he sat with the drink he can't go without but this time let his inner voice speak to him. Eyes as dark as twilight, he stared at the stars until they blinked out of existence while he mulled over his choice for tonight. In the end, his decision was cemented, he can only come up with one single con against his list of pros. The only con is never getting to know Stirling. What a journey it would have been to listen to his story, to learn about his life. It's obvious he is not from Patu, only expanding on the mystery of who he really is. But what is he to Stirling besides another one of these arrogant elitists? What will he think? Would he even care?

His ears perk up as Peyton asks Stirling. "You've won all those matches, how come you haven't updated your gear? Besides your goggles, everything else looks so umm—economical."

Quilan was not expecting Stirling's answer, but it rings true to his character, "That's because I made them myself. Well, me and a close friend. This is much more valuable to me than any of the gear I can buy."

It's more valuable. Quilan inspects the premium saddle he had custom made to bend effortlessly with his Quetzalcoatl's flexible spine. He had invested more money into the comfort of his dragon than it would take to build a house in Patu. But—he checks back at the self-made saddle—it's a harness tied together with a soft hide. Something as simple as that would have worked just as well, maybe even better.

"It doesn't impede your racing?" Peyton asks curiously.

Stirling shakes his head, "Not that I'm aware of, but I don't know any different." He pauses, "I have a question for you."

"Go for it," Peyton shrugs casually.

"Is the gear really what makes the racer?"

Quilan is stricken by the words. They echo in his mind, the answer bouncing back. No. The answer is no. Without this gear, without his training, his heart once loved racing. He once loved the adrenaline of it. It was in his blood, it pumped through his heart. *That* is what makes a racer. unlike you. Worthless. Rid yourself.

At the turning of curls, Quilan diverts his attention to his white gloves before he is caught staring. A spark is lit deep inside him. The ember catches the deadwood of his internal body. It's starting to feed and grow into a wildfire at the thought of a real race.

His eyes, beginning to glow, dart back to Stirling, "Good luck."

Hazel eyes widen with the unexpected, "Oh—uh—you, too."

Pulling back the corner of one side of his mouth into a crooked smile with a deep dimple creasing his cheek. "I don't need it."

He doesn't, not because he knows he will win, or believes he is above it. It's because the beating of his heart picking up rhythm, the blood beginning to surge in his veins in anticipation of the horn, is all he wanted to feel again. He wanted to *feel* again. He is excited to race Stirling and he hopes Stirling wins.

The crowd is wild in the stands beneath them. Banners and flags of the elite racer's colors wave about their heads as they call out to their favorite. Amongst the sea of robin egg blue is orange. The color started small, one single boy with wild curls and worn-out clothing. Like a blight in a crop field, it spread out infecting the crowd, the color orange growing and taking over.

I hope they never break who you are. Broken tash. I know I am.
"RACERS! ARE YOU READY!

Quilan shuts his eyes relishing the ambiance of life— the voices and cheers of joyous people carry up the sea cliff, the soft muttering of Stirling as he runs through the course under his breath, the beating of his own heart inside his chest, a sea breeze playing with his sunlight hair. What a beautiful day to be your last. His heavy eyelids lift, revealing the ocean to him. She never fails to dazzle as she shimmers endlessly out in front of him. He is ready.

At the sound of the horn, they are off, a cyclone of beasts tearing across the land and out over the waters.

As always, without any effort, Quilan begins to pull ahead. He refrains from checking Stirling's placement, he will not grant the other four the luxury of knowing he is concerned with their placement. He can only carry on and hope Stirling holds up. He should have warned him about the brutal last stretch, out of view of everyone, where the rules don't apply. Quilan shakes his head. Stirling didn't stay down when they attacked him with their fists, he won't be knocked down while he's flying.

The prairie air carries the fresh scent of long grass to fill his lungs. A crystal river snakes along the lush plains dotted with the shadows of clouds. Over here, on this side of the mountain, life seems to slow. He holds a hand out in front of his chest, out of view of the other racers, letting the invisible force curl around his fingers as they break through the air.

A family, the size of a village, jumps and dances, waving their arms as they pass overhead. Quilan breaks his rule and turns to see Stirling waving down to them. Patu. He could have said he was from anywhere, but he chose them. Why is that Stirling *of Patu*? What form of life is offered in a village so small it doesn't make the maps?

The image of the burly man and the loving girl crosses his mind. The homely smiles of friendship and belonging radiates as they laugh together. They willingly stand on either side of Stirling to be leaned on, to be his crutch, to keep him standing.

Oh. ALone. You'll die alone. Loser.

They enter the gorge of the last stretch. He has never participated in their battle royale. They have never been close enough to attempt to strike him down. Maneuvering the obstacles is the only hindrance to Aether. They devour these opportunities to test their flexibility in winding around the pillars and bridges without faltering, without slowing down.

Everyone should be lost to the stone forest by now, Quilan checks over his shoulder to see if Stirling had stayed afloat. He sees the four others flashing into view as they fight around the pillars, but there is no sign of the orange dragon. Odd. He twists in his saddle out of curiosity and checks the ravine below.

Quilan lets out a breathy laugh. The cheeky boy is running along the ground. He had avoided the onslaught of scales by using his dragon's advantage: sprinting. Quilan bites his lip, holding back a smile. Stirling still finds new ways to amaze him after this month of watching him compete. He deserves to be number one.

While he himself was born at the top with no ladder down, Stirling found the impossible rungs and dragged his beaten-down soul up to each new layer. He untied the weights of people holding him down and shrugged off the laughter and words weighing on his shoulders. Then when they reached up and pulled him back down, he always began again, only stronger.

With the excitement of a true race in his veins, Quilan flicks the reins of his dragon pushing it for the first time in his career. Untrained muscles strain to pull back his lips, a smile only the ocean will see stretches across

Quilan's face. This is why people race, *this* is why *he* wanted to race.

Stirling is nipping at his dragon's tail. There is a possibility he might lose. He can actually *lose* and he has never been happier.

They cross the finish line. His quetzalcoatl is a blue ribbon spiraling up the sea cliff to waft gently back to the shore of the roaring crowd. All remnants of his short-lived glee wipe clean from his face as he slips from his dragon and falls back into who he's written to be. His knees bend, almost betraying him and casting him to the ground. Unfamiliar with this body behavior, he lifts his hands to see them shaking. Perturbed, he drops his hands to find Stirling staring at the crowd in disbelief.

As if he is seeing land for the first time after being gone at sea, Stirling's jaw hangs slack and his eyes glaze over, submersed in the partying stands. Appearing lost he turns to witness the others cross the finish line, but Quilan doesn't remove his eyes from the second-place elite racer. He wants to keep this moment, to hold it close and protect it. He will shelter this single flame within his harbor. A single light to take with him when he sets sail.

Stirling's head whips back, locking his gaze with Quilan's. He feels his barely beating heart sputter. The muscles in his jaw clench holding his emotions steady. He blinks away the thoughts before they have time to affect his mind and breaks the contact. With a deep sigh, he shuffles his feet to the grooves in their size on the first-place podium.

Settling into the block people will remember him by, he can't help but take in Stirling's excitement. The jump in his step as he practically dances up to the second-place position beside him. How he's beaming as bright as the sun above, how his body vibrates with energy fighting the restraints to be expelled.

With his lips sealed shut, he struggles to contain himself. A shot of breath exhales through his nose as he holds back a laugh. Finding Stirling's enthusiasm entertaining, his dimples sink further into his cheeks.

"In second place we have Stirling of Patu!" the announcer's voice emphasized by a metal horn drowns out as the crowd cheers.

"WOO!" Stirling's hands shoot up into the air as he accepts the second-place prize from an employee.

"In first place, we have, Quilan of Leucasia!" the employee follows along with the announcer and bows as he offers the hefty velvet bag of coins to Quilan. With the sounds of the crowd cheering in the background, the announcer continues. "This concludes our final match of the annual Skylit Endeavor! You are granted permission to enter the racing grounds and meet our elite racers!"

Quilan disregards his winnings, hooking them to his belt. He has to catch Stirling before the crowd rushes them. He has one thing to tell him before the end of the day. He hops down from the podium. Stirling hugs the coins to his chest, grimacing at the stampede of people racing to them.

He clears his throat, stealing Stirling's attention, "Eh hem." The eyes shining with life are now covered in a film of fear as they turn to him. They bounce down to his outstretched hand and back to his face, "You're supposed to shake it."

"Oh–Uh," Stirling takes it in his grasp. The pure smile Quilan pulled out from his depths during the race re-emerges as the grip tightens in a firm handshake. This is not his practiced smile, it hangs offset one side of his mouth pulled farther than the other, with one dimple deeper in his cheek.

"Thank you," Quilan tells him.

Stirling tilts his head, "For what?"

Retracting his hand Quilan's shoulders fall to a slump before pulling back as if taken control by a puppeteer. He can no longer meet Stirling's eye, "A good last race." His gaze trails behind him to Stirling's friends. The bear-like man and the beautiful girl. He takes a couple of steps back creating distance between them. He can do one last thing for Stirling.

The flood has breached the gates and the masses surge upon them. Raising his hands Quilan fixes his smile and turns to catch the blunt force of the human tsunami. He won't be able to stop them, but he will slow them down enough for Stirling's friends to get to him first. They are what will keep Stirling afloat in this storm. They won't let him sink.

The people are an invading force filling in the space around him. Someone is shaking his right hand, another kissing his left. He can feel arms around his waist…two sets of arms. Fingers hooking around the crook of his arm, a kiss on his cheek. He's being pulled to the left, he is being pushed back into the wall forcing him forward. All these hands are reaching for him yet none of them are offering to help him stand.

He twists his neck, straining to find Stirling in the siege. His fake smile shows his true interior as it drops. The burly man, his lifeboat, is carrying him and the girl away. The space in his chest occupied by his heart tightens as he watches her slip her hand into Stirling's. He's knocked off balance by a force to his side, his focus brought back to the surrounding problem.

Wavering slightly, he's kept up by the tightly packed mound of flesh and bone. He turns back to where he last saw Stirling, his eyes scanning across the faceless heads. His neck bobs as he swallows the realization, there will be no one to save him from drowning.

Quilan's face flushes from the heat of the fire. He sits on one of the many plush sofas spread out across the center of the stadium. The sand pit has been transformed into a place of celebration. Torches line the top of the wall in a single ring of fire. His seat sits beside the roped-off center as a man blows fire into the air lighting up the dancers with staffs of flames. Quilan's blurred vision can barely focus on a man jumping through a burning hoop. The music falls on deaf ears. He takes a sip from his mug savoring the burn down his throat. He shouldn't have bothered coming here. *It* happened here.

"Quilan," a seductive voice whispers in his ear. Dead eyes remain fixated on the glow of the fire as he takes another sip. "What do you want to do?" Its soft lips nibble on his ear. A different mouth on his other side kisses his jawline.

He isn't alone on the velvet seat. Slender legs lay across his lap attached to the boy kissing his jaw. The girl kneels beside him, her fingers running through his hair. His body is numb, their advancements useless against an abandoned castle.

Why did he come here? He should have sat on the sea cliff and waited for twilight alone. With his legs hanging off the edge he would hold his flame, a single moment that he holds close to his heart. A scene of true emotion and it wasn't even his.

The pressure of touch slides across his chest beneath a thin hand. Fingers trace the lines of muscles and travel down to his thigh. The seductive voice is in his ear again, "What are you thinking about?"

Closing his eyes he pictures the tips of his shoes hanging over the crumbling edge, one-foot lifts and steps out over nothing. The hand interrupts his thoughts by slipping down to his inner thigh. His eyes open as

it begins to travel back up. *Not again. Toy.*

Downing the rest of his drink, he pushes the boy's legs off his lap ignoring his fussing exasperation, "Quilan!"

"Quilan! Where are you going? Quilan!" they both exclaim.

The clay mug slips through his limp fingers, dropping to the sand. Stranded in the middle of a storming sea, he sets off in the direction of land. The rough current of the drunken crowd threatens to pull him under. Voices cast out hooks to him, hands reach out to snag him, and everyone floating on the high of his success desires his attention. Quilan struggles to keep his head above the water he's swimming through.

They all want a sliver of Quilan of Leucasia's time when he desires no one's. He yearns to be left alone, to leap into the endless abyss where he will no longer belong to them. Then, and only then will he be free.

"QUILAN!" his mother squeals, a cascade of rainbow silks fluttering as she appears in front of him. He stops short. His body sways uneasily from his drinks. She reaches up pinching his cheeks. "Who's my number one?" she pauses waiting for an answer. "The answer is you, Quilan." She pokes his nose. "You're number one. That farm boy almost caught up to you, did you let him? Was it all for show, because that was a magnificent idea. You really added a little extra sugar to the end race."

Frowning, Quilan moves to step around her, but she holds her place in front and continues. "I bet that will bring even more people to the games next year. You put a lid on the farm boys' seemingly endless rise in the ranks, and people are going to want to watch you maintain it. You're going to be busy busy this year. I bet letters will be coming in from all over for you to have appearances. Next week there is—"

"Stop."

Her eyes bulge at his interruption. "Excuse me?"

"I said stop, just—" he shakes his head, his gaze drifting down. "Stop." He pushes past her.

She spins around. "Quilan? QUILAN!"

"Don't follow me," he grumbles, hugging his arms around his chest as he vanishes into the stadium's tunnels leading out.

Unperturbed by her son's behavior Florence's attention is immediately caught by another in the crowd. "Flora!" She waves her arm in the air calling out to her daughter. With a dancing twirl, she sets off into the crowd in her daughter's direction.

The coastal night air nips at his skin through the thin top. His feet drag across the dry brittle ground until they stop a step away from the ledge. With only his own voice talking in his ear as company, Quilan looks out across the harbor from the race's launch point. He scuffs the dirt with the bottom of his leather sole. How many times has he leaped from this very spot? How many times has he wished the wings weren't spread and he wasn't carried safely into the sky?

Every time.

No, it wasn't every time. There was once a time he lived for the force exerted the moment Aether caught the up draft and soared over the ocean at impeccable speeds. He was alive when his stomach dropped and his blood stopped. When did that cease? When did he lose his passion?

You never had it. It was never yours. It was your parents'.

He finds himself staring at the stadium. No, it was his passion at one time, but it wasn't lost, it was stolen. He was forced to perform repeatedly until it was dried of all meaning. He is empty yet they continue to squeeze every last drop from him.

You're used up, they'll bleed you dry and toss you aside.

They won't stop, not even after he is gone. They will mourn Quilan of Leucasia the number one racer, but they will not mourn him. They *can't* mourn him. They don't know who *he* is. You can't mourn someone you didn't know existed. Then they will move on, find another's life to feed off.

Let them. It won't be your problem.
He turns his head trailing his eyes down the length of the ledge. He sees the ghost of Stirling of Patu during his first race. How he was frozen with fear at the sound of the horn. Instead of succumbing to the fear he took initiative and finished the race.

You've already sacrificed him.
They will try to devour him—they are starving sharks that will chip away at his ship, slowly springing leaks until they can pull him off and into their depths. But they will keep him afloat, won't they? His friends from Patu? They were his barricade during the games. They put up a protective gate every day to keep him safe… but they aren't always around.

But you were, and you did nothing.
He closes his eyes. The night he failed Stirling is a parasite in his mind slowly eating away at his core. His friends weren't there to be his shield and he failed to be a blade. It would have taken only one word from him to make them stop. Stirling was injured because he allowed the attack to ensue.

You're pathetic. He's stronger than you. Give up already.
A golden streak lines the edge of the world when he opens his eyes the same color as the twilight sky. It's almost morning. If he steps off now, neither the stars nor the sun will have to witness what he is about to do.

The sun doesn't care, it will still rise regardless.
He edges closer, rolling pebbles beneath his sliding feet. He leans peering over the edge watching them fall

and disappear to the dark turf. One step. All he needs to take is one single step, then he can disappear.

Do it, join them, do it.
He must perform one more frivolous act for this audience of none and he will have his peace. Too many years of carrying this title. This name has worn through him. He had died ages ago, but his body was kept up by strings. His movements are controlled and forced to keep dancing, but the paint is peeling and the hinges are breaking. The body needs to be returned to the soul, and he can do that with one single step.

But why is it so hard?

Because you're weak, jump, jump now.
This is all he wished for, all he could think about. The one gift he wanted, he had promised himself this a month ago. Taking this step is the single aspect of his life he is granted control of. This is the one choice he is allowed to make. He is not someone's creation, not another's entertainment, he wasn't put here in this world to please them. He is human like them, but he wasn't allowed to be. He had to be more. He had to pretend he was cut from a different, sturdier cloth, but he wasn't. They are all made the same, so he stands here now, unraveled and frayed.

You can't even do this right, you have no free will. Puppet, useless puppet. Jump off.
His thoughts fall back to Stirling, how he mended his tears and didn't hide his stitches. He never did get to learn the truth about him. He would have enjoyed racing with him again, to have that adrenaline pumping through his veins in the heat of real competition.

Stop stalling. Rid yourself JUMP!
His body teeters on the crumbling edge, his gaze locked on the beams of light extending out over the water half obscured by the harbor's cliffs keeping Leucasia in the shadow. He hears a song playing in his thoughts, no

not just a song. It's *her* song. It's *her* voice. The song she was humming to Stirling to quell his nerves before the interview. He never did get to learn the girl's name.

What are they doing right now? Did they celebrate in Patu? How does a small village celebrate? He can feel the warmth of the sun on his skin as he pictures Stirling surrounded by people who love the curly-haired boy with worn-out clothing and not the number two elite racer.

He squints from the sun's rays. He hasn't heard his voice whispering to him since her song began to play. Besides the melody, it is silent in his mind for the first time in years.

A single slippered foot takes half a step back. It's the day after the annual games. The matching foot from the set steps farther back than its partner. He broke his promise to himself, he wasn't supposed to see this day. He can still go through with it. He can still leap.

He blinks, the ledge has moved away from him. It has been pulled back towards the ocean. His frame now stands several steps away and steadily retreating. It's not too late, the distance is now a running start. He can fulfill his promise to himself, he can do this. HE CAN DO THIS! This is his life, his choice to make, and no one else's. He puts his hand over his heart feeling the rapid beating. His name is Quilan and he is a person. He is alive.

Breathing in deep through his nostrils, Quilan fills his lungs with brisk morning air. Then without a word, he turns on the ball of his foot. Crossing his arms and with a hunch of his shoulders, Quilan walks away.

Acknowledgments

I'll start with the obvious, my family and my husband. My mom, for showing excitement for me by making a reusable bottle with pages from my book. My sister, for letting me read to her my roughest drafts and knitting me a stuffed Ignis. My dad, for taking the time to read the rough drafts, the final product, and being my number one fan. My husband, for dealing with me constantly talking about my book, hounding him with questions, and hovering over my laptop. I will, of course, love to thank my in-laws, who love my book no matter what.

I have to give a special shout out to some of my best friends. Taylor who helped me name my protagonist, Jessica who helped proofread, and Sophi who helped edit my book. That girl would sit in the cold, raining PNW forest with me while camping as we took turns reading the book out loud and making adjustments.

I'm also going to give thanks to my editor Belle Manuel. She was the one who helped change my book and characters for the better.

Then I'm going back to the roots, where it all started. I will not mention the place I had worked but let me say graveyard was so dull that I started writing this book. I will never forget those I worked with at the place that shall not be named. They supported me when the book was nothing but scribbles in a journal. They listened to me as I told them my idea and encouraged me to go for it. Four and half years later and its finally done because of their initial support.

Now I won't neglect to thank the later years. I had left that initial job and began somewhere else. My coworkers and supervisor watched me write furiously in my rough draft notebooks and type on the computer during down times. Instead of my supervisor telling me to put the notebook away and my coworkers getting upset that I was distracted at work, they supported me. Constantly asking me how my progress was going and putting positive vibes that I will one day finally complete it. Here it is guys. Except, I will still be typing at work because there's no stopping me now. So, you're stuck with me still click-clacking away, but after all these of watching me type, you must be used to it now.

Thank you, everyone.

About the Author

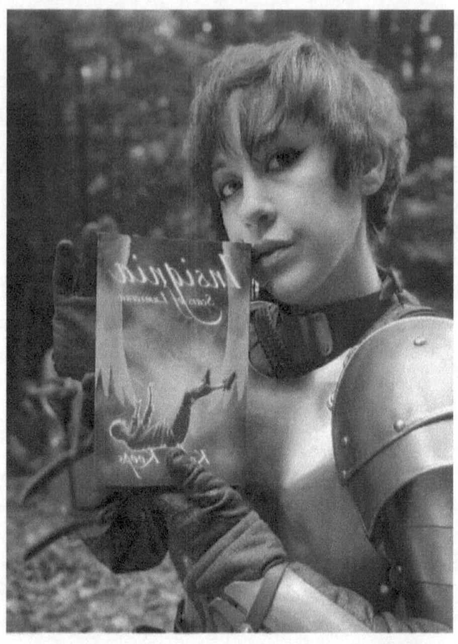

Born and raised in Thousand Oaks, California, I had changed what I wanted to be when I grew up numerous times like any child. Looking back through all my schoolwork and old notebooks, I loved story writing. The evidence was there, but I just ignored it. End of high school, I took that interest, believing I wanted to be a screenwriter. I wrote a full-length movie, but I didn't enjoy the lack of detail. I love writing detail, really building a mental picture of the world. I dropped out of college before gaining an associate degree and went straight into the workforce. I attempted to write another movie for the fun of it but never finished it. Looking back now, I don't know why I didn't just write those as books.

At 21, I had entirely given up on the idea of being a screenwriter but still liked writing as a hobby. I wrote a short story for only me to read, and it wasn't until I was 25 that it occurred to me to turn it into a full-length novel. Scars of Lumierna is the result.

When I'm not at my full-time job hovering over a computer, or at home sitting on the couch with my computer. I'm out camping, with my computer. With a rooftop tent mounted to my four-wheel drive Toyota, I love taking long drives through the Olympic Mountain's logging roads, even some roads that my car shouldn't be going on, and I had to do the sketchy backup and turn around. At the end of the day, my friend Sophi and I would pick a spot, make a fire and work on my book. There is no better place to work than in the middle of the forest with no one around except your best friend, some dogs, and the sound of the crackling fire.

Connect with me online at
Tiktok kelseakoops_author
Instagram kelseakoops_author
kelseakoops.com